MEMOIRS OF

MISS SIDNEY BIDULPH

Frances Sheridan was born in 1724 in Dublin. She married the Dublin actor and theatre manager, Thomas Sheridan, in 1747, and moved to London, where she spent the next ten years in debt and poverty. Of her four children, Richard Brinsley and Alicia Lefanu became well known writers themselves, and her friends included Sarah Fielding, Catherine Macauley, Samuel Johnson and David Garrick.

Her novels and plays were often written furtively in between household chores and include *The Discovery* (1763), *Memoirs of Miss Sidney Bidulph* (1767; posthumously published), and *The History of Nourjahad* (1767; posthumously published).

Frances Sheridan died at Blois in France in 1766.

Sue Townsend has had a number of plays staged: *Wombeang* (Soho Poly, London, 1979); *Dayroom* (Croydon Warehouse Theatre, 1981); *The Ghost of Daniel Lambert* (Leicester Phoenix, 1981); *Bazaar and Rummage* (Royal Court, Theatre Upstairs, 1982, BBC Television 1983). Her play *Groping for Words* was staged at the Croydon Warehouse in 1983 and is published – with *Womberang* and *Bazaar and Rummage* – by Methuen, as is her latest play, written for the Joint Stock Company, *The Great Celestial Cow*. She is also the author of *The Secret Diary of Adrian Mole Aged 13¾* and *The Growing Pains of Adrian Mole*. Part of *The Secret Diary of Adrian Mole* has been broadcast three times on BBC Radio.

MOTHERS OF THE NOVEL

Reprint fiction from Pandora Press

Pandora is reprinting eighteenth and nineteenth century novels written by women. Each novel is being reset into contemporary typography and reintroduced to readers today by contemporary women novelists.
The following titles in this series are currently available:

The History of Miss Betsy Thoughtless by Eliza Haywood (1751)
Introduced by Dale Spender

The Female Quixote by Charlotte Lennox (1752)
Introduced by Sandra Shulman

Belinda by Maria Edgeworth (1801)
Introduced by Eva Figes

Adeline Mowbray by Amelia Opie (1804)
Introduced by Jeanette Winterson

The Wild Irish Girl by Lady Morgan (1806)
Introduced by Brigid Brophy

Self-Control by Mary Brunton (1810/11)
Introduced by Sara Maitland

Patronage by Maria Edgeworth (1814)
Introduced by Eva Figes

The selection for Spring 1987 includes:

Memoirs of Miss Sidney Bidulph by Frances Sheridan (1761)
Introduced by Sue Townsend

A Simple Story by Elizabeth Inchbald (1791)
Introduced by Jeanette Winterson

The Memoirs of Emma Courtney by Mary Hays (1796)
Introduced by Sally Cline

Discipline by Mary Brunton (1814)
Introduced by Fay Weldon

Helen by Maria Edgeworth (1834)
Introduced by Maggie Gee

Forthcoming in Autumn 1987:

Munster Village by Lady Mary Hamilton (1778)
Introduced by Emma Tennant
and
The Old Manor House by Charlotte Smith (1794)
Introduced by Janet Todd

The companion to this exciting series is:

MOTHERS OF THE NOVEL
100 Good Women Writers before Jane Austen
by Dale Spender

In this wonderfully readable survey, Dale Spender reclaims the many women writers who made a significant contribution to the literary tradition. She describes the interconnections among the writers, their approach and the public response to their work.

MEMOIRS OF
MISS SIDNEY BIDULPH

Extracted from
her own Journal, and now
first published

FRANCES SHERIDAN

Introduced by Sue Townsend

London and New York

This edition first published in 1987 by
Pandora Press
(Routledge & Kegan Paul Ltd)
11 New Fetter Lane, London EC4P 4EE

Published in the USA by
Pandora Press
(Routledge & Kegan Paul Inc.)
29 West 35th Street, New York, NY 10001

Set in 10 on 11½pt Ehrhardt
by Columns of Reading
and printed in the British Isles
by Guernsey Press Co. Ltd
Guernsey, Channel Islands

Library of Congress Cataloging in Publication Data

Sheridan, Frances Chamberlaine, 1724–1766.
Memoirs of Miss Sidney Bidulph.

(Mothers of the novel)
Reprint. Originally published: London: R. and J. Dodsley, 1761.
I. Title. II. Series.
PR3679.S5M4 1987 823'.6 86–16982

British Library CIP Data also available

ISBN 0–86358–134–X

THE Editor of the following sheets takes this opportunity of paying the tribute due to exemplary Goodness and distinguished Genius, when found united in One Person, by inscribing these Memoirs to

THE AUTHOR

OF

CLARISSA

AND

Sir CHARLES GRANDISON

CONTENTS

INTRODUCTION

FAN LETTER TO A DEAD WRITER

Dear Frances,

I am writing to tell you how much I enjoyed your novel *Memoirs of Miss Sidney Bidulph*. If you were alive I would come to see you and kiss your cheek and thank you for the pleasure that your book had given to me. I would then leave before I made a fool of myself: I have no gift for critical analysis.

I understand that you wrote your fine book in between household chores and entertaining (often at breakfast) the literary figures of the day. James Boswell wrote that he often caught a glimpse of you carrying trays in corridors.

How you must have longed to fling the tray down in the corridor and run to a room in that busy house and shut yourself in, in order to write.

Did you also long to slam the door shut on Dr Johnson and Garrick when they came calling at all hours of the day and night? And were you never tempted to inform your husband Thomas that you were far too busy with your own writing to help him with his?

Were you bitter about the years you looked after your mad father, the same man who had previously forbidden you to learn to read and write? Thankfully you learned anyway with the help of your brothers; but so much secrecy, so much furtiveness, and then after many years of difficulty your book is finally published without your name on the cover. How this must have hurt you. I know this was the usual practice for women's work, but I believe it must have been painful and humiliating for the women writers every time it happened.

Your book is beautifully written, and is full of credible characters. It is also very funny. I laughed out loud many times at Sidney's commonsensical response to startling events. Your book could be described as a romantic melodrama, it is full of misinterpreted conversations, intercepted letters and misunderstood motives. Sidney sails through an incredibly complicated plot, with her morals and virtue intact, though why she didn't turn on her interfering old mother and beat her to a pulp I'll never know. She was equally forbearing with pompous George, her brother whose best friend is Orlando Faulkland, the hero of your book. I like the way you introduce Orlando: George is praising Orlando to Sidney, in fact he goes over the top. Sidney replies, 'Well brother, you have drawn a good picture, but to make it complete you must throw in generosity, valour, sweetness of temper *and a great deal of money*.'

Sidney is used to a certain standard of living and intends to keep it up. Good for her! Another thing I like about your book is the device you use of giving all the main characters long anecdotes to tell, using letters or their own voices. So we get not one story, that of Sidney and Orlando's on and off romance, but many subsidiary stories about women's lives. These short pieces are good enough to stand on their own and I suspect that you had written some of them earlier in your life and had slotted them in to your novel, thankful to have found a place for them at last. I am writing a novel at the moment and have also used stories I've written earlier. It's as if these unfinished pieces are waiting until they are called.

The overall structure of your novel is in diary form. Sidney writes to Cecilia her best friend who lives abroad. Never was there such a meticulous correspondent. Sidney tells Cecilia everything, however trivial, and thinks nothing of copying out in full an eight-sided letter. This is the reason your novel remains fresh and modern. It is directly written as to a friend, a friend who has known Sidney since childhood, one who loves and sympathises with her. There is a great tradition of letter-writing and diary-keeping in women's literature and your book is the first to combine these two forms and in my opinion turned it into an art form.

Your novel is very long, but is never dull. I was often loath to put it down and on a few occasions had it taken from me forcibly by people anxious to start a meal or to make sure I caught a train on time.

Your prose style is always a delight to read: precise and correct and seemingly effortless. As a friend of mine remarked on reading a section, 'What a lot of beautiful words she knew.' Yes, and how skilfully you took your beautiful words and arranged them into elegant sentences. Your son Richard was sufficiently impressed by

Miss Sidney to include several incidents from it in his famous play, *School for Scandal.* Naturally you received no acknowledgment. Perhaps you will take comfort from your contemporary women novelists Fanny Burney, Charlotte Smith, Maria Edgeworth and many others who all wrote or spoke about your work and acknowledged you as one of the finest writers of their time. You were truly the Mother of the Novel.

I wish I could spirit you back to London 1987 on the day your novel is republished. How delightful to hand you a copy of your novel with your name on the front cover, then to hand you a glass of champagne and to toast dead and living women writers everywhere. We know how difficult it is, and yet we do it because we love it and because in a dangerous world more of our female voices need to be heard.

Dear Francis, wherever you are I salute you and thank you for writing *Memoirs of Miss Sidney Bidulph.*

Love,

SUE TOWNSEND.

PS. I haven't mentioned the plays you wrote, or the sermons, or the fact that you had four children. Then there was your hectic social life of non-stop entertaining . . . and your husband Thomas Sheridan with his violent changes of mood and frequent theatrical speculations which led to poverty. I know you died aged 42, Frances. I'm not surprised, you must have been very, very tired.

VOLUME I

THE EDITOR'S INTRODUCTION

I WAS invited to pass a month last summer in Buckinghamshire by a friend, who paid annually a visit to his mother: a lady pretty far advanced in years, but extremely chearful, sensible, and well-bred.

She lived altogether in the country, in a good old fashioned house, which was part of her jointure; and it was to this hospitable mansion he carried me.

The lady received me very politely, as her son's friend; and I have great reason to be obliged to him for the introduction.

My friend and I generally dedicated our evenings to the entertainment of this obliging Lady. She loved reading, and was a woman of an excellent taste; but as her years rendered that employment not so easy to her as it had been, her son and myself usually spared her the task, and read to her such authors as she chose for her entertainment; nor was she so confined to particular studies, as not to allow us to vary our subjects as inclination led us.

It happened one evening, which was on the eve of the day appointed for our departure, that we had made choice of the tragedy of Douglas for our entertainment, when a neighbouring lady (a sensible woman) who had drank tea with us, desired to make one of our auditors.

After the tea-table was removed, we entered on our task; my friend and I reading alternately, to relieve each other, that we might not injure the performance by a wearied or flat delivery.

Neither of the ladies had ever seen or read this play before; and both gave that true testimony of nature to its merit, tears.

When we had finished the reading of it, they each in her turn bestowed high praises on it; but the visitor lady said, that notwithstanding the pleasure it had afforded her upon the whole, she had one great objection to it. We were all impatient to know what it was. I think said she, that the moral which in inculcates is a discouraging lesson, especially to youth; for the blooming hero of this story, though adorned with the highest virtues of humanity, truth, modesty, gratitude, filial piety, nobleness of mind, and valour in the most eminent degree, is not only buried in obscurity, by a severe destiny, till he arrives at manhood, but when he emerges into light, is suddenly cut off by an untimely death, and that at a juncture too, when we might (morally speaking) say his virtues *ought* to have been rewarded.

We each spoke our thoughts on the subject, as opinion led us, when the old lady drew our attention, which she always does, whenever she delivers her sentiments.

I should think as you do, madam, said she, if there were not too many melancholy precedents to give a sanction to the fable of that tragedy. I do not say but that the poet, who is at liberty to dispose as he pleases of the works of his own creation, may as well reward and punish according to the measures of justice in this life; it might perhaps make a better impression, and indeed afford a more prevalent example, to the generality of young people. I say therefore, I do not take upon me to defend an opposite conduct upon principles of poetic justice, but surely the poet who prefers that course, may be justified in it from every day's experience. If we always saw virtuous people successful in their pursuits, and their days crowned with prosperity, there would be more force in your objection; but the direct contrary is a truth, which every body who has lived but a moderate number of years, must have been convinced of from their own observation. Amongst heathens indeed, who looked no farther than *this* life for good and evil, and whose only incitement to virtue was the praise of men, or what *they* called glory, such morals might be dangerous; but surely amongst us Christians they *cannot*, at least *ought* not to have any ill effect.

On the contrary, I think it should serve to confirm that great lesson which we are all taught indeed, but which we seldom think of reducing to practice, *viz.* to use the good things of this life with that indifference, which things that are neither permanent in their own nature, nor of any estimation in the fight of God, deserve.

On the other hand, to consider the evils which befall us, as equally temporary, and no more dispensed by the great ruler of all things for punishments, than the others are for rewards; and by thus estimating both, to look forward for an equal distribution of justice, to that place only, where (let our station be what it will) our lot is to be unchangeable. It is in this light that I was instructed in my early days to consider the various portions that fall to the share of mankind; which very often, as far as we can see, appear extremely partial; and no doubt would really be so, were there not an invisible world where the distributions are just and equal. From this reflection I have drawn comfort in many trying incidents of my life; but in none more than the unhappy fate of a lady, who was my particular friend; and who, tho' a woman of most exemplary virtue, was, thro' the course of her whole life, persecuted by a variety of strange misfortunes. This lady, to use your expression, madam (addressing her friend), to all human appearance, *ought* at last to have been rewarded even here – but her portion was affliction. What then are we to conclude? but, that God does not estimate things as we do. It is ignorant, as well as sinful, to arraign his providence. We daily see its dispensations with our own eyes, in the various accidents of life. Why should we not then allow the poet to copy from life, and exhibit to our view events, the probability of which are founded on general experience?

We are indeed so much used to what they call poetical justice, that we are disappointed in the catastrophe of a fable, if every body concerned in it be not disposed of according to the sentence of that judge which we have set up in our own breasts.

The contrary we know happens in real life; let us not then condemn what is drawn from real life. – We may wish to see nature copied from her more pleasing works; but a martyr expiring in tortures, is as just, though not as agreeable, a representation of her, as a hero rewarded with the brightest honours.

We agreed with the venerable lady in her observations; and her son taking occasion from her mentioning that unfortunate person, who was her friend, told her, he would take it as a particular favour, if she would oblige me with the sight of that lady's story.

She answered, that as we had fixed up the next day for our departure, there would not be time for me to peruse it, but that she would entrust me with it to take it to town, that I might read it at my leisure. It is drawn up, said she, for the most part, by the lady herself, and the occasion of its being so was this. She and I had been intimate from our childhood; we were play-fellows when young, and constant companions as we grew up. We always called each other sister, and loved as well as if we had really borne that relationship to each other.

It was our continual practice from children to keep little journals of what daily happened to us; these, in all our short absences, were matter of great entertainment to us; we constantly communicated them when we met, or if we chanced to be separated by any distance, we made a mutual exchange by the post of our little diurnal registers, having made each a solemn promise, not to conceal an incident, or even a thought, of the least moment, from the other; and this promise I believe was religiously kept up during a correspondence of many years.

I had a brother about three years older than myself; a very promising young man. He was an only son, and the darling of his parents: when he had finished his studies, my father thought of sending him abroad, but his fondness for him made him resolve to accompany him himself.

A better tutor or a better guide he could not have found for him; my father was then in the prime of life, he had no other children but him and me. My mother, as fond of me as he was of his son, and perfectly affectionate to my father, expressed her wish to let both her and me be of his party. She said, she thought a young lady, under proper conduct, might improve as much by seeing foreign courts, and the various customs of different nations, as a young gentleman.

I was then about sixteen: my father readily consented, as he perfectly loved my mother; and we all four set out on our tour together. It was my lot, after I had been some time abroad, to marry an English gentleman, then resident at Vienna; this occasioned my continuing there some years, and it was during that space of time that I had the occurrences of my friend's life from her own hand. As she had kept up to the method we had agreed on of communicating every thing that happened, even to trivial matters, it generally encreased the bulk of the packets I used to receive from her to a prodigious size: these she sent off occasionally, at nearer or more distant periods of time, according as I gave her the opportunity, by letting her know our motions.

I have from those selected the most material parts of her history, and connected them so as to make one continued narrative.

There were long intervals of time between many of the most important incidents of her life; but as the passages which intervened were either foreign to the main scope of her story, or too trivial to be recorded, in copying her papers they were omitted.

I have myself prefixed to her story a very brief account

of the lady's family.

Thus much, Sir, added the good lady, I thought necessary to premise to you, for your better understanding her history, which I have never yet shewn to any body but my son.

When I took my leave, she put the manuscript into my hands, with a charge to be careful of it.

We returned to town, and in less than three weeks I had the mortification to hear that this respectable old Lady, by whom I had been entertained with so much friendship and politeness, was dead. Her son (my friend) was on this occasion obliged to go down into Buckinghamshire; it was some months before I saw him again, as he had a good deal of family business to settle.

When he came back to London, I offered to return him the manuscript, which he had quite forgot. He told me, as he had all the original papers, *that* copy was at my service.

I then expressed my wish that it were made public. To this he at first objected, as he said there were several persons living, related to the parties concerned in some of the principal events of the story, who might take umbrage at it. I told him, that this might easily be obviated, by changing the names both of persons and places, which I would undertake to do throughout the whole; and I was afterwards so urgent with him to comply with my request, that he at last yielded. With his consent therefore I give it to the world, just as I received it, without any alteration, excepting the proposed one of a change of names.

MEMOIRS OF MISS SIDNEY BIDULPH

MRS Catharine Sidney Bidulph, was the daughter of Sir Robert Bidulph of Wiltshire. Her father died when she was very young; and of ten children none survived him but this lady, and his eldest son, afterwards Sir George Bidulph. The family estate was not very considerable; and Miss Bidulph's portion was but four thousand pounds; a fortune however at that time but quite contemptible: it was in the beginning of queen Ann's reign.

Lady Bidulph was a woman of plain sense, but exemplary piety; the strictness of her notions (highly commendable in themselves) now and then gave a tincture of severity to her actions, though she was ever esteemed a truly good woman.

She had educated her daughter, who was one of the greatest beauties of her time, in the strictest principles of virtue; from which she never deviated, through the course of an innocent, though unhappy life.

Sir George Bidulph was nine or ten years older than his sister. He was a man of a good understanding, moral as to his general conduct, but void of any of those refined sentiments, which constitute what is called *delicacy*. Pride is sometimes accounted laudable; that which Sir George possessed (for he had pride) was not of this kind.

He was of a weakly constitution, and had been ordered by the physicians to Spa for the recovery of a lingering disorder, which he had laboured under for some time. It was just on his return to England that the busy scene of his sister's life opened. An intimate friend of hers, of her own sex, to whom she revealed all the secrets of her heart, happened at this juncture to go abroad, and it was for her perusal only the following journal was intended. That friend has carefully preserved it, as she thinks it may serve for an example to prove, that neither prudence, foresight, nor even the best disposition that the human heart is capable of, are of themselves sufficient to defend us against the inevitable ills that sometimes are allotted, even to the best. 'The race is not to the swift, nor the battle to the strong.'

THE JOURNAL

April 2, 1703

MY dear and ever-beloved Cecilia is now on her way to Harwich. How insipid will this task of recording all the little incidents of the day now appear to me, when you, my sister, friend of my heart, are no longer near me? how many tedious months will it be before I again embrace you? how many days of impatience must I suffer before I can even hear from you, or communicate to you the actions, the words, the thoughts of your Sidney? – But let me not grow plaintive, the stile my friend hates – I should be ungrateful (if I indulged it) to the best of mothers, who, to gratify and amuse me on this first occasion of sorrow which I ever experienced, has been induced to quit her beloved retirement, and come on purpose to London, to rouze up my spirits, and, as she expresses herself, to keep me from the sin of murmuring.

Avaunt then complainings! Let me rest assured that my Cecilia is happy in her pursuits, and let me resolve on making myself so in mind.

April 3

We have had a letter from my brother George; he is landed, and we expect him hourly in town. As our house is large enough, I hope he will consent to take up his quarters with us while we stay in London. My mother intends to request it of him: she says it will be for the *reputation* of a gay young man to live in a *sober* family. I know not how Sir George may relish the proposal, as our hours are not likely to correspond with those which I suppose he has been used to since he has been absent from us. But perhaps he may not refuse the compliment; Sir George is not averse to oeconomy. – How kind, how indulgent, is this worthy Parent of mine! she will not suffer me to stay at home with her, nay scarce allows me time for my journal. 'Sidney I won't have you stay within; I won't have you write; I won't have you think – I will make a rake of you; you shall go to the play to-night, and I am almost tempted to go with you myself, though I have not been at one since your father's death.' – These were her kind expressions to me just now. – I am indeed indebted to her tenderness, when she relaxes so much of her usual strictness, as even to *think* of such a thing.

April 5

My brother returned to us this day, thank God! in perfect health. Never was there such an alteration seen in a man; he is grown fat, and looks quite robust. He dropped in upon us just as we sat down to dinner: what a clutter has his arrival made! my mother was *so* rejoyced, and *so* thankful, and *so* full of praises, and asked *so* many questions, that George could hardly find words enough to answer the over-flowings of her kind inquisitiveness, which lasted all dinner-time.

When the cloth was removed, my mother proposed his taking up his abode with us: you see, said she, your sister and I have got here into a large house; there is full room enough in it for you and your servants; and as I think in such a town as this it will be a reputable place for you to live in, I shall be glad of your company; provided you do not encroach upon my rules by unreasonable hours, or receiving visits from such as I may not approve of for the acquaintance of your sister. I was afraid Sir George would disrelish the terms, as perhaps some of his acquaintance (though far from faulty ones) might fall within my mother's predicament: but I was mistaken, he accepted of the invitation, after making some slight apologies about the inconvenience of having so many servants: this however was soon got over.

To say the truth, I am very glad that my brother has consented to be our guest, as I hope by his means our circle of acquaintance will be a good deal enlarged. There is no pleasure in society, without a proper mixture of well-bred sensible people of both sexes, and I have hitherto been chiefly confined to those of my own.

I asked Sir George jocosely, what he had brought me home? He answered, perhaps a good husband. – My mother catched up the word – What do you mean, Son? I mean, madam, that there is come over with me a gentleman, with whom I became acquainted in Germany, who, of all the men I ever knew, I should wish to have for a brother. If Sidney should fortunately be born under the influence of *uncommonly* good stars, it may happen to be brought about. I can tell you (applying himself to me) he is prepossessed in your favour already; I have shewn him some of your letters, and he thinks you a good sensible girl. I told him you were very well in your person, and that you have had an excellent education. I hope so, said my mother, looking pleased; and what have you to tell us of this wonderful man that so much surpasses every body? Why, madam for *your* part of his character, he is the best *behaved* young man I ever saw. I never knew any body equal to him for sobriety, nor so intirely free from all the other vices of youth: as I lived in the same house with him for some months, I had frequent opportunities of making my observations. I have known him to *avoid* many irregularities, but never saw him guilty of *one*.

An admirable character indeed said my mother. So thought I too; but I wanted to know a little more of him. Now Sidney for your share in the description; I must tell you he is most exquisitely handsome, and extremely sensible.

Good sense to be sure is requisite, said my mother, but as for beauty it is but a fading flower at best, and in a man not at all necessary – A man is not the worse for it, however, cried my brother – No – my mother answered, provided it does not make him vain, and too fond of the admiration of giddy girls – That I will be sworn is not the case of my friend, answered Sir George, I believe no body with such a person as his (if there *can* be such another) would be so little vain of it; nay, I have heard him declare, that even in a woman he would give the preference to sense and virtue.

Good young man! cried my mother, I should like to be acquainted with him. (So should I, whispered I to my own heart).

Well brother, said I, you have drawn a good picture; but to make it complete, you must throw in generosity, valour, sweetness of temper, and a great deal of money – Fie my dear (said my good *literal* parent) a *great deal* is not necessary; a very moderate fortune with *such* a man is sufficient.

The good qualities you require in the finishing of my piece, answered my brother, he possesses in an eminent degree – will that satisfy you? As for his fortune – *there* perhaps a difficulty may step in – What estate madam (to my mother) do you think my sister's fortune may intitle her to?

Dear brother, I cried, pray do not speak in that *bargaining* way.

My mother answered him very gravely, Your father you know left her but four thousand pounds; it is in my power to add a *little* to it, if she marries to please me. Great matters we have no right to expect; but a *very* good girl, as my daughter is, I think, deserves something more than a bare equivalent. The equality, said my brother, (with a demure look) I fear is out of all proportion here, for the gentleman I speak of has but – six thousand pounds a year.

He burst out a laughing; it was not good-natured, and I was vexed at his joke. My poor mother dropped her countenance; I looked silly, as if I had been disappointed, but I said nothing.

Then he is above our reach, Sidney, answered my mother.

I made no reply – Have a good heart Sid, cried my brother; if my nonpareil likes you, when he sees you, (I felt myself hurt, and grow red) and without a compliment sister (seeing me look mortified) I think he will, fortune will be no objection. I have already told him the utmost extent of your expectations; he would hardly let me mention the subject; he has a mind for *my* sister, and if he finds her personal accomplishments answer a brother's (perhaps partial) description, it will be your own fault if you have not the prettiest fellow in England for your husband.

My mother reassumed her pleased countenance. Where is he? let us see him? I forced a smile, though I did not feel myself quite satisfied – We parted on the road, my brother answered; he is gone to Bath, for a few weeks; he has sent his servants and his baggage to town before him, and has commissioned me to take a house for him in St. James's Square, or some of the adjacent streets; so that we shall have him in our neighbourhood.

My mother enquired on what account he went to Bath. Sir George said, he complained of a weakness in one of his wrists, which was the consequence of a fever that had seized him on his journey, in their return to England. It seems he had finished his travels, on which he had been absent near five years, when my brother and he met in Germany. The liking he took to Sir George protracted his stay, and he resolved not to quit him while his health obliged him to continue abroad; they took a trip to Paris together, and returned home by Holland.

The name of this piece of perfection is Faulkland, Orlando Faulkland. What a pretty name Orlando is! My mother says it is romantic, and wonders how *sober* people can give their children such names.

Now am I dying with curiosity to see this man. A few weeks at Bath – what business he had to go to Bath till he had first settled his household at London? His wrist might have grown well without the pump. I am afraid he is gone to Bath only to shew himself, and that he will be snapped up before he comes to town. I wish Sir George had kept the account of him to himself, till he returned to London again.

April 7

We have settled Sir George's oeconomy within doors: my mother has been very busy all day in fixing trunks, portmanteaus, and boxes, in their proper places; and in appropriating the rooms for his men, which she has taken care shall be as remote from those of our servants as the house will admit. She says, she knows our own domestics to be orderly and regular, but she cannot answer for what other people's may be.

I begin to recover my spirits: my brother's arrival has given new life to the family; my mother thinks, that in *his* company, with a lady or two, there will be no impropriety in suffering me to go, at least, half a dozen times into public during the season, even without the sanction of her presence – How kind, how considerate is this dear mother! I find this was one (amongst others) of her principal reasons for wishing Sir George to be with us, as it will save her from the necessity of going to public diversions, which otherwise she would have done, rather than have me debarred the pleasure of partaking of them, through the want of a proper protector. Every day lays me under fresh obligations to her.

April 20

My brother has had another letter from Mr Faulkland. He has been but a fortnight at Bath, and already has found benefit from the use of the pump; I wish his wrist was quite well; I never was so impatient to see any body – But, Sidney, have a care – this heart has never yet been touch'd: this man is represented as a dangerous object. What an an ill-fated Girl should I be, if I should fall in love with him, and he should happen not to like me? Should *happen*, what a vain expression was that? I would not for the world any one should see it but my Cecilia. – Well, if he should not like me, what then? why, I will not like him. I have a heart, not very susceptible of what we young women call love; and in all likelihood I shall be as indifferent to him, as he may be to me – Indeed I think I ought to resolve on not liking him; for notwithstanding those fine out-lines of a character, which my brother gave of him in the presence of my mother, I have since drawn out of Sir George, who is always talking of him, some farther particulars, which do not please me so well; for I think he is made up of contrarieties.

Nature, says Sir George, never formed a temper so gentle, so humane, so benevolent as his; yet, when provoked, no tempest is more furious. You would imagine him so humble, that he thinks every one superior to himself; yet through this disguise have I discovered, at certain times, a pride which makes him look down on all mankind. With a disposition formed to relish, and a heart attached to the domestic pleasures of life, he is of so enterprising a temper, that dangers and difficulties rather encourage than dishearten him in the pursuit of a favourite point. His ideas of love, honour, generosity, and gratitude, are so refined, that no hero in romance ever went beyond him; of this I was convinced from many little incidents which occurred in the course of my acquaintance with him. The modesty and affability of his deportment makes every body fancy, when he is in company with them, that he is delighted with their conversation; nay, he often affects to be improved and informed; yet there is a sly turn to ridicule in him, which, though without the least tincture of ill-nature, makes him see and represent things in a light, the very opposite of that in which you fansied he saw them. With the nicest discernment, where he permits his judgment alone to determine, let passion interfere, and a child can impose on him. Though as I have already told you he is very handsome, he affects to despise beauty in his own sex; yet is it easy to perceive, by the nice care he takes in his dress (though the farthest in the world from a fop), that he does not altogether disregard it in his own person.

Are not these faults? yes, surely they are; yet Sir George protests he has none; or at least says, if these be such, they are so over-balanced by his good qualities, that unless it be *you* sister (flattering creature! though that is seldom his failing) I don't know the woman that deserves him. I did not thank him for the compliment he paid me, at the expense of the rest of our poor sex.

May 5

A month is past since my brother arrived, and Mr Faulkland does not yet talk of coming to town – If Sir George had drawn half such a flattering picture of me to him, as he has done of him to me, his curiosity would have brought him here sooner. – My mother has mentioned him several times, and asked when he is to be in town? My brother has taken a very handsome house for him in the Square. We are all in expectation of this blazing star's making its appearance in London. If he stays much longer, my patience will be so tired, that I shall not give a pinch of snuff to see him.

May 19

Six weeks, and no news of Mr Faulkland's coming! I'll positively give him but another week; I begin to think myself affronted by his stay.

May 23

Now, now, my Cecilia, I can gratify your curiosity at full: he is come at last; Mr Faulkland, I mean; Orlando is come! we had a message from him this morning, to enquire after all our healths; he was just arrived at his house in the Square: Sir George flew to him directly, and said he would bring him without ceremony to take a family dinner. My mother bid him do so; and she held a quarter of an hour's conference with her cook. She is always elegant and exact at her table; but we were more than ordinarily so to-day. My brother brought Mr Faulkland a little before dinner-time, and presented him to my mother and me, with that kind of freedom that almost look'd as if he were already one of the family.

We had both been prepossessed highly in favour of his figure, a circumstance that seldom is of advantage to persons on their first appearance: but here it had not that effect: Sir George did not overrate the personal accomplishments of his friend. Now you'll expect I should describe him to you, perhaps, and paint this romantic hero in the glowing colours of romantic exageration. But I'll disappoint you – and tell you, that he is neither like an Adonis nor an Apollo – that he has no hyacinthine curls flowing down his back; no eyes like suns, whose brightness and majesty strike the beholders dumb; nor, in short, no rays of divinity about him; yet he is the handsomest mortal man that I ever saw. – I will not say that his voice is harmony itself, and that all the loves and graces (for why should not there be male as well as female graces?) attend on his motions; that Minerva presides over his lips, and every feature has its attendant Cupid – But I will acknowlege that his voice in speaking is inexpressibly pleasing (you know how I admire an agreeable voice); that his air and motions are easy, genteel, and graceful; his conversation sensible and polite, and without the least tincture of affection, that thing, which of all others, would to *me* destroy the charms of an angel. – In short, without hyperbole, that he is, what every one must allow, a perfectly handsome and accomplished young man.

I never saw my mother appear so pleased with any one. The polite freedom of his address, the attention and deference he seemed to pay to her sentiments (and the dear good woman talked more to him, I think, than ever I heard her do to any one on so short an acquaintance), delighted her beyond expression. I bore no great part in the conversation, but was not, however, quite overlooked by Mr Faulkland. He referred to me in discourse now and then, and seemed pleased with me; at least I fancy'd so. My brother endeavoured to draw me out, as he said afterwards. The intention was kind, but poor Sir George is not delicate enough in those matters; I should have done better if he had let me alone. I thought of the conversations we had so often had about Mr Faulkland, and could not help considering myself like a piece of goods that was to be shewn to the best advantage to the purchaser. This reflection threw a sort of constraint over my behaviour, that (fool as I was) I had not courage enough to shake off, and I did not acquit myself at all to my own mind. I had, notwithstanding, the good fortune to please my mother infinitely. She told me, after our visitor was gone, that my behaviour had been *strictly* proper; and blamed Sir George for his wanting to engage me too often in conversation. You may assure yourself, son, she said, that a man of Mr Faulkland's understanding will not like a young lady the worse for her silence. She spoke enough to shew that it was not for want of knowing what to say that she held her tongue. The man who does not reckon a modest reserve amongst the chief recommendations of a woman, should be no husband for Sidney. I am sure, when I married Sir Robert, he had never heard me speak twenty sentences. Sir George agreed with her as to the propriety of her observation, in regard to a modest reserve; but said, people now a-days did not carry their ideas of it quite so far as they did when his father's courtship began with her; and added, that a young lady might *speak* with as much modesty as she could hold her tongue.

I did not interfere in the debate, only said, I was very glad to have my mother's approbation of my conduct. This put an end to the argument, and my mother launched out into high encomiums on Mr Faulkland. She said, upon her *truth*, he was the finest young man she ever saw, in every respect. So modest, so well bred, so very entertaining, and so unassuming, with all his fine accomplishments: She was quite astonished, and owned she almost despaired of finding a young gentleman, of the present mode of education, so *very* unexceptionable in his behaviour. If his morals answered to his outward deportment – there she stopped; or rather Sir George interrupted her. I hope you'll believe madam, that my knowlege of mankind is not so circumscribed, but that I can distinguish between a real and an assumed character; and I will venture to assert, that, in the whole circle of my acquaintance, I do not know *one* so unobjectionable, even in your strict sense of the word *morals*, as Mr Faulkland.

Well, said my mother, I have the pleasure to observe to you (and I think I am seldom mistaken in my judgment), that Mr Faulkland is at least as well pleased with Sidney as we are with him – What say you daughter? Ay, what *say* you sister? cry'd Sir George – I think madam, that Mr Faulkland is an accomplished gentleman, and – 'and that you could be content to look no farther, if matters are brought to bear; eh, Sidney?' (I need not tell you whose speech this was) – Brother, that is going a little too far, for the first time of my seeing him. A great *deal* too far, my mother said; let us first know Mr Faulkland's mind from himself, before we say a word more of the matter.

Sir George told us, that Mr Faulkland, at going away, had requested he would sup with him at his own house, as he said he had a few visits of form to pay, and should be at home early in the evening.

May 24

My mother and I were in bed before my brother came in last night, though he keeps very good hours in general. When we met this morning at breakfast, I saw by Sir George's face that he was brimful of something – Faulkland don't like you, Sidney, said he, abruptly – How can you or I help that, brother? cry'd I, colouring; tho', to tell you the truth, I did not believe him; for I knew, if it *had* been so, he would not have come out with it so bluntly. But my mother, who always takes every word she hears literally, took him up very short; 'If he does not, Sir, it is not polite in you to tell your sister so; I hope

Sidney may be *liked* by as good a man as Mr Faulkland,' and up she tossed her dear honest head. Sir George burst out a laughing. My mother looked angry; she was afraid her sagacity would be call'd in question, after what she had pronounced the evening before. I looked silly, but pretended to smile. Sir George was clown enough to laugh on; at last (to my mother) 'But my dear madam, can you believe me serious in what I said? have you so good an opinion of my veracity, or so ill a one of my breeding, as to suppose I would shock my sister by such a rude declaration, if I meant any thing by it but a joke?' Indeed, Sidney, (looking half smiling to me) I would not be as much in love with our sovereign lady the queen, as poor Faulkland is with you, for my whole estate.

This put me a great deal more out of countenance than what he had said at first. Nay, brother, now you are too extravagant the other way – My mother looked surprized, but recovered her good humour presently – Dear George, there is no knowing when you are in earnest and when not: but, as Sidney says, now you are rather too extravagant. You might say so to Faulkland, answered my brother, if you were to hear him; I could get nothing from him the whole night but your praises. I thought, said my pleased mother, he had not *disliked* the girl – Now you see, son, her *silence* did her no harm; and she smiled tenderly at me. Come, said Sir George, things are mighty well on all sides. Faulkland has begged of me, that I would use my interest with you, mother (whom he thinks one of the best of women), that he may be permitted in form to make his addresses to Miss Bidulph. *My* interest he knows he has, and I hope, madam, it will have your approbation – He desired me to explain minutely to you every circumstance of his fortune: what his estate is I have told you; and his family is of known distinction. He begged I would not *mention* Sidney's fortune; and said, that if, upon a farther acquaintance, he should have the happiness to be acceptable to my sister, he should insist upon leaving the appointment of her settlement to lady Bidulph and myself. I told him I would lay this proposal before you, and could for his present comfort inform him, that, as I believed my sister had no prepossessions in favour of any one else, I was sure, if he met with your concurrence, her's would follow of course.

A very discreet answer, said my mother; just such a one as I would have dictated to you, if I had been at your elbow. I believe we may venture to suppose, that Mrs Sidney *has* no prepossessions; and as this is as handsome an offer as can possibly be made, I have no objections (if you have none, my dear) to admit Mr Faulkland upon the terms he proposes.

What answer ought I to have made, Cecilia? Why, to be sure, just the one I *did* make – I have *no* prepossessions, madam, looking down and blushing, till it actually pained me, for I was really startled. My Cecilia knows I am not a prude.

My dear! cry'd my mother, and took me by the hand –

Poor Sidney, said Sir George, how you are to be pitied! Mr Faulkland purposes waiting on you in the afternoon, if he is not *forbid*; and he looked so teazingly sly, that my mother bid him leave off his *pranks*.

The day is ever – Mr Faulkland spent the evening with us; no other company but our own family. My mother likes him better even than before – Thy *mother* – disingenuous girl! why dost thou not speak thy *own* sentiments! (There is an apostrophe for thy use, my Cecilia). Well then, *my* sentiments you shall have; you have an undoubted right to know them on all subjects, but particularly on this interesting one.

I *do* think Mr Faulkland the most amiable of men; and if my heart were (happily for me it is not) *very* susceptible of tender impressions, I really believe I should in time be absolutely in love with him. This confession will not satisfy you: may be it is not enough – yet, in truth, Cecilia, it is all that at present I can afford you.

The thoughts of the aukward figure I should make in the evening visit, sat heavy on my spirits all day. – Can you conceive any thing more distressing than the situation of a poor girl, receiving the visit of a man, who, for the first time, comes professedly as her admirer? I had conceived a frightful idea of such an interview, having formed my notions of it only from romances, where set speeches of an ell long are made by the lover, and answers of a proportionable size are returned in form by the lady. But Mr Faulkland soon delivered me from my anxiety. His easy, but incomparably polite and sensible freedom of address, quickly made me lose my ridiculous fears. – He made no other use of this visit, than to recommend himself more strongly to our esteem, by such means as proved how well he deserved it. If he was particular to me, either in his looks or manner, it was under the regulation of such a nice decorum, that I (who supposed I must have sunk with downright confusion) was hardly disconcerted during the whole visit.

June 10

I do really think my good mother grows so fond of Mr Faulkland, that if he goes on at this rate, he will get the start even of Sir George in her affections – 'Mr *Faulkland* said so and so; Mr *Faulkland* is of opinion; and I am sure you will allow Mr *Faulkland* to be a good judge of such and such things.'

To say the truth, the man improves upon you every hour you know him. And yet I have discovered in him some of those little (and they are *but* little) alloys to his many good qualities, which Sir George at first told me of. The interest I may one day have in him makes me a closer observer than I should otherwise be. There *is* that sly turn to ridicule which my brother mentioned; yet, to do him justice, he never employs it, but where it is deserved; and then too with so much vivacity and good humour, that one cannot be angry with him.

We had a good deal of company at dinner with us to day; amongst the rest, young Sayers, who is just returned from his travels, as *he* calls it. You remember he went away a good humoured, inoffensive, quiet fool; he has brought no one ingredient of that character back with him but the last; for such a stiff, conceited, overbearing, talkative, impertinent coxcomb, does not now exist. His mother, who, poor woman, you know originally made a simpleton of the boy, contributes now all in her power to finish the sop; and she carries him about with her everywhere for a show. We were assembled in the drawing room before dinner: in *burst* (for it was not a common entry) Master Sayers, and his mamma, the cub handing in the old lady – *So* stiff, and *so* aukward, and *so* ungraceful, and so *very* unlike Mr Faulkland, that I pitied the poor thing, who thought that every body would admire him as much as his mother did. After he had been presented to the ladies (for it was the first time we had seen him since he came home), he took a turn or two about the room, to exhibit his person: then applying himself to a picture which hung over the door (a fine landscape of Claude Lorrain, which Mr Faulkland himself had brought over and given to Sir George), he asked my brother, in a tone scarce articulate, whether we had any *painters* in England? My mother, who by chance heard him, and by greater chance understood him, answered, before Sir George had time, *Painters*, Sir! yes, sure, and some very good ones too; why, you cannot have forgot *that*; it is not much above a year since you went abroad. (for you must know he had been recalled upon the death of an uncle, who had left him his estate). I observed Mr Faulkland constrained a very fly laugh, on account both of the *manner* of my mother's taking his question, and her innocently-undesigned reprimand. Sayers pretended not to hear her, but looking through his fingers, as if to throw the picture into perspective, that is a pretty good piece, said he, for a copy. Oh! cry'd his mother, there is no pleasing *you* – people who have been *abroad* are such connoisseurs in painting – No body making any immediate answer, Mr Faulkland stepped up to Mr Sayers, with such a roguish humility in his countenance, that you would have sworn he was a very ignoramus, said, 'Are you of opinion, Sir, that that picture is nothing but a copy?' Nothing more, take my word for it, Sir: When *I* was at Rome, there was a Dutchman there who made it his business to take copies *of* copies, which he dispersed, and had people to sell for him in different parts, as pretty good prices; and they did mighty well; for very few people *know* a picture; and I'll answer for it there are not many masters of eminence, but what have a hundred originals palmed upon them, more than ever they painted in their lives.

Mr Faulkland then proceeded to ask him abundance of questions, which any one, who did not know him well, would have thought he proposed for no other end but a desire of information; and the poor coxcomb Sayers plumed himself upon displaying so much travelled knowlege, to a wondering ignorant Englishman, who had never been out of his own country. The company were divided into little chattering parties, as is usual when people are whiling away an half hour before dinner. Mrs. Sayers, my mother, and I, were sitting together on a couch, near enough to hear the conversation that passed between the two gentlemen; at least as much as was not sunk in the affected, half-pronounced sentences of Mr Sayers. His mother, to whom he was the principal object of attention in the company, seemed mightily pleased at the opportunity her son had, from the inquisitiveness of Mr Faulkland (whom she did not know) of shewing his taste in the polite arts, and often looked about to observe if any body else attended to them. My mother, dear literal woman! (as I often call her to you) took every thing seriously, and whispered to me, how pretty that is, Sidney! how condescending in Mr Faulkland! you see he does not make a parade of his *own* knowledge in these matters, but is pleased to reap the benefit of other people's. I, who saw the latent roguery, could hardly contain myself. Indeed I was amazed at Mr Faulkland's grave inquisitive face, and was very glad my mother did not find him out.

Sayers, elated with having shone so conspicuously (for he observed that both my mother and I attended to his discourse) proceeded to shew away with an immensity of vanity and frothy chat, beginning every new piece of history with, 'When *I* was at Rome, or, when *I* was at Paris' – At last, unluckily for him, speaking of an incident (which made a good deal of noise, and happened at the first-mentioned place) in which two English gentlemen had been concerned, he said it was about eleven months ago, just before he left Rome. My mother, who had heard Mr Faulkland relate the same story, but with some very different circumstances, immediately said, Mr Faulkland, have I not heard you speak of that? you were at Rome yourself when the affair happened; and if I be not mistaken, it was through your interest with the cardinal of – that the business was made up.

If a spectre had appeared to poor Sayers, he could not have looked more aghast. He dropped his visage half-way down his breast, and for the *first* time speaking very *plain*, and very loud too, with a share of astonishment, Have *you* been at *Rome*, Sir? I was there for a little time, Sir, answered Mr Faulkland, with real modesty; for he pitied the mortified buzzard; and I know the story was *represented* as you have told it; the circumstances differed in a few particulars, but the facts were nearly as you have related them.

How obligingly did he reconcile the out-of-countenance Sayers to himself and to the company? Were you long abroad, pray Sir, said the coxcomb? About five years, Sir, answered Mr Faulkland; but I perceive, by the conversation I have had the honour of holding with you to-day, that many accurate and curious observations escaped me, which you made in a much shorter space of time; for the communication of which I think myself extremely obliged to you. Whether the poor soul thought him serious (as my mother did) I cannot tell; he made him a bow, however, for the compliment; but was so lowered, that he did not say a word more of Rome or Paris for the rest of the day: and in this we had a double advantage; for as he had nothing else to talk of, his mouth was effectually stopped, except when Mr Faulkland, out of compassion, asked him (as he often did) such questions as he thought he could answer, without exposing his ignorance: for he was contented to have enjoyed it in their tête à tête, and was far from wishing the company to be witnesses of it.

I think such a bagatelle may give you some idea of this man's turn.

I told it to Sir George; he laughed heartily, and said it was *so* like him! My brother loves even his faults, though he will not allow me to call them by that name.

July 4

You are unkind, Cecilia, and do not do justice to my sincerity, when you say, *you are sure I am in love with Mr Faulkland.* If I were, can you conceive it possible that I would deny it to you? Ah! my sister, must I suspect *you* of wanting candour by your making a charge of disingenuity against your friend? Indeed, Cecilia, if I *am* in love with him, I do not *yet* know it myself. I will repeat it to you, I think him the most aimable of men, and should certainly give him the preference, if I were left to a free choice, over all the rest of his sex; at least all that I have ever yet seen; though possibly there *may* be handsomer, wiser, better men, but they have not fallen within my observation. I am not however so prepossessed in his favour, as to suppose him a phoenix; and if any unforeseen event were to prevent my being his, I am sure I should bear it, and behave very handsomely.

And yet perhaps this may be only bragging like a coward, because I think a very short time will put it out of the power of fortune to divide us. Yet certain as the event of our marriage appears to me at present, I still endeavour to keep a sort of guard over my wishes, and will not, give my heart leave to center *all* its happiness in him; and therefore I cannot rank myself amongst the first-rate lovers, who have neither eyes, nor ears, nor sensations, but for one object. *This*, Mr Faulkland says, is his case, in regard to me. But I think we women should not love at such a rate, till *duty* makes the passion a virtue; and till *that* becomes my case, I am so much a philosopher in love that I am determined not to let it absorbe any of the other cordial affections, which I owe to my relations and my friends.

I think we ought always to form some laws to ourselves for the regulation of our conduct: without this, what an impertinent dream must the life be of almost every young person of our sex? You, my dear, though with an uncommon understanding of your own, have always been intirely conducted by your wise parents; and in this I make it my boast to have followed your example. I have been accustomed from my infancy to pay an implicit obedience to the best of mothers; the conforming to this never yet cost me an uneasy minute, and I am sure never will.

July 5

A little incident happened to-day, which pleased my mother wonderfully. She had been at morning prayers (as you know is her daily custom); when returning home in her chair, one of the men happened to flip his foot, and fell down just before Mr Faulkland's house. He was so much hurt, that he could go no farther; and the footman immediately opening the chair, told her she had better step into Mr Faulkland's, till he called another, or got a man to assist in carrying her home. One of Mr Faulkland's servants happened to be standing at the door; so that, without any previous notice, she was immediately conducted into a parlour, where Mr Faulkland was sitting at breakfast. She found with him two pretty little children at his knee, to one of whom he had given some cake; and the elder of the two, a boy of about five years old, he was gravely lecturing, though with great gentleness, for having told a lye. My mother asked him, with some surprise, whose children those were? He smiled, and told her they were his coachman's; and then ordered the footman to carry them down, bidding the little boy be sure to remember what he had said to him.

My mother enquired, if he permitted them to be in the house? He said, he did; and had been induced to do it from the distress he had seen their poor father in, a few days before. He is an honest careful fellow, continued Mr Faulkland, and has lived in my family from a boy. He was married to a good sort of a body, who took great care of these children, and helped to maintain them decently by her work. The poor woman died in childbed last week; and the person who attended her in her illness (for she had no servant) took that opportunity of robbing the lodgings; and after plundering the poor creature of every thing that was worth carrying away, locked up those two children, which you saw with me, and the new-born infant, with the corpse of their mother.

The poor little wretches continued in that dismal situation all night, having cried themselves to sleep, without being heard, though there were some other people in the house. The morning following I happened to make an early visit in the neighbourhood of this distressed little family, and my coachman, who was a very affectionate husband and father, took that opportunity of calling on his wife whom he had not been able to see for three days. The cries of his children (now awake and almost starved) obliged him hastily to break open the room door, where the poor fellow was shocked with the dismal spectacle of his wife lying breathless in her bed, the infant almost expiring at her side, and the other two poor little famished creatures calling to their dead mother for bread.

The sight almost deprived the man of his senses. He snatched up his two eldest children in his arms, and ran raving to the house where I was; tearing his hair like a madman. He told me his mournful story; with which I was so affected, that I ordered one of my footmen to carry the two children home to my house directly, and desired their father to look out for some body to take care of the young one, which he soon did.

The honest poor fellow was delighted, when he came home, to find his two children well and merry; for they were sensible of no want but their food. But his grief returned on him with great violence at the thoughts of his being obliged to put them into the hands of people, who, he said, he was sure would not be so kind to them as their own poor mother had been; and my man told me he did nothing but kiss them, and cry over them the whole day. To make his mind easy at once, I let him know they should remain here under his own eye, till they were old enough to be put to school; and accordingly directed my housekeeper to see that they were taken care of; which has made their father very happy.

The little rogues have found their way up to me, and I love some times to hear them prattle; but this morning the eldest having told me a lye of his brother, I was checking him for it when you came in.

My mother was so pleased with Mr Faulkland's conduct in his little history, that she repeated it to me word for word as soon as she came home, and concluded with observing, how *good a creature* Mr Faulkland must be, who in so tender a manner interested himself in his poor servant's misfortune. Most young gentlemen, said she, would have thought they had done enough in giving the servant money to have provided for his children how he could: it is in such trifles as these that we often discover the excellence of the heart.

You will suppose, my dear, that I am not displeased at any circumstance that can raise Mr Faulkland's character in my pious mother's esteem. I heard the story with great pleasure; but not making any comments on it, Sir George (who was present at the relation), said, Well, Sidney, you are either very affected, or the greatest stoic in the world; why, any other girl would be in raptures at such a proof of the honest tenderness of that heart which she knows she possesses intirely, and on which the whole of her future happiness depends. I am very sensible of Mr Faulkland's worth, brother, I replied, and I can feel without being transported. I will be hanged, said Sir George, if I think you love Faulkland, at least not half as well as he deserves; and I dare swear you have not been honest enough to tell him yet whether you do or not. It is time enough for that, I replied; if Mr Faulkland and I should be married, I hope I shall give him no cause to complain of my want of affection.

If you marry, said my brother! I know of no possible *ifs*, unless they are of your own making. I know of none neither, answered my mother; yet I think Sidney is in the right to be doubtful about all human events. Many things, added she gravely (for she has a great veneration for old sayings), fall out between the cup and the lip.

I think, mother, said Sir George, bluntly, *you* were disappointed in your *first* love; I have heard you speak of it, but I forget the circumstances. As I had never heard my mother make any mention of this particular, I begged she would oblige me with relating it.

When I was about one-and-twenty, daughter, said she, a match was concluded by my father between me and a very fine gentleman. I loved him, and (as I suppose all young women do in the like circumstances) believed myself equally beloved by him. The courtship had been of a year's standing; for you must know I was not very easily won. Every thing was settled, and the day appointed for our marriage arrived; when, instead of the bridegroom, whom we every minute expected, there came a letter from him directed to me. The contents were, that having formerly been engaged to a young lady by the most solemn vows, he had, unfortunately for them both, forgot them all on seeing me, and had broke through every obligation divine and human to obtain me. He intreated mine, and my family's pardon, in the most pathetic manner, for having engaged our esteem so far as to consent to an union, of which he found himself unworthy, and which it was impossible for him to accomplish; for, said he, the wrongs I have done the woman, whose youth I seduced, rise to my imagination with so much horror, that, for the empire of the world, I would not complete my guilt, by devoting that hand to another, to which she only has a right. He enlarged greatly on the sufferings of his heart, in the struggle between his love for me, and his duty to the person who had his first vows; and whom, he declared, his infidelity had almost brought to the grave. He claimed my pity, both on his own and her account; and repeatedly intreated my forgiveness of his fault.

The whole letter, which was very long, was so expressive of a mind overwhelmed with despair, that I was exceedingly shocked at the reading of it. What could I say? The plea he offered for his seemingly strange conduct, was too just to admit of any objections. I own the disappointment afflicted me, but I bore it with a becoming resolution. My family were at first exceedingly exasperated against my doubly unfaithful lover; but, upon enquiring into the facts, they found the truth to be as he had represented it. The conclusion was, that, upon the very day on which he was to have been married to me, and on which he had writ me that gloomy letter, he was seized with a melancholy, with increasing on him daily, soon after ended in absolute madness, and he was obliged to be confined for the remainder for his life. The young lady lived but a short time after the melancholy fate of her lover, and died, as it was said, of a broken heart.

It was a great comfort to me to reflect that my fate disposed otherwise of me than to this unhappy gentleman; for I am very sure, had these fatal events happened in consequence of my marriage with him, that I should never have survived it.

This extraordinary anecdote of my mother's life, which I had never had a hint of before (for she could not speak of it without great emotion), very much affected me. Sir George said, the story was more tragical than he had apprehended, and told my mother, *that* was an accident which fell out between the cup and the lip, with a vengeance.

My mother continued thoughtful for a good while; and I was sorry that the memory of this melancholy story had been revived; but Sir George talked and laughed us both in spirits again.

July 6

This Mr Faulkland is a princely man; he has sent me *such* a set of jewels! My mother says they are too fine for a private gentlewoman; but George tells her they are not a bit too fine for Mr Faulkland's *wife*, and only suitable to his fortune. You know I have but few of my own, those only which were my mother's when she was a maiden. The greatest part of her's, and by much the finest, were presented to her by my father; but those she reserves for Sir George, against the time of his marriage, as a present for his lady; for they are family jewels.

July 8

My probation is over, my Cecilia. – The formidable question has been put to me, and I have answered it – Ay marry, say you, but how?

In the *negative*, to be sure, my dear – No, no, my Cecilia; a valuable (psha! what an affected cold word that is), a lovely and most worthy man, with six thousand pounds a year, is a prize that a country girl must not expect to draw every day. Mr Faulkland, in *lover-like* phrase, demanded from me the time of his destined happiness: I referred him to my mother. She, good and delicate as she is, referred him back to Sir George. George blurted out some sudden day that startled us both, when Mr Faulkland reported it to us. I stammered out something; my mother hesitated; Sir George came in, and blundered at us all; so I think we compounded for the time, and amongst us fixed upon this day month – And full soon enough, says my Cecilia: you have known the man but about six weeks, and surely a month is as little time as you can take, in preparing fineries. True, my girl, true; but it is all George's doings. Indeed, my Cecilia, without affectation, I had much rather have had a longer day; though I think I *know* the man as well in those six weeks, as if I had been acquainted with him so many years; for he has spent most of his hours with us every day during that time; and my mother says he is one of those in *whom there is no guile*.

Sir George is downright insolent; he declares I am not sensible of my own happiness, and that I deserve to be married to some little petty Wiltshire 'squire. He so piques himself upon making this match, there is no bearing him. He has taken all matters of settlement upon himself, and insists on my mother's not interposing. She acquiesces, but charges my brother not to let Mr Faulkland's generosity carry him too far, and bids him remember what is due to his friend, as well as to his sister.

July 10

I really begin to be hurried. My mother, you know, is exactly punctilious in every thing. Such a quantity of things *are* brought, and such a quantity to *be* bought, that there is no end of journies into the city. Then milaners and mantua-makers! – One would think I was going to pass the remainder of my life in a remote country, where there were no kind of manufactures or artificers to be come at, and that I was to provide cloathing for half a century.

July 12

I have much upon my hands, and Sir George is so impatient, and troublesome, that I believe I must employ an amanuensis, to give you a minute detail of all our foppery; for I shall not have patience to do it myself.

July 17

Sir George has often told me, that he knows of no fault Mr Faulkland has, but a violence of temper when provoked. I saw an instance of it to-day, which I was sorry for, and the more so, as I was in some measure accessary to it. Mr Faulkland, my brother, a lady of our acquaintance, and myself, took a ride in Hide-Park this morning. We were to dine at Kensington (where my mother was to meet us), at the house of the lady (a relation of Mr Faulkland's), who was with us.

We rode into the stable-yard of her house, in order to alight. My horse, which happened to be a young one that Sir George had newly bought, saw some object that made him shy of advancing, and he turned suddenly about. A footman of Mr Faulkland's, who chanced to stand just behind me, very imprudently, though I am sure with design of harm, gave him a stroke with his whip, which made the animal plunge and throw me, as I had not time to recover my seat from the first short turn he made. I luckily received not the least hurt, and was on my feet in an instant. But Mr Faulkland, who had leaped off his horse even before I fell, was so enraged at the fellow, that he gave him two or three sound lashes with his whip across the shoulders, which fell on him as quick as lightning. I am inclined to think the servant was not sober; for he had the insolence to lay hold of his master's whip, and muttered an oath or two. Mr Faulkland's attention being quickly turned to me, he took no farther notice of the man. We went into the house; and after I had assured them all I was not in the least hurt, I begged of Mr Faulkland to forgive the footman, who had undesignedly caused the accident. He made a thousand apologies, for having let his anger so far transport him, as to chastise his servant in a manner he was not used to do; but the peril he put you into, madam, addressing himself to me, made me forget myself. I repeated, I hope, Sir, you have forgiven him. I wish, my dear Miss Bidulph, said he, that the fellow were guilty of no other fault but this, that I might shew you my readiness to obey you; but he is such an intolerable sot, that there is no keeping him with safety. I have forgiven him several idle things; but as I had determined to part with him before this happened, I hope you will be so good as not to insist on my retaining him. I could not intercede for the foolish fellow after this: so said no more.

This little incident convinces me that Mr Faulkland is of too warm a temper; yet I am not alarmed at the discovery; you know I am the very reverse; and I hope in time, by gentle methods, in some measure to subdue it in Mr Faulkland. His own good sense and good nature must incline him to wish it corrected. My brother says, he has often lamented this vice of his nature to him, and said he had taken infinite pains to get the better of it; and had so far succeeded, that he seldom was surprized by it, but on very sudden and extraordinary occasions; such as, I suppose, he looked upon this to be, which I have related.

We passed the day delightfully at Kensington, and did not return to town till late. I think I have got cold, as we walked a long time in the gardens.

July 13

I have got an ugly sore throat; my mother insists on my being let blood; I am afraid of alarming her by complaining, though I had very little rest all night. Mr Faulkland came early this morning to enquire after my health: my mother told him I was not well. How tenderly dejected were his looks, when I came into the room. Sir George made him stay to breakfast; he scarce tasted any thing; he was quite cast down. My brother rallied him (I thought it unreasonable) on the chance he had the day before of losing his wife. Mr Faulkland answered, I wish I had followed the first motion of my thoughts, and discharged that wicked fellow a month ago. Sir George said, as it happened, there had been no harm done; but he thought Mr Faulkland would do well to dismiss such an insolent rogue from his service. He has saved me that trouble, said Mr Faulkland, he has dismissed himself; but took care to first to rob me. To rob you! we all repeated in the same breath. Yes, said Mr Faulkland: I told him, after I got home, that he was to deliver up such things as he had in his charge to my own man, as I meant to discharge him in the morning. He made me no reply, for he was a sullen fellow; but when the family were asleep, he contrived to pick the lock of a bureau in my dressing room, where I sometimes keep money. I believe what induced him to it was, his having seen me yesterday morning, when I was going to ride (a precaution which I generally use), put my pocket book into this place, and I suppose he concluded there were bank notes in it, for he took *that* (I presume without staying to examine it) and all the money he could find besides, and very cleverly made his escape out of a back window, which was found open this morning.

My mother lectured Mr Faulkland a little, for suffering a servant, whose fidelity he was not sure of, to see where he deposited his money; which, she said, might prove a temptation to one, who was *not* so ill inclined as this man. Mr Faulkland acknowleged it was careless in him; but said, in his justification, he had been accustomed to very honest people about him, which rendered him less suspicious.

He appeared so anxious and unhappy about my indisposition, that I affected to make as light of it as possible; though indeed I find myself very much out of order. With what a kind sorrow did he observe my looks; sighs now and then stole from him, as his eyes were fixed on my face. I am obliged to him, yet I think I should be as much concerned for *him*, if he were ill.

Here is a whole cargo of silks and laces just sent in to me – Heigh-ho! I can't look at them – I am not well – and I have such a gantlope to run of visiting and racketting, that the thought makes me sicker.

July 27

After a fortnight's, a dreadful fortnight's intermission, I reassume my pen. I have often told you, Cecilia, I was not born to be happy. Oh! I prophesied when I said so, though I knew not why I said it.

I will try to recollect all the circumstances of this miserable interval, and relate them as well as I can. The last line in my journal (which I have not yet ventured to send you, as your stay at Paris is so uncertain) informs you that I was ill. I was let blood; but my disorder increased, and I was in a high fever before next morning. I remember what my reflections were, and am sure my apprehensions of death were not on my *own* account afflicting, but grievously so at the thoughts of what those should feel whom I was to leave behind.

My mother and Mr Faulkland, I believe, chiefly engaged my mind; but I did not long continue capable of reflection. The violence of my disorder deprived me of my senses on the fourth day, and they tell me I raved of Mr Faulkland. I remember nothing, but that, in my intervals of reason, I always saw my poor mother in tears by my bedside. I was in the utmost danger, but it pleased God to restore me to the ardent prayers of my dear parent. In about ten days I began to shew some symptoms of amendment, and enquired how Mr Faulkland did. My mother answered, he is well, my dear, and gone out of town, but I believe will return in a day or two. Gone out of town, said I, and leave me dying! Indeed that was not kind of Mr Faulkland, and I shall tell him so. My mother was sitting on the bedside, and had hold of my hand; my brother was standing with his back to the fire place. I observed they looked at one another, but neither made me any answer. Pray, Sir George, I cried, would you serve the woman so whom you were so near making your wife? My brother was going to reply, but my mother frowned at him; he looked displeased, and went out of the room. Dear madam, said I, there is something the matter with Mr Faulkland; don't keep me in suspence. I *know* there is something, which you and my brother would conceal from me. Is Mr Faulkland sick? Not that I know of, I assure you, answered my mother; he was well yesterday, for we had a message from him to enquire after your health, as we have had every day, for he is but at Richmond; and you know if he were in town, he could receive no other satisfaction than hearing from you, as you are too ill to admit of any visits. My mother rang the bell immediately, and asked me to take something; I saw she wanted to turn the conversation. My maid Ellen came into the room, and I asked no more questions.

My mother staid with me till it was time for her to go to rest; but avoided mentioning Mr Faulkland's name, or giving me any opportunity of doing it; for she tenderly conjured me to keep myself quite composed, and not to talk. The doctor assured her this night that he thought me out of danger; and she retired with looks of cordial delight.

She was no sooner gone, than I called Ellen to my bedside, and charged her to tell me all she knew concerning Mr Faulkland. The poor girl looked concerned, and seemed to study for an answer. Lord bless me, madam! what should I know of him more than my lady has told you? When did you see him, said I? Not for several days, she answered. Where is he? At Richmond, I heard Sir George say; but I suppose he will come to town as soon as he hears you are well enough to receive him. I catched hold of her hand; 'Ellen, I know there is something, relative to Mr Faulkland, which you all want to hide from me; don't attempt to deceive me; you may be sure, whatever it be, I must soon be informed of it; in the mean while, my doubts make me very unhappy.'

The good-natured girl's trouble and confusion increased as I spoke: My dear madam, she replied, when you are better my lady will tell you all: 'No, no, Ellen, I must know it now; tell it me this minute, or you must never expect to see me better under such uncertainty. What is the *all*, the frightful *all*, that I am to be told? How you have shocked me with that little word!' I know nothing, madam, answered Ellen, but what I gathered from Sir George's loud angry talk with my lady; and I should be undone if her ladyship were to know I mentioned it to you. I assured her my mother should not know it. Why then, madam (speaking lower), I am afraid that Mr Faulkland has misbehaved, or has been belied to my lady – She stopped at this – How? how? cried I eagerly; What has she heard of him? Something of another courtship, she replied; but I hope it is all false – You trifle with me – speak out, and say all you know. The poor creature started at my impatience: 'I know no more, madam, than that I heard my lady say to Sir George, I had rather Sidney were in her grave, than married to him. Sir George said, But why will not you not let Mr Faulkland justify himself, madam? Justify himself! my lady answered; What can he say? Is it not plain that he is false to another woman? They talked lower; but at last Sir George raised his voice, and said, he would give half his estate to have the villain punished – All this, madam, I over-heard by mere accident. Sir George was going abroad; his linen was lying ready for him in his dressing-room; and his man desired me to put a stitch in one of his master's point ruffles which was a little ripped in the gathering. I had come up the back stairs into the dressing-room, just as my lady (who was with Sir George in the bed-chamber) said the words I first repeated; and while I stood doing the ruffle, I heard the rest. There was a great deal more said, but I could not distinguish any thing besides, except a word here and there, which Sir George seemed to speak in a very angry tone. This was the second day of your illness. Mr Faulkland had been here in the morning to enquire how you did; my lady saw him, and I thought they parted very friendly. I met Mr Faulkland coming down stairs; he looked full of grief; my lady stood at the dining-room door, and wished him a good morning. About an hour after came a letter directed to you; it was brought by a porter, who said it required no answer. As you were too ill to read it, I gave it to my lady; and it was soon after this, that I heard the conversation between Sir George and her ladyship. Mr Faulkland came again in the evening. Sir George was not at home; but my lady had him above an hour in the drawing-room; and the footman, who let him out, said, he looked as if he were in sad trouble. He has never been here since, but sends constantly every day to know how you do. My lady ordered me, if any letters came for you, to deliver them to her. And has there any come to me? No madam; word was always sent to Mr Faulkland of your being so ill, that to be sure he thought it would be in vain for him to write to you.'

This was all I could gather from the maid. What a night did I pass? I scarce closed my eyes. Ellen lay in a field-bed by me; she had watched several nights, and I obliged her now to undress and go into bed. She slept soundly; how I envied her tranquility! If I forgot myself for a few minutes, my slumbers were distracted, and I started at the recollection of what I had already heard, and the dread of what I had *still* to hear. Mr Faulkland absenting himself from the house so long; my mother wishing me in the grave, rather than be his wife; my brother denouncing vengeance on the *villain*! These were the terrible ideas that haunted me till morning. What can he have done, I cried aloud several times? I summoned to my aid all the fortitude I was mistress of, and resolved not to sink under the calamity, be it of what nature it would.

My mother, ever kind and tender, came early the next morning into my room. She enquired after my health, and looked as if she *pitied* me. I was ready to cry at her compassionate glances; they mortified me, but I was determined not to let her perceive it. I told her I was much better; and, what is surprizing, I was really so, notwithstanding the uneasy state of my mind. She talked of indifferent things, and said, she hoped I should soon be able to go into the country for a few days, to recover a little strength. I answered, I hope so too, madam. We were both silent for a while; my mother had her indulgent eyes fixed upon me; mine were cast down: at last I resolved to speak out. Madam, said I, looking steadfastly at her, what is the cause of your coldness towards Mr Faulkland? 'Tis in vain for you to hide it longer; you say he is *well*, and gone out of town. If he has shewn any slight towards me, tell me so at once; and do not entertain so mean an opinion of your daughter, as to suppose she cannot bear the news. Your tenderness, I see, would conceal *something* from me; but believe me, madam, I am prepared for the worst.

My dear, replied my mother, it gives me great pleasure to hear you say so. I pray God preserve my child, and grant her a better lot than she could hope for in a union with Mr Faulkland. What has he done, madam? My dearest Sidney, she answered, this is the first trial you have ever had of your patience; but I have no doubt that your goodness and discretion will teach you to act as becomes your character.

I did not intend to have spoken to you on the subject, till you were better able to bear the knowlege of what I am going to acquaint you with; but your prudence, I think, makes you equal to every thing; and

I hope your health will not be endangered by the discovery of Mr Faulkland's baseness. (What a dreadful preface!)

The day after you were taken ill, a letter, directed to you, was brought hither by a porter, which your maid (very discretely) delivered to me. As you were not in a condition to read it yourself, I thought proper to open it. The cover contained a few lines addressed to you; and in it was inclosed a letter directed to Mr Faulkland. Good God, added she, taking the papers out of her pocket, how little reliance ought we to have on a fair outside!

Here are the letters; read what is in the cover first. I did so; it was ill writ, and worse spelt. These were the contents:

> Madam,
>
> I hear you are soon to be married to Mr Faulkland; but as I think it a great pity that so virtuous a young lady should be thrown away, this is to inform you, that he does not deserve you.
>
> The inclosed letter, wrote to him by a fine and beautiful young lady that he decoyed, shews you how false he is. When you tax him with it, he will know from whence you got your information; but let him deny it if he can.
>
> I am, madam,
>
> You unknown friend,
>
> and humble servant.

The letter to Mr Faulkland, in a very pretty female hand, and the date but a week old (from the time it was sent to me) was as follows:

> "Oh! Mr Faulkland, I am the most unfortunate woman in the world! Fatal have you been to me, and I am undone for ever – I was in hopes that our mutual fault might have been concealed; for, while we staid at Bath, I kept my aunt intirely ignorant of what passed between us, though she often pressed me to confess the truth; but it can now no longer be concealed. I am but too sensibly reminded of the unhappy consequences of my own weakness, and your ungoverned (would I could call it) love. I never meant to trouble you with complaints; but my present condition calls loudly for your compassion. Are you then really going to be married? There wants but this to complete my destruction! Oh! Sir, before it is too late, take pity on me! I dare not continue in the house with my uncle much longer. My aunt

says, that, when my affliction becomes so conspicuous as not to be any longer hid, she will form a pretence, on account of my health, for me to be absent for some months, under colour of going to Bath, or to London, for better advice than I can have here. But what will this avail me? I have no relations, no friends, nor acquaintance, that I can trust with the secret of my miserable situation. To whom then can I fly, but to you, the cause of all my sorrow? I beseech you, for Heaven's sake, write to me, and tell me, if indeed you are going to give your self away for ever! If you are, your intended bride, perhaps, may have no other advantage of me, but what you in an evil hour deprived me of. Write to me, dear, though cruel as you are; and think of some place of refuge for your unhappy

A. B."

When I had read these letters, my mother asked me, What I thought of Mr Faulkland? Indeed, I was so astonished, that I scarce knew what answer to make; but replied, Madam, are you satisfied that this letter is not forged, with a design to injure Mr Faulkland? Ah! my dear said she, I am sorry you strive to catch at so slender a twig; you may be sure I am but too well convinced that the letter is genuine, or you should never have had a moment's uneasiness by the knowlege of it. Mr Faulkland himself does not deny it, and it is with his permission that I kept it. I promised to return it, but desired leave to retain it for a few days. He could not refuse me this, though he might easily imagine I designed to shew it to you. That, indeed, *was* my intention, when I desired to keep it a little while in my hands, and I did so, that I might have your judgment on the letter itself, as well as fully to justify my own proceedings in what I have done. Ah! dear madam, cry'd I, scarce knowing what I said, I rely on your maternal goodness; I am sure you have done what is proper. Yet has Mr Faulkland nothing to say for himself? – But I will ask no more questions – I know too much already – My love, said my mother, you have a right to know every thing relative to this affair.

I shewed the letters to your brother, as soon as I received them. Sir George at first seemed quite confounded, but afterwards, to my very great surprize, he smiled, and said, he knew of that foolish business before. I asked him, if he knew of it before, how he could answer it to his honour, his conscience, or the love he ought to bear his sister, not to divulge it immediately? Why, said he, I assure you it is a *trivial* affair, that ought not to make you uneasy.

What, George! I answered I, a trivial matter for a man to ruin a fine young lady, forsake her, and dare to involve an innocent creature in his crimes! Do you call this a *trivial* affair? If you knew the *circumstances*, said he, you would not view it in so disadvantageous a light. Faulkland certainly gained the affections of a young lady, though without seeking to do so; he never courted her, never attempted to please her, much less to win her heart, and least of all to ruin her virtue. I know that is an action he is not capable of committing. How comes it to pass then that he *did* so, said I, interrupting him? Why, the girl was silly, and she was thrown in his way by a vile designing woman that had the care of her, 'And was he (again stopping him) to take advantage of her folly, and join with that *vile designing* woman, to destroy a poor young creature's honour?' The *best* men, said he confidently, may fall into an error; and if you expect to find a man entirely free from them, you look for what is not possible in human nature.

I may expect to find a man without flagrant crimes to answer for, I hope; and I believe I spoke it with warmth. Do you call *this* one, madam, said he, with still more assurance? I hope Sidney will not be such a chit as to think in this manner, when she comes to hear the affair explained. I really grew down-right angry, and could not forbear saying, I would rather see you married to your grave than to such a man. Your brother then begged I would hear Mr Faulkland *justified*, and be a little cool till that was done. I told him there was a terrible fact alleged, of which I could not conceive it possible for him to acquit himself.

George said, he had a letter to shew me on the subject, which he had received from Mr Faulkland while he was at Bath, and which he was sure would convince me, that the whole affair was so trifling, it ought by no means to be objected to Mr Faulkland, nor, in his opinion, even mentioned to him.

I told him I was sorry to find that he and I thought so differently; for that I was determined to speak to Mr Faulkland immediately about it, and, if he could not satisfy me intirely on the score of the injured lady, that he must never think of Sidney more.

Your brother said, that the letter which was sent to you had come from the revengeful dog who had robbed his master, and that he would give half his estate to have the villain punished as he deserved. Mr Faulkland, it seems, had told him this himself. The fellow found it in the pocket-book which he had taken out of the escrutore, and his disappointment, perhaps, at not getting a better booty, (for he found but twenty moidores besides), joined to his malice against his master, incited him to make the use he did of this letter. Now, continued my mother, though the fellow is undoubtedly a vile creature, yet, my dear, I think *we* are obliged to him for this discovery, providentially as it has come, to save you from what, in my opinion, would be the worst of misfortunes.

The loss of this letter had alarmed Mr Faulkland so much, that he put an advertisement into the papers next day, worded in so particular a manner, as shewed how very fearful he was of that letter's coming to light; for, no doubt, he suspected the man might make a dangerous use of it. The advertisement said, that if the servant, who had absconded from his master's house in St James's Square the night before, would restore the papers which he took with him, they should be received without any questions being asked, and a reward of twenty guineas paid to any person who should bring them back. This advertisement, which, to be sure, the fellow either did not see at all, or had not time enough to avail himself of it, shews you to what sad resources people are driven, who, having done unwarrantable actions, are often in the power of the lowest wretches. I own this circumstance gave me a very ill impression of Mr Faulkland. Your brother says, he remembers this man was one of the servants he took with him to Bath, and, without doubt, he knew of his amour. The advertisement has since been changed, by Sir George's advice. I find the man is named, his person described, and a reward of fifty pounds offered for the apprehending him; but I take it for granted he has got out of reach.

Though his little digression was very pertinent, I was impatient to know what had passed between my mother and Mr Faulkland on the fatal subject, and could not forbear asking her.

I shall tell you, said she, in order. Your brother and I had some farther altercations; and indeed, my dear, it amazes me to find, that a young man, educated as Sir George was, in the early part of life, in the strictest principles of virtue, and the son of parents, who, thank God, always gave him the best example, should have so far deviated from the sober paths he was brought up in, as to treat the most glaring vices with a levity that shocked me. But, I suppose, the company he kept abroad, among whom this hypocrite Faulkland was his chief, has quite perverted him. He gave me the letter to read, which he had received from his friend whilst he was at Bath; and which, he said, was to convince me that it was such a *trifling* affair, that we ought not to take the least notice of it. And all his reason for this was, truly, because that loose man treats the subject as lightly as he does. I am afraid Sir George is no better than himself, or he would not have ventured to make him the confidant of his wild amours; and that at a time too when he was encouraged to address you. He tells him of a very pretty young lady (innocent he says too) that he got acquainted with, who came to Bath under the care of an aunt and uncle; he talks some idle stuff of avoiding her, when he found she liked him, and that the aunt (wicked woman!) contrived to leave them together one evening, when, I understand, the poor young creature fell into the snare that was prepared for her. For, would you believe it, my dear, the monstrous libertine, notwithstanding his pretences, owned that he had paid a price for the girl to her aunt. The betrayed creature herself knew not of this.

I own I had not patience to read the letter through. To say the truth, I but run my eye in a cursory manner over it; I was afraid of meeting, at every line, something offensive to decency. And *this* was the account, which, in your brother's opinion, was entirely to exculpate Mr Faulkland. I think I never was so angry. I threw the letter to George with indignation, telling him, I was ashamed to find, that he, after knowing an incident of this kind, had so little regard to the honour of his sister, as to promote a marriage between her and such a rake. He answered, if I kept you unmarried till I found such a man as *I* should *not* call a rake, you were likely to live and die a maid. that for his part, he was very sorry, as well for Mr Faulkland's sake as yours, he had ever proposed an union, which he found was likely to be overthrown by unseasonable scruples. And the gentleman, in a violent passion, flung out of the room, without deigning even to take up the letter which had fallen on the floor.

I presume he went directly to his friend Faulkland, and told him all that had passed; for the plausible man came to me in the evening, and with looks, full of pretended sorrow, but *real* guilt, begged I would hear him on the subject of a letter which he said he found had unfortunately prejudiced me against him. To be sure he was prepared, and had, with George's help, contrived an artful story to impose on me. He took me unawares; but I was resolved not to give him the advantage of arguments, but proceed to ask him a few plain questions. I therefore cut him short at once, by saying, Mr Faulkland,

I am extremely concerned and shocked at what has happened; I will say but a few words to you, and desire to hear nothing more than answers to my questions: he bowed, and remained silent.

I then asked him, taking the young lady's letter out of my pocket, whether that was from the same person, of whom he had written an account to my son whilst he was at Bath? He answered, It is, madam; and I hoped from that letter, which I find Sir George has shewn you, you would be induced to believe that I never formed a thought of injuring that young lady, till some unfortunate circumstances combined, and suddenly surprized me into the commission of a fault that has made us both unhappy. Sir, said I, I don't pretend to know people's hearts, I can only judge of them from their actions. You acknowlege that she was a fine young woman, and you believe innocent: What excuse can you offer for being her destroyer? Dear madam, don't use so severe an expression – Sir, I can use no other: How can you extenuate the fault, by which you merit so severe an appellation? To a lady of your rigid delicacy, madam, said he, perhaps what youth could offer, in extenuation of the fault, might appear but a weak plea: yet 'tis most certain, that I was surprized into the fatal error: I am under no promises, no ties, no engagements whatsoever to the lady. No ties, Sir! (interrupting him) Is your own honour no tie upon you, supposing you free from any other obligation? You see the consequence of this fatal error, as you call it: here is a young person, of fashion, perhaps (I don't enquire who she is, but she seems to have had no mean education), who is likely to bring a child into the world, to the disgrace of herself and her family. On you, Sir, she charges her dishonour, and mentions your marrying another, as the blow which is to complete her ruin. Mr Faulkland, is not all this truth? Be so good as to give me a direct answer. Madam, I cannot deny it; you have the proof of it in your hands: from all that appears to you, I am indeed very blameable; nay, I do not pretend to vindicate my folly; but, Madam, do not aggravate my fault in your own thoughts, by considering the affair in a more unfavourable light than what even her letter puts it! I conjure you, madam, to suffer Sir George to be my advocate on this occasion; he is acquainted with every particular of the transaction, and can give you a detail that I will not presume to do. Be pleased, Sir, replied I, to tell me what you mean to do in regard to this lady? I mean to do all that I *can* do, answered he; I shall provide a place of retreat for her, where she will meet with the utmost care, tenderness, and respect; and where she may continue with privacy till she is in a condition to return home again to her friends. You may be sure, madam, as to the rest, I shall acquit myself consistently with honour. That is as much as to say, Sir, said I, that you will take care of the maintenance of your poor babe. He looked as if he had a mind to smile, forward man! but constrained it. Doubtless, madam, I shall do all that is now in my power to do, in every circumstance relating to her.

I felt myself exceedingly displeased with him; I was so disappointed in my opinion of him, that it increased my resentment. Sir, I proceeded, I must inform you, that there is as much *now* in your power as ever there was. You are still unmarried; the way is open to you, to repair the mischief you have done: I will never bring down the curses of an injured maid upon my daughter's head, nor purchase her worldly prosperity at the expence of the shame and sorrow of another woman, for ought I know, as well born, as tenderly bred, and, till she knew you, perhaps as innocent as herself. For heaven's sake, madam! he cry'd, don't, don't, I beseech you, pronounce my fate so hastily – You must pardon me, Sir, said I, if I beg to hear no more on this subject. Sir George has already said every thing you could expect of your friend to say in your justification, and more than became him to utter. All I can find by either you or him, is, that you think the loss of honour to a young woman is a trifle, which a man is not obliged to repair, because truly he did not *promise* to do so. This young creature, I understand, is a gentlewoman, very charming in her person, by your own account; one who loves you tenderly, and will shortly make you a father. Is not all this so? I grant it madam, said the criminal. Then, Sir, what reason can you urge in your conscience for not doing her justice? None – but your own inconstant inclinations, which happen now to be better pleased with another woman, whom, perhaps, you might forsake in a few months.

I cannot pretend to repeat to you all he said upon this last article: worse of course, you may be sure. He intreated, over and over again, that I would permit Sir George to plead for him. I told him, that after the facts he had granted, it was impossible that either he or Sir George could make the affair better; that I was very sorry to find myself disappointed in a person of whom I had conceived so high an opinion; and added, that as your illness made it very improper to let you know any thing of the matter for the present, I should take it as a favour if he would permit me to retain the lady's letter to him for a few days, or till you were in a condition to have the matter broke to you. In the mean while, I requested that he would dispense with my receiving any more visits from him.

He said some frantic things (for the man seems of a violent temper); but finding me peremptory, took his leave with respect.

I understand from Sir George, that he flew directly down to Richmond, to a little house he has there, where he has remained ever since; but sends every day to enquire after your health. Sir George, I am sure, sees him often; for he frequently goes out early in the morning, and stays abroad till night. The increase of your illness, from the time I received the last visit from Mr Faulkland, to such a degree as to alarm us for your life, I suppose, prevented your brother from reassuming the subject; though I can perceive he is full of anger and vexation on the occasion. You are now, my dear, God be praised, in a hopeful way of recovery, and I expect that George (who has, by espousing this man's interests so warmly, very much offended me), that George, I say, will renew his sollicitations in his favour. What do you say, my child? I should be glad to know your thoughts, with regard to the part I have acted, as well as with respect to Mr Faulkland's conduct.

Shall I own my weakness to you, my dear Cecilia? I was ready to melt into tears; my spirits, exhausted by sickness, were not proof against this unexpected blow; a heavy sigh burst from my heart, that gave me a little relief. You know my mother is rigid in her notions of virtue; and I was determined to shew her that I would endeavour to imitate her. I therefore suppressed the swelling passion in my breast, and, with as much composure as I could assume, told her, I thought she acted as became her; and that, with regard to Mr Faulkland, my opinion of his conduct was such, that I never desired to see him more. This answer, dictated perhaps by female pride (for I will not answer for the feelings of my heart at that instant), was so agreeable to my mother, that she threw her arms about my neck, and kissed me several times; blessing, and calling me by the most endearing names at every interval. Her tenderness overcame me; or, to deal with sincerity, I believe I was willing to make it an excuse for weeping. Oh! my dear mother, cry'd I, I have need of your indulgence; but indeed your goodness quite overpowers me. My dear love, said she, you deserve it all, and more than it is in your mother's power to shew you. What a blessed escape have you had, my sweet child, of that wild man! Little did I think, my Sidney, when I told you the story of my first disappointment, that a case so parallel would soon be your own.

With respect to you and me indeed, the incidents are nearly alike; but there is a wide difference between the two men. My lover had the grace to repent, and would have returned to his first engagements, if a dreadful malady had not overtaken him; but this graceless Faulkland persists in his infidelity, and would make you as culpable as himself. I own to you, daughter, that the recollection of that melancholy event which happened to me, has given me a sort of horror at the very thoughts of a union between you and Mr Faulkland. You remember the sad consequences which I related to you of an infidelity of this kind; the poor forsaken woman died of grief, and the dishonest lover ran mad. Think of this, my child, and let it encourage you to banish such an unworthy man from your heart. I was afraid your regard for him might make this a difficult task; but I rejoice to find your virtue is stronger than your passion. *I* loved as well as you, but I overcame it when I found it a duty to do so; and I see your mother's example is not lost upon you.

The honest pride that my mother endeavoured to inspire me with, had a good effect, and kept up my spirits for a time. She told me, she was sure that Sir George would quarrel with us both, when we came to talk upon the subject of the marriage; but she was entirely easy as to that, now she knew that *my* sentiments corresponded with her own.

You know my mother has ever been despotic in her government of me; and had I even been inclined to dissent from her judgment in a matter of this importance, it would have been to no purpose; but this was really far from my thoughts.

I was as much disgusted with Mr Faulkland as she was, and as heartily pitied the unhappy young creature whom he had undone.

You may recollect, my dear, that my mother, tho' strictly nice in every particular, has a sort of partiality to her own sex, and where there is the least room for it, throws the whole of the blame upon the *man's* side; who, from her own early prepossessions, she is always inclined to think are deceivers of women. I am not surprized at this bias in her; her early disappointment, with the attending circumstances, gave her this impression. She is warm, and sometimes *sudden*, in her attachments; and yet it is not always difficult to turn her from them. The integrity of her own heart makes her liable to be imposed on by a plausible outside; and yet the dear good woman takes a sort of pride in her sagacity. She had admired and esteemed Mr Faulkland prodigiously; her vexation was the greater, in finding her expectations disappointed; and could I have been so unjust to the pretensions of another, or so indelicate in regard to myself, as to have overlooked Mr Faulkland's fault, I knew my mother would be inflexible. I therefore resolved in earnest to banish him from my thoughts. I found my mother was mightily pleased with her own management of the conversation she had held with Mr Faulkland. I think I talked pretty *roundly* to him, said she; but there was no other way; he is an artful man, and I was resolved not to let him wind me about. He would make a merit of having *formed no designs* upon the young lady; why, possibly, he did not, till he found the poor soul was so smitten with him, that he thought she would be an easy prey. Sir George impudently insinuated, that a man *must* not reject a lady upon these occasions. I was ashamed to hint to Mr Faulkland at the circumstance of his having actually paid a price for the girl; it was too gross; and I think, had I mentioned it, must have struck him dumb: though very likely he might have had some subterfuge, even for that aggravating part of the story.

How I am shock'd, my Cecilia, to think of this! I was glad my mother had spared his confusion on this particular; for though probably, as she observed, he had come prepared with some evasion to this charge, yet what a mean figure must a man make, who is reduced to disingenuous shifts, to excuse or palliate an action, despicable as well as wicked!

My brother came in, during our discourse, to ask me how I did. My mother answered his question before I had time to speak. She is pretty well, thank God! and not likely to break her heart, though she *knows* your friend Mr Faulkland's story (and she spoke it scornfully). My brother said, Sidney, Are *you* as averse to Mr Faulkland as my mother is? I replied, Brother, I wonder you can ask me that question, after what you have been just now told. I always said, answered he, that you did not know the value of the man, and now I am convinced of it. I wish he had never seen you! I wish so too, said I. Sir George walked about the room, and seemed vexed to death. For Heaven's sake, madam, (turning to my mother) now my sister is tolerably recovered, suffer her to see Mr Faulkland; let her hear what he has to say in his own vindication: I think you may trust to her honour, and her discretion; and if the affair appears to her in so heinous a light as it does to you, I will be contented to give Mr Faulkland up; but don't shut your own ears, and your daughter's too, against conviction.

Sir, you are disrespectful, said my mother angrily. Dear brother, I cry'd, I beg you will spare me on this subject; my mother *has* given me leave to judge for myself; she has repeated all that you have said, and all that Mr Faulkland has been able to urge on the occasion; and I am sorry to tell you, that I think myself bound never to have any farther correspondence with him; therefore you must excuse me for not seeing him. And so the match is broke off, cry'd Sir George. *It is*, said my mother peremptorily. It is, echoed I faintly. Why then, replied Sir George (and he swore), you will never get such another whilst you live. A pretty figure you'll make in the world, when you give it for a reason that you refused *such* a man, after every thing was concluded upon, because truly you found that he had had an intrigue! Why, Sidney, you'll be so laugh'd at! He addressed himself to me, though I knew he meant the reproof for my mother. Sir, answered she, neither your sister nor I shall trouble ourselves much about the opinion of people who *can* laugh at such things. You may put the matter into as ridiculous a light as you please: but this was no common intrigue; *you know* it was not, however you may affect to speak of it. I don't suppose *any* of you are *Saints*, but I trust in Heaven, some are better than others. Oh! madam, madam, said my brother, if you knew the world as well *I* do, you would think that Mr Faulkland is one of the best. God forbid! my mother answered coolly. Well, well, madam, cry'd Sir George, I see it is to no purpose to argue; there are many families of more consequence than ours, and ten times the fortune, that will be very proud of Faulkland's alliance; and will hardly make it an objection to him, that he was led into a foolish scrape by the wickedness of one woman, and the folly of another. If you make my sister wait for a husband, till you find a man who never offended in that way, I think, mother, you had better take a little boy from his nurse, breed him up under your own eye, and by the time Sidney is a good motherly gentlewoman, you may give her the baby to make a play-thing of. For my own part, I am heartily sorry I ever interfered. – People of such nice scruples had better chuse for themselves; but I cannot help thinking, that both Faulkland and I are very ill used. I told you (said my mother to me) how he would behave. Sir George, I desire you will not distress your sister thus (She saw me sadly cast down: I was ill and weak): if you have no respect for *me*, have a little tenderness for her. – I beg your pardon, child, said he, I did not mean to distress you, I pity *you*, indeed Sidney. I could have cry'd at his using that expression, it humbles one so. Madam (to my mother), you shall be troubled no farther by my friend or myself; all I shall say is this, that whenever my sister gets a husband of your ladyship's chusing, I wish he may have half the worth of the poor rejected Faulkland.

My brother left the room with these words. My mother was downright in a passion, but soon cooled on his withdrawing.

My spirits were quite fatigued; and my mother left me, that I might take a little rest.

What a strange alteration have a few days produced! our domestic peace broke in upon by the unlucky difference between my mother and my brother. My near prospect of – of – oh! let me be ingenuous, and say Happiness, vanished – Poor Mr Faulkland! *Poor* do I call him? for shame, Sidney – but let the word go; I will not blot it. Mr Faulkland forbid the house, myself harassed by a cruel disorder, and hardly able to crawl out of bed. All this fallen on me within these last fourteen black days. Then I dread the going abroad, or seeing company, I shall look so silly; for the intended wedding began to be talked of; – and the curiosity of people to know the cause of it's being broke off – What wild guesses will be made by some, and what lies invented by others! Then the ill-natured mirth of one half of the girls of my acquaintance, and the *as* provoking condolements of the other hand – I am fretted at the thoughts of it – but it cannot be helped; I must bear it all – I wish I were well enough to get into the country, to be out of the reach of such impertinence.

I long to know who this ill-fated girl is, that has been the cause of all this. *A gentlewoman, and very pretty; one that loves Mr Faulkland, and will shortly make him a parent.* Thus my mother described her to Mr Faulkland, and he assented to it. Oh! fie, fie, Mr Faulkland, how could you be so cruel to *her*? How could you use *me* so ill? and Sir George knew of all this, and makes light of it! it is a strange story! My mother is severe in her virtue, but she is in the right – My brother would sacrifice every consideration to aggrandize his family – To make a purchase of the unhappy creature, and that without her knowlege too, it is horrid! Away, away from my thoughts, thou vile intruder – Return to your Bath mistress, she has a better right to you than I have; she implores your pity; she has no refuge but you; and she may be every way preferable to me – I wish I knew her name, but what is it to me; *mine* will never be Faulkland, *hers* ought. Perhaps Mr Faulkland may be induced to marry her, when he sees her in her present interesting situation. He says he will provide a retreat for her; to be sure he will have the compassion to visit her: and then who knows what may happen? If I know my own heart, I think I do most sincerely wish he may make her his wife; but then I would not chuse to have it known suddenly; that might look as if he forsook me for her. *That*, I own, would a little hurt my pride. I wish not the truth to be known, for Mr Faulkland's sake; but then I should not like to have a slur thrown on me.

I will add no more to this, but send the packet off at all events; I think it will find you at Paris.

August 1

My health promises to return: my mother praises me, and calls me a Heroine. I begin to fancy myself one: our pride sometimes stands in the place of virtue.

Sir George went to Richmond yesterday. We have scarce seen him since the tift he had with us the other day. What strange creatures these men are, even the best of them! and how light they make of faults in one another, that shock us but to think of!

My mother takes his behaviour very ill: he staid all night with his friend, and returned to town this morning: he only looked into my room, to ask me how I did: my mother was sitting with me. I believe that hindered him from coming in; for he looked as if he wanted to speak to me. He bowed to my mother, but said not a word; he went abroad again as soon as he was dressed, and did not come in till late. I fear his conduct will oblige us to separate; for my mother will not brook any liberties to be taken with her: she hinted as much, and said she believed Sir George was tired of living regularly.

She anticipated the request I intended to make to her, of letting me go out of town; for she said, as soon as I was able, I should remove into the country for a while. Sidney Castle is too long a journey for me at present to think of undertaking, and she talks of going into Essex, on a visit to Lady Grimston, which we have long promised her. I shall like this better than going down to Wiltshire, where the want of my Cecilia would make my old abode a melancholy place, especially at this juncture.

August 4

Sir George continues sullen and cold to us: he never has had an opportunity of saying any thing particular to me since the day he said so much. My mother scarce ever leaves me; he seems nettled at this. I believe he would endeavour to work on *me*, as he knows the attempt would be vain in regard to *her*. As I am now well enough to receive the visits of our intimate acquaintance, I am never without company. I am really in pretty good spirits, and bear my disappointment (as I told you I would) very handsomely. I never hear Mr Faulkland's name mentioned, no more than if such a man did not exist. We are to set out for lady Grimston's house on Tuesday; it is but twenty miles from London; and I am already strong enough to bear a longer journey.

My mother told Sir George, that if he liked it, the house we are now in was at his service during her time of it, of which there are some months to come; for she said, she meant to go directly home from Essex. Sir George thanked her, but did not say whether he would accept of her offer or not.

August 5

I have been obliged to turn away my poor Ellen. She was so imprudent as to receive a letter for me from Mr Faulkland's man, contrary to my mother's express commands. She brought it to me, and I gave it to my mother unopened; who put it directly into the fire without reading it, and told me it would oblige her, if I would part with the servant who had presumed to take it after her prohibition. I instantly obeyed, and have just discharged her. I should have a sad loss of her, only I am in hopes of having her place well supplied by an old acquaintance and play-fellow of ours, poor Patty Main; her father is dead, and she is obliged to go to service, for he has left a widow with six children. The eldest son, you remember, served his time to his father, and is just now setting out in business; but a young surgeon in a country town must take some time to establish himself; though he is a very worthy youth, and I hear clever in his profession.

Patty came to town last week with a lady from our neighbourhood, who applied to my mother to recommend the girl to wait on some person of fashion. My mother has been looking out for a suitable place for her; but she told me today, she thought I could not do better than take her to myself; I shall be very glad to have her, for she is an amiable young woman.

August 6

We go out of town at seven o'clock to-morrow morning, as we are to dine at Grimston-hall, and purpose going at our leisure. I will steal a few minutes from sleep, though it is now very late, to give you a short scene which passed in my chamber about an hour ago.

Sir George (who, according to his late custom, had been abroad all day) came into my room, where my mother and I were sitting together. He asked us, Did we hold our purpose of going out of town next day? Yes, certainly, my mother said. And you intend going from lady Grimston's to Sidney Castle? We do. Then, madam (to my mother), as it is the last trouble you are likely to have from Mr Faulkland, I hope you will not refuse to read this letter, which he has sent you; and he took one out of his pocket, and presented it to her. She did not make an offer to receive it, but answered, Sir George, it is to no purpose for Mr Faulkland to sollicit me; you know I don't easily alter my resolutions when once they are fixed: he has given himself an unnecessary trouble; pray excuse me: it was not handsome of him to write to my daughter, after he knew my sentiments. You need not be afraid of fresh sollicitations, madam, said my brother; I knew enough of your *firmness* (and he spoke the word firmness reluctantly, as if he would rather have used another, perhaps less respectful term); I knew enough to assure Faulkland there was not the least hope left for him; and though I do not know the subject of that letter, I can venture to assure you, it is not intended to move you in favour of his pretensions: this he declared to me, before I would take the letter from him; but what puts it past doubt, is, that he set out this very evening from London, in order to embark for Germany. I could not help breathing a sigh when Sir George said this; but no body heard me. He still held the letter in his hand, and again offered it to my mother; you need not be afraid of it, madam; I presume it may be no more than to take a civil leave of you. I wish him well, said my mother, taking the letter; if that be all, what he says may keep cold; and she put it into her pocket without opening.

This being the eve of our journey, some little domestic matters, which my mother had to settle, called her out of the room. Sir George took that opportunity to ask me, whether my mother had shewed me the letter which he had received from Mr Faulkland while he was at Bath, relative to that cursed affair, as he called it. I told him, my mother had repeated great part of the contents of it to me; and that the principal observation she had made, was not favourable to *him*, on account of his being made the confidant of such an affair.

I am very sorry for your sake, Sidney, said he, that our mother is of so inflexible a temper; you have lost by it, what you will have reason to regret as long as you live. Such amazing obstinacy! such unaccountable perverseness! I do not want to shake your filial obedience; but I, for my own part, think that nothing but infatuation can account for your mother's conduct – Does she want a man without passions? Or have *you* filled your head with such chimærical notions as to – I interrupted him (for my brother is not always nice in his choice of words); – Dear Sir George, say no more; I am very well contented as I am. I will not increase your uneasiness, said he, by telling you what Faulkland has suffered on this occasion. If ever love was carried to adoration, it was in the breast of that generous, charming fellow – but you have lost him – and I have lost him; thanks to my wise scrupulous mother for that. I begged of him to drop the subject. My mother came in to us again. Sir George bid us good night, and wished us a good journey. The parting was cool enough. I am glad, however, there is not a total rupture. I believe he will continue in our house in town for a time, at least.

Patty Main, who gladly accepted of the offer of my service, came home to me this evening. She is grown very tall and genteel. I hardly know how to treat her as a servant; but the good girl is so humble, that she does all in her power to make me forget that I ever knew her in a better situation; but in this she fails of her purpose, for it only serves to remind me the more strongly of it: she is so ready, and so handy, that she does twenty little offices that do not belong to her place, and which are not expected of her. My mother is exceedingly pleased with her, and says it is such a happiness to have about me a young person virtuously brought up, that she almost considers her as one of the family.

Grimston-hall, August 8

We arrived here yesterday, and met a most friendly reception from the lady of this mansion. But before I say any more of her, I will hasten to a more interesting subject. I have got Mr Faulkland's letter to my mother; she has just put it into my hands; and while she walks in the garden with lady Grimston, I will make haste to transcribe it. Thus it is:

Madam,

I submit to the sentence you have passed on me. I am miserable, but do not presume to expostulate. I purpose leaving England directly; but would wish if possible (a little to mitigate the severity of my lot), to convince you, that the unhappy rejected man, who aspired to the honour of being your son-in-law, is not quite such a criminal as he now appears to you.

To Sir George's friendship I know I am much indebted for endeavouring to vindicate me. It was not in his power, it was not in my own; for you saw all which I, in unreserved freedom, wrote to him on the subject of my acquaintance with Miss B.

I have but one resource left; perhaps, madam, you will think it a strange one. To the lady herself I must appeal. She will do me justice, and I am sure will be ready to acknowlege that I am no betrayer of innocence, no breaker of promises; that I was surprized into the commission of a fault, for which I have paid so dear a price.

Her testimony, madam, may perhaps have some weight with you; though I propose nothing more by it, than that you may think of me with less detestation. You have banished me from your presence: I am a voluntary exile from my country, and from my friends: submit to the chastisement, and would do anything to expiate my offence against you and Miss Bidulph. There is but *one* command which you can possibly lay on me, to which I would not pay a perfect and ready obedience; but that act, perhaps, is the *only* one which would make me appear worthy of your esteem.

The lady whom it has been my ill fate to render unhappy, and by whom I am made unutterably so, will, ere long, come to a house at Putney, which I have taken on purpose for her. I have placed in it my housekeeper, a grave worthy woman, under whose care she will be safe, and attended with that secresy and tenderness which her condition requires.

I have written to her a faithful account of every thing relative to my hoped-for alliance with your family, and the occasion of the treaty's being broken off. As she must, by this means, know that your ladyship is acquainted with her story, I have told her, that, perhaps you might, from the interest you took in her misfortune, be induced to see her in her retirement. Let me, therefore, conjure you, madam, by that pious zeal which governs all your actions, and by the love you bear that daughter so deservedly dear to you, to take compassion on this young lady. She has no friends, nor any acquaintance in this part of the kingdom; her situation will require the comfort of society, and perhaps, the advice of wisdom. It will be an act worthy of your humanity to shew some countenance to her.

I think she will be in very good hands with the honest woman who waits her coming; but if any thing should happen otherwise than well, it would make me doubly wretched.

To one who has no resources of contentment in her own bosom, solitude cannot be a friend; this I fear may be the lady's case; and this makes me with the more earnestness urge my request to you. Forgive me, madam, for the liberty I take with you; a liberty, which, though I confess it needs an apology, yet is it at the same time a proof of the confidence I have in you, which I hope will not affront either your candour or your virtue.

If you will condescend to grant this request, I shall obtain the two wishes at present most material to my peace; the one to secure to the lady a compassionate friend, already inclined to espouse her cause; the other, to put it in your power to be satisfied from the lady's own mouth, of the truth of what I have asserted. I trust to her generosity to deal openly on this occasion.

I wish you and Miss Biddulph every blessing that Heaven can bestow, and am, with great respect,

Madam,
Your ladyship's
Most obedient humble Servant,
ORLANDO FAULKLAND.

P.S. The lady will go by the name of Mrs Jefferis: you will pardon me for not having mentioned her *real name*. I never yet told it even to Sir George; but I presume she will make no secret of it to you, if you honour her with a visit.

Poor Orlando! unhappy Miss B! I could name a third person, that is not *happy* neither. What a pity it is, that so many good qualities, should be blotted by imperfections! how tender is his compassion for this poor girl! how ingenuous his conduct! but still he flies from her. I fear she can never hope to recover him. There is but *one* thing, he says, which *he would not do; the only act, perhaps, by which he could make himself appear worthy of my mother's esteem.* The meaning of this but too plainly shews him determined against marrying Miss B. I don't know any thing else which would reconcile my mother to him.

I make no doubt of her complying with Mr Faulkland's request in seeing the lady; she is very compassionate, particularly to her own sex.

What a *strange resource* indeed is this of Mr Faulkland's, to appeal to the lady herself! What am I to judge from it, but that the unfortunate victim, ignorant of the treachery that was practised against her by her wicked aunt, and that her destroyer paid a *price* for her dishonour, exculpates him from the worst part of the guilt, and perhaps, poor easy creature, blames her own weakness only for the error which a concealed train of cunning and perfidy might have led her into?

But even supposing Miss B. were generous and candid enough (and great indeed must be her candour and generosity) to justify this guilty man, What would it avail? Did not my mother tell me she conceived a *sort of horror at the bare idea of an union between Mr Faulkland and me?* This arises from the strong impression made on her by the unlucky event which blasted her own early love. Strong and early prejudices are almost insurmountable.

My mother's piety, genuine and rational as it is, is notwithstanding a little tinctured with superstition; it was the error of her education, and her good sense has not been able to surmount it; so that I now the universe would not induce her to change her resolution in regard to Mr Faulkland. She thinks he *ought* to marry miss B. and she will *ever* think so. I wish he would; for I am sure he never can be mine. The bell rings for breakfast; I must run down. My mother came up to dress just now, and stepped into my room. I returned her the letter, and she asked me, What I thought of Mr Faulkland's request? madam, you are a better judge of the propriety of it than I am. I shall have no objection to seeing the unhappy lady, said she, since it seems he has apprised her of my knowlege of her affairs. I am glad he has the grace to shew even so much compassion for her: perhaps it may be the beginning of repentance, and time may work a thorough reformation in him, if God spares him his life and his *senses*. You see which way my good mother's thoughts tended. I did not, she added, intend to return to London again; but this occasion, I think, calls upon me; and I believe I shall go for a while, in order to see and comfort this poor young creature. She cannot yet be near lying in; and I suppose she will not come to the house Mr Faulkland speaks of, till she can no longer remain undiscovered at home; so that a month or two hence will be full soon enough for me to think of going to town.

I saw my mother rested her compliance with Mr Faulkland's request, merely on one point; that of compassion to the girl. As for the other motive, said she, the hearing him justified from the *Lady's own mouth*, I am not such a novice in those matters, but that I know when a deluding man has once got an ascendency over a young creature, he can coax her into any thing. Too much truth I doubt there is in this observation of my mother's.

But it is time to say something of lady Grimston. My Cecilia has never seen her, though I believe she has often heard my mother speak of her. They are nearly of an age, and much of the same cast of thinking; though with this difference, that lady Grimston is extravagantly rigid in her notions, and precise in her manner. She has been a widow for many years, and lives upon a large jointure at Grimston-hall, with as much regularity and solemnity, as you would see in a monastery. Her servants are all antediluvians; I believe her coach horses are fifty years of age, and the very house-dog is as grey as a badger. She herself, who in her youth never *could* have been handsome, renders herself still a more unpleasing figure, by the oddity of her dress; you would take her for a lady of Charles the first's court at least. She is always dressed out: I believe she sleeps in her cloaths, for she comes down ruffled, and towered, and flounced, and fardingal'd, even to breakfast. My mother has a *very* high opinion of her, and says, she *knows more of the world* than any one of her acquaintance. It may be so; but it must be of the old world; for lady Grimston has not been ten miles from her seat these thirty years. 'Tis nine years since my mother and she met before, and there was a world of compliments passed between them; though I am sure they were sincerely glad to see each other, for they seem to be very fond. They were companions in youth, that season wherein the most durable friendships are contracted. I believe her really a very good woman; she is pious and charitable, and does abundance of good things in her neighbourhood; though I cannot say I think her amiable. There is an austerity about her that keeps me in awe, notwithstanding that she is extremely obliging to me, and told my mother, I *promised to make a fine woman*. Think of such a compliment to one of almost nineteen. My mother and she call one another by their christian names; and you would smile to hear the two old ladies (begging their pardons). *Lettying* and *Dollying* one another. This accounts to me for lady Grimston's thinking *me* still a child; for I suppose she considers herself not much past girlhood, though, to do her justice, she has not a scrap of it in her behaviour.

August 10

All our motions here are as regular as the clock. The family rise at six; we are summoned to breakfast at eight; at ten a venerable congregation are assembled to prayers, which an ancient clergyman, who is curate of the parish, and her ladyship's chaplain, gives us daily. Then the old horses are put to the old coach; and my lady, with her guests, if they chuse it, take an airing; always going and returning by the same road, and driving precisely to the same land-mark, and no farther. At half an hour after twelve, in a hall large enough to entertain a corporation, we sit down to dinner; my lady has a grace of a quarter of an hour long, and we are waited on by four truly venerable footmen, for she likes state. The afternoon we may dispose of as we please; at least it is a liberty I am indulged in, and I generally spend my time in the garden, or my own chamber, till I have notice given me of supper's being on the table, where we are treated with the same ceremonials as at dinner. At ten exactly, the instant the clock strikes the first stroke, my lady rises with great solemnity, and wishes us a good night.

August 14

You cannot expect, in such a house as this is, my dear, that I can be furnished with materials to give you much variety. Indeed these four last days have been so exactly the same in every particular, excepting that the dishes at dinner and supper were changed, that I had resolved to hang up my pen till I quitted Grimston-hall, or at least resign it to Patty, and let her plod on and tell you how the wind blew such a day; what sort of a mantua lady Grimston had on such a day (though by the way it is always the same, always ash-coloured tissue); what the great dog barked at, at such an hour, and what the old parrot said at such a time; the house and the garden I have exhausted my descriptive faculties on already, though, they are neither of them worth describing; and I was beginning to despair of matter to furnish out a quarter of an hour's entertainment, when the scene began to brighten a little this auspicious day, by the arrival of a coach full of visitors. These were no other than a venerable dean, who is the minister of our parish, his lady and daughter, and a Mr Arnold, a gentleman who is a distant relation of lady Grimston's. He has a house in this neighbourhood, and is just come to an estate by the death of his elder brother.

This visit has given me hopes that I may now and then have a chance for seeing a human face, besides the antiques of the family, and those which are depicted on the arras. Though not to disparage the people, they were all agreeable enough in their different ways. The old dean is good humoured and polite; I mean the true politeness, that of the heart, which dictates the most obliging things in so frank a manner, that they have not the least appearance of flattery. Being very near sighted, he put on a pair of spectacles to look at me, and turning to Mr Arnold, with a vivacity that would have become five-and-twenty, he repeated

'With an air and a face,
'And a shape and a grace, &c.'

The young man smiled his assent, and my mother looked so delighted, that the good-natured dean's compliment pleased *me* for *her* sake. Lady Grimston, who is passionately fond of musick, has a very pretty organ in one of her chambers; Mr Arnold was requested to give us a lesson on it, which he very readily obliged us with. He plays ravishingly; the creature made me envious, he touched it so admirably. I had taken a sort of dislike to him when he first came in, I cannot tell you why or wherefore; but this accomplishment has reconciled me so to him, that I am half in love with him. I hope we shall see him often; he is really excellent on this instrument, and you know how fond I am of musick.

August 15

This packet is already so large that I am sure it will frighten you. I will therefore send it off before I increase it; especially as I am now so much in the hum-drum way, that I ought, out of policy, to make a break in my narrative, in order to encourage you to read it. Positively, if things do not mend, and that considerably too, – Patty shall keep the journal, for I find myself already disposed to sleep over it.

August 20

I have looked over what Patty has writ for the five last days; upon my word she is a very good journalist, as well as amanuensis; and she has given you, to the full, as good an account of matters and things as I could.

My time passes rather more tolerably than I expected. The dean's family seem to have broke the solitary *spell* that hung over the house, and we have company you see every day. Mr Arnold never fails. I always make him play; he is very obliging, and, if he were not good natured, I should tire him.

August 22

I have had a letter from Sir George; he mentions not Mr Faulkland; I too am endeavouring to forget him. When my mother goes to London, I will try to prevail on her to let me go down to Sidney-castle. I have no inclination to go to town, and less to stay here. We are to have a concert to-morrow, at Mr Arnold's house. My lively good old dean touches the bass viol, his daughter sings prettily; I am to bear my part too; so that we begin to grow a little sociable.

August 30

Are you not tired of my Grimston journal, my Cecilia? Day after day rolls on, and the same dull repetition! Lady Grimston, the Dean, and Mr Arnold, perpetually! there is no bearing this, you cry. Well, but here is a new personage arrived to diversify the scene a little. Lady Grimston's daughter, a sweet woman; but her mother does not seem fond of her. It amazes me, for she is perfectly amiable, both in temper and person; she is a widow of about eight and twenty. Lady Grimston appears to treat her with a distance very unmaternal; and the poor young woman seems so humbled, that I pity her. She is come but on a visit, and we shall lose her in a week, for which I am very sorry, as I have taken a fancy to her.

September 1

Poor Mrs Vere! that is the name of Lady Grimston's daughter. I can now give you the cause of her mother's coldness to her; I had it from herself; she told me her little history this evening in the garden, with a frankness that charmed me.

How happy you are, dear Miss Bidulph, said she! you seem to be blessed with one of the tenderest of parents. I am indeed, I answered; she is one of the best of mothers, and the best of women. She sighed, and a tear started into her eye; I too was happy once, said she, when my indulgent father lived. I hope, madam, Lady Grimston is to you, what my good mother is to me. She shook her head: No, Miss Bidulph, it must be but too obvious to you that she is not. I should not have introduced the subject, if the cold severity of her looks were not so apparent that you must have taken notice of them. My mother is, undoubtedly, a very good woman; and you may naturally suppose, that my conduct has been such as to deserve her frowns; I will therefore tell you my melancholy, though short story. It is now about twelve years since Mr Vere paid his addresses to me. He was the eldest son of a gentleman of family and fortune, who then lived in this country. I was about sixteen, and the darling of my father; who was perhaps the more indulgent to me, as he knew my mother's severity. Mr Vere was but two years older than myself, and a childish courtship had gone on for some time between us, before it was suspected by any body; and to say the truth, before I was well aware of the consequences myself. It happened, that an elderly gentleman of a great estate, just at that time saw and liked me, and directly made proposals to my mother, as she was very well known to hold the reins of government in her family.

This offer, I suppose, was advantageous; for she immediately consulted my father upon it, or rather gave him to understand that she meant to dispose of her daughter in marriage.

My father, who had no objection to the match, told her he was very well satisfied, provided I liked the gentleman; but said, he hoped she would not think of putting any force on my inclinations. My eldest sister had been married some time before by my mother's sole authority, and quite contrary to her own liking; the marriage had not turned out happily, and my father was resolved not to have me sacrificed in the same way.

My mother told him, she was sorry he had such romantic notions, as to think a girl of my age capable of having any ideas of preference for one man more than another; that she took it for granted I had never presumed to entertain a thought of any man as yet, and supposed her precepts had not been so far thrown away upon me, as that I could let it enter into my head that any thing but parental authority was to guide me in my choice.

My father, from the gentleness of his nature, had been so accustomed to acquiesce, that he made no other reply than to bid my mother use her discretion. He came directly to me notwithstanding, and told me what had passed. It was then, for the first time, that I discovered I loved Mr Vere. I burst into tears, and clinging round my father's neck, begged of him him to save me from my mother's rigour. My gesture and words were too passionate for him not to perceive that there was something more at my heart than mere dislike of the old man. He charged me to deal sincerely. I loved him too well, and was myself too frank to do otherwise. In short, I confessed my inclination for Mr Vere, and his affection for me.

Though my kind father chid me gently for admitting a lover without his or my mother's approbation, yet at the same time he told me, he would endeavour to dissuade her from prosecuting the other match; though he could wish, he said, I would try to bring myself to accept of it; adding, he was afraid my mother would be much incensed by a denial.

My mother was fond of grandeur; and would not like to have me marry any one, who could not at once make me mistress of a fine house, and a fine equipage; which I knew I must not expect to be the case with Mr Vere. His father had several children, and was very frugal in his temper: besides, as he was but of the middle age, and of a very healthy constitution, his son's prospect of possessing the estate was, to all human appearance, at a very great distance.

These discouragements, however, did not hinder me from indulging my wishes. My father's tenderness was the foundation on which I built my hopes. I told Mr Vere the designs of one parent, and the kind condescension of the other. Emboldened by this information, he ventured to disclose his love to my father, begging his interest with my mother in his favour. He had a great kindness for the youth, and was so fond of me, that he would readily have consented to my happiness, if the fear of disobliging my mother had not checked him. He represented to her in the mildest manner, the utter dislike I had expressed of the proposed match, and conjured her not to insist on it. My mother, unused to be controuled, was filled with resentment both against him and me; she said, he encouraged me in my disobedience; and that, if he did not unite his authority to hers, in order to compel me to marry the gentleman she approved of, it would make a total breach between them.

My good father, who loved my mother exceedingly, was alarmed at this menace. Unwilling to come to extremities either with her or me, he was at a loss how to act. His paternal love at length prevailed, and he determined, at all events, to save me from the violence which he knew would be put upon my heart.

My mother had never condescended to talk to me on the subject: she thought my immediate obedience ought to have followed the bare knowlege of her will. She forbad me her sight, and charged me never to appear before her, till I came with a determination to obey her.

However severe this prohibition was, I yielded to it with the less reluctance, as my father's tender love made me amends for my mother's harshness. Perhaps, had she vouchsafed to reason a little with me, tempering her arguments with a motherly kindness, she would have found me as flexible as she could wish; but the course she took had a very contrary effect. I thought myself persecuted, and that it was for the honour of my love to persevere. On the other hand, my father's secret indulgence encouraged me in the sentiments I entertained, and I now determined, not only to refuse my old lover, but to have my young one.

My mother had given me a stated time in which I was to come to a resolution, and if I did not, at the expiration of it, acquiesce, I was to be pronounced a reprobate, and to be no more considered as her child. In this emergency I had recourse to my father. I told him there was nothing which I was not ready to suffer, rather than marry the man I hated: my greatest affliction was the uneasiness I saw him endure on my account; for my mother reproached him daily with my obstinacy.

My father said, he thought the alternative offered by my mother, was to be avoided but in one way, and that was, by marrying Mr Vere; For, added he, when she finds you resolute in your refusal of her choice, not even my paternal authority will be able to screen you from her severity, and your life will be made miserable, without your father's being able to relieve you. On the other hand, when you are out of her house, she cannot distress you, nor prevent me from doing you the justice which I owe my child. Nay, possibly in time, I may be able to work out a reconciliation between you; but she must not know that I was consenting to this marriage, lest an irreconcileable quarrel should ensue. I fell at my father's feet, and embraced his knees, for this tender and unexpected proof of his affection.

Mr Vere's father was no stranger to his son's attachment, and we were very sure he would readily come into the proposal which my father intended to make.

The two parents had a meeting secretly, where all the terms of portion and settlement were speedily and privately adjusted. Mr Vere the father, who had been long intimate in our family, knew very well the necessity there was for keeping the secret. After this, my lover and I were to be married privately, without the knowlege, seemingly, of any one in either family, excepting one of the Miss Veres, who was to be present; and when the time of my probation was expired, my father was to let my mother into the knowlege of this affair, as a thing he had just discovered; and to pacify her anger as well he could.

Every thing was conducted in the manner proposed. I was married with the utmost privacy, and continued in my father's house till the day arrived, when I was to give my definitive answer.

Unfortunately for me, my mother chose to receive it from my own mouth, and called me into her presence. I appeared before her trembling and terrified: I had not seen her for a fortnight, and I was in dread, lest the discovery I had to make, should banish me her sight perhaps for ever, unless my father might influence her in time to forgive me. She asked me, with a stern brow, What I had resolved on? I had not courage to make her an answer, but burst into tears. She repeated her question; and I could only reply, Madam, it is not in my *power* to obey you. She did not comprehend the meaning of my words, but imputing them to obstinacy, commanded me to leave the room, and not to see her face till I came to a proper sense of my duty; at the same time ordering me into my chamber, where I was to be locked up.

I flew to my father, and conjured him to let my mother know the truth at once, that I might be no longer subject to such harsh treatment; for I knew the being sent home to my husband would be the consequence of her being told that I had one.

My poor father was almost afraid to undertake the task, though he had been the chief promoter of my marriage, and his authority ought to have given sanction to it. He ventured however to let her know, that I had confessed to him what my fears of her immediate resentment would not suffer me to discover whilst I was in her presence; and what my aversion to the man she proposed to me, and the rigours I had been threatened with, if I refused him, had driven me to. The rage my mother flew into, was little short of phrenzy, and my father made haste to send me out of the house.

Mr Vere's whole family received me with great tenderness; but I was sorry at leaving my father, whose visits to me were made but seldom, and even those by stealth.

My situation, though I was united to the man I loved, and caressed by all his family, was far from being happy. My mother's inflexible temper was not to be wrought upon, notwithstanding my father did his utmost to prevail on her to see and to forgive me; and she carried her resentment so far, that she told my father, unless he cut me off entirely in his will, she was determined to separate herself totally from him. This was an extremity he by no means expected she would have gone to.

In a fit of sickness, which had seized him a few years before, he had left me ten thousand pounds; five of this he had secretly transferred to Mr Vere on the day of my marriage, and had promised him to bequeath me five more at his death.

In consequence of this disposition, he purposed making a new will, so that he the less scrupled giving my mother up the old one, with a promise of making another agreeable to her request.

My mother's jointure was already settled on her; my eldest sister had received her portion; so that there was little bequeathed by this testament, but my fortune, and a few other small legacies.

My mother tore the will with indignation, and not satisfied with my father's promise, insisted on his putting it into execution immediately. In short, his easy temper yielded to her importunities, and he had a will drawn up by her instructions, in which I was cut off with one shilling, and my intended fortune bequeathed to my eldest sister. My mother was made residuary legatee to every thing that should remain, after paying all the bequests. This would have amounted to a considerable sum, if the half of my portion, which was already paid without her knowlege, had not made such a diminution in the personal estate, that after paying my sister the whole of what was specified in the will, there was scarce any thing likely to remain.

Had my mother known this secret, she would not perhaps have been so ready to have made my father devise all my intended fortune to my sister. My father, who was aware of this, durst not however inform her at that juncture, how much she hurt herself, by forcing him to such measures. She insisted upon his leaving the whole of what he designed for me to my eldest sister; as well as to convince him, she said, that she had no self-interested views, as to be an example to other rebellious children.

My father had no remedy on these occasions, but a patient acquiescence: the will was made, and my mother herself would keep it.

My father took an opportunity the same day to inform me what he had done, but assured me, he would immediately make another will, agreeable to his first intentions, and leave it in the hands of a faithful friend.

This was his design; but alas he lived not to execute it. He was seized that night with a paralytic disorder, which at once deprived him of the use of his limbs and his speech. They who were about him believed he retained his senses, but he was not capable of making himself understood even by signs. Alarmed with this dismal account of my beloved father's situation, I flew to the house without considering my mother's displeasure; but I was not permitted to see him. I filled the house with my cries, but to no purpose; I had not the satisfaction of receiving even a farewell look from him, which was all he was capable of bestowing on me.

He languished for several days in this melancholy condition, and then, in spite of the aid of physic, expired.

The loss of this dear father so entirely took up my thoughts, that I never reflected on the loss of the remaining part of my fortune; but it was not so with my father-in-law. There had been a settlement made on me in consequence of the fortune promised; though not equal to what it demanded, yet superior to the half which was paid. He relied on my father's word for the remainder, and had no doubt of its being secured to him, knowing his circumstances, as well as his strict integrity, and that my sister had actually received the same fortune which I was promised.

Mr Vere had four daughters, and it was on this fortune he chiefly depended to provide for them.

The news of my being cut off with a shilling exceedingly surprized and exasperated him. Unluckily I had not mentioned to him, nor even to my husband, the will which my father had been obliged to make. The assurances he gave me, of immediately making another in my favour, prevented me; as I thought it would only be a very severe proof of my mother's enmity to the family, which I could have wished to conceal from them; especially as I did not imagine it would have affected me afterwards. Mr Vere the elder was from home when my father died, and his business detained him for more than a month after his funeral was over. My husband, on this occasion, shewed the tender and disinterested love he bore me; he affected to make as light as possible of this unexpected disappointment, but at the same time expressed his uneasiness, lest his father should carry matters to an extremity with my mother, from whom we knew we were to expect nothing by mild methods.

It was now thought adviseable, that I should write to my mother, to condole with her on my father's death; again to intreat her forgiveness of my fault, and, as some mitigation of it, to acknowlege that it was not only with my father's privity, but even with his consent and approbation, that I had married.

I wrote this letter in a strain of the utmost humility, without mentioning a word of my fortune; *that* I thought it would be time enough for me to do, if I could prevail on my mother to see me, and would at all events come better from my husband or his father, than from me. But I gained nothing by this, only some unkind reflections on my father's memory, and a message, that since he thought proper to marry his daughter in a manner so highly disagreeable to her mother, he should have taken care of providing for her; as he could not expect a parent, so disobliged as she had been, would take any notice of me.

My mother had been left sole executrix to my father's forced will; and she took care to put my sister, and the other legatees, into possession of what was bequeathed to them in a very short time after his decease. She found there was an unexpected deficiency in his personal fortune, insomuch that there was barely enough to pay his debts; and that her being left the residue, after the specified legacies were paid, amounted to nothing. On the contrary, had my father's just intentions taken place, in leaving me five thousand pounds, she would have come in for the other five; but the whole ten thousand now went to my sister.

She was not long however at a loss to know how this came to pass. Mr Vere determined to assert his own, and his son's right; and being exceedingly provoked at my mother's behaviour, wrote to her immediately on his return home; and having informed her of the settlement made on me, on account of the fortune already paid, and what was farther agreed on to be paid by my father, told her, he expected that this promise should be punctually fulfilled. He said, he knew she had it in her power to do this; and since it was by her contrivance I had been robbed of my just right, if honour, and the duty of a parent, would not induce her to make me proper amends, she must excuse him, if he made use of such means as the laws allowed him, in order to compel her.

Such a letter, to a woman of my mother's temper, met with such a reception as might be expected. She tore it before his messenger's face; and desired him to tell his master, that as what he had already obtained was by fraud, so he was at liberty to make use of force to recover the remainder; but with her consent, he never should have a single shilling.

This exasperating reply, made my father-in-law directly commence a suit against her, in which the other legatees were made parties. The distress I felt on this occasion is scarce to be imagined; the breach was now so widened between my mother and my husband's family, that there remained not the least hope of its ever being closed. Mr Vere unwillingly joined with his father in pursuit of these measures. He would for my sake much rather have yielded up his expectations, than supported them at the expence of my quiet; but his father's will, and justice to the rest of his family, compelled him to proceed, and deprived me of any pretence for interposing.

The law-suit was carrying on with great acrimony on both sides, when an event happened, that made me then, and has indeed ever since, look with indifference on every thing in this life; it was the death of my husband. He was snatched from me by a violent fever, before he reached his twentieth year.

I will not pretend to describe my sufferings to you on this sad occasion; they were aggravated by my being near the time of lying-in.

Whatever affliction Mr Vere felt for the death of his only son, it did not make him forgetful of what he owed his daughters; and he was resolved to carry on the law-suit with the utmost vigour.

You may suppose the house wherein I had lost a beloved husband appeared a dismal place to me, especially in my present situation. I thought too, my father's looks began to grow colder to me than they used to be; and I begged I might have his permission to remove for a while. He did not oppose it, and I went, at the pressing intreaties of your favourite, the good old dean, to his house; where he and his lady behaved to me with more than parental tenderness. My health was in so declining a way, that this worthy man (as I have since learned) made several applications to my mother to see me, but without success. At length the hour of my delivery arrived, and I was brought to-bed of a dead female child. The estate, in case of Mr Vere's dying without issue, devolved on his sisters; and I was in hopes that this circumstance, so favourable to the young ladies, would have induced their father to have been less rigorous in persisting in his claim. But in this I was deceived; he loved money, and was besides full of resentment against my mother. I thought however of an expedient, which I flattered myself might work upon him; and by good fortune it succeeded.

Mr Vere, though I had left his house, visited me constantly, and kept up a shew of tenderness, which I am sure he had not in his heart. I told him one day, whilst I was still confined to my bed, that as I had now lost both my husband and my child, a very moderate income would be sufficient for me; and that as I valued my mother's peace of mind, beyond any selfish consideration, I was very willing to give up half my jointure, provided he would drop his suit. Mr Vere seemed surprized at the proposal: he said, he wondered I could be so blind to my own interest, and that all he was doing was purely for my sake. I thanked him for his pretended friendship, but assured him, he could serve me no way so effectually, as by coming into the measure I proposed. Mr Vere said, I talked like a child; but he would consider of it. The following day he called on me again, and told me, that to make me easy, he was willing to come into my proposal; that he would have the proper instruments drawn, by which I would relinquish half my jointure; and he in consequence to give up all claim on my father's estate.

I was much better pleased, at this losing agreement, than if I had acquired a large accession of fortune.

Mr Vere soon got the proper deeds ready, and they were executed in form.

I now relapsed into an illness, from which I was supposed to have been quite recovered, and my life was thought in great danger. I have since been told, that Mr Vere repented his agreement at that juncture, and told some of his friends, that if he had not been so hasty, he should have had a chance for my jointure and my fortune too.

I begged of the dean to go to my mother, and use his last efforts on her, to prevail with her to see me and forgive me before I died; at the same time, I sent her the release I had procured from Mr Vere, which I knew was the most acceptable present I could make her. The dean urged the danger I was in, without its seeming to make much impression on her. I am willing to believe, that she thought the dean exaggerated in his account of my illness. He owned to me himself, that he was shocked to find her so obdurate. At length, he took the paper out of his pocket, and presenting it to her, I am sorry, madam, said he, I cannot prevail with you to act like a parent or a christian; your daughter I fear will not survive her present malady; but she will have the comfort to consider, that she has left nothing unattempted to obtain that forgiveness, which you so cruelly deny her. I hope, lady Grimston, your last hours may be as peaceful, as hers I trust will be from this reflection. There, madam – she has by that instrument left you disengaged from a troublesome and vexatious law-suit, that would, if pursued, infallibly turn out to your disadvantage; it was all she *could* do, and what few children, used like her, *would* have done.

My mother, a great deal alarmed at the dean's manner of speaking, now examined the contents of the paper. She seemed affected, and called him back, as he was just leaving the room. She told him, she was not lost to the feelings of nature; and that if he thought her presence would contribute to ease my mind of the remorse it must needs labour under, she was not against seeing me.

The good man, glad to find her in this yielding disposition, told her she could not too soon execute her intention; and pressed her to come to his house directly. She suffered him to put her into his coach, and he carried her home with him. The interview, on my side, was attended with tears of joy, tenderness, and contrition. My mother did not depart from her usual austerity; she gave me but her hand to kiss, and pronounced her forgiveness and her blessing in so languid a manner, as greatly damped the fervor of my joy.

She staid with me not more than a quarter of an hour, and having talked of indifferent things, without once so much as mentioning what I had done, she took a cold and formal leave.

This interview, as little cordial as my mother's behaviour was to me, had so good an effect on me, that I began perceptibly to mend from that hour. She sent indeed constantly to enquire how I did; but avoided coming, lest, as she said, she should meet with Mr Vere, whom she could never forgive. As soon as I was in a condition to go abroad, I went to pay my duty to her. She received me with civility, but no tenderness; nor has she ever from that time made me the least recompence for what I have lost; her permitting me to see her, she thinks sufficient amends.

I did not chuse to return to Mr Vere's house, as I had only a polite, not a kind invitation. One of his daughters, she who had been present at my marriage, and who always had shewn most affection towards me, was about this time married to a gentleman, whose estate lay in another country. When the bride went home, she pressed me to go with her so warmly, that I could not refuse her; and during the time I staid with her, I received so many marks of tenderness from her, that I resolved to settle in her neighbourhood; and have now a little house near her, where I have resided constantly ever since. I come once or twice a year to pay a visit to my mother, but my reception, as you may see, is always cold, and I seldom stay more than a few days.

Old Mr Vere is dead; and his daughters, who were coheiresses to his estate, are all married, so that the family is intirely dispersed; but notwithstanding this, and the number of years that have passed over since my marriage, my mother cannot yet endure the name of the family: and always, as you may have observed, calls me by my maiden name.

I was much affected at the story of the amiable Mrs Vere. The sweet melancholy, which predominates in her countenance, shews that the spirits, when broken in the bud of youth, are hardly to be recovered. What a tyrant this lady Grimston is! I did not admire her before, but I now absolutely dislike her. What a wife and a mother has she been to a husband and a daughter, who might have constituted the happiness of a woman of a different temper! And yet she passes for a wonderful good woman, and a pattern of all those virtues of a religion, which meekness and forgiveness characterise. She is mistaken, if she thinks that austerity is necessary to christianity. The most that my charity allows me to believe of such people is, that they impose on *themselves*, at a time when the most discerning perhaps think that they are endeavouring to impose on others.

What an angel is my good mother, when compared to this her friend, whom her humility makes her look upon as her superior in virtue! I am very angry with Sir George, who in his resentment, said to me once, that she was like lady Grimston. I then knew but little of that lady's character, or I should have reproved him for it.

I conjured Mrs Vere to make her visit longer than she had at first intended. She told me, she would most gladly do it; but that it was a liberty she did not dare to take, unless her mother asked her to prolong it; which, she said, she possibly might do, in complaisance to me.

September 4

My mother I find has made lady Grimston her confidant in relation to my affairs; the dear woman never keeps her mind to herself on any subject. Lady Grimston highly applauds her conduct in that business; and bestowed a few civil words on me for my filial duty, intermixed with an ungrateful comparison of her own daughter's behaviour. And she condoled with herself, by saying, that *good parents* had not always *good children*. She told my mother, that she wished to see the child (meaning me) happily disposed of; for that, notwithstanding the prudence of my behaviour, the world would be apt to cast reflections on me, on account of the abruptness with which the match was broken off, without the true reasons being known: and my illness, she said, might be imputed to the disappointment; which might incline people to suspect the rejection had been on Mr Faulkland's side. What a provoking hint was this my dear! it has really alarmed my mother, who depends much on the judgment of her friend, and has at the same time so nice a regard to the honour of her family. I wish that formal old woman would mind her own business.

September 6

My mother and lady Grimston have had abundance of private confabulation these two days, from which Mrs Vere and I are excluded. I wish there may not be some mischief a brewing. One thing, however, has given me pleasure; lady Grimston has invited her daughter to stay at Grimston-hall as long as my mother and I continue here.

Mrs Vere tells me, she suspects the subject of their conferences; but she is perverse, and will not tell me what she thinks, for fear, as she says, she should have guessed wrong, and her surmises would only teaze me.

September 10

A packet sent me from London – A letter from Sir George – one from my Cecilia – and so soon too! Welcome, welcome, thou faithful messenger, from the faithfullest of hearts!

Thou dear anticipating little prophetess! What put it into thy head to call Mr Arnold a new conquest, upon my but barely mentioning him to you? I was just going to tell you all; and behold your own whimsical imagination has suggested the most material part to you already. You desire me to be sincere: was that necessary, my sister, from *you* to *me?* You say, you are *sure Mr Arnold is, or will be my lover*; and insist on my being more particular in my description of him. What a strange girl you are! again I ask you, What put this into your head? What busy little spirit of intelligence flew to you with the news before I knew it myself? For as to the fact, it is but too certain.

This has been the subject of my mother's and lady Grimston's private conferences; and Mrs Vere (sly thing as she is) guessed it. It seems Mr Arnold disclosed his passion to lady Grimston, in order to ask her advice about it. She loves mightily to be consulted; and ill-starred as I am, did me the honour to recommend me strongly to him; and she has prepossessed my mother too in favour of this new man. I wish the meddling old dame had been dumb. Now shall I go through another fiery tryal! Heaven help me, if lady Grimston were to be my judge! But my mother is all goodness.

Well, but you want a description of this man. I will give it to you, though I have scarce patience to write about him. Indeed, Cecilia, I am vexed; I foresee a great deal of trouble from that quarter. – But come, I will try what I can say.

The man is about thirty, genteel, and handsome enough; at least he is reckoned so, and I believe I should think him so, if I were not angry with him. He is very like your brother Henry; and you know he is an allowed handsome man. He seems to have plain good sense, and is good humoured I believe: I do not know of what colour his eyes are, for I never looked much at him. Lady Grimston says he is a *scholar* (a thing she pretends to value highly), and a mighty sober, pious, worthy gentleman. He is of a very good family; and has an estate of about fifteen hundred pounds a year, upon which there is a jointure of three hundred pounds a year, paid to his brother's widow. Part of the estate is in Kent, and part in this county of Essex, where he has a mansion-house, a well-enough looking old-fashioned place, something in the Grimston-hall stile, at about a mile distance from this; where he passes most of his time.

I have told you already, he plays divinely on several instruments; this is the only circumstance about him that pleases me.

He has not yet made his addresses to me in form; yet we all know that he intends it, from his uncommon assiduity towards me; but he has a sort of reserve about him, and loves to do every thing in his own way.

Bless me! – here he is – his chariot has just driven into the court; and Mrs Vere peeps in upon me, and with a most vexatious archness, bids me come down to the parlour; but I will not, unless my mother desires me. I will go into the garden, to be for a while out of the way.

September 11

Yesterday evening was productive of nothing but looks and compliments, and bows, and so forth; except two or three delightful pieces of musick, which he executed incomparably. But, this morning, my Cecilia, Oh! this morning! the man spoke out, told me in down-right plain English, that he loved me! How insipid is such a declaration, when it comes from one, who is indifferent to us! I do not know how it was, but instead of being abashed, I could have smiled in his face when he declared himself; but you may be sure I did not, that would not have been pretty.

I was sitting in the little drawing-room, reading, when he came in. To be sure he was sent to me by the ancient ladies, otherwise he would not have intruded; for the man is not ill-bred. The book happened to be Horace; upon his entering the room, I laid it by; he asked me politely enough, what were my studies. When I named the author, he took the book up, and opening the leaves, started, and looked me full in the face; I coloured. My charming Miss Bidulph, said he, do you prefer this to the agreeable entertainment of finishing this beautiful rose here, that seems to blush at your neglect of it? He spoke this, pointing to a little piece of embroidery that lay in a frame before me. I was nettled at the question, it was too assuming. Sir, I hope I was as innocently, and as usefully employed; and I assure you I give a greater portion of my time to my needle, than to my book.

You are so lovely, madam, that nothing you can do needs an apology. An apology, I'll assure you! did not this look, my dear, as if the man thought I ought to beg his pardon for understanding Latin? For this accidental, and I think (to a woman) trivial accomplishment, I am indebted, you know, to Sir George; who took so much pains with me, the two or three summers he was indisposed at Sidney Castle.

He then proceeded to tell me how much he admired, how much he loved me! and that having been encouraged by lady Grimston's assuring him that I was disengaged (observe that), he presumed to tell me so. Oh! thought I, perhaps thou are thyself a Grimstonian, and do not think it necessary that the heart should be consulted. I answered him mighty civilly, and mighty little to the purpose. Sir, I thank you for your favourable sentiments – Lady Grimston does me a great deal of honour – I think myself happy in her good opinion – But he was not to be so put off, he pressed me to give him hopes, as he called it. Alas! I have no hopes to give him. He said, he would not presume to mention his love to my mother, though lady Grimston pressed him to it (it was like her), till he had first declared himself to me. This was not indelicate; my heart thanked him for it, though I only returned him a bow. We were seasonably (to me at least) interrupted here, by the arrival of my friend the dean. He had come to see lady Grimston, just as Mr Arnold had entered into conversation with me; the old gentleman had a mind to walk in the garden; the little drawing-room, where we were, opened into it, by a glass door; so that lady Grimston and my mother were obliged to bring him that way. Though I was glad that the conversation was broke off, yet I could have wished that I had first had an opportunity of throwing a little cold water on Mr Arnold's *hopes*, lest he should have put too favourable an interpretation on the reception I gave him, and mention the thing to my mother, before I had time to speak to her.

I was in some confusion at their entering the room. Mr Arnold had at that time laid hold of one of my hands, and I had but just time to withdraw it, when the door flew open to give entrance to the two ladies and the good man: the latter lifting up both his hands, as if conscious of having done something wrong, with a good-humoured freedom, asked pardon; but with a look that seemed to indicate, he thought the apology necessary both to Mr Arnold and me. This disconcerted me more; my mother smiled, and lady Grimston drew up her long neck, and winked at the dean. I took up my hat, that lay in a window, without well-knowing what I did, and said, I would wait on them into the garden. Mr Arnold followed my example; but looked at me, I do not know how – impertinently – as if he thought I did not dislike him. I took one turn with them, and then slipped away, under pretence of going in to dress. I ran directly into Mrs Vere's room, and told her what had passed between Mr Arnold and me. She laughed, and said, she could have told me long ago it would have come to that. I knew Mr Arnold admired you, said she, the first time I saw you in his company; he is no contemptible conquest I can tell you. He assured my mother, that you were the only woman he ever saw in his life that had made an impression on him; and I am inclined to believe him, for he is not a man of an amorous complexion; nor did I ever hear of his making his addresses to any one, though he might have his choice of the best fortunes, and the best families in the country; for the ladies, I must inform you, admire him exceedingly; and when you are known to be his choice, you will be the envy of all the young women in the country. I sighed, (I don't know why) and said, I desired not to create envy on that account. Mrs Vere said, why really Miss Bidulph, if your heart is at liberty, I know of no man more worthy of it than Mr Arnold; but perhaps (looking with a kind earnestness on me) that may not be your case. I told her, my heart was not engaged (as it really is not; for indeed, Cecilia, I do not think of Mr Faulkland); but that I did not find in myself any great inclination towards Mr Arnold. Oh! my dear, said she, if you find no disinclination, it is enough. I married for love, yet I was far from being happy. The vexation that I occasioned in my own and my husband's family, was a counter-ballance to the satisfaction of possessing the man I loved. Mr Arnold, besides being very amiable in his person, has good sense, and good temper; and if you marry him with nothing more than indifference, gratitude will soon produce love in such a breast as yours. Were there anything like aversion in your heart, then indeed it would be criminal in you to accept of him.

Mrs Vere delivered her sentiments with such a calm sweetness, such a disinterested sincerity, that what she said made an impression on me. We are apt, contrary as it may seem to reason, to be more wrought upon by the opinion and advice of young people like ourselves, than by that of persons, whose experience certainly gives them a better right to form judgments: but we have a sort of a natural repugnance to the being dictated to, even by those who have an authority to do it; and as age gives a superiority, every thing that comes from it carries a sort of air of prescribing, which we are wonderfully inclined to reject.

Had lady Grimston said this to me, it would have put me upon my guard, as suspecting a design on my liberty of choice. Even my good mother might have been listened to on this subject not without uneasiness; though my duty to her would not suffer me to give her a moment's pain, unless I was sure that my eternal as well as temporal happiness was at stake. I told Mrs Vere that I had no aversion to Mr Arnold; on the contrary that if I had a sister, I should wish her married to him. Now, my Cecilia, the mischief of it is, there *can* be no reasonable objection made to him: he is a very tolerable man; but I knew a man once that I liked better – but fye fye upon him! I am sure I ought not to like him, and therefore I will not. I am positive, if I were let alone, I should be as happy as ever.

I told you I got a letter from my brother; he says in it, he has had one from Mr Faulkland, who is now in your part of the world. He tells Sir George, that 'if my lady Bidulph will be so good as to see Miss B. and converse with her, he is not without hopes that she may so far exculpate him, as to induce my lady to repeal his sentence of banishment.' Sir George adds his own wishes for this, but says (to give you *his* words) he fears the wench will not be honest enough to do Faulkland justice – Justice! what can my brother mean by this?

How ungenerous these men are, even the best of them, in love matters! He knows the poor girl doats on her destroyer, and might perhaps take shame to *herself*, rather than throw as much blame on him as he deserves. I think this is all the justice that can be expected from her; and how poor an extenuation would this make of his guilt! It would only add to the merit of *her* sufferings, without lessening his fault.

To what purpose then would it be? I know my mother's sentiments already on that head. I would not shew Sir George's letter to her, he had said so many ridiculous things about lady Grimston in it, which I know would have offended her highly; otherwise, on account of Mr Faulkland's paragraph, I should have been glad she had seen it.

September 12

Ah! my sister! my friend! What shall I do? Oh! that officious lady Grimston – What ill star drove me to her house? Nothing would serve her but she must know what Mr Arnold said to me in the drawing-room conference; and how I had behaved. She made her enquiry before my mother and the dean, after I had left them in the garden. What could the man do? He had no reason to conceal what passed, and frankly owned he had made me an offer of his heart. Well, and how did Miss receive it, asked lady Grimston? With that modesty and polite sweetness that she does every thing, answered Mr Arnold. He could say no less, you know.

He thence took occasion to apply particularly to my mother, apologizing at the same time for his not having done it before. What the self-sufficient creature added, I know not; for my mother, from whom I had this account, did not repeat all he said; but it seems it was enough to make her imagine I had not heard him reluctantly, and accordingly she gave him her permission to win me and wear me.

I could cry for very vexation, to be made such a puppet of. This eclaircissement I dreaded before I had time to explain myself to my mother. That best of women, still anticipating what I had to say, congratulated me on my extraordinary prudence, in not letting a childish misplaced attachment keep such a hold on my heart, as to make me blind to the merits of a more deserving object.

Dear madam, said I, sure Mr Arnold did not say that I had encouraged his addresses. Encouraged, my dear! why sure the hearing, from a young lady of your education, is encouragement enough to a man of sense. – I heard him with complaisance, madam, because I thought *that* due to him; that it was my wish to remain single, at least for some time. My mother looked surprized. 'Sidney, this is not what I expected from you; I flattered myself you thought no longer of Mr Faulkland.'

She contracted her brow a little. Madam, I do not; indeed I think no more of him; but may I not be permitted to continue as I am?

Had you never had any engagement with Mr Faulkland, answered my mother, I should be far from urging you on this occasion; but, circumstanced as you now, are, I think your honour is concerned.

Lady Grimston has put your affair in such a light to me, as I never considered it in before. How mortifying must the reflection be, my dear, to think that it may be said Mr Faulkland perhaps flew off, from some disadvantageous circumstance he discovered in regard to you. The world wants not envious malicious tongues enough to give it this turn. Your unluckly illness, and your brother's ill-timed assiduity in going so often to him when he was at Richmond, looks as if we had been endeavouring to recall him. Every body knows the marriage was almost concluded; and Lady Grimston, though she thinks our reasons for breaking it off were extremely cogent, yet as she knows the world well, thinks it has not virtue enough to believe those to be the true reasons, and that it will be much more apt to put an invidious construction on the affair, that may be very detrimental to you in your future prospects. These considerations alone ought to determine you; but there is one still of greater moment, which I hope, from the goodness of your heart, will have still greater weight with you. That unfortunate young lady, who *ought* to be the wife of Mr Faulkland, if you were once put beyond the reach even of his most distant hope, would stand the better chance for having justice done to her; at least it would leave him void of that pretence which he at first pleaded, and which probably he will continue to do, while you remain single. Think seriously of the matter, my love. I shall only add, that Mr Arnold is every way an unexceptionable match, and that your acceptance of him will be extremely agreeable to me; as, on the contrary, your refusal will give an uneasiness to your indulgent mother, which she never yet experienced from you.

She left me with these cruel words, cruel in their kindness – Oh! she knows I am flexible by nature, and to *her* will, yielding as air. What can I do? My heart is not in a disposition to love – Yet again and again I repeat it, Mr Faulkland has no interest there. What he once had he has lost; but I cannot compel it to like, and unlike, and like anew at pleasure. Fain would I bring myself chearfully to conform to my mother's will, for I have no will of my own. I never knew what it was to have one, and never shall, I believe; for I am sure I will not contend with a husband.

I have told Mrs Vere what my mother said to me; she is intirely of her mind; every body is combined against me; I am treated like a baby, that knows not what is fit for it to chuse or to reject.

September 15

I have been searching my heart, my dear Cecilia, to try if there remained a lurking particle of my former flame unextinguished; a flame I call it, as we are allowed the metaphor, but it never rose to *that*; it was but a single ray, a gentle glow that just warmed my breast without scorching: what it might have arisen to I will not say; but I have the satisfaction to find, that the short-lived fire is quite extinct, and the mansion is even chilled with cold.

This was a very necessary scrutiny, before I would even entertain a thought of Mr Arnold; and believe me, had I found it otherwise than I say, I would rather have hazarded my mother's displeasure by owning the truth to her, than injure any man, by giving him my hand with an estranged heart.

I will acknowlege to you, my sister, that it was not without a struggle I reduced my mind to this frame. My heart (foolish thing) industrious to perplex itself, would fain have suggested some palliating circumstances in Mr Faulkland's favour; but I forbid it to interpose. Trifler, said I, let your guardian, your proper guide, judge and determine for you in this important cause, whereupon so much of your future peace depends. It sighed, but had the virtue to submit; and I arraigned Faulkland before a little tribunal in my breast, where I would suffer reason only to preside. The little felon, love, knocked at the door once or twice, but justice kept him out; and after a long (and I think a fair) trial, he was at length cast; and in order to strengthen my resolves, and justify my mother's, as well as my own conduct, these are the arguments which I have deduced from the evidences against him.

If Mr Faulkland feared the frailty of his virtue, why did he not fly when he was first alarmed with the knowlege of the lady's passion for him? If not for his own sake, yet at least for her's. If he could not return her love, was he not cruel in suffering her to feed a hopeless flame? But since his evil fate urged him on, and the unhappy girl lost her honour, was he not bound to repair it? He had never seen me at that time, was under no personal engagements to me, and might easily have acquitted himself to my brother, from so justifiable a motive.

What if I had married him, ignorant of this secret, and it had afterwards come to my ears, how miserable would it have made me, to think that I had stood between an unfortunate young creature and her happiness? For had Mr Faulkland never heard of me, had he not been prejudiced in my favour, this young woman's beauty and innocence (which he acknowleges) might have then engaged his honest vows; the wicked aunt would not have been tempted to betray her trust, nor he (shocking thought! whenever it recurs) to buy that favour he might have obtained on virtuous terms. His prior engagements to my brother was the final plea that undid them both! Had he not been furnished with this excuse, her hopes might have supported her virtue; or, if ignorant of this, she fell, what pretence could he offer, after the injury *was* done, for not fulfilling an obligation of so much importance? I could not have suffered by not obtaining a man I never saw; Miss B. is undone by losing him: Yet his word to Sir George, the breach of which could have been attended with no ill consequence, was to be preferred to an act of justice. This is that false honour upon which the men pique themselves so much. An innocent child stigmatized; an amiable woman abandoned to shame and grief! I thank Heaven I made not myself accessary to this. *Had* I married Mr Faulkland, *knowing* his fault, I could not say so, nor have blamed any thing but my own imprudence, if *I* in my turn found myself deserted. Who knows but he might (after having bound me in chains), return to his neglected mistress; and *that* love, which, when it would have been meritorious in him, he disrelished, he might have pursued with eagerness when interdicted. This might have been the case. I believe you may remember an instance of it among our own acquaintance. Mr Saunders, who refused a young lady for his bride, from an absolute dislike of her person, took uncommon pains to debauch her when she became the wife of his friend. Had Mr Faulkland so behaved, what a wretch it would have made me! You know I have not a grain of jealousy in my composition, yet I am sure a neglect of this kind would make me very miserable.

You have not forgot, I believe, that about two years ago there was a match proposed to my mother by the bishop of B. between me and his nephew. The young man was heir to a good fortune, was reckoned handsome and accomplished, and I think he really was so: I was intirely free from prepossessions in favour of any one, and had no objection to him, but that I knew he had a most lamentably-vulnerable heart, for he had been in love with two or three women of my acquaintance. My mother mentioned him to me upon the good old prelate's recommendation, and I gave her this as my reason for disliking the offer, which she approved of so intirely, that the thing went no farther. Indeed I think that woman is a fool, who risques her contentment with one of a light disposition. Marriage will not change men's natures; and it is not every one who has virtue or prudence enough to be reclaimed. Upon the whole, I am satisfied with my lot; and am sure I could hear with pleasure, that Mr Faulkland was married to that Miss B. I wish I knew the other letters that compose her name.

September 16

My mother asked me to-day, Had I considered of what she had been saying to me? I told her I had, and only begged a little more time. She kissed me, with tears in her eyes. To be sure, my dear, as much as you can reasonably desire. I know my Sidney is above trifling. Mrs Vere was present when my mother left the room. Oh! Miss Bidulph, said she, who would refuse to gratify such a parent as that? Had *my* mother condescended to treat me so, I am sure she could have wrought on me to do any thing she liked, even though it had been repugnant to my inclination. Dear madam, I replied, how sweetly you inforce my duty – Yes, I will obey that kindest best of mothers. I believe I spoke this, tho' without intending it, in a tone that implied something like making a merit of this concession; for Mrs Vere immediately answered, There's a good child! that, to oblige its mamma, will accept of a very handsome young gentleman, with a good estate, and one that many a girl in England would give her eyes for. I felt the rebuke; but turning it off with a smile, said, but you forget, my dear, that I am not dying for him.

September 20

How will you plume yourself on your sagacity, Cecilia, when you read this account of my love, which you so wisely foretold? I can tell you I am trying to like Mr Arnold as fast as I can; I make him sing and play for this purpose from morning till night, for he is here every day and all day. Lady Grimston holds her head a quarter of a yard higher than she did before; and looks, as who should say, it was *I* that brought this about. The dean is as frolick as May-day upon it; for he is very fond of Mr Arnold; but tells him he will not forgive him for robbing him of his second wife; for such, he says, he intended me. I think his daughter (a pretty girl of about seventeen) looks a little grave of late. I hope she does not like Mr Arnold herself. I wish my mother would take it into her head that she was in love with him, and that Mr Arnold had promised to marry her; then should I a second time crown me with a willow garland. But there is no fear of this, or rather no hope.

Lady Grimston has given my mother *such* a character of Mr Arnold, that if you will take her word for it, there is not a man like him in the world; and my mother firmly believes every syllable she says. She told me to day she would write to Sir George, to give him an account of the matter, and desire his advice. This is a compliment she would not omit paying, for any consideration, tho' I know my brother's judgment has now lost all credit with her; and that, let his opinion be what it will, she is firmly resolved on her new plan. Knowing as you do my mother's firmness, when once she is possessed with a thing, you will not wonder that I did not make attempts to alter her mind, which I knew would be fruitless. She likes Mr Arnold prodigiously; she piques herself on her skill in physiognomy, and says, if she is deceived in this gentleman, she will never again rely on that science. Lady Grimston is so fond of him, that I wonder she did not marry him herself.

September 23

We have received two letters from Sir George; one in answer to my mother's letter, the other to me. I will give them both to you: the following is a copy of that to my mother.

Madam,

I thank you for the honour you do me in asking my advice, in regard to the proposal of marriage you have received for my sister; but I am entirely disqualified from giving you any, as I am an absolute stranger both to the person and character of the gentleman you mention; and know no more of him, than that I have heard there *is* such a person, who has some estate in the county where you now you are.

As you are absolute mistress of your daughter's will, as well as of her person, I shall not presume to interfere in this nice point. If the marriage is not *already* agreed upon (which may be the case, notwithstanding the compliment you do me the favour to pay me), I think it would be generous in you to see Miss B. and hear what she has to say, before you proceed farther; but in this, as in every thing else, your own discretion must guide you.

I am,

Madam,

Your affectionate son,

and most obedient servant,

GEORGE BIDULPH.

London,
Sept. 22.

My mother was exceedingly displeased with this letter. She said Sir George had a haughtiness in him that was very offensive to her. I have acquitted myself in applying to him, and shall give myself no farther trouble about him or his opinion. As for Miss B. I think she can hardly be under a necessity of coming to town as yet, and that affair may keep cold, for I have but little curiosity to hear what the poor Soul may be prompted to say, as I am sure I shall be time enough to afford her any assistance she may stand in need of. This was the whole of her observation. My brother's letter to me is as follows:

Dear Sidney,

I received with concern (though I own not with surprize) an account from my mother, of a new treaty of marriage that is on foot between you and a Mr Arnold, of whom I know nothing. Instead of congratulating you upon this occasion, I cannot help condoling with you; for I have a better opinion of your heart than to suppose it can have so soon renounced poor Faulkland. I do not reproach you for your acquiescence in giving him up: I *know* you could not do otherwise; but why in the name of precipitancy are you to be hurried into wedlock already? You went into the country to recover your health, I thought; prithee, how comes this new husband into your way? I know, child, it is not of your seeking, and do from my heart pity you.

I would by no means have you guilty of a breach of duty to our mother; but for Heaven's sake, why don't you try your influence over her, to have this sudden scheme of matrimony suspended, till she sees and talks to this girl that Faulkland refers her to? If the wench owns that he was not to blame so much as she herself was, and relinquishes all pretensions to him, don't you think she (my mother I mean) would in that case remain bound in honour to yield you to his prior claim?

Indeed, Sidney, I must blame you for this part of your conduct; it looks like a strange insensibility in you.

I know you will urge your perfect submission to your mother's will; and I know too, that *will* is as absolute as that of an Eastern monarch. I therefore repeat it, I do not mean to reproach you with your compliance, but I am vexed to the heart, and must give it vent.

I see plainly that old piece of formality, lady Grimston's infernal shrivelled paw in all this. For my mother of herself, I am sure, would not have thought of disposing of you, without your liking, so soon after an affair that had created you so much uneasiness, unless it had been suggested to her by somebody. Prithee tell me what sort of man this Arnold really is, for I do not depend on the partial representations I have had of him.

I wish Miss B. were come to town, but she is not yet arrived. I enquired for her of Faulkland's housekeeper, by the name of Jefferis. The woman is at the house at Putney waiting to receive her, but does not know how soon she will come. Would she had been buried before Faulkland saw her!

I shall expect a letter from you soon. How comes it that you never mentioned Mr Arnold to me in any that you have writ? But I excuse you, and am

Your affectionate brother,

London, Sept. 22. G.B.

You see this is Sir George himself, my dear, a mixture of petulancy and indelicacy. There is one thing in him, however, commendable; his steady adherence to his friend's interests. You find how impossible for me it is to shew such a letter to my mother: by his strange unguarded manner of writing, which he does not consider, he defeats his own purposes; for if any use could be made of that part of his letter relative to Miss B. I could not shew my mother part, without letting her see the whole: but that is not to be done; and I can only thank my good fortune that I received this, and the last letter from him, without her knowlege.

I will now give you my answer to this letter, which I wrote, by the return of the post.

Dear Brother,

I thank you for your condolements, but can assure you my heart is not in such a situation as to require any. I own I had all the esteem for Mr Faulkland, which I thought his merit deserved. Duty to my good mother, and an undeniable blemish in his character, first wrought a change in my sentiments towards him: my own peace of mind now requires me to improve that change into indifference.

You do me justice in supposing that I should never think of seeking a husband; and you have formed as right a judgment in regard to lady Grimston's being the promoter of this union. As for Mr Arnold, though perhaps (had I never known your friend) he might not have been the man of my choice, yet have I no dislike to him. I believe him to be a very worthy gentleman; and that my mother has not been partial in her representations. I am sure, at least, she has said nothing of him but what she has seen, or been told, and has good reason to believe.

I wish, dear brother, you had writ with more caution, that I might have laid before my mother what you said in relation to Miss B. It may have its weight with me, though I cannot answer for its having any with her. Do you forget her having told me, that she conceived a sort of horror at the thoughts of my marrying Mr Faulkland? She cannot but be sensible, that Miss B. is not without her share of blame in that affair, which has so perplexed us all. But you know too that does not exculpate Mr Faulkland. The young lady's relinquishing her hopes (for a claim I think she does not make), would only the more excite my mother's compassion, and interest her in her favour. To sum up the whole in one word, my mother is resolved, and you yourself acknowlege that her will is absolute. She has used the most irresistible argument to obtain my consent, *viz.* that it would make *her* happy. Spare then, my dear brother, unkind reflections on any part of my behaviour; for I am determined to pursue, through life, that rule of conduct, which I have hitherto invariably adhered to; I mean that of preferring to my own the happiness of those who are most dear to me.

I am, &c.

September 25

Mr Arnold has so many advocates here, that his interest cannot fail of being promoted. Mrs Vere admires him; the Dean commends him; my mother praises him; lady Grimston extols him to the skies. No one is silent, but the young girl that I mentioned to you before; she only colours and hangs down her head when he is spoken of. I really begin to fear that the poor thing loves him; but he never made any addresses to her, and I hope does not suspect it.

Things are now gone so far, that my mother and lady Grimston talked to day of settlements. Mr Arnold receives but twelve hundred pounds a year from his estate; his brother's widow, as I have already told you, having a jointure upon it of three hundred pounds a year. She lives intirely in London, and is, I am told, a very imprudent woman, and not at all esteemed by the family. The elder Mr Arnold and she were married several years, but never had a child; the last two years of his life his wife and he lived separate, her conduct having given room for some suspicions, very injurious to her husband's honour.

The Arnold estate was originally a very considerable one, but has been dissipated by the extravagance of the successive possessors. What remains, however, is quite clear, and is likely to be kept so by the good management of the present owner. His late brother was exceedingly remiss in his affairs, and spent most of his time in London; and if it had not been for Mr Arnold, the mansion-house would have fallen to the ground; but his brother lent it to him, and he kept it in repair for his own use, as he is fond of the place: though he has a pretty house in Kent, belonging to another estate of about three hundred pounds a year, which came to him by his mother, for he is the son of a second marriage. And this, till his brother's death, was the whole of his income; but he is so good an oeconomist, that he always made a genteeler figure on his three hundred pounds a year, than his brother did on twelve.

My mother, who you know is integrity itself, thinks that I ought not to have more settled on me than the widow of Mr Arnold's brother had, whose fortune was superior to mine. Mr Arnold makes a much handsomer proposal; lady Grimston is for laying hold of it. The Dean was for striking a medium. I do not care how they settle it; but I fancy my mother will have her own way in this.

She purposes going to town next week, that the wedding – (bless me! whose wedding is it that I am talking of so coolly?) well – that it may be celebrated in her own house. This to be sure will send Sir George directly out of it. I cannot help it; I am born to give, and to receive vexation.

Mr Arnold speaks of taking a house in London, where my mother is to have an apartment whenever she chuses to be in town. This is a pleasing circumstance to me; and she likewises proposes our being sometimes with her at Sidney-castle. That is a prospect which loses much of its charms, by the reflection that my dear Cecilia is not there.

October 1

All preliminaries are settled. There has been a fuss with parchments this week past. My mother has carried her point, in regard to the jointure; and has made choice of that little estate in Kent to be settled on me, as it is a complete three hundred pounds a year, detached intirely from the rest, and has a pretty house on it. This was all she would accept of, though, to do Mr Arnold justice, he would have been much more liberal; but, my mother says, a single woman, bred in retirement as I have been, who cannot live on that, does not deserve to live at all; adding, that as the estate was already subject to one jointure, and the widow so young a woman; if it should be also my misfortune to become one early, a great part of the fortune would be swallowed by dowagers, and the heir not have enough to support his rank.

October 2

This morning my mother, lady Grimston, the Dean, and Mr Arnold (who is the idol of them all) took a rumbling together in the old coach, by way of taking the air, in a dusty road; and what do you think was the result of their deliberations in this jaunt? Why truly lady Grimston, proud of her handy-work, would needs see it accomplished; and nothing will serve her, but I must be married at her house. My mother opposed it at first, but the Dean seconded the proposal, that he might have (as he expressed himself) the satisfaction of contributing *himself* to make Mr Arnold happy; and Mr Arnold (audaciously expecting, I suppose, that this would hasten the ceremony) joined his intreaties so effectually, that my mother was obliged to yield.

What a tormenting old woman is this lady Grimston! I hoped, at least, for the respite of a month, by getting to London. I thought first to have delayed the time of our going to town, and then to have faddled away a good while longer under pretence of preparations; though there is but little room for that now, as all my fineries, destined I thought to another purpose, are lying quietly in my trunks at home. But then one might have contrived many little occasions of delay. There was a house to be fixed upon, and I had twenty things to do, and, as my mother says, many things fall out between the cup and the lip. But all my expectations are blown away, and I have but one poor fortnight given me to recollect my scattered thoughts, when they are all to be centered in Mr Arnold. I am not merry, my Cecilia, but I am determined not to appear sad; neither am I so; I hope I have no reason.

My mother purposes writing again to Sir George, to desire his presence at my marriage. I hope he will behave respectfully to every one here, if he should come.

October 5

Mr Arnold has writ to town, to bespeak a new chariot; he will do nothing in regard to the house, till I am on the spot to please myself. I intend sending Patty to town, to bring me down my bridal trappings.

Mr Arnold has given some necessary orders for the new decking of his person, as well as some of the apartments in the old mansion-house, which seem a little to want refurnishing; most of the goods having been inhabitants there since the time of his great grand-father.

October 9

My mother's last letter to Sir George has produced the following answer, which he sent by Patty, when she returned down here with my cloaths.

Madam,

I am sorry I cannot accept of the invitation you favour me with, to be present at my sister's nuptials. Some affairs in Wiltshire require my immediate attendance; and I had settled matters before I received your summons, so as to set out as on this day. I wish you all imaginable satisfaction in your new son-in-law; and my sister abundance of happiness in her spouse.

I am, Madam, &c.

London, October 8

I am glad Sir George does not come down; I am sure if he did, his behaviour would be such, as would render him no very acceptable guest at Grimston-hall.

A week, but a short week, to come, before my fate is irrevocably fixed; or revocable only by the hand of death! This reflection, solemn as it is, does not alarm me; because, after again calling my heart to the strictest account, I think I *can* pronounce it intirely free. Mr Arnold will soon have an indisputable right to it; and it is my firm purpose to use my utmost endeavours to give him intire possession of it. He every day gains upon my esteem. If his talents are not so glittering as I have seen some others possessed of, he is nevertheless master of an exceedingly good understanding, which a sort of diffidence in his manner does not suffer him to shew at once to the best advantage. His temper is extremely sweet, and he seems to have an openness of heart (when he throws off a little shyness which he has contracted) that is exceedingly engaging. His love for me appears as fervent as I believe it sincere; and I should be ungrateful not to do my utmost to return it.

October 14

How precipitate has been my fortune? Twice within these three months have I been almost at the eve of my intended nuptials. Those which *were* to have been, I thought as certain as those which are *now* to be solemnized within two days. Who knows what may still happen to frustrate our present designs? – No – there is not another Miss B. to interpose. Mr Arnold seems to be one of those who are born to pass quietly through life. He has already attained to the age of thirty, without one event ever happening to him, but such as happen to every man every day. May no future storm ever interrupt his or my tranquility! for they will soon be one and the same thing.

October 16

The die is thrown, my Cecilia, and thy Sidney is the wife of Mr Arnold! This day we were married; the good Dean joined our hands, and his daughter was one of my bride-maids. The poor girl was taken ill during the ceremony, and was obliged to leave the church, which has confirmed me in my suspicions – Oh! how I pity her! I believe indeed she only feigned illness for an excuse to retire. Mrs Vere went out with her, but she would not suffer her to attend her home. She promised to dine with us, if she should be better; and so she did, and seemed chearful and pretty well; but I thought she looked as if she had been crying. She made my heart ache – but I am in hopes it is but a slight wound; she is exceedingly lively, and, I dare say, will soon get the better of it.

Lady Grimston was downright tiresome with her compliments; and preached an hour long about the duty of children to their parents; and how good a wife that woman was likely to make, who had always been exemplary in her filial obedience. Ah! lady Grimston, thought I, by what I have heard of you, you did not seem to number obedience amongst wife-like virtues in your own case, though you can preach it up to others. But I knew this sermon was chiefly intended for poor Mrs Vere's use. My mother was all kindness and complacency. She seemed so delighted, that I rejoiced in having had it in my power to give her so much happiness. Lady Grimston did the honours of her house on this occasion with great magnificence, and I believe I need not tell you, with most exquisite decorum. Indeed this wedding was conducted with such a decent festivity, so rationally on all sides, and such a comfortable privacy, that I was not half so much shocked as I expected to have been.

We have no company here besides the family of the house, my dear good old Dean, his lady and daughter, one young lady more, and a relation of Mr Arnold's; a gentleman who came from London on purpose to be present on this (as it is called) joyful occasion.

We shall leave this house to-morrow, Mr Arnold and I, I mean. I am to be put into possession of the old mansion of Arnold-abbey. My mother is to continue with lady Grimston a week or a fortnight longer, and then she goes to London on no other call, as she says, but to see and administer comfort to poor Miss B. who she supposes will be by that time come to her retreat.

I believe I shall remain in the country while the weather continues pleasant, but am not yet determined.

October 17

We took leave of lady Grimston this morning, or rather of her house; for her ladyship, my dear mother, and all the good folks that were our guests at Grimston-hall, are to dine with us to-day at Arnold-abbey. I desired I might be permitted to go home without any parade, and in as private a manner as possible; for you know how I hate a bustle. Mr

Arnold very obligingly indulged me in this request, and conducted my sweet Mrs Vere and me home in his coach, at eight of the clock this morning. I found every thing in exact order at Arnold-abbey. The house is very spacious and convenient, though very old-fashioned. Some of the rooms, however, are newly fitted up, perfectly neat and handsome. The servants are orderly and well-behaved, and every thing seems to be exactly well regulated. You may be sure I have taken my own Patty home with me; I intend to constitute her housekeeper, and give her an additional salary for her additional trouble. Mr Arnold had nobody in that capacity before, as his household had not been settled since the acquisition of his fortune, and he reserved the chusing of so material a domestic to me; but as I do not love to multiply servants, and know that Patty is very capable of the place, I shall take no other.

October 21

Visitors still in abundance: all the gentry in the neighbourhood for some miles about have been to pay us their compliments; at least, I hope by this time they have *all* been here, for we have not had a minute to ourselves these three days. It will take me up ten to return them, as many of the families live at a good distance from hence.

Mr Arnold, whose mourning has been laid aside since our wedding day, seems to have a very good taste in dress; he is perfectly well shaped, and appears to great advantage in colours; in short, he is more amiable than I thought he was. It is with great pleasure that I observe my young acquaintance, on whose heart I feared Mr Arnold had made an impression, has recovered her usual vivacity. With people extremely full of spirits, love is not apt to sink very deep, or last long, when it does not meet with a return.

October 30

My mother sets out for London to-morrow, and Mr Arnold has proposed to me, that he and I should accompany her. He says, he wants to look out for a house, and should like to fix in one before the weather advances; and that we may take up our abode at my mother's till our house is ready for us. My mother is charmed at this proposal: she dreads the thought of parting with me; and as she intends going (after a convenient stay in London) down to Sidney-castle, if I remain here, our separation must be immediate. I know this is Mr Arnold's kind reason for desiring me to go; he thinks I shall be less affected at parting with my mother, when in the midst of the various scenes which London affords, than I should be if I were to continue here. He does not give this for a reason, but I know it is his true one; for he is not fond of London himself, especially at a season of the year, when the country is so much more agreeable. I thanked him for this mark of his tenderness, and am determined to go.

October 31

Once more returned to London in very good spirits, after a stay of little more than two months in Essex, in which time so material and unexpected a change has been made in my condition.

Lady Grimston took a most affectionate leave of my mother and asked her, with more tenderness than I thought her capable of, How many ages would it be before they should meet again? As for Mr Arnold and me, she considers us her neighbours. The Dean pleases himself with that expectation too; and the dear Mrs Vere, who shed tears at bidding me adieu, promises herself the happiness (as she kindly expressed herself) of spending many delightful days with me next summer. She set out on her return to her own house, at the same time that we left ours to go to town.

My brother is still in Wiltshire; but I find he did not leave town at the time he mentioned in his letter to my mother, nor for some days after. This Patty learnt from the servants; but I hope it will not come to my mother's ears, for she would take it extremely ill of him.

Mr Arnold, for the first time, mentioned, that he was very much disappointed in not having had the honour of seeing Sir George at his house in the country; but he hoped, when he came to town, his brother and he should make up for this, by being the more together. I wish Sir George may behave as he ought to this deserving brother. Mr Arnold little imagines how much he was an enemy to this match, and much less his reason for it. I should be very sorry Mr Arnold were to know how near I was being married to another man; it might give a delicate mind pain, lest there should remain any traces of this former attachment in the breast of the woman he loves; but I hope there is no danger of his hearing of it, certainly no one would be so indiscreet as to mention it to him. Mr Arnold has lived chiefly in the country, and may never have heard of Mr Faulkland, as he was so short a time returned from his travels, on which he had been absent more than five years; and as he is now out of the kingdom, probably he will not be spoken of. I have begged of my mother, who is naturally communicative, never to name Mr Faulkland to Mr Arnold, and have given my reasons for desiring this. She says, she thinks it would be better to tell him the whole affair at once; but I cannot agree with her in that opinion; and have at last prevailed on her to promise me she will not speak of it.

November 2

My mother drove out in my new chariot to-day (a very gay fine one it is), and went to Putney, to enquire after Miss B. by the name of Mrs Jefferis. She soon found the house, a very neat box, with a pretty garden behind it. The door was opened by a servant maid; and my mother being told the lady was at home, sent in her name; and was immediately conducted up stairs into a very elegant little dressing-room, where the lady was sitting at her toilet; and Mr Faulkland's housekeeper (whom my mother had seen before) assisting to dress her head. On my mother's entering the room, Miss B. rose off her chair, and soon discovered by her shape (for she was without her stays), that it was high time for her to seek a place of concealment. The housekeeper immediately withdrew; and the young lady seemed in the utmost confusion; my mother says, she herself was at a loss how to begin the conversation, but Miss B. relieved her, and spoke first. She thanked her for the honour she did her by so charitable a visit, which, she said, Mr Faulkland had long ago made her hope for; and which she must consider as the greatest consolation in her present unhappy circumstances.

My mother placed herself by her. Madam, said she, Mr Faulkland made it a point with me before he left England, that I should see you, and afford you all the assistance in my power, or that you should stand in need of. You seem to be commodiously situated here, and I understand have a very careful good woman to attend you.

I have so, madam, she answered; but the most material circumstance is wanting to my relief: Mr Faulkland! – He is not here. Tears started into her eyes as she spoke. You were apprised of his absence, said my mother, before you came to town. I was, madam, and with the cause of it; she hung down her head and was silent.

My mother reassumed the conversation. She told her, she thought it a most providential discovery, that had given her the knowlege of Mr Faulkland's ill behaviour, time enough to prevent his marriage with her daughter; assuring her, she would not, for the universe, have had me the wife of a man under such ties, as she must consider Mr

Faulkland to be. Miss B. brightned up a little upon my mother's saying this. Did Mr Faulkland ever tell you, madam, how the unhappy affair happened? My mother told her, she knew not particulars; that she had been referred to her for a full explanation; that Mr Faulkland had always endeavoured to excuse himself; and went so far as to say, He was sure the lady herself would acquit him in a great measure. Ah! madam! Miss B. cried, and shook her head. 'Tis as I suspected, said my mother, Mr Faulkland is an ungenerous man. A young lady of your modest appearance, I am sure he must have taken more pains to seduce, than he will acknowlege. Miss B blushed exceedingly – Oh! madam, you have a charitable, generous heart, I was *indeed* seduced. I knew it, replied my mother. Did he promise to marry you? She coloured deeper than before. I will not accuse him of that, madam. My mother proceeded; You have a relation, madam; I understand she was accessary to your misfortune. Yes, the barbarous woman, answered the lady, she was the contriver of my destruction; and if I could have avoided it, I would never have seen her face again. Tears of grief and indignation again burst from her eyes. Have comfort, madam, said my mother, all may end well yet. I can have no hopes, answered Miss B. Mr Faulkland flies me, you see, nor can I ever expect to recover his heart, since so charming a young lady, as I hear Miss Bidulph is, has possession of it; and though your goodness disappointed him in his late views, he may not yet despair. I found by this, continued my mother, that Miss B knew nothing of your being married, and made haste to tell her. I never saw joy so visible in a countenance. She clasped her hands together; Dear madam! what do you tell me? How you revive my drooping heart! then I am not *quite* hopeless, there is a *possibility* in my favour.

She then asked my mother if Mr Faulkland had acquainted her with her real name, or that of her relation. My mother, who had once or twice called her by the name of Jefferis, assured her he had not. That was generous in him, said she; he *can* be generous in *some* points. But I have no reason to conceal it from so prudent and worthy a lady as you are; my real name is Burchell; that of my cruel relation I will forbear to mention, out of respect to my good uncle, whose wife she is. Mr Faulkland, she added, left a Bill of five hundred pounds with his housekeeper, to provide every thing for me that I should want; with assurances that he would take the tenderest care of – the poor young creature hesitated, and could proceed no farther; but my mother said she understood her meaning. They had a good deal more discourse: my mother promised to see her often during her confinement, and took her leave.

She tells me, she is extremely pretty, and has such an air of innocence and simplicity, as very much engages one in her favour.

I have set down this whole conversation, with every other particular, exactly as my mother related it.

She, who has a most circumstantial memory, repeated it word for word; and I, from a custom of throwing upon paper every thing that occurs to me, have habituated myself to retain the minutest things.

I know not, my dear, whether you will be of my opinion; but I cannot help thinking, that there was something like art in Miss Burchell's behaviour, far from that candour which Mr Faulkland seemed to expect from her. My mother mentioned the *pains* that she supposed had been taken to *seduce* her; her deep blush at this hint, makes me suspect that her answer was not dictated by sincerity. She saw my mother was not acquainted with the particulars, and that she was willing to pass a favourable judgment on her fault; it looks to me as if she laid hold of this prejudice – and yet she *owned* that Mr Faulkland had never promised to marry her – I know not what to think; but there appears to me, upon the whole, something evasive and disingenuous in her conduct. My mother, who is all openness and integrity, saw it not in this light. But be it as it may, it is no longer of any consequence to me, which was most to blame, the gentleman or the lady: Miss Burchell is certainly the injured Person; perhaps I too may have wronged her in my surmises; if I have, I beg her pardon; the observations I have made on her behaviour are only *en passant*, and I do from my heart wish Mr Faulkland would make her his wife. You may perceive, from what I have told you, how little this interview was likely to produce in Mr Faulkland's favour, had it even been brought about sooner. My mother is now more than ever confirmed in her opinion, that the poor young creature has been deceived; and she prays, that Mr Faulkland may not be overtaken with a judgment, which she thinks nothing but his marrying the girl can avert.

November 10

We have at length fixed upon a house to our liking, a handsome convenient one in St James's-street. We are preparing to get it furnished as fast as we can, that we may go into it; for if my brother should come to town, I know *our* being with my mother will be an objection to his lodging in her house: this I should be sorry for, as she told him he might make use of it while it remained in her hands.

November 15

Thank my stars! I have got over the fatigue of receiving and paying a second round of bridal visits, and I am really so tired of it, that, uninviting as the season is, I could wish myself in quiet at Arnold-abbey; but I cannot think of leaving London while my mother continues in it, and she is now resolved to do so till Miss Burchell, or rather, on this occasion, Mrs Jefferis, is brought to-bed. You can't imagine how sollicitous she is about her; every time she sees her she seems more and more pleased with her. I am very glad it has happened so, for the poor young woman's sake; my mother is as warm in her attachments as in her resentments. She visits her almost every second day; for the poor thing it seems is ill at present, and can't leave her chamber. She tells me she is extremely melancholy, and seems much to dread the approaching hour. I greatly honour my mother for her humanity towards her: in her terrifying situation she must want the tenderness of a well-bred as well as a sensible friend; for it must be a melancholy thing, in such circumstances, to have no one about her but servants, and those strangers too.

She told my mother, that her altered looks, and frequent sicknesses, gave her aunt (who was privy to the cause of it) a pretence for asking her uncle's permission for Miss to go to Bath, which she told him would do her more good than any thing. He consented, and supposed she was actually gone thither under the care of a lady, whom her aunt named, who was really going there in order to settle for life, and to whose house she went for a day or two to give a colour to this story. Her aunt contrived that she should not take any servant with her; giving it for a reason, that as she might be as well attended by the lady's servants with whom she lodged, and be considered by her as one of the family, a maid would only be an unnecessary incumbrance. She added, that her uncle was so afflicted with the gout, that he never stirred abroad, and saw very little company, so that it was not likely he should ever be undeceived.

November 20

We have just received a very odd piece of news, that I own has a little alarmed me. It is, that the widow of Mr Arnold's brother is found to be with child. There was no mention of this at the time her husband died, nor indeed any cause to suspect it; but the strongest presumptions in the world to the contrary, as her husband and she lived a-part. It has not been even whispered, till since our arrival in town. The lady pretends that she was not conscious of it herself till within this fortnight; yet her husband has been dead four months. This I am told is very possible, though not very common. She has herself wrote a letter to Mr Arnold, to inform him of it; at the same time declaring, that she and her late husband had been reconciled a little before his death; and that, had he recovered, she was to have lived with him again. All this is very strange. The elder Mr Arnold killed himself with excessive drinking. His death approached him by slow degrees; but as he could never be persuaded to think it near, he took not the least care either of his spiritual or temporal concerns. His brother was in the country when he was seized with his last illness, which he had precipitated by some extravagant excess. He was almost at the last extremity before he could be prevailed on to let a physician attend him, or suffer his brother to be sent for. In regard to the latter, he told those about him, that as he was his heir, of course he had made no will. He mentioned not his wife. The jointure which had been settled on her, he allowed her for a separate maintenance. They had for a long time pursued separate pleasures, and none of his friends knew that they had ever met, or so much as seen one another from the time they parted. My Mr Arnold arrived in town just time enough to close his brother's eyes; he was speechless when he came, and expired in less than an hour after he entered his chamber.

As his wife had been very obnoxious to the family, there was little notice taken of her by them, more than what common forms require. She seemed as indifferent about the death of her hubsand, as she had been towards him in his life-time; and did not then hint a word of this reconciliation between them, or of her having had an interview with him. I am told, she is a very weak, as well as a very loose woman; and Mr Arnold thinks she has got into the hands of some designing person. However that matter may be, it is a serious affair; and he designs to take the opinion of an eminent lawyer upon it. My poor dear mother is frightned sadly. If this child should make its appearance in the world time enough to prove the possibility of its being the offspring of the late Mr Arnold, she says, it must be considered by the law as his heir, notwithstanding the husband and wife lived apart. Mr Arnold laughs, or affects to laugh at this; we shall, however, wait with patience till the lady is brought to bed.

November 25

Our house is intirely fitted up, and we shall remove into it this evening; my mother chuses to continue in her own, though Mr Arnold presses her to accept of an apartment in ours; but we shall be near neighbours, and she does not like to change.

We have received the opinion of our lawyers, who tell us, that in case the child should be born within such a period of time, as to give colour to its claim, yet the lady must prove her assertion, in regard to the pretended meeting between her and her husband; which it is imagined is not in her power to do; and her indifferent character, together with several favourable circumstances which Mr Arnold has on his side, makes them quite sanguin in their expectations of overturning her claim. We are, however, likely to be engaged in a disagreeable law-suit; but as Mr Arnold seems perfectly easy about the issue of it, I will make myself so too.

December 10

I am more and more reconciled to my lot, my dear Cecilia, every day that I live. Mr Arnold's assiduity and tenderness towards me deserve the gratefullest return my heart can make him; and I am convinced it is not necessary to be passionately in love with the man we marry, to make us happy. Constancy, good sense, and a sweet temper, must form a basis for a durable felicity. The two latter I am sure Mr Arnold possesses; Oh! may I never experience his want of the former! I hope my own conduct will for ever ensure to me his love. That only can secure the tranquility of my future days.

December 11

My brother arrived in town last night; and came this morning in company with my mother (and I am sure at her request) to make us a formal visit. My kind Mr Arnold received him with tenderness; Sir George was coldly polite. He owned, however, to my mother, upon her asking him his opinion of his brother-in-law, that he seemed to be a *good clever sort of a fellow*. I wish I could cultivate a friendship between them; it will not be Mr Arnold's fault if there is not; but Sir George, you know, is not of a very pliant disposition.

He asked my mother, when they were alone, Whether she had yet seen Miss B or Mrs Jefferis (for he knew her by no other name) and what she had to say for herself? My mother told him, he had better not touch upon that string. I will be hanged, replied Sir George, if the artful young baggage has not imposed upon you. My mother, who is always angry at having her sagacity called in question, told Sir George he was rude, and she should give him no satisfaction on that head. My brother answered, as it was *now* of no consequence, what the wench affirmed or denied, he had no farther curiosity about her. My mother called him a bear, and so the enquiry ended.

December 20

I congratulate you, my sister, my friend, my ever beloved Cecilia. Happy! happy may you be in your nuptials! but in the midst of my joy for your being so nobly and worthily bestowed, self-love forces a sigh from me. I have lost the pleasing hope of seeing you, at the time fixed for your return. The station your husband holds at the court of Vienna, will, I fear, long detain my beloved in a foreign land. But you are not amongst strangers; a husband, a brother, and tender parent, must make every part of the globe equally your home. I will therefore seek for my contentment in your's, and rest satisfied with believing that you will always continue to love me.

January 10, 1703-4

I begin to find my thoughts so dissipated, that I am angry with myself; Mr Arnold's excessive indulgence will spoil me; he is always contriving new scenes of pleasure, and hurries me from one to the other. I do not wish to be perpetually fluttering about. The calm domestic life you know was always my choice; but I will not oppose my kind Mr Arnold in his fond desire of pleasing me: besides, I find that by his constantly gallanting me to public places, he begins himself to acquire a sort of relish for them, which he did not use to have; at least his prudence made him so to conform to the necessity of his circumstances, while his fortune was small, that he never indulged himself in any of the fashionable expensive amusements; nor does he now in any, but such as I partake of with him. I find he is by nature open and liberal to excess. I must take care, without his being conscious of it, to be a gentle check upon his bounteous spirit; I mean only so far as it regards myself: indeed this is the most material point, for in every other instance his generosity is regulated by prudence. I am every hour more obliged to him, and should hate myself if I did not find that he had an intire possession of my love.

Sir George hardly ever comes near us but by formal invitation, and then his behaviour to Mr Arnold is so very civil, and so very distant, that it mortifies me exceedingly. Mr Arnold cannot but perceive it; but either his tenderness for me makes him take no notice of it, or else, not being well enough acquainted with my brother to know his disposition, he may impute his coldness to his natural temper.

My mother says, he never names Mr Faulkland or Miss Burchell to her. I wish Sir George could entirely forget that unhappy affair.

February 1

There is a story propagated by the widow Arnold, about the meeting between her and her husband; the circumstances of which are as follows:

She says, she had dined one day in the city, and was returning home to her lodgings in York-buildings in a hackney coach; that the driver, by his carelessness in coming along the Strand, had one of his fore wheels taken off by a Waggon, which accident obliged her to alight: the footboy, who was behind the coach, had by the jolt been thrown off, and received a hurt, which made it necessary to have him carried into a shop for assistance. That the lady herself, being no otherwise injured than by a little fright, found that she was so near home, that she did not think it worth while to wait for another carriage, but pursued her way on foot. It was a fine dry evening, about nine o'clock; and though there was no light but what the lamps afforded, yet as the streets were full of people, she had no apprehensions of danger.

In this situation she was accosted by two gentlemen, who, seeing a lady well dressed and alone, insisted on seeing her safe to her lodgings. However disagreeable such an encounter was, she said she did not give herself much concern about it, as she was so near home, and expected to shake off her new acquaintance at the door of the house where she lodged; and accordingly, when she got there, she told them she was at home, and wished them a good night; but the impertinents were not so easily to be put off. The door having been opened by the maid of the house, they both rushed in; her landlady, a single woman, happened to be abroad and there was no man in the house.

Mrs Arnold thought she had no way left, but to run up to her dining-room, and lock herself in; but in this she was prevented, as the gentlemen, whom the servant of the house vainly endeavoured to oppose, got up stairs almost as soon as she did. Her own maid, on hearing the rap at the door, had lighted candles in the dining-room; the two sparks entered with her; but how was she surprized to find that one of them was her husband. Her fright, she said, had prevented her from discovering this sooner, as she had not looked in either of their faces, though there was a light in the hall; and Mr Arnold's being half drunk, she supposed, was the reason of his not perceiving sooner who she was.

The astonishment that they both were in, and the exclamation that each made in their turn, soon informed the companion of Mr Arnold who the lady was. He congratulated them both on this fortunate mistake, and saying, since chance had been so propitious to Mr Arnold as to throw him into the arms of so charming a woman, he hoped his discovering her to be his wife would not render her the less agreeable to him; but that this unexpected meeting might be a means of re-uniting them in their former amity.

Mr Arnold, she says, in the presence of this gentleman, advanced with open arms to embrace her, which she not declining, his friend having again felicitated them on their reconciliation, took his leave, and Mr Arnold remained with his lady.

That at parting, which was not till late, (as she would not, on account of her reputation, permit him to pass the night at her lodgings) he promised to bring her home to his house in a day or two; but unfortunately for her he was taken ill in the interim, which she did not know of, till she had an account that Mr Arnold had lost his senses. The reason she assigned for not enquiring after him sooner was, that her pride would not suffer her to make any advances to a man, who had been so injurious as to part with her; and she thought it his duty to recall her, without her taking any step towards it.

This story seems plausible; yet none of our friends believe a word of it, and imagine somebody has contrived it for her. The gentleman, who was the companion of Mr Arnold that night, she says, can at a proper time be produced as a witness, as also her own maid, who can testify the truth of this story. In the mean time this maid is kept out of the way, and nobody can guess at the gentleman, for his name is kept a profound secret.

I am delighted at the sweetness of Mr Arnold's temper: vexatious as this affair is likely to be, even at the best, he does not suffer it to interrupt our pleasures or his own good humour. On the contrary, he is the more studious of promoting every thing, which he thinks will entertain me.

February 28

At length the poor Miss Burchell is happily rid of her burden; a pretty little boy, my mother says it is: it was, immediately after its birth, at which my mother was present, privately baptized by the name of Orlando, and sent away with its nurse, a careful body, who had been before provided for it. It passes for the son of a captain Jefferis, abroad with the army. Miss Burchell would never suffer the nurse to see her; for as she intends to reassume her own name, as soon as she shall be in a condition to leave her present retirement, she would not chuse to be known by the woman, in case of her going to see her child. Every thing was managed with so much privacy, and Miss Burchell has lived so perfectly recluse, nobody visiting her but my mother, that in all probability this affair will always remain an intire secret.

My mother says, that as soon as Miss Burchell (to whom she considers herself as a kind of patroness) is tolerably recovered, she will go down to Sidney-castle; for she thinks herself in a strange land any where but there. And would you believe it my dear, she has taken such a fancy to Miss Burchell, that she talks of inviting her down with her, if she can obtain her uncle's leave. The girl must certainly have some very amiable qualities, so to captivate my mother, or she has an immensity of art. I dare say the young lady will gladly accept of her invitation; it will undoubtedly be a most eligible situation for her. I do not know what Sir George may say to her carrying her humanity so far, as he hates the name of this poor girl; but no matter, it may be a means of preserving her character, which probably she might not long keep, if she returned to live with so vile a woman as I conclude her aunt to be; nor can she have any colour for quitting her, whilst her uncle lives; for I find she is an orphan, and has no relation but him. She must however go home for a while, in order to get leave from him for this visit to Sidney-castle.

March 26, 1704

I am told the widow Arnold computes the time of her lying-in about the latter end of the next month; if it should so happen, she saves her distance, as her husband died in July, a little before we went to Grimston-hall. Mr Arnold treats the affair very lightly, and is only concerned at seeing my mother so much affected by it. For my part, I form my behaviour upon Mr Arnold's conduct, and as long as he appears easy, I shall certainly be so too.

My brother throws out some unkind reflections: he says, he wonders the old Sybil at Grimston-hall did not foresee this; and congratulates me on my good fortune, in having my jointure settled on that part of the estate which is not disputed. I really think he shews a sort of ill-natured triumph even in his condolements; for he generally concludes them with thanking his stars that *he* had no hand in the match. I trust in God we shall none of us have any cause to repent it. I am sure I never shall; for if Mr Arnold were reduced to the lowest ebb of fortune, I should find my consolation in his kindness and affection.

March 27

My mother is preparing to leave town. Miss Burchell is quite recovered, and purposes going down to the country, to obtain her uncle's consent for the intended visit. She says, she can easily tell him she made an acquaintance with lady Bidulph in her late excursion to Bath, from whom she received an invitation, and she is sure he will not refuse to let her accept it.

Sir George laughs exceedingly at this plan. He says his mother ought not to be surprized at Faulkland's falling into the girl's snares, since she herself has done the same; but he supposes my mother thinks she is doing a very meritorious action, in affording an asylum to this injured innocence. I give you my brother's words, for I assure you, as to myself, I approve of my mother's kindness to her, and think it may be a means of preserving the girl from future mischief.

April 2

Miss Burchell is gone to the country, and this morning, for the first time, severed me from the best of mothers. I cannot recover my spirits; I have wept all day. Mr Arnold, ever good and obliging, would needs accompany her some miles on her journey; you may be sure I was not left behind. Sir George was so polite as to say, He would escort her down to Sidney-castle. I was surprized at it; for he does not often do obliging things. My mother gladly accepted of his company, and said, she would make him her prisoner, when she had him there; for she should be quite melancholy without me for a time. Now though I should be very unwilling not to allow the merit of a good-natured action to Sir George, yet do I attribute this in some measure to its answering a purpose of convenience to himself. You know, before his illness sent him to the Spa, he always spent his summers with us at the Castle, though he has another very convenient house on his estate. When he was in London, he never had any thing but lodgings, for which I have often been angry with him. My mother, since his return, made him a compliment of her house; but as the time she took it for is now expired, and it is let to another family, he could no longer continue in it. Mr Arnold, in the most affectionate manner, pressed him to accept of an apartment with us, which he declined. Now as he could not, without shewing us an apparent slight, continue in town in other lodgings, I believe he, for this reason, preferred going down with my mother. Be it as it may, I am very glad that she will have his company; for I make no doubt of his staying with her some time, unless Miss Burchell should frighten him away.

April 5

I have been so cast down since my mother's departure, that Mr Arnold's obliging tender assiduity to please and entertain me seems redoubled; but indeed I am wearied with a continual round of noisy pleasures, and long to get back to Arnold-abbey. I hope to be there in about three weeks, or a month at farthest. My mother has dispensed with our going down to her this summer. She thinks it might be attended with inconveniences to me, and talks of coming to town again in a few months; but I shall insist on her not giving herself the fatigue of so long a journey, unless she comes to stay all the next winter with us.

April 20

My mother writes me word that Miss Burchell has obtained leave of her uncle, and is come to Sidney-castle: she says, she never saw a better behaved young creature. Sir George has taken so much offence at her coming, that he talks of going to his own house. My mother adds, 'He behaves however, with manners, but I shall not press him to stay.'

May 6

An important birth, my Cecilia! the widow Arnold has produced a young miss. I assure you the little damsel has been ushered into life with all the ceremony due to a young heiress; and her mother introduces her as one, whom an unjust uncle debars of her right.

Now you must know, that upon an exact calculation, this little girl has made her appearance just twelve days later than she ought to have done, to prove her legitimacy, dating the possibility of her being Mr Arnold's, from the very day whereon he took that illness of which he died, and which confined him for five days to his bed. In all that time, his servants never left him for a minute; this has occasioned various speculations; our lawyers say that it is enough to destroy her pretensions; but some physicians, who have been consulted on the occasion, are of a contrary opinion; and declare they have known instances of children being born, even so long after the stated time alloted by nature for their coming into life.

It is a very unlucky affair, and has involved us in a law-suit. Who the person is that secretly abets the widow, we cannot find out; but it is certain she has somebody; every one believes this is an infamous and unjust claim; and the woman's folly almost frees her from the suspicion of its being of her own contriving.

May 10

You cannot imagine, my Cecilia, how happy I think myself, after such a hurrying winter as I have had, to find myself once more restored to my favourite pleasures, the calm delights of solitude. Arnold-abbey seems a paradise to me now.

Lady Grimston shewed me a specimen of her humour this morning, in talking of the widow Arnold. She said she was an *harlot*, that having already disgraced the family, now wanted to beggar them; but that if Mr Arnold did not make an example of her, she would never own him for a kinsman.

My chearful old Dean says, he is now completely happy, having lived to see his daughter married (while we were in town) very much to his and her satisfaction. I am heartily glad of it, neither am I sorry (for her sake) that she has left the country.

May 11

Mrs Vere is come to spend a few weeks with me according to her promise. She is a truly amiable creature; her disposition so gentle, her temper so mild, such a sweet humility in her whole deportment, that it astonishes me her mother can still persist in her unkindness to her. But the eldest daughter was always her darling, who I understand is pretty much of her mother's own cast; and makes a very termagant wife to a very turbulent husband. So that notwithstanding their title (for he is a Baronet) and immense riches, they are a very miserable pair.

They were lately to pay lady Grimston a visit; but there happened such a frecas, that probably it may be the last she will ever receive from them. The husband, it seems, though very rough and surly in his nature, is, notwithstanding, a well-meaning man, and not void of humanity; which had induced him to give a small portion to a young girl, a distant relation of his own, who had been left an orphan. She was beloved by the son of a substantial farmer, a tenant of the baronet's, and had an equal affection for him; but the young man, depending entirely on his father for his future prospects, durst not take a wife without something to begin the world with; for his father had just put him into the management of one of his farms. The young lady and her mother (who was a widow, and is but lately dead) had boarded for some years at this honest farmer's house, and in that time a mutual love had been contracted between the young people. The old man himself liked the girl so well for a daughter-in-law, that his only objection was her want of fortune; but this was such an obstacle as was not to be surmounted by a man, who, being accustomed to earn money by indefatigable industry, put the utmost value upon it. His regard to his son's happiness, however, made him resolve to try an experiment in his favour, and accordingly he plucked up courage, and went to his landlord. He told him, in his own blunt way, that he came to speak to him in behalf of a poor young gentlewoman that was his (Sir William's) relation. I have a son that loves her, said he, and she loves him, but I cannot afford to let the boy marry a wife that has nothing; and you know she has no portion. I would not desire much with her, for she is a good girl, and very housewifely; but if you will be so kind to give her something to set them a going a little, I shall be content; if not, you will be the cause of my son's losing a wife, for he swears he will never marry any other woman, and she, poor thing, may pine away for love. I do not desire this match out of the ambition of having my boy related to you, but because I think the girl is an honest girl, and may make him happy.

The rough honesty of the farmer pleased his landlord so well, that he gave the young woman five hundred pounds, to set them a going, as the old yeoman termed it. Though this sum was but a trifle to a man of his fortune, and the giving it was a praise-worthy action, yet did it exceedingly displease his lady, especially as he had not thought proper to consult her on the occasion. She was not contented with venting her indignation on her husband at home, but she renewed the quarrel, by complaining to lady Grimston, that her opinion and advice were not only despised, but that Sir William was lavishing away the fortune *she* had brought him upon a *tribe* of poor relations of his own. Lady Grimston immediately took fire; she could not bear the thoughts of having her daughter's authority of less weight in his family, than her own had been, and she attacked her son-in-law with acrimony on the subject. His answer to her was short. Look ye, lady Grimston, you made a very obstreperous wife to a very peacable husband; your daughter, I find, is mightily disposed to follow your example; but as I am not quite so tame as my father-in-law was, I will suffer her to see as little of it as may be. With this he turned from her, and ordering his coach and six to be got ready immediately, with very little ceremony he forced his wife into it, and carried her home directly, leaving lady Grimston foaming with rage. The altercation had been carried on with so little caution, that the servants heard it, and the story is the jest of the neighbourhood.

I confess I am not sorry for this breach; it may be the better for poor Mrs Vere; for though her mother's jointure reverts to a male relation, on whom the estate was settled, yet as lady Grimston has a large personal fortune, it is in her power to make her daughter full amends for the injury she did her.

May 20

Mr Arnold is improving his gardens, and taking in a great deal more ground to enlarge them. I do not express the least dissatisfaction at this, tho' I own I could wish he would not engage in new expences on an estate which is now in litigation; but our lawyers are so sanguin, that they encourage him to proceed.

[*The following is writ in the hand of the lady, who gave the editor these papers: 'Here follows an interval of four months; in which time, though the Journal was regularly continued, nothing material to her story occured, but the birth of a daughter, after which she proceeds.'*]

September 25

How delightful are the new sensations, my dear Cecilia, that I feel hourly springing in my heart! Surely the tenderness of a mother can never be sufficiently repaid; and I now more than ever rejoice in having, by an obedience, which perhaps I once thought had some little merit in it, contributed so much to the repose of a parent, to whom I have such numberless obligations. I never see my little girl, but I think such were the tender sentiments, the sweet anxieties, that my honoured and beloved mother felt when her Sidney was such a brat as this. Then I say, surely I have a right to all the duty, all the filial love that this creature can shew me, in return for my fondness. As for Mr Arnold, he idolizes it; you never saw so good a nurse as he makes. Lady Grimston declares, we are both in a fair way of ruining the child, and advises us to send it out of the house, that we may not grow too fond of it; but we shall hardly take her counsel.

September 28

I informed you before that Miss Burchell had been summoned home by her uncle, who was then very ill. She has lately written an account to my mother of his death; and that as she has now her fortune in her own hands, she intends immediately to quit her aunt, and look out for some genteel and reputable family in London (where it seems she chuses to reside) to lodge with.

My mother, in her letter to me, expresses great satisfaction at her resolution to leave her aunt, but is not without her fears, that so pretty a young woman, left to her own guidance, may be liable to danger; though she thinks both her natural disposition, and her good sense, sufficient to guard her against actual evil.

Our lawyer writes us a word, that he has had an offer of a composition, proposed by the widow Arnold's people: he says, though the sum they mention is a very round one, yet it plainly indicates the weakness of their hopes; and concludes with telling Mr Arnold, that if six-pence would buy them off, he should not, with his consent, give it to them; as it would tacitly admit the legality of their claim, and might be productive of troublesome consequences hereafter; and therefore he would by all means have the issue fairly tried. Mr Arnold laughs heartily at the proposal, but says he is very much obliged to the lady for condescending to give up more than half, when her daughter has a right to the whole; without whose consent he supposes it is not in the mother's power to make terms.

I wish we were rid of this troublesome affair, as it must hurry us to town sooner than we intended, and the country is still delightful.

London, October 1

Again we have quitted our sweet retirement for the noise and bustle of London; but this law-business, it seems, must be closely pursued, though our antagonist's motions seem a little dilatory. We cannot find out the secret spring that sets the machine a-going; the wheels however do not seem to move with such alacrity as they did; though the widow still talks big, and says, we shall repent of having rejected her offer.

October 3

My brother is arrived in town, but took care to settle himself in handsome commodious lodgings before he paid us a visit, for fear, I suppose, that we should again press him to accept of apartments in our house. I see he is determined to keep up nothing more than an intercourse barely civil. Mr Arnold cannot but be disgusted with his behaviour, but he is too delicate to take notice of it to me.

October 17

I am disappointed in my hopes of seeing my dear mother in town this winter. Her apartment was ready for her, and I delighted myself with the thoughts of seeing her in possession of it, at least for a few months; but she writes me word that her old rheumatick complaint is returned on her with such violence, that she cannot think of undertaking the journey. Sadly am I grieved at this news, and shall long to have the winter over, that Mr Arnold and I may fly to Sidney-castle; he has promised me this satisfaction early in the summer.

My mother informs me that Miss Burchell constantly corresponds with her: she tells her that her aunt is come to town to sollicit for her pension, but that she never sees her; and as she means to drop all correspondence with her, she does not intend even to let her know where she lodges. I commend Miss Burchell highly for this, as the acquaintance of such a woman may be hurtful to her reputation.

[*Here ensues another interval of nine months, in which nothing particular is related, but that Mrs Arnold became mother to a second child. This last circumstance, with a few others preceding and succeeding that event, are related in the Journal by her maid Patty; after which Mrs Arnold herself proceeds.*]

July 1, 1705

Again, my dear Cecilia, I am able to reassume my pen. I have read what Patty has writ, and find she is admirable at the anecdotes of a nursery. Am I not rich, think you? Two daughters, and both perfect beauties, and great wits you may be sure!

The new-born damsel was baptized this day by the dear-beloved name of Cecilia. I am angry with Mr Arnold, he takes so little notice of this young stranger; his affections are all engaged by Dolly: indeed, I am almost jealous of her; for he spends most of the time he is at home in the nursery.

Our antagonist is grown alert again, and has renewed her efforts, which we thought began to flag a little, with fresh vigour. Whence she derives those revived hopes is a mystery; but she now says, she would not accept of a composition if it were offered. My poor Mr Arnold begins to fret a little, it now and then makes him thoughtful; not that he says he has the least doubt about his success, but he has been much harrassed with the necessary attendance that the cause requires, and downright tired with dangling after lawyers; besides, they say the cause cannot come to an hearing in the ensuing term, though they before made us hope, that it would be at an end long before this time.

July 3

I am mortified exceedingly, my dear Cecilia: I find I am not likely to see my mother this summer. I thought I could not have lived so long from her sight. Indeed it was purely in the hope of making her this visit, that I prevented her coming to town in the spring, which she purposed doing, though far from being well enough to undertake the journey. I own I have been impatient under my confinement, as that, and my previous circumstances, detained us so long in town, and I this day asked Mr Arnold when we should set out for Sidney-castle. He answered me, that he feared it would not be in his power this season to pay the intended visit to my mother: he says, he has not been near his estate in Kent these five years, except for a day or two at a time, and that he thinks it necessary to see what condition it is in. I believe I have told you that there is a pretty house on it. The place is called South-park, and is that which my mother chose for my settlement. Mr Arnold, who always preferred Arnold-abbey to it, hardly ever visited this place; and as he never resided there, and only lay at an inn when he went down, the house is unfurnished, excepting a room or two, which a man who receives his rent has just made habitable for his own convenience.

But that I have laid it down as a rule never to oppose so good, so indulgent a husband as Mr Arnold is, in any instance, wherein I do not think a superior duty requires me to do so, I should certainly show some disapprobation of what he now purposes doing. It will be attended with so much trouble, so much expence too: he has ordered the house at South-park to be completely furnished, and says, he hopes I shall like it so well as to be induced to pass the remainder of the summer there. Most sure it is, every place will be delightful to me where I can enjoy his company, and have my dear little babes with me; but methinks two country houses are an unnecessary charge, and more than suits our fortune. I pray God this tender husband may not have a strong and prudent reason for this conduct, which out of kindness he conceals; perhaps he thinks this little spot at South-park may some time hence be the whole of our dependence, and he has a mind to be before-hand with ill fortune, in rendering that retreat agreeable to me, and rather an object of choice than of necessity. If this be his motive, How much am I obliged to him? He has not hinted any thing like it; nor would I dash the pleasure he seems to promise himself there, by insinuating the least suspicion of what his reasons are for going to it. If we lose Arnold-abbey, and the whole estate belonging to it, I shall only regret it for his sake.

July 8

We are to set out to-morrow, my Cecilia, for our place in Kent. I have made the best apology that I could to my mother, and Mr Arnold too has writ to her; but I know she will be extremely disappointed at not seeing us.

July 12

We are lately arrived at South-park, Mr Arnold in high spirits; and my two young travellers bore the fatigue extremely well.

I am not surprized Mr Arnold liked the old family seat better than this. I cannot say I am much charmed with it, but I will not let him see that. I affect to admire, and seem pleased with every thing that affords me the least opportunity of commendation. The house is a very neat one; it has not been many years built, and is in perfectly good repair. It is genteely, though plainly furnished, and we have a tolerable garden; but as the whole domain is let, we are obliged to take a few fields from one of our tenants, to supply our immediate want. We are in a very genteel and populous neighbourhood, and within a mile of a good market town.

July 20

I have regretted nothing so much in my absence from Arnold-abbey, as the being cut off from the hope of seeing my amiable Mrs Vere. We can have but *one friend* to share our heart, to whom we have no reserve, and whose loss is irreparable; but I perceive the absence of a pleasing acquaintance, whose society is no farther necessary to us, than as it contributes to enliven solitude, and gets a preference to others merely by comparison, is a loss easily supplied; this I find by experience. There are Mrs Veres every where; but, alas! there is but *one* Cecilia!

I was visited today by two ladies that I am charmed with, though it is the first time I have seen either of them. The one is lady V of whom you have formerly heard. Her Lord and she came together; their seat is within a mile of us, and Mr Arnold had a slight acquaintance with lord V before. My lady is about forty, and has that kind of countenance that at once invites your confidence; I never saw integrity, benevolence, and good sense, more strongly pictured in a face; her address is so plain, so perfectly free from affectation, or any of the little supercilious forms of ceremony, that a person, ignorant of what true politeness consists in, would imagine she wanted breeding; yet she received her education in a court; but she seems to let good sense and good nature preside over all her words and actions rather than form. She told me she had deferred her visit to me, longer perhaps than the laws of decorum would admit of, as we were such near neighbours; but, said she, I was determined not to be overlooked in the crowd of visitors that have been thronging to you every day, since you came down. The character I have heard of you, makes me wish for an intimacy with you, and you are not to look upon this as a visit of ceremony, but as an advance towards that friendship I wish to cultivate.

She spoke this with so frank an air, that, flattering as the compliment appeared, I could not help believing her sincere; and thought myself, that my appearance did not diminish that good opinion which she said she had conceived of me from report.

Lord V— is many years older than his lady; a robust man, as plain in his way as my lady is in her's; though *his* way and *her's* are very different; for he is frank even to bluntness, but the best humoured man living.

The other lady whom I mentioned is a widow; her name is

Gerrarde, and she lives upon a little estate she has in this neighbourhood. I think I never beheld so fine a creature; she is about six and twenty; her stature, which is much above the common size, is rendered perfectly graceful and majestic by one of the finest shapes in the world; if her face is not altogether so regularly beautiful as her person, it is, however, handsome enough to render any woman charming who had nothing else to boast of. Whether her understanding be of a piece with the rest, I have not yet been able to discover. Her visit to me was but short, for she had not sat with me an hour when lady V— came in, and she then took her leave; but by what I could observe in that little time, she seems to have as much vivacity and agreeable humour, as I ever met with in any one. She pressed me to dine with her at her cottage, as she calls it, to-morrow, and I like her too well to refuse the invitation.

These two charming women, I think, I shall single out for my chief intimates, from the crowd which have been to compliment me, on my coming into this country.

Mr Arnold is mightily pleased with them both; but he gives the preference to lady V—, whom, tho' he had a slight acquaintance with her lord, he never saw before. But he is almost as great a stranger in this place as I am: he is highly delighted at my having met with people who are likely to render it agreeable to me.

July 21

We dined to-day according to appointment with Mrs Gerrarde. A cottage she called her house, nor does it appear much better at the outside, but within it is a fairy palace. Never was any thing so neat, so elegant, so perfectly well fansied, as the fitting up of all her rooms. Her bedchambers are furnished with fine chints, and her drawing-room with the prettiest Indian sattin I ever saw. Her little villa is called Ashby, and her husband, she told me, purchased it for her some time before his death, and left it to her; but she has since had a considerable addition to her fortune, by the death of a relation.

Our entertainment was splendid almost to profusion, though there was no company but Mr Arnold and I. I told her, if she always gave such dinners, it would frighten me away from her: indeed it was the only circumstance in her whole conduct that did not please me, for I was charmed with the rest of her behaviour. They must surely be of a very churlish disposition, who are not pleased, where a manifest desire to oblige is conspicuous in every word and action. If Mrs.

Gerrarde is not as highly polished as some women are, who, perhaps, have had a more enlarged education, she makes full amends for it by a perfect good humour, a sprightliness always entertaining, and a quickness of thought, that gives her conversation an air of something very *like* wit, and which I dare say passes for the thing itself with most people.

July 24

I have returned lady V—'s visit, and am more delighted with her than before. Mr Arnold went with me; but my lord not being at home, he went to ramble about the grounds, so that I had a long *tête à tête* with lady V—. She is an admirable woman, so fine an understanding, such delicacy of sentiment, and such an unaffected complaisance in her manner, that I do not wonder my lord perfectly adores her. There is a tenderness, a maternal kindness in her behaviour towards me, that fills me at once with love and reverence for her; and, next to my Cecilia, I think I never met with any woman whom I could so highly esteem as lady V—. She is an admirable mistress of her needle, and every room in her house exhibits some production of a very fine genius, united with very great industry: for there are beds, chairs, and carpets, besides some very pretty rural prospects in panels, executed with inimitable skill, and very excellent taste. She tells me, if I will give her leave to bring her work with her, she will live whole days with me.

I am rejoiced now that Mr Arnold thought of coming to South-Park. How valuable is the acquaintance of such a woman as lady V—! and I might never have known her, but for a circumstance to which I was at first so averse. And then my agreeable lively Mrs Gerrarde! My acquaintance at Arnold-abbey begin to fade upon my memory: to say the truth, I think of none of them with pleasure, but Mrs Vere, and my good humoured old Dean.

August 4

Mrs Gerrarde is a little saucy monopolist; she grumbles if I do not see her every day, and is downright jealous of my intimacy with lady V—. They are acquainted, but I don't find there is a very close intercourse between them: Mrs Gerrarde says, her ladyship is too good a houswife for her; and as she is not very fond of needle-work herself, she cannot endure people that are always poring over a frame. I find indeed, that this sprightly rogue is fonder of cards than of work; she draws Mr Arnold and me in very often for a pool at piquet: at her house I am obliged to submit; but at my own, I often take up a book, when she and Mr Arnold are engaged at their game, and make them decide the contest between them. Nay, I threaten that I will, some night or other, steal to-bed and leave them; for she is unconscionable at late hours; and as she lives very near us, and keeps a chariot, she does not scruple to go home at any hour of the night. What a pity it is so amiable a woman should be thus fondly attached to so unprofitable an amusement! for I begin to see play is her foible; though, to do her justice, she never engages but for very trifling sums, and that only in our own little domestic way. But this passion may grow upon her, and she may be led unawares into the losing more than her fortune can bear.

August 12

I never was so disconcerted as I have been this day: you will be surprized when I tell you, it was by my good lady V—. She came to pass the day with me, Mr Arnold being engaged abroad.

We were both sitting at work in the parlour: lady V— had continued silent for a good while; at last looking at me with a most benign smile, for I had at the same instant cast my eyes at her; I was just then thinking, my dear Mrs Arnold, said she, that I once (though perhaps you did not know it) flattered myself with the hopes of being related to you. Her words threw me into confusion, though I did not know their meaning. It would have been both an honour and a happiness to me, madam, I replied, though I don't know by what means I was ever likely to possess it. She continued smiling, but seemed in suspence whether she should proceed. You will pardon my curiosity my dear, said she, but give me leave to ask, whether Mr Arnold was not once near losing the happiness he now enjoys? I felt my face glow as she spoke. There was once a treaty of marriage on foot, madam, I answered, between me and another gentleman. I am sorry I mentioned it, said my lady, observing my confusion; but as I was no stranger to the affair while it was transacting, and Mr Faulkland is a kinsman of mine, I hope you will forgive my inquisitiveness; for I own I have a curiosity, which I believe no body but yourself can gratify; and if I did not think you the most candid, as well as the best tempered creature living, I durst not push my enquiry. My lord, you are to know, was in London, at the time Mr Faulkland was first introduced to you; and as they are extremely fond of each other, Mr Faulkland did not scruple to disclose his passion to him, nor the success it then appeared likely to be crowned with, giving him at the same time such a character of you, as I have since found you deserve.

When my lord returned to V— hall, which he was obliged to do very soon after Mr Faulkland had made this discovery to him, he informed me of the alliance my cousin Faulkland was going to make; and we were pleasing ourselves with the thoughts of congratulating him on his happiness, when we received a letter from him that put an end to all our expectations; this letter contained but four distracted lines: he told my lord, in broken sentences, that he had lost all hopes of Miss Bidulph; that an act of indiscretion had been construed into a capital crime; and that being banished from the presence of the woman he adored, he was immediately about to bid adieu to England, perhaps for ever.

This was the substance of what he wrote to us: we have heard from him since a few times, but he never cleared up the matter to us, nor even so much as mentioned it. I have not been in London since; my lord has; but he never could get any light into the mystery: he heard from some of our friends, who knew of the intended match, that it was broke off nobody knew why. There were, however, several idle surmises thrown out; some laid the blame on Mr Faulkland, and some on you; but the truth I believe still remains a secret. Now, my dear, if my curiosity is improper, or if there was any particular motive to this disappointment of my kinsman's hopes, which you don't chuse to reveal, forgive my enquiry, and think no more of it; but take up that book, and read to me while I work.

Though my lady gave me this kind opportunity of evading her question, I did not lay hold of it: I did not indeed chuse to reveal the whole of this affair, because I did not think myself at liberty to divulge Miss Burchell's secret, however I might discover my own. I told my lady in general terms, that though Mr Faulkland might pretend to a lady every way my superior, yet there was an objection to him of no small weight with us; that my mother had been informed of a very recent piece of gallantry he had had with a person of some condition, and that it had disgusted her so much, she could not think of uniting me with a man whose passions were not a little more staid; and that this was the sole reason of her dislike to a gentleman, who was in every other respect unexceptionable. I am glad it was no worse, said lady V—, smiling; I am sure Mr Faulkland is not capable of a *base* action; youthful follies he may have had, though I believe as few even of those to answer for as most men of his years. I make not the least doubt, however, that lady Bidulph was guided by prudence in what she did. She certainly could not be too cautious in the disposal of *such* a child as you; and whatever Mr Faulkland's disappointment may be, *you* I hope are happy. Lady V— looked at me as she pronounced these words, with an inquisitive, though tender regard. I was glad of an opportunity of enlarging on the merits of Mr Arnold, and told her, I was as happy as my heart could wish, or the worthiest of men could make me. I am glad of it, said she, with a quickness in her voice, but don't imagine, my dear Mrs Arnold, (and she took me by the hand) that I introduced this conversation merely to gratify a curiosity, which I fear you must condemn in your private thoughts, though you have been so good as to satisfy it: I had another reason, a much stronger one. What is it dear madam? almost starting with apprehensions of I did not know what. Don't be alarmed, said she smiling, it is only this; a great aunt of Mr Faulkland's is lately dead, who has left him a considerable personal estate, and he is coming over to take possession of it; otherwise I don't know when we should have seen him in England. My lord had a letter very lately from him; he was then at Turin, where he had met with our eldest son, who is now on his travels: he told us he had letters and some tokens of love to deliver us from him; and that he should immediately on his arrival in England come to V— hall, where he would pass a month with us. Now as we expect him daily, I had a mind to apprize you of his intended visit, that you might not be surprized, by perhaps unexpectedly meeting him at my house. I thanked her ladyship for her obliging caution, though I thought it had something in it that mortified me. I told her, that though I should not seek to renew my acquaintance with Mr Faulkland, yet had I no reason to avoid him. Lady V—, who is extremely quick of apprehension, replied, Without doubt, madam, you have not; but you might be surprized at seeing him notwithstanding.

She presently turned the discourse; but made me happy the whole day, by that inexhaustible fund of good sense and improving knowlege, of which she is mistress.

Mr Arnold came not home 'till very late; he complains that he is got into a knot of acquaintance that like the bottle too well; but I am sure his natural sobriety is such, that it will not be in the power of example to lead him into intemperance; though I am vexed he has fallen into such acquaintance, because I know drinking is disagreeable to him: yet a country gentleman must sometimes give a little into it, to avoid the character of being singular.

August 22

Surprized I was not, because I came prepared; but I own I was abashed, at seeing Mr Faulkland to-day. Mr Arnold and I were invited to dine at Lord V—'s, and his lordship, and his guest, came in from the fields where they had been walking, just as we were ready to sit down to table.

There happened to be a good deal more company; Mr Faulkland was not introduced; so that there was no room for any thing constrained or improper of either side. I presently recovered the little embarrassment, that his first entrance into the room occasioned. I am sure nobody took notice of it; for dinner being immediately served, there was a sort of bustle in hurrying out of the drawing-room. The crowd we had at table destroyed all conversation; and nothing particular was said during dinner. Lady V— soon withdrew, and all her female friends followed her. I observed she frequently glanced her penetrating eyes at Mr Faulkland while we were at table, but I did not chuse to make any observations on him. We had not been long seated at our Coffee, when four of the gentlemen slipped from their company and came to us: these were Mr Arnold, Mr Faulkland, and two others. My lord is pretty free at his bottle, and none of these gentlemen I suppose were fond of that entertainment. Lady V— and I were sitting on a couch: I called to Mr Arnold, and placed him between us: Mr Faulkland approached me, and then, for the first time, with a respectful distance, enquired after my mother and Sir George, telling me he had missed of the latter, when he was in London, being told he was at Sidney-castle. After a few more indifferent questions, he took a dish of coffee, and retired with it to a window. Mr Arnold asked me in a whisper, if I was acquainted with Mr Faulkland; I could only answer, that I was formerly very well acquainted with him. Nothing more passed between Mr Faulkland and me the whole evening: he returned soon to the company in the next room, and I saw no more of him.

I can with the utmost sincerity assure my Cecilia, that I now behold Mr Faulkland with as much indifference as I do any other man of my acquaintance. Time, joined to my own efforts, must, without any other help, have intirely subdued an inclination, which was always restrained by prudential motives, and rendered subservient to my duty; but I have, besides this, now acquired a shield that must render me invulnerable; I mean the perfect and tender affection I bear my husband: this has completely secured me against the most distant apprehensions of being alarmed from any other quarter; yet notwithstanding all this, I can't say that I am quite satisfied at this renewal of my acquaintance with Mr Faulkland. I hope, and indeed it is reasonable to suppose, that I have now as little interest in *his* heart as he has in mine: it is but natural to believe that a gay young man like him, should not be so weak as to nourish a hopeless passion for more than two years, especially as he has never once seen the object of it in all that time; and must, without doubt, have had his attention engaged to others in all likelihood much preferable to her; so that I think I have reason to be as easy on his account as on my own. But still I am disquieted in my mind; I have a delicacy that takes alarm at the veriest trifles, and has been a source of pain to me my whole lifetime: it makes me unhappy to think that I am now under an almost unavoidable necessity of sometimes seeing and conversing with a man, who once had such convincing proofs, that he was not indifferent to me.

Mr Arnold's ignorance of our former connnections makes it still worse. At the time I was so averse to his knowing any thing of this affair, I flattered myself I should never see Mr Faulkland more, or at least never be obliged to have any intercourse with him; but I now lament that I did not take my mother's advice, and disclose the whole affair at first. Oh! my Cecilia, when the smallest deviations from candor (which we suppose discretion), are thus punished with remorse, what must they feel whose whole life is one continued act of dissimulation? If Mr Arnold had been acquainted with my former engagements, my heart would be more at ease, and I should then converse with this man with all the disengaged freedom of a common friend. I wish Mr Arnold's curiosity would excite him to ask me some questions relative to my acquaintance with Mr Faulkland, that I might have an opportunity of telling him the secret. But the enquiry he made at lady V—'s was in a careless manner; he was satisfied with my reply, and spoke not of him since.

You will laugh perhaps when I tell you that I have not courage to mention it first; Mr Faulkland is reckoned a very fine gentleman, and I think it would have such an air of vanity to tell my husband that I refused him: then it would bring on such a train of explanations, and poor Miss Burchell's history must come out; for a husband on such a subject might be disgusted with concealments of any kind; and I doubt whether even some circumstances in my particular share of this story might not displease him. In short, I am bewildered, and know not what to wish for; but must e'en let things take their course, and rest satisfied in the integrity of my own heart.

August 26

Oh! my dear! I am mortified to the last degree, lest Mr Arnold should, from some indiscreet tongue, have received a hint of my former engagement; he may think me disingenuous for never having mentioned it, especially since Mr Faulkland has been in the neighbourhood: I think his nature is too open to entertain any suspicions essentially injurious to me; yet may this affair, circumstanced as it is, make an unfavourable impression on him. I wish I had been before-hand with any officious whisperer: he has got so many new acquaintance, and is so much abroad, that the story may have reached his ears. God forbid it should affect his mind with causeless uneasiness! I would Mr Faulkland were a thousand miles from V— hall. I think Mr Arnold is altered since his arrival there – Colder he appears to be – I hope I but *fancy* it – yet there *is* a change – his looks are less kind – his voice has lost that tenderness, that it used to have in speaking to me – yet this may only be his temper – a man cannot *always* be a lover – Oh! I sicken at the very thought of Mr Arnold's entertaining a doubt of my true affection for him. I would not live in this suspence for millions. I would rather he should treat me roughly – if I discovered that to be his humour, though it would frighten me, yet should I patiently conform to it.

August 30

That which was ever the terror of my thoughts is come upon me – Mr Arnold – Ah! my dear Cecilia! Mr Arnold is no longer the same! Coldness and indifference have at length succeeded to love, to complacency, and the fondest attention – What a change! but the *cause*, my dear, that remains a secret locked up in his own breast. It cannot be that a whisper, an idle rumour should affect him thus. What if he *has* heard that Mr Faulkland loved me once? That we were to have been married? Cannot he ask me the question? I long to set his heart at ease – yet cannot mention the affair first, after so long a silence; it would look like a consciousness. A consciousness of what? I have nothing to accuse myself of.

September 1

I am no longer in doubt. – The cause, the fatal cause of Mr Arnold's change is discovered. This miserable day has disclosed the secret to me; a black, a complicated scene of mischief.

Mr Arnold rode out this morning. He told me he was to dine wtih a gentleman at some miles distance, and should not return till late in the evening.

He was but just gone, when a lady of my acquaintance called in upon me, to request I would go with her to a play, that was to be performed at night. You must know we have had a company of players in the neighbourhood for some time past, and it was to one of those poor people's benefits that she desired my company. I promised to attend her, though you know I don't much admire those sort of entertainments in the country, and seldom go to them.

The lady and her husband called upon me at the appointed hour, and I went with them in their coach. The place which the players had fitted up for their purpose, had formerly been a pretty large school-room, and could, with the addition of a gallery (which they had made) with ease contain above three hundred people. The play had been bespoke by some of the principal ladies in the neighbourhood, who had used all their interest for the performer, so that the house was as full as it could hold. The audience consisting chiefly of fashionable people, it was with difficulty that we reached the places which were kept for us in the pit, as they happened to be on the bench next the stage, and the door was at the other end of the house. The first object that I observed on my coming in was Mr Faulkland; he bowed to me at a distance, but made no attempts to approach me. The play was come to the latter end of the fourth act, and the curtain was let down to make some preparation on the stage, when we were alarmed with the cry of fire.

It happened that the carpenters, who had been employed in fitting up this extempore theatre, had left a heap of shavings in a little place behind the stage, which had been converted into a dressing-room; a little boy belonging to the company had found a candle in it, and having piled up the shavings, set them on fire, and left them burning: the flame communicated itself to some dry boards which lay in the room, and in a few minutes the whole was in a blaze. Some persons, who heard the crackling of the wood, opened the door, when the flame burst out with such violence, that the scenes were presently on fire, and the curtain, which as I told you was dropt, soon caught it.

The consternation and terror of the poor people, whose *all* was destroying, is not to be described: the women shrieking, threw themselves off the stage into the pit, as the smoke and flames terrified them from attempting to get out any other way, though there was a door behind the stage.

The audience were in little less confusion than they; for as the house was composed chiefly of wood, every one expected it would soon be consumed to ashes.

The horror and distraction of my mind almost deprived me of the power of motion. My life was in imminent danger; for I was scorched with the fire before I could get at any distance from the stage, though the people were rushing out as fast as they could.

The lady who was with me was exceedingly frightned; but being under her husband's care, had a little more courage than I had. He caught her round the waist, and lifted her over the benches, which were very high, giving me what assistance he could with his other hand. But the terror and hurry I was in occasioned my foot to slip, and I fell between two of the benches, and sprained my ancle.

Some people pushing to get out, rushed between me and my company; the excessive pain I felt, joined to my fright, made me faint away; in this condition Mr Faulkland found me, and carried me out in his arms; for my companion was too anxious for her own safety, to suffer her husband to stay to give me any assistance, so that he had only time to beg of the men about him not to let me perish.

I soon recovered, upon being carried into the open air, and found myself seated on some planks, at a little distance from the booth, Mr Faulkland supporting me, and two or three other people about me, whom he had called to my assistance.

Indebted to him as I was for saving my life, my spirits were at that time too much agitated to thank him as I ought.

He told me, he had stepped behind the scenes to speak to somebody, and was there when the stage took fire; that he then ran to give what assistance he could to the ladies that were in the house (observe he distinguished not *me* in particular), and had just come in when he saw me meet with the accident, which had occasioned my fainting away; and when the gentleman, who was with me, was calling for help, but at the same time getting out as fast as he could.

I now began to recollect myself; I was uneasy at Mr Faulkland's presence; I wished him away. I beseeched him to return once more to the booth, to see if every one had got out safe, for I told him I had seen several of my female acquaintance there, for whom I was alarmed. With the assistance of the people about me, I said I could make a shift to get to the nearest house, which was not above a hundred yards off, from whence I should send home for my chariot, which I had ordered to come to me after the play. He begged I would give him leave to see me safe to that house, but I would not permit him; and he left me in the care of two women and a man, who had come to be spectators of the fire.

With the help of these people, I contrived to hobble (for my ancle pained me exceedingly) to the place I mentioned, which happened to be a public house. All the rooms below were full, and the woman of the house very obligingly helped me up stairs into her own chamber. I called for a glass of water, which was immediately brought me, and I desired the woman to send some one to my house, which was at about a mile's distance, to order my chariot to come to me immediately.

While the woman went to execute my instructions, I had thrown myself into a chair that stood close to the wainscot. I heard a bell ring, and presently a waiter entered, and asked if I wanted any thing; I told him, no. He ran hastily out of the room, and entering the next to that where I was sitting, I heard a voice, which I knew to be Mr Arnold's, ask, Were the servants found? The man replying that they were not, Then, said Mr Arnold, tell your mistress she will oblige me if she will let me have her chaise to carry this lady home. The waiter presently withdrew, and without reflecting on the particularity of Mr Arnold's being there with a lady, about whom I formed no conjectures, I was about to rise off my chair to go in to him; but being almost disabled from walking, I was obliged to creep along, holding by the wainscot; when a tender exclamation of Mr Arnold's stopped me. My dearest creature, said he to his companion, you have not yet recovered your fright. A female voice answered him with some fond expressions, which I could not hear distinctly enough to discover whose it was; but I was soon put out of doubt, when the lady added, in a louder tone, Do you know that your wife was at the play to-night? Mr Arnold answered, No; I hope she did not see me. Mrs Gerrarde, for I perceived it was she who spoke, replied, I hope not, because perhaps she might expect you home after the play. Though Mr Arnold, in his first emotion of surprize at hearing that I was at the play, was only anxious lest I should have observed him, yet he was not so lost to humanity as to be indifferent whether I escaped the flames or not: I am surprized I did not see her, said he; I wish she may have got out of the house safe. You are very sollicitous about her, replied Mrs Gerrarde, peevishly; there was one there perhaps as anxious for her preservation as you are – The conversation I found here was likely to become extremely critical for me; but I was prevented from hearing any more, by the woman of the house, who just then entered the room to ask me how I did, and to know if I wanted any thing.

I had heard enough to convince me that my presence would be very unacceptable both to Mr Arnold and his companion, and I resolved not to interrupt them; nor, if possible, ever let Mr Arnold know that I had made a discovery so fatal to my own peace, and so disadvantageous to him and his friend.

The messenger who had been dispatched for my chariot met it by the way, and was now returned with it; I was told that it was at the door; and it was with difficulty I got down stairs, leaning on the woman of the house.

I found Mr Faulkland at the door; he saw that I wished to disengage myself from him after he had carried me out of the booth; and though probably he did not take the trouble to excuse the sham commission I gave him, which was indeed with no other view than to get him away, yet I believe he had too much respect to intrude on me; and came then with no other design than to enquire if my chariot had come for me, and how I was after the terrible condition he had left me in, sitting at night in the open air, with nobody but two or three ordinary people about me, and those strangers. This was a piece of civility which humanity, had politeness been out of the question, would have obliged him to. He told me the fire was extinguished, and happily nobody had received any hurt; and that he had only called at that house to know if I were safe, and recovered from the fright and pain he had left me in. I thanked him, and was just stepping, assisted by Mr Faulkland, into the chariot, when Mr Arnold appeared at the door: he was alone, and I concluded, that having heard the chariot rattle up the court-yard, he supposed it was the carriage he had ordered for Mrs Gerrarde, and came down to see if it was ready to receive her.

The light which the servant, who attended me out, held in his hand, immediately discovered Mr Arnold and me to each other. I could easily distinguish surprize mixed with displeasure in his countenance. He asked me abruptly, How I came to that place? Which I told him, in few words. The cold civility of a grave bow passed between him and Mr Faulkland, who leaving me in my husband's hands, wished me a good night, and got into my lord V—'s coach, which waited for him.

Though I knew, from the discourse I had overheard, that Mr Arnold did not mean to go home with me, yet as I was now seated in the chariot, I could not avoid asking him. He told me, he was engaged to sup with company at that house, and that probably he should not be at home till late. I knew this beforehand, and, without troubling him with any farther questions, drove home.

I have thrown together the strange occurrences of this evening, as well as the tumult of my spirits would give me leave: I shall now lay down my pen, to consider of them a little more calmly. My heart sinks in me – Oh! that I had remained in ignorance! –

Is it possible, my Cecilia, that Mr Arnold, so good a man, one who married me for love, and who for these two years has been the tenderest, the kindest husband, and to whom I never gave the most distant shadow of offence, should at last be led into – I cannot name it – dare not think of it – yet a thousand circumstances recur to my memory, which now convince me I am unhappy! If I had not been blind, I might have seen it sooner. I recollect some passages, which satisfy me that Mr Arnold's acquaintance with Mrs Gerrarde did not commence at South-park. I remember lady V— once asked me, had she and I been acquainted in London? I said, No. My lord laughed, and in his blunt way said, I will swear your hubsand was, for I have seen him hand her out from the play more than once. I never asked Mr Arnold about this; it made no impression on me at the time it was spoke, and went quick-out of my thoughts.

'Tis one o'clock: I hear Mr Arnold ring at the outer gate; I tremble all over, and feel as if I feared to see him. Yet why should I fear? *I* have not injured *him*.

September 2

Mr Arnold staid long enough in his dressing-room after he came in last night, to give me time to go to-bed before he came up stairs. Not a word passed between us: I slept not the whole night: whether he did or not I cannot tell. He asked me this morning, when he rose, how I did: I told him in great pain. My ancle was prodigiously swelled, and turned quite black, for I had neglected it last night. He said, you had better let a surgeon see it, and went carelessly out of the room. How new is unkindness to me, my friend! you know I have not been used to it. Mr Arnold adds cruelty too – but let it be so; far be reproaches or complaints from my lips; to you only, my second self, shall I utter them; to you I am bound by solemn promise, and reciprocal confidence, to disclose the inmost secrets of my soul, and with you they are as safe as in my own breast. –

I am once more composed, and determined on my behaviour. I have not a doubt remaining of Mr Arnold's infidelity; but let me not aggravate my own griefs, nor to a vicious world justify my husband's conduct, by bringing any reproach on my own. The silent sufferings of the injured, must, to a mind not ungenerous, be a sharper rebuke than it is in the power of language to inflict.

But this is not all: I must endeavour, if possible, to skreen Mr Arnold from censure. I hope his own imprudence may not render these endeavours ineffectual. I am resolved not to drop my acquaintance with Mrs Gerrarde. While we continue upon a footing of seeming intimacy, the frequent visits, which I am sure Mr Arnold makes at her house, will be less taken notice of.

How Sir George would triumph at the knowlege of Mr Arnold's deviating from virtue! How my poor mother would be amazed and afflicted! But I will, as far as lies in my power, disappoint the malice of my stars; my mother shall have no cause to grieve, nor my brother to rejoice; the secret shall die with me in my own bosom, and I will wait patiently, till the hand of time applies a remedy to my grief. – Mrs Gerrarde sent a message to enquire how I did. Conscious woman! she would not come herself, though she knew not I had discovered her.

My dear good lady V— hurried to see me the instant she had breakfasted: Mr Faulkland had told her of my disaster, and her tenderness soothed and comforted me much. She sat by my bed-side two hours, and her discourse alleviated the pain both of my mind and body; but now she has left me, I must again recur to the subject that wrings my heart. Mr Arnold is enslaved to one of the most artful of her sex. I look upon his attachment to be the more dangerous, as I believe it is the first of the kind he ever had; and no woman was ever more formed to please and to deceive, than she who now holds him in her chains. Into what hands am I fallen! Mrs Gerrarde must have heard my story, and by the hint I heard her drop, what cruel misrepresentations may she have made to Mr Arnold! Mr Faulkland, she can have no enmity to; but me she certainly hates, for she has injured me.

'Tis noon: I have not seen Mr Arnold since morning; he has been abroad ever since he rose; Good God! is this the life I am condemned to lead?

A new scene of affliction is opened to me: surely my fate is drawing towards a crisis. Mr Arnold has just left me. What conversation have we had!

After entering my room, he walked about for some minutes without speaking; at last stopping short, and fixing his eyes upon me, How long have you, said he, been acquainted with Mr Faulkland? I told him my acquaintance began with him some months before I was married. He was once your lover I am informed. He was, and a treaty of marriage was concluded on between us. You would have been happier perhaps, madam, if it had taken place. I do not think so Mr Arnold, you have no reason to suppose I do. I had a very great objection to Mr Faulkland, and obeyed my mother willingly, when she forbid me to see him. I ask not what that objection was, said he; but I suppose, madam, you will without reluctance obey *me*, if I make the same request to you. Most chearfully; you cannot make a request with which I should more readily comply. But let me beseech you, Mr Arnold, to tell me, what part of my behaviour has given you cause to think such a prohibition necessary? I do not say, answered Mr Arnold, that I have any suspicion of your virtue; but your acquiescence in this particular is necessary to *my* peace and your *own* honour. A lady's being *married* does not cut off the hopes of a gay man. You give me your promise that you will not see him any more. I *do*, said I; I will give up lady V—, whose acquaintance I so much esteem: I will go no more to her house while Mr Faulkland continues there; and I know of no other family, where I visit, that he is acquainted with.

My pride would not suffer me to enquire where he had got his information: I already knew it too well; and fearing he would rather descend to an untruth than tell me his author, I declined any farther questions. He seemed satisfied with my promise, but quickly left me, as if the whole end of his visit to me was accomplished in having obtained it.

September 8

What painful minutes am I obliged to sustain! Mrs Gerrarde has been to see me, gay and assured as ever. She affected to condole with me on the accident that happened to my foot, with such an overstrained concern, such a tender solicitude, that her insincerity disgusted me, if possible, more than the other part of her behaviour. She told me, she herself had been at the play, but very luckily had got out without receiving any injury. I said, I was surprized I had not seen her there. O, replied she, I was in a little snug corner, where nobody could see me; for having refused to go with some ladies that asked me, I did not chuse to be visible in the house, and so squeezed myself up into what they called their gallery, for I took nobody with me but my maid. Audacious woman! – Is it not strange, my dear, that Mr Arnold could be so weak as to humour her in the absurd frolick of going with her to such a place? for so it must have been; or perhaps she appointed him only to call for her at the play; and he might have arrived but just in time to assist her in getting out. No matter which it was.

September 9

I was born to sacrifice my own peace to that of other people; my life is become miserable, but I have no remedy for it but patience.

Mr Arnold spends whole days abroad; at night we are separated on account of my indisposition; so that we hardly ever converse together. What a dreadful prospect have I before me! O! Cecilia, may you never experience the bitterness of having your husband's heart alienated from you!

Lady V—, that best of creatures, is with me constantly; she presses me to come to her house, as my ancle is now pretty well, yet I am obliged to excuse myself. I am distressed to the last degree at the conduct I shall be forced to observe towards her, yet dare not explain the motive. Causeless jealousy is always the subject of ridicule, and at all events Mr Arnold must not be exposed to this.

September 12

I am weary of inventing excuses for absenting myself from V— hall. My lady has done solliciting me, yet continues her friendly and affectionate visits; I fear she guesses my situation, though she has not as yet hinted at it; but her forbearing to press me any more on the subject of going to her, and at the same time not requring a reason for this breach of civility as well as friendship, convinced me, that she suspects the cause of my restraint. I am now perfectly recovered, yet do I still confine myself to my house, to avoid as much as possible giving umbrage to lady V—: but this restraint cannot last much longer; Mrs Gerrarde teazes me to come to her, and I have promised to make her my first visit.

September 27

Said I not that my fate was near its crisis? Where will this impending ruin end? Take, my Cecilia, the occurrences of this frightful day.

Mr Arnold rode out this morning, and told me he should not return till night. He asked me, with that indifference which now accompanies all his words, How I meant to dispose of myself for the day? I told him, I had no design of going abroad, and should spend my time in reading, or at my needle. This was my real intention; but Mr Arnold had but just left the house, when I received a message from Mrs Gerrarde to know how I did, and to tell me she was not well, and much out of spirits, or she would come and pass the day with me; but that she insisted on my dining with her. As I had told Mr Arnold I did not mean to go out, I really had neither intention nor inclination to do so. But shall I confess my weakness to you? I suspected that he purposed spending the day (as he often did) with Mrs Gerrarde, and the more so from the question he had asked me on his going abroad; he thought I might probably pay her a visit; and this intrusion was a circumstance he had a mind to be guarded against, by knowing before-hand my designs. I had not been to see Mrs Gerrarde since my recovery, and it was natural to suppose I would return her visits. Possessed as I was with this opinion, her message gave me a secret satisfaction, as it served to convince me Mr Arnold was not to be with her, for she generally detained me late when I went to her house. From what trivial circumstances will the afflicted draw consolation, or an additional weight of grief? So it was, I felt a sort of pleasure, in thinking, that for all that day at least Mr Arnold would absent himself from my rival – My rival! mean word, she is not worthy to be called so; from his mistress let it be. In short, I resolved to go, especially as she had sent me word she was not well, and I knew my husband would be pleased with my complaisance.

I went accordingly to her house, a little before her hour of dining, which is much later than any body else's in this part of the world. I found her dressed out, and seemingly in perfect health. She looked surprized when she saw me; and I then supposed that she hoped to have received a denial from me, and was disappointed at my coming;

though I wondered that the answer she received to her message had not prepared her. This thought rushed into my mind in an instant, and I was sure she expected Mr Arnold. I told her, if I had thought I should have found her so well, that her message should not have brought me to her; for that I had determined not to stir out that day, till her invitation prevailed on me to change my mind. Sure, my dear, said she, there must have been some mistake in delivering the message to you, it was for to-morrow I desired the pleasure of your company to dine with me; for today I am absolutely engaged. However, I am very glad you are come, for I shall not go out till seven o'clock. I was vexed and mortified: either your servant or mine made a mistake, said I, for I was told you desired to see me to-day; besides you sent me word you were not well. She seemed a little abashed at this: I *was* very ill in the morning, she said; and though I was engaged to spend the evening abroad, did intend to have sent an excuse; but finding myself better, I changed my purpose.

Dinner was immediately served, and I sat down, but with a reluctance that prevented me from eating. I would have taken my leave soon after dinner, but Mrs Gerrarde insisted on my staying, and told me, if I refused her, she should think I had taken something amiss of her. She called for cards; I suffered myself to be persuaded, and we fell to piquet.

I played with disgust, and without attention, every minute wishing to break away. Coffee was at length brought in; I begged to be excused from staying, telling Mrs Gerrarde, I was sure I prevented her from going abroad, but she would take no denial. I was constrained to take a dish of coffee, and was hastening to get it down when the parlour door flew open, and lo! Mr Faulkland entered the room. If an object the most horrible to human nature had appeared before me, it could not, at that instant, have shocked me half so much. I let the cup and saucer drop from my hand: to say I turned pale, trembled and was ready to faint, would be too feeble a description of the effect this spectre had on me. I was senseless, I almost died away. Mrs Gerrarde pretended to be greatly alarmed; she ran for drops, and having given me a few in a glass of water, I made a shift to rise off my chair, and telling her, I should be glad of a little air, tottered to the street door. I determined to go home directly, but the universal tremor I was now in, disabled me from walking, and I sat down in the porch to recover myself a little. Mr Faulkland's having been a witness to the agony his presence had thrown me into, did not a little aggravate the horror and confusion of my thoughts. Whatever *his* were, he had not spoke to me, nor was it possible for me to have remarked his behaviour: I staid not more than two minutes in the parlour after he entered. In this situation you will think my distress would hardly admit of any addition; but the final blow was yet to come. Mrs Gerrarde had staid a minute in the parlour to speak to Mr Faulkland after I went out, but presently followed me, and was soothing me with the kindest expressions, when I heard the trampling of horses, and presently beheld Mr Arnold alighting at the door. I now gave myself up for lost. My mind suddenly suggested to me that Mrs Gerrarde had contrived a plot upon my innocence; but how she had been able to bring it about, my thoughts were not then disengaged enough to conceive. My mind was all a chaos; I was not able to answer Mr Arnold when he spoke to me. He soon perceived my disorder, and enquired the cause. Mrs Gerrarde took upon her to answer, that I was just preparing to go home, when I was taken suddenly ill. I was going abroad, said she, and as I ordered the chariot much about this hour, I fancy it is ready, and may as well carry Mrs Arnold home; you had best step into the parlour, my dear, (to me) till it is brought to the door.

I am now able to walk, madam, said I; there is no occasion to give you that trouble. Mr Arnold said, I should not walk by any means; and Mrs Gerrarde immediately calling to a servant to order the chariot to the door, said, as she was going out, she would leave me at home herself. Mr Arnold answered, it would be the best way, and that he should follow soon. The chariot was presently at the door, and I was preparing to get into it, when Mrs Gerrarde cry'd, Bless me, I had forgot, it will not be so civil to leave the gentleman behind, without saying any thing to him. Mr Arnold hastily asked, What Gentleman? Mrs Gerrarde replied, Mr Faulkland, *who took it into his head* to make me a visit this evening. She went quickly into the parlour, and strait returned with Mr Faulkland; who bowing carelessly to Mr Arnold, and civilly to me, walked away.

Mrs Gerrarde stepped into the chariot to me, and ordered it to drive to my house, leaving Mr Arnold standing motionless at her door.

A total silence prevailed on my side during our short journey home, except to answer in monosyllables Mrs Gerrarde's repeated enquiries after my health. She set me down at my own door, and took her leave without alighting. When I found myself alone, I began to consider the consequences of this evening's fatal interview; an interview, which, though unthought of by me, I judged was contrived to ensnare me. I laid all the circumstances together, and endeavoured to unravel the clue. 'Tis plain to me Mr Arnold was expected by Mrs Gerrarde this evening. She sent for me on purpose to betray me; the message, which she pretended was delivered wrong, was only an artifice, in order to impose on Mr Arnold, that he might imagine she did not expect me. Indeed, he could not possibly think she should send for me on the very evening he was to be with her; and she had so well guarded her contrivance, that it was not easily to be detected. She had sent her message by word of mouth, though she generally wrote them down on paper, but this way would not have been liable to misconstruction: she had told me she was engaged in the evening, yet detained me longer than I meant to stay. From the first of these circumstances, it must appear to Mr Arnold, that as I had come unwished for, she wanted to get rid of me; the latter obviously served her own purpose; for it is as clear as daylight that she laid her plan so as that Mr Arnold should find Mr Faulkland and me together. All this I have deduced from a long train of reasoning on the circumstances. But the inexplicable part of the mystery is how she contrived to get Mr Faulkland, with whom I did not think she was acquainted, to visit her at so fatally critical a juncture. Sure some evil spirit must have assisted her in this wicked scheme: she knew, no doubt, of the promise Mr Arnold had exacted of me, never to see him. The apparent breach of this promise, she may have art enough to persuade Mr Arnold was concerted on my side. But I hope I shall be able to clear myself of this cruel imputation to my husband. Truth *must* force its way into his mind, if he is not resolved on my destruction. Perhaps Mr Faulkland may be secretly Mrs Gerrarde's admirer, and Mr Arnold is the dupe to her perfidy, as I am the sacrifice to her malice and licentiousness. – 'Tis all a strange riddle, but I cannot remain long in this dismal state of suspence; Mr Arnold, perhaps, may discover her treachery, while she is endeavouring to destroy me in his good opinion.

I am waiting here like a poor criminal, in expectation of appearing before my judge. I wish Mr Arnold were come in, yet I dread to see him.

I might have spared myself the anxiety. Mr Arnold is just returned, but he has locked himself into another chamber. I will not molest him tonight; to-morrow, perhaps, he may be in better temper, and I may be able to justify myself to him, and dispel this frightful gloom that hangs over us.

September 13

Hopes and fears are at an end, and the measure of my afflictions is filled up.

I went to bed last night, but slept not; the hours were passed in agonies not to be described. I think all griefs are magnified by silence and darkness. I well knew, prepossessed as Mr Arnold was by my artful enemy, I should find it difficult to excuse myself, or persuade him, that chance, or Mrs Gerrarde's more wicked contrivance, had been the sole cause of what had given him such offence. I was resolved, however, to vindicate my innocence, and was, in my own thoughts, preparing my defence the greatest part of the night. Towards morning, weariness and grief overpowered me, and I fell asleep, but I enjoyed not this repose long. Some noise that was made in the house suddenly awakened me; I saw it was broad day, and looking at my watch, found it was past seven o'clock. I rang my bell, and Patty entering my room, I enquired if her master was yet stirring. The poor girl looked aghast, He is gone away on horseback, madam, said she, almost two hours ago; and he ordered his man to put up some linnen and a few other things in a small portmanteau. I believe he means not to return to-night; for he bid me to deliver this letter to you. I opened the letter with trembling hands, from whence I received my doom in the following words:

'You have broken your faith with me, in seeing the man whom I forbad you to see, and whom you so solemnly promised to avoid. As you have betrayed my confidence in this particular, I can no longer rely on your prudence or your fidelity. Whatever your designs may be, it will be less to my dishonour if you prosecute them from under your husband's roof. I therefore give you till this day se'nnight to consider of a place for your future abode; for one house must no more contain two people, whose hearts are divided. Our children remain with me, and the settlement which was made on you in marriage, shall be appropriated to your separate use.

'I have left home to avoid expostulations, nor shall I return to it till I hear you have removed yourself. Spare the attempt of a justification, which can only aggravate the resentment of your already too-much injured husband.'

I have for a while suppressed the tumult in my soul, to give you this shocking letter.

O my Cecilia! What a wretched lot is thy unhappy friend's! To be neglected, forsaken, despised, by a husband that I love! Yet I could bear that: but to be suspected, accused too! to be at once the miserable object of jealousy and scorn! Surely they know nothing of the human heart, who say that jealousy cannot subsist without affection; I have a fatal proof to the contrary. Mr Arnold loves me not, yet doubts my honour. Cruel, mean, detestable suspicion! Oh that vile woman! 'tis she has done this; like a persecuting dæmon she urges on the ruin which she set on foot.

What can I do? Whither can I fly? I cannot remain here any longer; my presence banishes Mr Arnold from his home. If I go to my mother under such circumstances, it will break her heart; yet she must know it. I must not wait to be turned out of my own doors. That thought is not to be borne. I will go this instant, no matter whither.

September 15

God preserve me in my senses! I have passed two days and two nights I know not how; in silence and without food, Patty tells me. But I think I am a little recovered. I will write to my mother, and beg of her to open her arms to receive her miserable child. I am collected enough, and know what to say.

I had just dispatched my letter, incoherent as it is, and blotted with my tears, when Patty brought me one that had come by the post. I knew my dear mother's hand on the superscription, and kissed it before I opened it. See, my sister, how the tenderest of parents write to her unhappy child, whom she fondly believes to be the darling of her husband, and blessed with domestic felicity.

My beloved Sidney,

I find age and infirmities are advancing a-pace upon me. My last illness shook me severely, and has left a memorandum of what I may expect in the next visit it makes me. Your family cares are now so much enlarged, that I cannot expect, nor do I desire that you should undertake a journey to Sidney-castle to pay me a short visit; yet, my dear, as you are the comfort of my age, I cannot, in the present precarious state of my health, bear to be at such a distance from you; while God permits me strength I will lay hold of his bounty, and endeavour to get to London. You have told me that you are not conveniently circumstanced at South-park as to room; I will not therefore incommode you, but shall content myself with waiting your arrival in town, at your house in St. James's-street; but do not hasten your departure from the country on this account. I am in no immediate danger, my dear, only willing to lay hold of an interval of health, to get nearer to you. If God prolongs my life, what joy will it be to me to spend next winter with my darling, and her dear good Arnold, and to feast my eyes with my lovely grandchildren!

If I am called from you, I shall have the comfort of my child's affectionate hands to close my eyes; and shall leave the world without rgret, as I have lived to see my Sidney happy in the arms of a good man, who will supply the loss of parents, and unite in hmself those tender ties which nature must soon dissolve.

My prayers for yours, and my dear son's prosperity, I never fail to offer up to Heaven. Your brother George is with me, and desires to be remembered to you; he purposes staying here the greatest part of the winter.

As I hope to reach London by the latter end of the week, direct your next to me at your own house in town.

I am,

My dear love,

Your most sincerely,

affectionate mother,

DOROTHY BIDULPH.

My heart is bursting – O Cecilia! What will become of my fond, my dear, venerable parent, when she finds this daughter, this comfort of her age, this beloved of her soul, a poor abandoned outcast; lost to her husband's love, turned out of his doors, despised, disgraced! My children too – I must leave them behind – My God, for what calamities hast thou ordained thy creature! Tears, tears, you may well flow!

So! I am relieved, and will endeavour to fortify my soul against the two events, that appear to me horrid as an approaching execution to a guilty wretch, the parting with my children, and the meeting with my mother. As the letter I wrote will miss of her at Sidney-castle, I shall write to London, to prepare her to receive the wretch whom her imagination has figured to her so happy.

Lady V—! I hear her coming up stairs – I cannot conceal my

affliction, nor my disgrace.

Lady V— has left me: left me in astonishment and new horror. Mrs Gerrarde! Who do you think Mrs Gerrarde is? She is the aunt of Miss Burchell, that aunt who betrayed her to destruction. Sure this woman was sent into the world for a scourge!

I cannot collect myself to tell you with any method, the conversation that passed between lady V— and me. She found me with the marks of tears on my face; they streamed again at the sight of her; I could not conceal the cause, and I put Mr Arnold's letter into her hands, for I was not able to tell her the purport of it.

This is Mrs Gerrarde's doing, said she, the detestable creature! How could she work on your infatuated husband, to drive him such horrid lengths? I know not, said I, but I hope my lady V— believes me innocent. Innocent, she exclaimed! My dear creature, your sufferings almost make me mad. Do you know that Mrs Gerrarde has an intrigue with your husband? I fear so, madam, I replied, but I hoped it was not publick. Poor child, said lady V—, his attachment to her has been no secret, ever since he came down to this country, though probably you were the last to suspect it. I have often dreaded the consequences of it, but never imagined it would have come to this; I always had a bad opinion of the woman, and only kept up a face of civility to her in her husband's time, on account of her niece, a charming girl that then lived with her; but since Miss Burchell has left her, I have almost dropt my acquaintance with her; though my lord, who had an old friendship for captain Gerrarde, persuades me to be civil to her.

The name of Miss Burchell had struck me speechless. The clue was now unravelled. With what an unremitting zeal has this base woman gone on in her career of iniquity? Lady V—, who was intirely taken up with the thoughts of my unhappiness, took no notice of my silence or confusion. What do you mean to do, my dear Mrs Arnold, said she? Do you think it is not possible, by the interposition of friends, to disabuse your unfortunate husband? For unfortunate he is, in a higher degree than yourself, as you have conscious innocence to support you. Oh madam, said I, it is in vain to think of it! Mrs Gerrarde has struck the blow effectually. Were Mr Arnold left to the workings of his own heart, he might, perhaps, relent; but that woman, like my evil genius and his, will take care to keep his suspicions alive. She possesses his whole heart, and my removal is become necessary, to the quiet of them both. I have taken this resolution, I will immediately quit this house, and leave it to a righteous God to vindicate me in his own time. You should go no where but to my house, said lady V—, with tears n her eyes, but that I think it an improper situation for you, while Mr Faulkland is my guest. He will be distracted when he hears of this. I conjured lady V— not to tell him: my being parted from my husband cannot long be a secret, said I, but the cause may. Lady V— told me that Mr Faulkland was that very morning set out for Sidney-castle, to see my brother; having received a letter from him the day before, in which he told him that my mother was going in a day or two to London, and begged he would come and spend a week with him. She added, that Mr Faulkland purposed doing so, and then to return to V— hall, as my lord had obtained a promise from him to stay some time longer with them; at least till the old lady's affairs were settled, who had left her fortune to Mr Faulkland, and to whom my lord V— was executor.

I told lady V— I depended on her friendship, to keep this affair a secret from Mr Faulkland, lest the heat of his temper should make him take such notice of it, as might render my separation from Mr Arnold doubly injurious to my character. Lady V— saw the necessity of this caution, and promised to observe it. She expressed great surprize at Mr Faulkland's visiting Mrs Gerrarde, whom she said, she did not imagine he had been acquainted with. He is no stranger, said she, to your husband's amour with her, as it has often been a topic of discourse between my lord and me; and I can hardly think he would be so indelicate as to carry on a love-affair with such an abandoned creature; especially as I have often heard him express the utmost detestation of her, on account of her robbing you of your husband's affection; which I had observed for a good while. But there is no knowing mankind, added she: if that should be the case, you may depend upon it that vile Gerrarde has laid her plan deeper than we are aware of, and would out-swear us all, that Faulkland came to her house for no other purpose, than to have an opportunity of seeing you; who to be sure, she said, had given him a private hint to meet you there. Now the worst of it is, it is impossible to have this matter cleared up to your husband, without Mr Faulkland's concurrence, and that you will not consent to. By no means, I replied, I would not for the world have Mr Faulkland interfere in my justification. If the affair should really be as you have suggested, a little time may, perhaps, discover this wicked woman to Mr Arnold, and it will not then be so difficult to clear my innocence. At present, her influence over him is too powerful for me to combat with; and I know he wishes for nothing more than to free himself from the restraint that my presence lays him under.

Lady V— acquiesced in my opinion, and said, she hoped a little time would chace away the dark cloud that now hung over me. She staid with me the whole day; it was a day of tears: the dear woman was quite subdued at parting with me. I see you no more, dear lady V—, said I; I shall go to London in two days – Preserve your fortitude, dearest Mrs Arnold, she replied; the time will come when your husband will repent of the bitter distress he has occasioned to you; my lord and I will use our utmost endeavours to convince him of his error. – We shall meet in London, my dear, I shall go thither early in the winter on purpose – Have courage – Your innocence *must* be cleared. I answered her not, my heart was too full. We embraced, and lady V— parted from me in silence.

I have written to my mother, and directed my letter to St James's-Street. I would have her prepared for the shock before she sees me; a shock, which I fear she will not be able to sustain.

September 16

Mrs Gerrarde has never called or sent to me since I was at her house. She has effected her purpose, and is contented without a triumph.

I am prepared for my departure. To-morrow I turn my back upon my husband's house, and upon my children. I have been weeping over them this hour as they lie asleep in their nurse's arms. But I will look at them no more. – Poor Patty is almost dead with grief; she would fain go with me, but I have persuaded her to stay: I can rely on her fidelity and her tenderness towards my children; she says, she *will* be as precious of them as the apple of her eyes, and will give me an account of their welfare from time to time. Sure Mr Arnold will not turn *her* out too; she is an excellent manager, and he cannot do without a housekeeper.

I have been debating with myself whether I should write to Mr Arnold or not, and have at length determined to depart in silence. It is an easy matter for the guilty to make as bold asseverations as the innocent, and nothing which I could now assert would make an impression on him. Had I only his suspicions to combat, there might be hopes: but his *heart* is alienated from me; and while it continues attached to another, I despair of his listening to the voice of reason or of justice. If ever his eyes are opened, his error will prove sufficient punishment to him – Perhaps my mother or my brother may put me in a way – My conduct, in time, I hope, may justify me – Mean while I will not condescend to the weak justification of words.

September 18

I have bid adieu to South-park, and arrived this morning in London in a hired carriage, for I would not take one of Mr Arnold's. I found my mother at the house in St James's-street, where I now am: she got here late last night, and my letter had thrown her into agonies, from which she had not yet recovered. What have you wrote to me, said she, as she held me in her arms? your dreadful letter has almost killed me – Sure, sure, my dear child, it cannot be true that you have left your husband! What is the cause? What have *you* done? or, What has *he* done? I begged my mother to compose herself a little, and then related to her every circumstance, in the same manner you have had them as they occurred. Her lamentations pierced my heart; she wrung her hands in bitterness of anguish; Why did not the grave hide me, said she, before I saw shame and sorrow heaped upon my child. I came to die in peace with you – You might have lengthened my days for a while – But you cut them off – My eyes will close in affliction – A wounded spirit who can bear! Had you died in your cradle, we had both been happy. My child would now have been a cherub, an angel you would have been in my eyes, and I am punished for it; but that was *my* crime, not your's. But you are a martyr to the crimes of others.

My mother wept not all this time; I wished she had; her passionate looks and tones affected me more than tears could. My eyes began to run over, her's soon accompanied me, and it a little relieved the vehemence of her grief.

She then began to reproach herself for having listened to lady Grimston's suggestions in favour of Mr Arnold, and for her own solliciting this fatal marriage. But I stopped her, on a subject which I knew would so much torment her thoughts. I conjured her not to reflect on it in that manner; I told her I knew she had acted for the best, and that nothing but an extraordinary fatality, which could neither be foreseen nor avoided, had made me unhappy. I said I was sure Mr Arnold had been seduced by the wiles of a wicked woman, for that he was by nature a good man, and that he had more of my pity than of my resentment.

I found it necessary to reconcile my mother to herself on this head; she seemed willing to lay hold on the hint, and turned all her indignation against Mrs Gerrarde. A *practised* sinner, she called her, for whom nothing could be said in extenuation of her crime.

We now turned our thoughts towards fixing on some other abode. You may be sure Mr Arnold's house is no place for us; and my mother declared she would not stay another night in it: accordingly we have dispatched her maid to take us lodgings immediately.

September 21

We have quickly shifted the scene, my dear Cecilia, and are settled, at least for the present, in very handsome lodgings in St Alban's-street. We came to them last night, and my mother seems a little less disturbed than she was. I pray God spare her life, but I fear I shall not long enjoy that blessing. She is sadly altered since I last saw her; a dropsical complaint is stealing on her fast, her legs are swelled, and she has intirely lost her appetite; yet if her mind were a little more at ease, I should hope, that by the assistance she can have here, she might be enabled to hold out against this disorder for a good while. I endeavour to suppress my own grief, that I may not increase her's.

VOLUME II

September 21

I WAS surprized to-day by a visitor to my mother. Miss Burchell came to pay her respects to her: I have told you they corresponded. My mother, it seems, had given her notice of the time she intended being in town: the young lady had been to wait on her in St James's Street, and was from thence directed by the servant, who kept the house, to our new lodgings.

She is really a very lovely young woman; and there is something so insinuating in her manner, that there is no seeing her without being prejudiced in her favour. She changed colour when my mother presented me to her by my name; but, at the same time, surveyed me with a scrutinous eye. My mother asked her, had she seen Mr Faulkland since his return to England. She answered, No, with a sigh; but that she believed he had been to Putney. To see his son, said my mother? without reflecting, that Miss Burchell had avoided mentioning that circumstance, and stopped upon naming the place where the child was at nurse. Yes, she replied, in a timorous accent, and stealing a look at me. The woman told me, that a young gentleman had been there about six weeks ago, who said he came from the child's father abroad, and made her a handsome present. As I did not then know Mr Faulkland was returned to England, I should not have suspected it was he himself who had called, if his housekeeper (that gentlewoman in whose care he left me) had not come to me from him. She is settled now in a lodging-house; and Mr Faulkland, on his coming to London, went to her, to enquire where the child was. She told me he inquired civilly after me, and gave her a letter for me, which the good-natured woman joyfully brought me; but it contained nothing but a bill of a hundred pounds, with two or three lines, polite indeed, but not kind, to inform me it was for the child's use; and I have heard nothing of him since.

My mother told her, that as Mr Faulkland was returned again, probably to continue in England, she did not despair of his being brought to do her justice; especially as she must suppose the sight of the child had made an impression on him. She then, without ceremony, entered into a detail of my unhappy story: she was full of it; and being, as you know, of a very communicative temper, made no scruple to inform Miss Burchell of every particular. She seemed very much affected with the story, and grew red and pale by turns; especially at finding her aunt so deeply concerned in it. She exclaimed against her barbarity, reproached Mr Arnold for his injurious suspicions, and condoled obligingly with me on the wrongs I had received; and yet, my Cecilia, would you believe it, I thought I could discover, through all this, that Miss Burchell was not entirely free from doubt in regard to my innocence. This observation I gathered only from certain looks that she cast at me, as my mother related the passages. There are little minute touches on the countenance sometimes, which are so transient they can hardly be overtaken by the eye, and which, from the passions being strongly guarded that give rise to these emotions, are so slight, that a common observer cannot discover them at all. I am sure my mother did not; but my sensibility was particularly rouzed at her relating a story that I did not then wish to have divulged; and I was too much interested in the narrative, not to attend precisely to its effects on the hearer. I am neither angry with, nor surprized at, Miss Burchell, for her scepticism on this occasion. She loves Mr Faulkland, and had not herself the power to resist him: she knows he once loved me, and may fancy he does so still; nay, thinks perhaps I am not indifferent towards him: she is a stranger to *my* heart; but is convinced, that her aunt is base enough, first to ensnare to vice, and then to betray. Upon the whole, there is nothing unnatural in her suspicions; but I think they could not proceed from a virtuous mind.

Upon Miss Burchell's taking leave, my mother gave her a general invitation to come to her as often as she had leisure; telling her, she must not take it amiss if she did not return her visits, as her health would not permit her to go much abroad.

Miss Burchell, it seems, has a house (not lodgings) in a retired street in Westminster, where she has been ever since she quitted her aunt, to whom she never discovered where she lived. Her fortune enables her to appear very genteelly in the private manner she chuses to live. She goes but seldom into publick, and has but a narrow circle of acquaintance. Those are all of her own sex, and of the best character; and she has had the good fortune to preserve her reputation unsuspected; so that, I hope, she may yet retrieve her error by an advantageous match, should Mr Faulkland still continue averse to her.

September 28

I have had a letter from Patty: she tells me, her master is returned home; and adds, 'To be sure, that vile wicked wretch let him know you were gone.' She says, he called for the two dear babes, and kissed them both. Patty carried the youngest to him in her arms, the other in her hand, and she says, he looked troubled. How came you not to follow your lady, Mrs Martha, said he? She replied, My Lady was willing, Sir, that I should stay to look after the children – And to be a spy upon my actions, I suppose: Is that not to be part of your employment too? Ah! Patty, Patty; Mrs Arnold had better have looked to her own conduct. Patty made no answer, but retired in tears. Every one in the house, she writes, is broken-hearted; but that Mr Arnold is never at home, spending his whole time with Mrs Gerrarde, whom the girl, in the overflowings of her zeal for me, heartily execrates. She informed him, that I was gone to London, and purposed living with my mother, who was now there.

October 7

I have just received a letter from Lady V—. She tells me she sent twice to Mr Arnold to dine with them, in order, if possible, to lead him into a conversation, by which they hoped, in some measure, to have cleared my innocence, as my lord could take upon him to justify Mr Faulkland; but he declined coming, not knowing, perhaps, that Mr Faulkland was absent from V— hall. She said, her lord had gone to South-Park; but either Mr Arnold was not at home, or denied himself. My Lady adds, 'It is a delicate affair to interpose in; yet would I have ventured to have wrote to your husband, if I had been sure that you had no objection to my telling him, that you had made me privy to the cause of your parting: 'tis plain, by his avoiding us, it is a subject he does not care to come to an explanation upon. Let me have your sentiments, and I will act accordingly.'

I shall answer Lady V—'s letter directly, and beg of her to leave the matter as it is. Mrs Gerrarde's testimony will have more weight than all my good lord or lady could urge in my favour: besides, they are not furnished with sufficient weapons to combat against such an enemy: they know nothing of Miss Burchell's story; my regard to *her* character prevented me from giving my lady this specimen of her aunt's baseness. I suppose the same reason may have closed Mr Faulkland's lips on that subject: so that they have nothing to allege against Mrs Gerrarde, which would help to invalidate her testimony with regard to Mr Faulkland and me. Mr Arnold, indeed, knows that she has forfeited her pretensions to modesty; but the delusion of self-love blinds a man in those cases; and he can believe, that *truth*, *sincerity*, and *justice*, inhabit the bosom of her, whose passion for *him* alone has caused a deviation from chastity.

I cannot think of exposing the poor Miss Burchell by giving up her secret. Though it might contribute to clear me, by turning Mr Arnold's suspicions on Mrs Gerrarde, yet would she have great reason to resent it; more especially as she is now, by a blameless life, endeavouring to blot out the memory of her fault. Though my Lady V— is very prudent, her zeal for me, and my lord's good-natured earnestness in my cause, might render them unguarded on the occasion; and should they attempt to make use of this secret, in order to eliminate Mrs Gerrarde, it might, at the same time, bring malicious censures both on Miss Burchell and Mr Faulkland.

I think, upon the whole, my mother is the properest person to mediate on this occasion. When Mr Arnold comes to town, she can, with due tenderness to the young lady, disclose the whole affair to him. The knowlege of this black part of Mrs Gerrarde's character, joined to her arguments, may perhaps have some weight; though, to tell you the secret bodings of my heart, I expect not much from this. I have lost my husband's love; Mrs Gerrarde possesses it all; and who knows whether he even wishes to lose his pretence for abandoning an unhappy wife. I wish, however, Mr Faulkland were returned to V— hall: should Mr Arnold know of his absence at this juncture, he might imagine possibly he was gone in quest of me.

October 12

How the scene is changed, my sister! What a melancholy reverse is here, to my late prospect of domestic happiness! I pass my nights in tears, and bitter reflections on my dismal situation. My days are spent in a painful constraint, to conceal the anguish of my own heart, that I may not aggravate that of my poor mother. My endeavours to be chearful, I perceive, have a good effect on her; she is much more composed, and seems resigned to our fate, patiently waiting for a change. I think too she is rather better in her health; she has had the advice of a physician of eminent skill; the medicines prescribed, he gives us hopes, will keep her disorder at least from gaining ground; and that she may hold out for some years.

I have prevailed on her not to give Sir George an account of my unhappy story, till I hear that Mr Faulkland has left him; because I know my brother would conceal nothing from him; and, if possible, I would have Mr Arnold's suspicions of *Him* concealed. I have many reasons for this; my own delicacy would receive a wound by it; for who knows what judgment Mr Faulkland might form on this knowlege? But my most material objection is, should he attempt to vindicate his own honour, what might be the consequence! I shudder to think of it. I know Mr Faulkland is rash, when provoked. Rather let my sufferings and my disgrace lie wrapped in oblivion, than bring any disaster on the father of my children.

October 16

Another letter from Lady V—. She tells me, that Mr Faulkland is returned from his visit to my brother. He was soon informed of my parting with Mr Arnold; 'tis the talk of the neighbourhood; every body lays it on Mrs Gerrarde. Mr Faulkland was very inquisitive to learn particulars from my lady, which, he said, he was sure I had told her; but she took care not to give him the least hint which could lead him to suppose that *He* had any share in my fate. She says, he raves like a madman; and that she finds it absolutely necessary to keep him in ignorance of the truth. She was obliged to tell him, that my having discovered Mr Arnold's amour with Mrs Gerrarde, she believed, was the sole cause of our separation. He asked her, Was she *sure* there was no other? adding, That he thought my temper had been too gentle, to fly, on a sudden, to such extremes. My lady took occasion to ask him, Whether he did not visit Mrs Gerrarde? He replied, He did sometimes, having formerly known her at Bath. She concludes with telling me, That Mr Arnold is become quite invisible to every friend he has, Mrs Gerrarde engrossing him wholly.

I hope Mr Faulkland may not suspect how much *He* is concerned in my misfortune: my absenting myself, for some time before I left home, from V— hall, and my departure from my husband, immediately after my interview with Mr Faulkland at Mrs Gerrarde's, may raise some distrust in his mind; but, while it continues merely surmise, he can have no pretence for requiring an explanation from Mr Arnold; so that, if my husband keeps his own council, which he seems inclined to do, and my lord and lady V— preserve the secret, I shall rest satisfied.

October 20

My mother has written to Sir George, and given him a full account of my situation, with a request, which I prevailed on her to make, that he would not take any notice of the affair till he saw us. My brother, perhaps, may think of a way, with tenderness and safety, to remove Mr Arnold's doubts, without farther exposing my reputation, or laying my husband open to mischief. A prudent, cool, and at the same time zealous friend, might devise some means to effect this; but I fear my brother's disregard to Mr Arnold, his diminished love for me, and his resentment to my mother, will prevent him from engaging with that alacrity or precaution that the nicety of circumstances may require. I will, therefore, wait with patience, till God, in his own time, shall raise me from the state of humiliation into which I am fallen.

October 22

With what a tortoise pace does time advance to the wretched! how dismal are those hours which are spent in reflecting on lost happiness. O Faulkland! how light was thy transgression, if we consider the consequences, compared to that which has driven me from my home, and from my children! steeled my husband's heart against me, heaped infamy on *my* head, and loaded my mother's age wth sorrow and remorse! All this is the fatal consequence of Mr Arnold's breach of his marriage-vow: all this, and much more, I fear, that is to come.

We keep ourselves entirely concealed from the knowlege of all our acquaintance: not a mortal visits us, but, now and then, Miss Burchell; and I have never stirred out of doors but to church.

October 28

Sir George has answered my mother's letter, just as I feared he would: he speaks of Mr Arnold with more contempt and aversion, than he does of me with pity or brotherly kindness. He says, 'It is well for him, that Mr Faulkland knows not of his injurious suspicions of him, or he would vindicate himself in a manner he little thinks of.' He tells us, He does not know (at this distance) how to advise; but that, as I am of so *patient* and *forbearing* a spirit, he thinks my wrongs may sleep till he comes to town, which cannot yet be these three or four weeks, having leases to renew with his tenants, and abundance of other business to do in the country. – So much for George's tenderness.

October 29

My comforts are circumscribed within a very narrow compass; for I cannot reckon one, but what I receive from poor Patty's letters, who never fails to send me weekly an account of my dear little children. They are well, thank God, and not yet abandoned by their father; but even the knowlege of this is imbittered by repeated hints of Mr Arnold's lost condition. Lost, I may call it; for his whole soul is absorbed in the mad pursuit of his own ruin. The poor girl, in the bitterness of her indignation, tells me, he has made Mrs Gerrarde a present of a favourite little pad of mine: she says, she had a mind to tear her off, when she saw her mounted upon it.

I wish not to be told of any of Mr Arnold's motions, and should forbid Patty to write to me any thing upon the subject, but that I fear my letter might fall into Mr Arnold's hands: his curiosity might lead him to open it (for the conscious mind will descend to meannesses); and, if he should see my prohibition, he would be satisfied that his servant was too free in her censures. I am sure he is quite unconcerned at *my* knowing his conduct; but I would not, nevertheless, for my children's sake, bring this tender, faithful, poor creature into disgrace with him, by convincing him of the liberty she takes, though he may very naturally suspect it.

October 30

A lady of our acquaintance, who happened to see me at church, came to pay me a visit to-day. It seems, she is intimate with the widow Arnold, who told her,very lately, that she was impatient for the commencement of term, as she then expected the cause depending between her and us would be brought to a final issue, and determined intirely in her child's favour. This account alarmed my poor mother so much, that she could not be easy till she sent for our lawyer, who was so obliging as to come upon the first summons. She acquainted him with the cause of her apprehensions; and asked him, whether there was any likelihood of the widow's succeeding. He laughed at my mother's fears, and at our antagonist's flourishes, as he called them; and said, he would not give a bent six-pence to ensure Mr Arnold's estate to him, which the ensuing term, he says, will put out of the reach of doubt. This assurance has quieted our anxiety on that head. The loss of our suit would indeed be a dreadful blow, as we should have nothing then remaining but my small jointure, for the support of Mr Arnold, myself, and our two children; not to mention Mrs Gerrarde, who, I have reason to believe, has been no inconsiderable sharer in Mr Arnold's fortune.

November 4

Six melancholy weeks are gone since I have been here, I may say, both a prisoner, and a fugitive. I count the days as they pass, as if I expected some revolution in my fate; yet, whence is it to come? No prospect as yet opens to me. Mr Arnold's law-affairs will soon call him to town: something may then happen – But does not Mrs Gerrarde come too? He cannot live without her; and I shall reap no benefit from this, but the chance of seeing my children sometimes perhaps; though he may not bring them with him, or, if he does, he may be cruel enough to refuse me the sight of them. Sir George is cold and dilatory: were he on the spot, something might be done; he might expostulate: my mother too could join arguments to intreaties: Mr Arnold perhaps might be recovered from his delusion; it is but a perhaps.

November 15

My brother is arrived in town sooner than we expected, and came this evening to pay us a visit. My altered and dejected looks, I believe, shocked him; but George wants tenderness, or at least a capacity of shewing it. After a recapitulation of my story, he asked me, 'Could I be so mean-spirited a creature as ever to think of living with Arnold again, even though he should be inclined to desire it?' I told him, he considered the matter in a wrong light; and that he ought to reflect on my reputation, and the future welfare of my two poor little girls, who would be material sufferers, from the want of my care and attention, as they grew up; not to mention the disadvantages they would enter life with, by my continuing under an aspersion which might in time become very public, as I made no doubt but that Mrs

Gerrarde would take pains to propagate it wherever she went. My mother added, Mr Arnold too might be saved from perdition, if he could be so far convinced of his wife's innocence, as to be reconciled to her, and live with her again. And pray, said Sir George, how is this to be done, if that damned woman has put it into his head, that Faulkland and you are fond of one another? Do you imagine that he will believe what *you* say? what your brother, or your mother, or even Faulkland himself, could say to the contrary? I own to you very fairly, that I so much despise the man, that, unless you will give me leave to talk to him my own way, I will have nothing to say to him at all. Would you have me *sue* to him for a reconciliation, and try to persuade him out of the belief of an imaginary injury, which probably he was glad to make a handle of to get rid of you? No, Sidney; you may be as tame as you please yourself, but it does not become your brother to be so. When I go to him, I must insist upon not having rules prescribed to me: your delicacy, in regard to Faulkland's asserting your innocence, I have nothing to say against; but there can be no objection to your brother's vindicating the honour of his family. I saw Sir George's resentment was rouzed to the highest pitch; his eyes sparkled with indignation, and his whole frame seemed agitated.

Dear brother, said I, I conjure you, (and I fell upon my knees and clasped both my arms around his) do not add to my affliction, by involving yourself and my husband in a fatal quarrel. What difference would it make to me, if Mr Arnold should fall, whether it is by your hand or Mr Faulkland's? The loss would be the same; the misfortune, the publication of my disgrace, the same. Your husband, said he, breaking from me, though a little softened, would have as good a chance as I, if it came to the hazard; or perhaps he might condescend to take you again (if you will have it so), without coming to these extremities, if I am suffered to argue properly with him. – I will not consent to your seeing him at all, said I, eagerly. The cause is now my own, he answered, coolly; but I will do nothing to aggravate your distress. I did not like the manner in which he spoke. My mother, who till now had been silent, caught the alarm. Let me intreat you, son, said she, to drop the thoughts of any violent methods with Mr Arnold. If you value your sister's peace, or have any regard to the obedience you owe me, I insist on it, that you neither see him nor write to him, without our knowlege and consent; and if you do not promise me this, I renounce all ties of kindred or affection to you: your mother has as just a sense of the honour of her family as you can have; but it is not on so hot a head, and so weak an arm, that she depends to see it justified to the world. Sir George, who was nettled at my mother's spirited rebuke, made her a low bow. No doubt of it, madam, said he, there will be a miracle wrought in my sister's favour. I would have you let her try the experiment of the ordeal: I dare say she would come off victorious, and then Mr Arnold would do you the favour to take her home again. I wish, said my mother, gravely, that there was a possibility of bringing my dear child's innocence to such a proof; I would not hesitate a minute to put it to the trial: but since there is no such a thing *now-a-days*, I will wait till God, in his own righteousness, shall judge her cause, and clear her to the world. Therefore, son, I insist upon your promise before you leave me.

I give you my word, madam, answered Sir George, I will not attempt to hold any conference with Mr Arnold without your knowlege. Will that satisfy you? It does, answered my mother; for I think I can rely upon your word. Sir George left us not very well satisfied with each other; his pride and resentment piqued to the highest. I cannot censure him for it here: he has cause; but the case is a nice and difficult one. The gratification of a private spleen ought not to enter into the measures he should pursue. Glad I am that my mother's properly-exerted resolution has tamed him a little. Though George sometimes fails in the respect which he owes her, yet I never knew him wilfully to disobey her commands, or oppose her inclinations. 'Tis well there is any hold on a disposition so ungentle and self-willed as his.

November 18

My brother has taken a very handsome house in Pall-mall, and told my mother, between jest and earnest, he is going to give her a daughter-in-law, to make up for the loss of her son-in-law. He is, in reality, making his addresses to Lady Sarah P the daughter of a new-created peer. She has a great fortune, he tells me; but I know nothing more of her. I wish him better success in his nuptials (if they take place) than I have had.

November 20

Mr Arnold is arrived in town: he came late last night, and his man called this morning to enquire how I did. The poor fellow stole out before his master was up; and was afraid of staying a minute, lest he should be wanted at home. I called him up to the dining-room: I saw an honest shame and sorrow in his countenance. How does your master do, Frank, said I? Has he brought the children to town? No, madam, said he; but they are pure and hearty. I believe my master thought it a pity to bring them out of the fresh air, as long as Mrs Patty is there to look after them. They are better where they are. I asked him, was Mr Arnold come to town to make any stay? I believe for good and all, said he. This ugly law-suit, to be sure, will detain him; but he is come *alone*, said he, with an intelligent nod: I don't suppose though he will continue long so. Well, Frank, said I, I am glad to hear your master and the children are well. Ah, madam! shaking his head as he opened the door to go out, it was a woeful day for us when you left South Park. God give every one their reward!

November 22

I have not seen my brother these two days: he does not know, I believe, that Mr Arnold is come to town; though, if he did, I am sure he will not break his word; so that I am easy on that particular. My mother says she will go to Mr Arnold herself, to *reason* with him a little. I shall not oppose it, though I have no hopes of her being able to effect any thing in my favour: she is now laid up with a cold, and is not able to come out of her room; but she pleases herself with the thought of this visit, as soon as she is able to make it. She has planned what she intends to say to him; and is resolved to let him into the whole history of Miss Burchell, that he may know, she says, the full extent of Mrs Gerrarde's wickedness; as what is there of which that woman is not capable, who could set to sale the honour of an innocent, unsuspecting creature, left to her guardianship?

November 23

Amazing, my dear Cecilia! I thought I should wonder no more at any thing, yet is my wonder now raised to astonishment – I have just received a letter from Lady V—. I have read it over and over again, and can yet scarce believe my senses. Here it is in her own words.

> 'I suppose you know, my dear Mrs Arnold, that your husband is in town; and that he left Mrs Gerrarde behind him for no other reason, I imagine, but that he did not chuse to be quite so scandalous as to let her travel with him; for we heard that she purposed following him in a few days. Patty, I conclude, may have informed you of thus much; but the extraordinary part of

the intelligence, I believe, is reserved for me to acquaint you with. Know then that Mrs Gerrarde is eloped, no-body knows whither. *Good*, you say; good, should *I* say too; but for the conclusion of my story. It is with Mr *Faulkland* she is eloped: 'tis positively true; she went off with him in triumph last night in her own chariot, and neither of them have been heard of since. I own I am so much confounded at this, I scarce know what I write.

'I am very glad, for your sake, that bad creature has quitted your husband; but that she should have drawn my cousin Faulkland in, is a matter of serious concern to me. It is evident the plan was previously concerted between them; for I am informed to-day, that Mrs Gerrarde's maid decamped at the same time, and took with her every thing valuable belonging to her mistress, several of her drawers being found open and empty. Mr Faulkland's servants have also disappeared; so that we cannot conjecture which way they are gone.

'Mr Faulkland, who was about leaving us, asked my permission to give a ball to the neighbouring ladies in our new room, which is just finished. As I concluded he would ask nobody but our own acquaintances, I readily consented; and my lord, you know, is fond of those frolics. I own I was surprized to see Mrs Gerrarde amongst the company, as undaunted as the *modestest* face there. I would not however confront Mr Faulkland so much, as to shew any disrespect to one, who was, at that time, *his* guest; but I was out of all patience to find that *she*, along with several others, was asked to supper; my too-good-natured lord joining in the invitation. Mr Faulkland made a pretence to wait on her home, and the audacious creature took that opportunity to march off with him.

Now, as Faulkland really purposed leaving V— hall the next day, I think it would have been but decent in him to have forbore this piece of barefaced libertinism, till he was fairly from under *our* roof. He might have made his assignation in any other place; but, I suppose, the lady had a mind to shew the world she is above restraint, and chose to make her infamy a sort of triumph.

'I am quite angry with my lord, for only laughing at this, and calling it a piece of spirited gallantry in them both. He says, he is delighted to think how your good man will shake his ears, when he hears his mistress has left him in the lurch, and gone off with another lover. I should smile too; but that it makes me sad to think, that Mr Faulkland, of whom I had so good an opinion, should so impose upon my judgment, and forfeit his own character, for so vile a creature.

'Pardon me, my dear madam; I am so full of my own reflections, on the interest *I* take in this affair, that I have been forgetful of how much more moment it may be to *you*. Heaven grant that your husband may think of making himself amends, in returning to a faithful and amiable wife, for the loss of a deceitful, jilting mistress. Surely this event must open his eyes, or he deserves to lose them. I hope to embrace you in London in a very little time; till then, believe me,

'My dear Mrs Arnold,

'Your most assured friend and servant,

V— hall, Nov. 12 'A.V.'

Well, my Cecilia, what say you to this? Are you not as much surprized as I am? Mr Faulkland to emerge at last the favoured gallant of Mrs Gerrarde! Prodigious! I confess, my dear, I am so selfish as not to participate with Lady V— in her uneasiness on this occasion. That Mrs Gerrarde flies from my husband, I am glad; and that Mr *Faulkland* is the very man she chose to fly with, I am still gladder: he, of all men living, I would have wished (though least expected) to be the person. This explains every thing that is passed. Surely, as Lady V— says, this *must* open Mr Arnold's eyes. I can now discover a double reason for my poor deluded man's having his imagination poisoned with jealousy. Mrs Gerrarde did not aim singly at separating my husband and me: this, perhaps, was but a secondary consideration; or who knows whether it was at all intended? But she most certainly designed to secure herself against all suspicions, by making me the object of them; and effectually to blind Mr Arnold, persuaded him, that Mr Faulkland's visits, made to her, were only in the hope of seeing me.

Let her views have been what they would, this event was beyond my hopes. Some glimmerings of comfort begin to break in upon me. Methinks my heart feels much lighter than it did. How Sir George will stare at this account! My mother will lift up her eyes; but she has no opinion of Mr Faulkland's morals, and therefore will be the less surprized. I pity Miss Burchell: this is an irremediable bar to her hopes; faint and unsupported as they were before, they must now entirely vanish.

November 24

I gave you a copy of Lady V—'s letter, while the subject was warm at my heart, and before I shewed it to any one; but my mother and my brother have now both seen it. My mother (just as I expected), without any great emotions of surprize, only exclaimed against their wickedness; but said, she could not help rejoicing in it, as *I*, she hoped, would derive happiness from their accumulated crimes. Sir George read the letter twice over before he uttered a word; and then said, It was *strange*; upon his soul, most unaccountable; and that either Faulkland was run mad, or that woman had bewitched him. When he was with me, said he, at Sidney Castle, he did not so much as mention her. I asked him, whether he was acquainted with Mr Arnold (for I had written him word of your marriage, when he was abroad)? He told me, he had seen both you and him, two or three times, at Lord V—'s; but that as he did not wish to renew his acquaintance with you, he had never visited your husband. I presume he was not then a stranger to his connection with Mrs Gerrarde; at least to the conjectures of the neighbourhood upon it: but as it was then but a matter of opinion, and he knew not of the difference between you and your husband, 'tis probable he did not chuse to disgust me more against my brother-in-law, by hinting at this circumstance. He expressed great acknowlegements to my mother, when I told him of the notice she had taken of Miss Burchell; though, he said, he found (from my account of your marriage) that she had deferred her conference with that young lady, till it was too late for her testimony to be of any service to him. As I knew nothing of what had passed between my mother and Miss Burchell, I could give him no satisfaction on that subject; and the recollection of past transactions being equally disagreeable to us both, I avoided ever mentioning them after our first conversation; nor do I remember that Mrs Gerrarde's name occurred once.

My mother now began to exult over Sir George, and took advantage of the surprize and consternation that Lady V—'s letter had thrown him into. This is your boasted friend, said she; the man whose *honour* and *generosity* were not to be questioned, and whose *utmost* crime was a youthful folly that he was surprized into with a silly girl. I am pleased, however, that *this* has proved I was not so grossly mistaken in believing him a loose man. Mrs Gerrarde is the fittest mate for him, and I am glad they are gone together.

Sir George was too much mortified at the flagrant misconduct of his friend to attempt excusing him: he contented himself with repeating, It was the strangest thing he ever knew in his life.

My mother then told him Mr Arnold was come to town; and that, as things had taken such a turn, she hoped herself to be able to bring him to the use of his judgment; and therefore thought it would not be at all necessary for my brother to interfere. Sir George said, With all his heart; if her ladyship should be able to patch up a reconciliation that would save his sister's credit, and she could be so *extremely* pliant as to think of living with such a husband again, he should not give himself any farther trouble about the matter; but, in *his* opinion, the affair wore a much odder aspect than it did before. I find Mr Faulkland's behaviour sticks with him, and has a little cooled his zeal towards him.

November 25

I have had a letter from Patty, who confirms my Lady V—'s account of the lovers flight; and she tells me one of Mrs Gerrarde's servants is gone off express to town; I suppose, to bring Mr Arnold the news: for they are all in confusion at her house, and know not what is become of their mistress; but they are certain she is gone with Mr Faulkland. Patty adds, The servants believe this scheme had long been concerted, Mr Faulkland having been a private visitor to their mistress for a good while.

I must confess I am astonished at it: it has sunk the man extremely in my opinion.

November 26

Miss Burchell has just been here. Poor creature, she is quite stunned with the news: she could scarce believe it at first, till my mother desired I would shew her Lady V—'s letter, and Patty's, which corroborated all she said. She then gave way to tears and lamentations; saying, That cruel woman was born to be the destruction of every-body she had any connection with. *I* have found it so; *you*, madam (to me), have done so too; Mr Arnold, I believe, has been a great sufferer; Mr Faulkland is *now* her victim. Inconsiderate and barbarous as he is, I grieve for him.

November 30

I have heard nothing of Mr Arnold. Indeed it is hardly possible that I should: we are shut up here from all commerce with the world. My mother's illness has confined her to her bed-chamber; we admit no visitors, and I never leave her. I long to know how he takes the ingratitude of his mistress; but I see nobody who converses with him. My brother and Miss Burchell are the only people we see. The latter is pretty often with us; as for Sir George, he only looks in upon us now and then, and we all seem in an aukward situation. I wish my mother were well enough to call on Mr Arnold: I am very anxious to know what his sentiments are; at least in regard to Mrs Gerrarde.

December 6

I have been almost asleep, my dear Cecilia, for this week past; but I have been rouzed this morning in a most extraordinary manner. Sir George called on us; he ran up stairs in a violent hurry; and had a countenance, when he entered the room, that spoke wonders before he opened his mouth. He hardly gave himself time to ask me how I did (though he had not seen me for three days), before he took a bundle of papers out of his pocket, which he gave me. 'Tis from Faulkland, said he, and may be worth your knowlege. Upon opening the cover, I found it contained, at least, four sheets of paper, written on every side. Bless me, brother, said I, do you expect I should take the trouble to read all this? He answered, You may read it at your leisure: you will find it will pay you for the mighty trouble of a perusal. Sir George left me presently; and having read this extraordinary letter to myself, for I happened to be in my own room when my brother came to me, I sate me down to give you a copy of it. My mother, who coughed almost the whole night, is now endeavouring to get a little sleep; so that I will scribble on as fast as I can, while I have no interruption.

Boulogne, Nov. 30, 1704.

My dear Bidulph,

I am in haste to vindicate myself to you, but in much more haste to do so to Mrs Arnold; who, if she bestows a thought at all on me, must, I am sure, hold me in the utmost contempt; and great reason would she have, if things were always as they appear. Methinks I see her beautiful scorn at hearing I had carried off Mrs Gerrarde. What a paltry fellow *you* must think me too. And yet I *have* carried her off, and she is now in my possession, not displeased with her situation; and I might, if I would, be as happy as Mrs Gerrarde can make me: but I assure you, Sir George, I have no designs but what are for the good both of her soul and body; and I have hitherto treated her like a vestal. What a paradox is here, say you? But have patience till I tell you the story of my knight-errantry.

You are to know then, that as Arnold's amour with Mrs Gerrarde was no secret at V— hall, from the moment I heard it, I meditated a design of breaking the detestable union; not out of regard either to him or her, but in hopes of restoring, to the most amiable of women, a besotted husband's heart, which nothing but downright magic, infernal witchcraft, could have robbed her of. The woman is handsome, 'tis true; but she is a silly toad, and as fantastic as an ape. I had formed this design, I say, from the first notice I had of the intrigue; and, in consequence of this, resolved to renew my acquaintance with Mrs Gerrarde: for I had *known* her before; known her to my cost. She it was, this identical devil, whom I have now in my power, that was the cause of Miss Burchell's misfortune; and therefore the remote cause of my losing Miss Bidulph. Had it not been for her, I should never have had the fall of that unhappy girl to answer for. *I* should not, I say (mark that); for the mercenary witch was determined to sell her to somebody, when my ill stars threw me in her way. I do not rank this affair in the number of capital crimes; and yet I never think of it without a pang. If half of my fortune would retrieve the girl's peace of mind, I would give it freely: but it is past now, and cannot be helped. She had the good fortune never to be suspected; and, if she keeps her own council, probably never will. If I die a bachelor (as I believe I shall), I will leave her my whole fortune. What can a man do more?

How I ramble from my subject! I meant only to tell you what my design was in carrying off Mrs Gerrarde. In order to effect it, as I said before, it was necessary for me to renew my acquaintance with her; and accordingly I put on a bold face, and made her a visit. She was not surprized at this, our former intimacy giving me a sufficient pretence for it. She received me with a pleased familiarity, which convinced me my company was far from being disagreeable to her; and I am sure, had my views been other than they were, I should have met with as kind a reception as my heart could have wished; for she certainly thought of retaining me in her service unknown to Arnold. I was soon aware of this; for, though she often desired to see me, she always contrived it at such times, as she was sure of not being surprized by him. This was, in some measure, meeting my purpose half way; but though I wanted to disengage her from Arnold, I did not mean to sacrifice myself to her; and our views, in the material point, were very different: mine were only to part her from her gallant; her's were to share her favours between us: for she did not intend to let go her hold on him; and I believe my backwardness, in pushing my good fortune, began to disgust her; but the time for carrying my plan into execution was not yet arrived; it could not be till Arnold's departure from South-Park. I meant to carry Mrs Gerrarde away with the appearance of her own consent; and I knew this was impossible, whilst her lover remained so near her. I had formed but a rough sketch of my plan when I received your letter, which summoned me to Sidney-Castle; and I resolved not to apprize you of it, till my enterprize was crowned with success; more especially as you were then quite ignorant of your sister's wrongs.

On my return from visiting you, the first news I heard at V— hall was, that Mr Arnold and his lady were parted. I curst my own dilatoriness, that I had not executed my plan before things were brought to such extremities; for I well knew it was that artful fiend who had occasioned it, though I then little thought how fatally *I* had contributed towards the misfortune of the ever-amiable and most-respectable of women.

Lady V— told me, that your sister, having discovered her husband's infidelity, had left him on that account; but my lord soon let me into the whole secret. Oh! Sir George, that angel, who deserved the first monarch in the universe, to be cast off by an undiscerning dolt! and *I*, though innocently, the accursed cause. I cannot think with patience of what the divine creature has suffered on my account; but was it not all, from the beginning, owing to Mrs Gerrarde, that avenging fury, sent on earth as a scourge for the sins of me and of my ancestors? – I rave – but no wonder – I am mad upon this subject. – But to return: I then recollected, that the day before I set out for Sidney Castle, I received a message from Mrs Gerrarde in the morning, desiring my company to drink coffee with her that evening. I obeyed the summons, little expecting to meet Mrs Arnold at her house, whom I had never seen there before. The effect my presence had on her extremely surprized me: she presently quitted the room. Mrs Gerrarde took that opportunity of telling me, that she had dropped in on her very unexpectedly; but, as she supposed she would go directly away, we should have an hour to chat by ourselves. She then followed your sister out, and I remained alone in the parlour. Whilst I was reflecting on this odd encounter, which I did not then imagine had been brought about by design, Mrs Gerrarde came in to me, saying, your sister was so ill she was under a necessity of accompanying her home, and had ordered her chariot for that purpose: she made an apology for being obliged to leave me, and said she should be glad to see me the next day. I took my leave, and in going out saw Mr Arnold at the door, which I judged was the true reason of Mrs Gerrarde's dismissing me.

I set out for Wiltshire the next morning; and though there was something odd in the whole of this incident, I believed it was owing to chance alone, and thought no more of it; till, upon my Lord V—'s telling me the true cause of your sister's disgrace, I found that this serpent had laid the whole plan on purpose to destroy her. You see (for to be sure you know all the particulars) how she seduced the innocent Mrs Arnold into this fatal visit, having first engaged me to come at the very point of time when she knew the husband would surprize us; for *his* coming, you may be satisfied, was not unexpected.

I own to you, Sir George, in the first motions of my rage, I could have stabbed Arnold, Mrs Gerrarde, and myself; but my Lord V— calmed my transports, by telling me, that it was your sister's earnest request that this detestable secret should be kept from my knowlege; and that Lady V—, who had intrusted him with it, would never forgive him, if she knew he had divulged it. This reflection brought me back to my senses, and I burned with impatience to execute my first plan, which Mrs Gerrarde's repeated crimes now called upon me to accelerate. I communicated my design to Lord V—, who was delighted with it; for he perfectly adores your sister. This, said he, though not such a vengeance as that wicked woman deserves, must in the end be productive of what you wish, and Mrs Arnold may be restored to her peace, without injury to her character, or mischief to any-body.

Having settled my measures with Lord V—, I went to pay a visit to Mrs Gerrarde. The cockatrice affected to speak with surprize and concern of your sister's separation from her husband. I asked her, had she, who was so intimate with both, heard any reason assigned for it? She shook her head, and by a pretended sorrow in her looks, and a mysterious silence, invited me to press for an explanation of her meaning. She told me at length, with a seeming reluctance, that 'poor Mrs Arnold, though to be sure she was a sensible woman, was not without the little frailties and passions of her sex; and that, *astonishing* and *groundless* as her suspicions were, she had taken it into her head to be jealous of Mr Arnold; and with whom do you think, of all people, she suspects him?' I cannot imagine, said I. Why truly with *me*, replied the undaunted Jezebel, and looked as if she expected *I* should be as much amazed as she pretended to be. I affected to laugh at it; and changing the discourse, put an end to my visit.

The measures I had to observe required some management. It would not answer the full extent of my purpose to rob Mr Arnold of his dear, if it did not appear at the same time that she had left him with her own consent. To bring about this, it was necessary that the flight on her part should seem premeditated; which would not carry any face, unless she took with her such of her moveables as were most valuable. This I knew could not be done without the assistance of her maid, whom I therefore not only resolved to trust, but also to make her a partner in her mistress's elopement.

Having settled thus much of the plan in my own mind, I began my operations, by making the maid presents every time I visited the mistress; and I took care to give those visits as much the air of an amour as I possibly could. I dare swear the girl thought Mrs Gerrarde and I were upon the best terms imaginable. I affected to come at such hours as I was sure Mrs Gerrarde was alone; I always made my visits short, as if through fear of being surprized with her; and went so far as to leave my chariot (when I came in it) at a distance from the house, and walked to it alone, with the caution of one fearful of being observed. It was a matter of indifference to me whether Mrs Gerrarde knew of this or not; my business was only to excite suspicions of an intrigue amongst her servants, in order to answer a future purpose: but if she were to know with what extreme precaution I visited her, my prudence could not but be very agreeable to her: she had her measures to observe as well as myself. As it was of consequence to her to conceal our acquaintance from Arnold's knowlege, she must necessarily be pleased at the pains I took (without her laying herself open in making the request) to conceal it from him; and she saw I was as careful as she could wish never to interfere with him.

In short, we carried on a private intercourse, that, if it could not be called gallantry, was something very like it; for I amused, complimented, and flattered her so agreeably, that I believe she began to think herself sure of me, and wondered I did not make a better use of the favourable disposition she was in towards me; but I trifled with such dexterity, that even she, with all the cunning she is mistress of, could not possibly fathom my design.

Having thus laid the foundation of my plot, I made no doubt of being able to execute it, with my Lord V—'s assistance: he was in raptures at the thought of our enterprize, and swore he would never have forgiven me, if I had not allowed him a share in it. He said, I would give my right-hand to make Mrs Arnold happy; adding, besides it will save her husband from destruction; for, to my knowlege, that woman has already almost ruined his fortune.

I asked him, might we venture to let my lady into the secret? He said, by no means; my lady was too squeamish to be trusted with such a notable exploit; but, when the affair was over, he would take upon him to excuse me to her, after he had diverted himself a little with her surprize.

I fretted to death at Arnold's staying so long in the country, as it delayed my enterprize. There was one circumstance indeed that a little compensated for this vexation; and that was, that my long stay at V— hall, which could be no secret to him, though he dropped visiting there on purpose to avoid me, might in some measure help to efface his injurious suspicions with regard to his lady and me; besides, it gave the better colour to my other designs.

At last the long-sought-for opportunity arrived. Arnold was obliged to go to London on his law-affairs. I took care to inform myself of the day from Mrs Gerrarde's maid; and learnt at the same time that her mistress purposed going to town in a week after; for she still endeavoured to save appearances, and dared to the last to pretend to reputation. I proposed giving a ball, to take my leave of the ladies, on the night subsequent to the day fixed for Arnold's departure from South-Park. My lord, almost as anxious for the event as myself, immediately dispatched invitations all over the neighbourhood: there was not a person of any fashion left unasked. Mr Arnold and Mrs Gerrarde, you may be sure, were not forgot. From the former, as we expected, we received a civil apology; from the latter, a message that she would be sure to come.

This was at the distance of eight days from the appointed time. In the interim, I continued to visit Mrs Gerrarde as usual, and took care to bespeak her for a partner. Arnold went to town as opportunely as we could wish. I called on Mrs Gerrarde the same morning; and having my lord's permission for it, engaged her to come early enough to drink tea, as there were a good many more ladies invited for the same purpose; and, at going away, I dropped a few mysterious hints to her maid.

In the evening there was a very large company met at V— hall; and having concerted my whole plan, when the ladies were engaged at the tea-table, I slipped out, mounted my horse, and rode to Mrs Gerrarde's house. I desired to see her maid; and, taking her aside, told her not to be surprized; but that her lady was to go off with me that night: that the thing had, for certain reasons, not been determined on till that very evening: that I had just snatched a minute to desire her to get all her ladies trinkets together, and whatever money and bills she might have in her escruitore. In order to this, I gave her a parcel of small keys, which I had carried in my pocket for the purpose; and bid her hold herself in readiness against seven o'clock, when a person should call on her, who would conduct her to a place where she should find her lady and me.

I needed no arguments to persuade the girl; the thing appeared plausible enough: she was fully convinced of the intimacy between her mistress and me; and knowing her too well to have a doubt of her baseness, she concluded I acted by Mrs Gerrarde's directions, and promised punctually to obey them. She said, she could easily carry away in the dark as many things as she could conveniently carry; and, to avoid observation from the rest of the servants, she would wait at a cottage hard by, which she named to me, till her conductor arrived.

Whether any of the keys I gave her would fit the locks or not, I was not much concerned; if they did not, I concluded she would think her mistress had made a mistake; and that she would force them open, rather than fail. Having settled this material point, I got back to my Lord V—'s, without having been missed by the company.

Our ball was very well conducted; I danced with Mrs Gerrarde, and we passed a very agreeable evening. We supped at twelve, and she had ordered her chariot to come a little after that hour; but I had given my fellows their cue. As the dancing was not renewed, the company broke up between one and two. Mrs Gerrarde was one of the first that offered to go; but as her servants were not to be found, she was detained till every-body else had taken their leave. At length her coachman and footman were found in the cellar, with one of my mean, all so drunk that they were not able to stand. Her servants were really so, and mine counterfeited so well, there was no discovering the cheat. In this emergency, nothing was more natural than the offering my servants to attend her home, and of course to wait on her myself to see her safe. She readily accepted the first offer, but declined the other. This was easily got over; I handed her into her chariot, and stepped in after her. Our route was settled;: we drove from my Lord V—'s door; and turning short from the road that led to Mrs Gerrarde's house, we struck down a lane which was to carry us by cross-roads to our first destined stage, which was at the distance of seven miles. This was no other than a poor gardener's house, to which place two of my emissaries had been dispatched that day to wait our coming, with a travelling chariot, and four stout horses. I had taken care, according to promise, to send a trusty groom for the maid, with a boy to carry her luggage. They were both well mounted, and had orders to carry her to an inn on the road to Rochester, and within about a mile of the town. This inn was kept by a fellow, who had formerly been my servant; I had placed him there, and he was intirely at my devotion. He had already received his instructions, and his house was to be our second stage. I concluded the maid had arrived there long before us, having had six or seven hours the start of us, and the place was not more than twenty miles from her own house.

Mrs Gerrarde was not immediately aware of our going out of the road; she was in high spirits, and I kept her in chat. As soon as she perceived it, she cried out, with some surprize, Lord, Mr Faulkland! where is the fellow carrying us? He has missed his way. She called to him; but the coachman, who had orders not to stop unless I spoke to him, only drove the faster. Pray do call to him, said she; the wretch has certainly got drunk with the rest of the servants. I told here there was no possibility of turning in the narrow road in which we then were: that when we got out of it, I would speak to the coachman; and begged of her, in the mean while, not to be frightened. The lane was a very long one, but our rapid wheels soon carried us to the end of it, where I had appointed Pivet and one of my footmen to meet us on horseback. I had another servant behind the chariot, whom I purposed to send back with it in the morning.

At the sight of two horsemen, who were apparently waiting for us, she screamed out, Oh! the villain; he has brought us here to be robbed. She had a good many jewels on her; and, to say the truth, had some reason for her fears. The chariot had now got on a good open road, and the horses rather flew than galloped. The two horsemen joined us, and kept up with us at full speed. I saw she was heartily frightened, and thought it time to undeceive her. I was not ill-natured enough to keep her longer under the apprehensions of highwaymen, and thought she would be less shocked at finding there was a design upon her person, than on her diamond ear-rings. Now, said I, taking one of her hands with rather more freedom than respect, since we are out of all danger of discovery, or any possibility of pursuit, I will tell you a secret; and I spoke with an easy assured tone. She drew her hand away. What do you mean, Sir? Nothing, madam, but to have the pleasure of your company in a little trip I am going to take: believe me, you are not in the least danger; you are under my protection; those are my servants that you see riding with us; and you may judge of the value I set upon you, by the pains I have taken to get you into my possession. Lord, Mr Faulkland! why sure you can't be serious! Never more so in my life, madam; I have long had a design upon you; but your connection with Mr Arnold – *My* connection with Mr Arnold, Sir! interrupting me; I don't understand you! – Come, come, Mrs Gerrarde; you and I are old acquaintance, you know; 'tis no time for dissembling. He has been a happy man long enough: 'tis time for a woman of your spirit to be tired of him; especially as I think I may say, without vanity, you do not change for the worse in falling into my hands. The lady had now recovered her courage; she was no longer in fears of being robbed, and her spirits returned. You audacious creature! how dare you treat me thus? Have you the assurance to insinuate that there was any thing criminal in my attachment to Mr Arnold and his family? My dear madam, I accuse you of no attachment to any of his family; he himself was the only-favoured person – Sure there never was such an impertinent wretch! – But I know the author of this scandal: it was Mrs— (and she dared to prophane your sister's honoured name); but I despise her; and Mr Arnold shall soon know how I have been affronted; and she fell a crying. – My dear Mrs Gerrarde, I beg your pardon; I did not mean to offend you: if Mr Arnold admired you, he did no more than what every man does who sees you. I beseech you to compose yourself; by all that is good, I mean you no harm: be calm, I conjure you, and don't spoil the prettiest face in England with crying. A daring, provoking creature, she sobbed; what could put such an attempt as this in your head? and to what place are you carrying me? Only to France, my dear creature? have you have been there? To France! to France! she exclaimed; and do you dare to think you shall carry me there? Oh! you'll like it of all things, said I, when you get there – What do you think her reply was: Why, neither more nor less than a good box on the ear. I catched hold of her hand, and kissed it: you charming vixen, how I admire you for your spirit! She endeavoured to wrest her hand from me; but I held them both fast, for fear of another blow. Base, insolent, ravisher, villain! As she rose in her epithets, I replied with, lovely, charming, adorable, tender, gentle creature – She cried again; but they were spiteful tears, and did not create in me the least touch of that pity, which, on any other occasion, they might have moved me to.

I was glad our altercations had a short truce, by the chariot's stopping at the gardener's cottage, where I had ordered my equipage to wait. All the family were in bed but the man's wife, who came curt'sying to the door. I led, or rather lifted, Mrs Gerrarde out of the chariot; for she would not give me her hand; and begging she would repose herself for a few minutes, whilst I gave orders to my servants, put her into the good woman's hands. She went sullenly in, without making me any answer: and seeing nobody but the old woman, she was convinced that complaints, or an attempt to escape, would be equally fruitless, and so prudently acquiesced. I soon dispatched my orders: I made the footman, who came behind the chariot, mount the box, and directed him to drive to an inn in the next village to Mrs Gerrarde's house, and from thence to send it home by some one who did not know to whom he belonged. I then ordered my own equipage to the door; and entering the cottage, told the lady I was ready to attend her. The old woman presently vanished; so that seeing nobody to apply to, she suffered me very quietly to put her into my chariot, and I placed myself by her. It was made on purpose for travelling, and I took care to have nothing but wooden windows; to which I had the precaution to add a couple of spring-locks, which shut on drawing up, and were not without difficulty to be opened. One of the windows was already up, and I flurted up the other as soon as I got into the coach. It was a fine moon-light morning, the postilion cracked his whip, and, though the roads were deep and dirty, the four horses darted away like lightning.

I believe, madam, said I, you are by this time convinced that my scheme is too well laid to be baffled by any efforts you can make. I mean to treat you with due respect, and beg you will use me with a little more gentleness than you have done; that is all the favour I shall ask in return, till you yourself are disposed to shew me more.

You are the most amazing creature, said she, that ever breathed! What is the meaning that, in the whole course of our acquaintance, your behaviour never gave me room to believe that you were serious in your designs on me, and now at once you souse upon your prey like a hawk? I'll answer you in two words, said I. When we first met, you had a husband; since the renewal of our acquaintance (you'll pardon me), it was no secret that you had a favoured lover in Mr Arnold: I am not of a temper to solicit a lady by stealth, and I would not give a pinch of snuff for the woman who is not intirely at my disposal. Your attachments to Arnold forbad this, and I was determined to have you all to myself. My attachments to Mr Arnold! cried she, impudently, again. Ay, said I, coolly, it began to be talked of so openly, that your reputation was mangled at every tea-table in the country; and had you staid much longer there, you would have found yourself deserted by every female of character that knew you. Mr Arnold's parting with his wife, was by every-body charged to your account; and as she is reckoned a very *good sort* of a woman (was not that a pretty phrase?), every one took her part, and were not sparing in their invectives against you. Add to all this, that Arnold has certainly run out his fortune, and is so involved that it will not be possible for him long to make those returns of generosity which your merit deserves. – You and I have been acquainted long; I am no stranger to your circumstances; I know, at Captain Gerrarde's death, your pension as his widow, and the very small jointure at Ashby, was the whole of your income. Arnold's love, it is apparent, has hitherto been bountiful; how long it could be in his power to continue it so, may be a question worth your considering.

I found I had mortified her pride, by mentioning the narrowness of her circumstances, and the demolition of her character. If all you say *were* true, Sir, which is far from being the case (with a toss of her head), you will find it no very easy matter to make me amends for what I shall perhaps lose for ever by this violence of yours, notwithstanding the *smallness* of my income, which you seem so well informed of. I have a considerable sum of money, and some valuable jewels, lying by me, of which my servants may very probably rob me. I assured her, upon my honour, I would make good to her every thing she should lose through my means, and would take care her situation should never be upon the same precarious footing which it had been. I did not chuse to mention the circumstance of my having secured her maid and her money too; I reserved that for an agreeable surprize. I had measures to observe; I did not want to be on good terms with her too soon for obvious reasons, as nothing was farther from my heart than a thought of gallantry.

For this purpose, I assumed a more distant behaviour, and affected to shew her something like respect. I did not drop the least hint of my knowing that Mr Arnold had made his lady uneasy on my account, much less that I suspected her for the wicked contriver of that mischief. I deferred the discussing of this point till a more favourable opportunity should offer, when it would be in my power to make a better use of it.

My design was by degrees to make her satisfied enough with her situation, not to wish to return to Arnold. When I had once brought her to this, I judged it would not be difficult to carry her still farther, to the point I aimed at; and that was, to write a letter to him of my dictating. You will think this was a strange expectation, and yet it was what I resolved to accomplish. I knew the turn of the mind I had to deal with: bring a woman of this sort into good-humour, and it is easy to wheedle her into compliance. She has no solid understanding; but possesses, in the place of it, a sort of flashy wit, that imposes on common hearers, and makes her pass for what is called clever. With a great deal of vanity, and an affectation of tenderness, which covers the most termagant spirit that ever animated a female breast, her ruling and governing passion is avarice; and yet, strange to tell! generosity is of all things what she professes to admire, and is most studious of having thought her characteristic. Her pretensions to this virtue I have opposed to her vice of avarice, as the terms appropriated to each seem most contrary in their natures; yet I do not mean by generosity, that bounteous disposition which is commonly understood by the word: no, no; she aimed at the reputation of this virtue in our most exalted idea of it, and would fain be thought a woman of a *great soul.* This phrase was often in her mouth; and though her whole conduct gave the lye to her professions, she would tell you fifty stories, without a word of truth in any of them, to prove how nobly she had acted on such and such occasions. On the knowlege of this part of her temper, I chiefly built my hopes of success.

I kept up a sort of forced conversation during the rest of our journey. She was sullen, but not rude. As I was far from desiring to come to an eclaircissement with her, I did not wish to have her in better temper.

We reached the inn, which was about a mile on our side

of Rochester, at eight o'clock in the morning. This was a favourable hour, as by that time every traveller must have left the stages they lay at. The house stood alone, and luckily enough had no company in it. My old servant, Lamb, had received my instructions by letter, and was prepared accordingly for our reception. This was the place to which I had ordered the maid to be carried; she had arrived there some time before us, and was safely lodged.

The chariot drove into the court-yard close to the door of the inn; the step was let down in an instant, and Mrs Lamb appeared to receive us. We both darted into the house. Dressed as we were for a ball, we made an odd appearance as travellers at that hour of the morning. I believe this consideration made Mrs Gerrarde very readily hurry upstairs with the woman of the house.

I enquired for Mrs Gerrarde's maid, having given orders to Lamb that she should not been seen till I first spoke to her. I was carried into the room where she was: she seemed very glad that we were arrived. I desired her to lay out her lady's toilet, which I concluded she had brought with her; for that Mrs Gerrarde would presently put herself in a proper habit for travelling. The maid told me she had brought her mistress's riding-dress with her, and as many other things of her wearing apparel as she could conveniently carry. I saw a vast heap of things lying unpacked on a bed which was in the room, and asked her how she had managed so cleverly as to get such a number of things together without observation. She told me she had lost no time, from the minute I left her, till the arrival of her guide; but had employed the interval in carrying out some of the best of her lady's cloaths piece by piece, and conveying them to the cottage, which she could easily do without the servants seeing her; for as it was dark, she passed in and out without observation. Here she huddled them into a large portmanteau. After this she went to examine her lady's escruitore; but was a long time puzzled in endeavouring to open it, as none of the keys I had given her answered. She endeavoured to force it open with as little noise as possible, but in vain. She then had recourse to a second trial of the keys, when one of them, which probably had been passed by before, luckily opened the lock; and she secured all the money and jewels she could find. These, said she, kept me in continual dread all the way as I travelled; for I have eight hundred pounds in bank notes; and though my lady has such a quantity of jewels on her, I am sure I have as many more about me, which I have hid in different parts of my cloaths.

I commended the girl's diligence, as indeed it deserved; and having before ordered tea and coffee into Mrs Gerrarde's room, I now went in to breakfast with her. I found the woman of the house still with her, at which I was not at all uneasy; for as she had been tutored by her husband, I knew she was not to be wrought upon, if Mrs Gerrarde had attempted it.

As I did not at that time desire a *tête à tête* with her, I contrived to keep Mrs Lamb in the room, by desiring her to drink tea with us.

When we had done breakfast, I told Mrs Gerrarde, that as I feared she was a good deal fatigued, if it was agreeable to her, we would remain where we were for that day; and that I would by all means have her think of taking some rest. She said she was extremely tired, and should like to get a little sleep. I think, madam, you had better go to bed, said Mrs Lamb; I have a very quiet chamber ready, where no noise in the house can disturb you. Shew me to it, answered Mrs Gerrarde, with a tone of weariness and ill-humour. The woman obeyed; I followed: she carried her to the door of the room where the maid was, and throwing it open, Mrs Gerrarde, who supposed she was attending her, went in: I stepped in after her; Mrs Lamb withdrew.

Mrs Gerrarde's astonishment at the sight of her maid, is past description. Rachael! in a tone of admiration. Rachael, who did not think there was any thing unexpected or extraordinary in their meeting, quite at a loss to guess at what her mistress wondered, answered her in her turn with some surprize, Madam! and waited, expecting she would give her some orders; which finding the lady did not, the maid asked her, very composedly, Would she please to undress? I hope, Madam, said I, stepping forward, that Mrs Rachael has taken care to bring you every thing you may have occasion for; I shall leave you in her hands, and wish you a good repose. Strange, astonishing creature! said Mrs Gerrarde, looking at me with less anger than surprize. I bowed, and left the room.

I ordered Mrs Lamb to have an eye to my prisoners; and heartily tired as I was, between dancing and travelling, I undressed and threw myself into bed. I slept till six o'clock in the evening; then rose, and put myself into a habit fitter for my journey than that in which I came; and which I had sent in a post-trunk before me, by the messenger whom I had employed to apprize Lamb of my coming.

Mrs Gerrarde was not yet stirring. I called for Rachael, and asked her how she had come off with her lady, upon telling her the manner of her falling into my snare. Rachael told me her lady wondered mightily at my art, and said I was the *strangest gentleman* that ever was born. My friend Rachael softened the expression I fancy; I am sure Mrs Gerrarde did not call me a strange *gentleman*. She said her mistress smiled two or three times at her relation, particularly at my giving her the keys. I found, upon the whole, that my conduct in securing to her her money and her jewels, together with the attendance of her maid, had a good deal appeased her resentment.

Mrs Gerrarde did not rise till near eight o'clock. I had ordered as elegant a dinner as the house could afford; and the lady having put herself into a genteel dishabille, with great alacrity sat down to table, and did not appear to have fretted away her appetite. I would suffer no one to attend but Rachael. I told Mrs Gerrarde that I purposed setting out for Dover that night, and that as it could not be supposed her maid should be able to ride so far, and that a second carriage with four horses (as less might not be able to keep pace with us) would be liable to observation, I would, if she pleased, resign my place in the chariot to Mrs Rachael, and attend her myself on horseback. She answered me coldly, Since she *must* go, it was indifferent to her who was to be her companion. Though the motive I offered for this manner of travelling was not without its weight, yet my true reason was to avoid being boxed up so long again with Mrs Gerrarde. My time was not yet come for explanations, and I was afraid of being upon good terms with her too soon.

The remainder of the evening was spent by her and her maid in carefully packing up their baggage, which had been brought in a confused huddle to the inn. Mrs Gerrarde had a convenient trunk bought at Rochester for the purpose, and assisted herself in laying them up safely.

She equipped herself in a smart riding-dress, and at eleven o'clock, without any great reluctance, permitted me to put her and her maid into the chariot. The inn had no company in it, at least that we saw; and our host was too discreet to let any of his servants be in the way. I mounted my horse, and triumphantly galloped off with my prize.

We reached Dover early next morning, and immediately got on board the packet. The lady by this time appeared so perfectly serene, that I believe in my soul I should not have got rid of her, if I had desired her to have gone back again; but she had assumed a new air, and affected a fine tender melancholy in her countenance. I guessed at her thoughts, and found afterwards my conjecture right. Will you believe me, Sir George, when I tell you the baggage had formed serious *honourable designs* upon my person? Fact, upon my word. I saw it presently (you know my knack of reading people's minds in their faces), and was not sorry for the discovery; for though I determined not on any account to encourage such a wild expectation, yet I intended to make a *discreet* use of it; besides, I knew it would afford me a handle for keeping a *respectful* distance.

We landed next evening. She had been very sick at sea, and continued so much out of order, that she was put to bed as soon as we got to the inn. She ordered her maid not to stir from her; the very thing I wished; so that I had nothing to do but to be very troublesome in my enquiries after her health, and very sorry for her indisposition.

The next morning however set all to rights; and after congratulating her on her recovery, and the revival of her beauty, I told her I meant to carry her to Boulogne, whither I had sent Pivet the night before to take lodgings for us, in a private house which he knew. I found that neither Mrs Gerrarde nor her maid spoke French; a circumstance I was very glad of, though the former bitterly lamented her having *forgot* it. She made not the least objection to the travelling from Calais to Boulogne, as she had done before: her late indisposition gave me a pretence for insisting on Rachael's attending her in the chariot.

The lodgings Pivet had taken were very handsome; our apartments were on the same floor, separated only by a lobby. Mrs Rachael had a little bed fitted up for her by my directions in her lady's dressing-room. Thus far I had sailed before the wind; but now came the difficult part of my task. It was impossible for Mrs Gerrarde to conceive that any thing, but down-right love for her person, could have induced me to do what I had done. I had actually run away with her, put myself to some hazard, and, what in her estimation was no small matter, some expence too. No other motive had appeared in all my conduct towards her; and tho' I had not absolutely made love to her, yet what other construction could my actions bear? for my words, to say the truth, were equivocal. She must necessarily have concluded that I had no other view but a piece of gallantry with her. Her designs on me were of a much more serious nature; and her vanity made her imagine, that, notwithstanding my thorough knowledge of her character, her cunning, joined to my passion, might lead me into her snare.

Now, I had two nice points to consider of, and two difficulties to surmount. The first was, not, by any part of my conduct, to carry the deception so far as to give her the least room to hope I could be mad enough to marry her. This, bad as *she* is, and extravagant as *I* am, I could not think of doing, even to gain my favourite point. The other was, to keep up such an appearance of gallantry towards her as she must naturally expect, and at the same time avoid all approaches which usually forerun the catastrophe of an amour; than which nothing was more repugnant to my wishes.

To steer between these two extremes was the difficult task, particularly the latter; for, between ourselves, I began to be much more afraid of her than she was of me. I knew it would be impossible for me to keep up the farce long; the sooner it was over the better; and therefore I determined to enter on my part directly.

I had been ruminating on my project all the way as I rode. When we arrived at Boulogne, I found myself a little out of order, having caught cold; and as I was really somewhat feverish, a thought started into my head, that this illness might aid me in my design. When we came to our lodgings, I made my excuses to Mrs Gerrarde for not being able to attend her: I told her I found myself ill, and must be obliged to go to bed. She said she was *very sorry*, and perhaps she spoke truth.

I left her in possession of her new apartment with her maid Rachael. Their being strangers to the language of the country cut off all communication with the people of the house, who could not speak English. I introduced Pivet to them, whom they had never seen before (for he had taken particular care to keep out of their view during the whole journey), as a gentleman who was to be their interpreter; and having thus settled my household, I retired to my bed-chamber.

Not well, nor sick enough to go to bed, I threw myself however down on it; and after revolving in my mind all the occurrences of the three or four past days, I started up again, sat down to my desk, and have given you, my Bidulph, a faithful narrative of my proceedings down to the present period of time, being November 20, eight o'clock in the evening.

You may soon expect to have the second part of this my delectable history; 'Shewing how Orlando, not being able to prevail, with all his eloquence, on the as fair and beautiful, as fierce and inexorable,

Princess Gerrardina, to put the finishing hand to his adventures and most wonderful exploits, did, his wrath being moved thereby, like an ungentle knight, bury his sword in her snow-white, but savage and unrelenting breast; whereat, being stung with remorse, he afterwards kills himself.'

Would not this be a pretty conclusion of my adventures? No, no, Sir George, expect better things from thy friend. I hope my knight-errantry will not end so tragically. But hasten to make my peace with that gracious creature your sister: yet why do I name her and myself in the same sentence? She cares not for me, thinks not of me, or, if she does, it is with contempt. I said this before, and I *must* repeat it again; but tell her, what I have done was with a view to promote her happiness. Oh! may *she* be happy, whatever becomes of me. I know the means I have used will make her angry; but try to make her forgive the means for the motive's sake. Tell her as much of this wild story as you think proper; but do not let her see it in my wild rambling language; that is only fit for your own eye.

Your mother, I know, is out of all patience with me. I am black enough in her opinion already. This last action, as far as she has yet known of it, will dye me ten shades deeper; but pray put in a word for me there too. I know she will say, that 'we are not to return evil for evil; and that it is not lawful to do evil, though to bring forth good.' But put her in mind that there are such things as *pious frauds* (though, by-the-bye, I do not take this of mine to be one of them); 'that wicked people are to have their arts opposed by *arts*; and that good people have not only been permitted, but commanded to execute vengeance on sinners.' And you may hint at the children of Israel's being ordered to spoil the Ægyptians, though far be it from me to spoil Mrs Gerrarde of any thing she has. This however, and as many wise sayings as you can collect for the purpose, you may string together; and be sure you tell her I have hopes of reclaiming Mrs Gerrarde from her *evil* courses, and do not despair of prevailing on her to go into a nunnery; for Mrs Gerrarde, you must know, was bred a Roman Catholic, though she conformed on marrying Captain Gerrarde.

Now put all this into decent language, fit for that very good woman's ears; for *good* I must call her, notwithstanding she was inexorable to me.

I am fatigued with writing so long a letter – I feel my disorder increase upon me; I will be let blood, and hope soon to give you a good account of my undertaking. Mean while, if I am not quite reprobated, write me a line, directed under cover to Monsieur Larou, at the Post-house, Boulogne. Farewel, my dear Bidulph; sick or well, I am ever your's,

O.F.

December 7

Was there ever such a piece of knight-errantry? What a mad-cap is this! Pray, my dear, are you not astonished at him? I am sure I am. I had not an opportunity to finish the copying of this very long letter, which I began yesterday morning, till very late this night. My poor mother has been so restless, and so much out of order, these two days, I desired her leave to read to her Mr Faulkland's history (for I can call it by no other name) as I sat by her bed-side. She told me, I might let her know the substance of what he said, as it would fatigue her too much to attend to so long an epistle.

You would have smiled, my Cecilia, at my good parent's amazement, when I told her Mr Faulkland's proceedings, and his reasons for them. She would scarce give credit to it at first, and I was obliged to repeat several circumstances to her over again. And so, said she, this was all on *your* account, and he had *really* no ill design on Mrs Gerrarde. I am glad of this for Miss Burchell's sake, and shall be impatient to tell her of it. I begged of my mother to wait a while for the result of Mr Faulkland's adventure, before she mentioned any thing of the matter to Miss Burchell. We do not yet know, said I, how this matter may turn out; Mr Faulkland, to be sure, will make haste to communicate to my brother the issue of this odd affair, and it will then be time enough to inform the young lady.

My mother unwillingly consented to postpone a discovery which she knew would be so agreeable to Miss Burchell. I applaud her humanity; but think that, good and prudent as she is, she is too unreserved in her confidences. This strange business is, I think, at present in too critical a suspence to trust the knowledge of it to any-body. If Mr Faulkland fails in his design, his avowal of it will be far from serving me. Sir George was with us for a few minutes to-day, only to exult in Mr Faulkland's recovered credit. Has he not well explained himself, said he? Oh! I knew there must have been some mystery at the bottom of that conduct which surprized us all so much. *There's* a man for you! Shew me another who would carry his noble distinterested love to such lengths!

My mother did not like that he should run on in that strain, and therefore stopped him. The end crowns all, Sir George: let us see how your friend will conduct himself *through* this ticklish affair. Let him get through it how he will, answered my brother a little bluntly, I think Sidney has obligations to him she ought never to forget.

December 16

More intelligence, my dear; stranger and stranger still! I am sorry I sent off my last packet, as I am sure you must be impatient for the conclusion of Mr Faulkland's adventure; and then what sorry stuff has the interval been filled up with! but I will now make you amends. My mother is better too, thank God! and every thing promises well.

Sir George has had a second packet from Boulogne. Take the continuation of Mrs Gerrarde's history as follows:

How rude is the hand of sickness, my Bidulph! it had like to have spoiled one of the best projects that ever was undertaken, and consigned to oblivion an action worthy of immortality. I have been very ill since I last wrote to you; the disorder, which I then complained of, turned out to be an ugly fever; and I was for three days in extreme danger. Mrs Gerrarde was, during that time, closely attended by Pivet, whose services I dispensed with on that account. He told me she appeared uneasy at my situation, and enquired constantly, and *kindly* too, after my health. When I grew well enough to sit up, I begged the favour of seeing her in my chamber. She came very readily, and seemed downright anxious for my recovery. I told her I hoped she had been treated with proper care and respect during my sickness. She said Mr Pivet was a very obliging, good-natured man, and had endeavoured to make her confinement as easy to her as possible.

The plan she had formed of turning to the most lasting advantage the inclination she supposed I had for her, inclined her to assume a very different behaviour from what was natural to her. The weakness of my condition, while it afforded me a pretence for a more cold and languid behaviour than I could with any colour have put on at another time, gave her an opportunity of playing off her arts, and facilitated my design beyond my hopes.

She was seated at my bed-side: our first conversation consisted of nothing but complaints on my side, and condolements on her's. I sighed several times, and she sighed in return. Mrs Gerrarde, said I, you are afflicted; but my illness has no share in your concern. Something else oppresses you; you regret the being separated from Mr Arnold, and I am always the object of your hatred. Neither one nor t'other, answered she, in a kind voice. 'Tis impossible to hate you; you know it is not in nature for a *woman* to hate such a man as Mr Faulkland. As for Mr Arnold, though I *own* my former weakness in regard to him, yet I hope I have something to plead in my excuse. I was married very early to an old man, and had never experienced the happiness of reciprocal love: he died, and left me destitute. Mr Arnold's generous, though I must confess unwarrantable passion, rescued me from distress. I did not know he was married when I first unwarily accepted of his addresses, and it was too late to retreat before I found it out; otherwise the universe should not have tempted me to have listened to him.

In the midst of the affluence I obtained from him, it often grieved me to think of the injury I did his wife. There is nothing, Mr Faulkland, so grating to a generous mind, and I think I may venture to assert that *mine* is one, as to live in a state of dependence, and, at the same time, owe that very dependence to a vice that you disdain.

I was delighted to find that she had got into this strain; it was the thing I wished, but durst hardly hope for without abundance of trouble on my part, and a dissimulation that was irksome to me. I knew she had studied this speech, and got it by rote to answer her own purpose; but in this, as is generally the case of designing people, she overshot herself, and became the dupe to her own artifice. I laid hold of the cue she gave: Oh! madam, you charm me! go on, go on; now indeed you shew a generous mind: happy would it be for all your sex, after having deviated from the paths of virtue, if they could return to them with so good a grace, so just a sense of their errors! To *you*, Sir, said she with a solemn air, I am indebted for my present resolutions: I hope from this time forward that my life will be irreproachable. *I* hope so too, madam. I guessed she understood these words as favouring her design: it was not meet to undeceive her (a little mental reservation, you know, Bidulph): she went on, little thinking she was forwarding *my* plan, when she only meant to promote her *own*. I hope Mr Arnold will be as sensible of *his* fault as I am of *mine*, and that he will never fall into the like indiscretion again. I believe there can be no true happiness but between a *married* pair, who sincerely love each other.

Good! Good! thought I; sure my better genius prompts the woman to speak thus. Ah! Mrs Gerrarde, how exactly do your thoughts correspond with mine! How just are all your sentiments! What a true relish have you for virtue! Yes, I hope with you that Mr Arnold will be able to tread in your steps: it is a pity he has not your noble example before him. Mrs Arnold is a good woman, and he might still live with her in tolerable contentment, if he can get the better of his irregular passion for you. What a noble triumph of virtuous resolution would this be, if you yourself were the instrument to bring this about. For Mrs Arnold's and her brother's sake, as well as your own, I wish this were feasible.

I would do any thing in my power, said she (thinking she obliged me by the declaration); but I know not by what means such an event can be brought to pass.

I was afraid to urge the matter farther: I was within an hair's breadth of gaining my point, but did not think it prudent to press too forward. We'll think of it another time, said I, and groaned heavily, as if my spirits were fatigued with talking. She took the hint. I am afraid I have tired you; you have talked too much. I answered her faintly, You are very good! She curtesied to me, and retired with a majestic step. I saw her no more that day: she had got upon stilts, and it was not yet time to take her down. To-morrow may produce a wonder: I will wait for it. I am really weak, but begin to recover my spirits.

Boulogne, December 6.

Nothing is so conducive to the body's health, as the mind's being at ease. I have proved the truth of this observation: my soul had been racked with suspence and uncertainty during my illness; the uneasy state of my mind increased my disorder; the disorder itself had chiefly given rise to my apprehensions, as pain and sickness are naturally accompanied with a gloominess of thought. Thus the cause and its effects were united in mutual league against me, and reciprocally assisted each other to plague and torment me.

My fears were intirely on Mrs Arnold's account. What, thought I, would be the consequence of my project, in case of my death? Mrs Gerrarde will return back to England; and, upon telling her story, will be received again by Arnold; their union perhaps established as firmly as before, and poor Mrs Arnold's hopes ruined for ever. Then I thought what a wretch I must appear in her eyes, doubtful, may be, of my sincerity as to the motives I urged to you for my conduct. On the other hand, if these motives should by any means happen to be suspected by Mrs Gerrarde, it might be the means of producing the direct contrary effect from what I intended; and instead of banishing Arnold's cruel suspicions of his lady, only serve to strengthen them; for I knew Mrs Gerrarde would leave nothing unsaid or undone for this horrid purpose; and it is not every one, Sir George, whose hearts are enlarged enough to suppose a man may now and then take a little pains from disinterested principles. This last suggestion of my thoughts made me almost mad, and actually brought on a delirium; and what may seem a paradox, though it is literally true, the total deprivation of my senses for two days was the means of my recovering them afterwards; for I am sure, had I retained enough of them to have ruminated longer on this fatal supposition, and my disorder had still threatened me with death. I should have run mad. The care of a skilful physician recalled me from the precincts of the grave; the strength of a constitution, naturally good, joined to all the resolution I could muster, did the rest.

The first use I made of my recovered reason, was to consult with myself in what manner, or by what means, I should prevail on Mrs Gerrarde to lend a helping hand to my design. Her leaving Arnold to go off with me, and to all human appearance with her own consent, was a material point gained; but the most important of all, and without which every thing else would be fruitless, was to get her to acknowlege, under her own hand, the injury she had done Mrs Arnold by her vile insinuations to her husband. This was the grand object of all my wishes. This, you will say, was difficult: I confess it did then appear so to me. I had not at first weighed all the consequences of my enterprize with that deliberation that I ought. The principal object I had in view, was the separating Mrs Gerrarde and Mr Arnold, and raising his indignation against her, on account of the apparent infidelity on her side. To say the truth, I had not considered what I was to do with her when I had her. Two things I had resolved on; the one was, not to let her return to England; the other, to provide for her in whatever way she would put it in my power (the devoting myself to her excepted), in such a manner as should leave her no room to reproach me with having injured her temporal welfare.

During my illness, I had resolved all these things in my mind; the last, viz. the providing for Mrs Gerrarde, was not a matter in which I expected to meet many difficulties; the other appeared very formidable. Several methods presented themselves, but none of them pleased me, and I rejected them one after the other; and, to tell you my mind honestly, I was almost resolved on using compulsion, and frightening the poor woman into compliance; for I preferred even this to artificial dealings. I had already used more than I could have possibly brought myself to on any other occasion in the world; and I think I should have threatened her with a nunnery, the bastile, or even an inquisition, sooner than have failed, if she herself had not beyond expectation, beyond hope, almost beyond the evidence of my senses, led me as it were to request the thing of her, which of all others I most despaired of her consenting to, or even hearing proposed with patience. And yet, notwithstanding the seeming strangeness of this, it was nothing but what was very natural, and most consonant to her own designs. Blinded, and, as I may say, infatuated by vanity, she imagined, that as I had taken such uncommon pains to obtain her, I must love her with an uncommon degree of passion; and that her steadily refusing any dishonourable proposals, might induce me, rather than lose her, to make her my wife.

In order to prepare me the better for this, no means were more natural, than for her to assume the air of a penitent, to seem sorry and ashamed of her past sins, and resolve on a virtuous course for the future. At the worst, that is, if she found *I* was not disposed to be as virtuous as herself, she knew she might play an after-game; and could easily relax by degrees from the severity of her chastity, accordingly as I made it worth her while.

This was the master-key to her behaviour, and once I had got it, which I soon did, it was easy to unlock her breast.

She came into my room the next morning without an invitation, and only the previous ceremony of sending Rachael to enquire how I did, and to tell me, if I were well enough to *rise* (observe her nicety), she would sit half an hour with me. I had enjoyed such tranquility of heart since my last conference with her, and had rested so well the preceding night, that I found myself quite another thing from what I was the day before; and, excepting a little weakness, I was as well as ever I was in my life. I was up and dressed, and you may be sure sent a suitable answer to her kind message, which soon brought the lady, sailing wtih an imperial port, into my chamber. After some civilities past on both sides, she, by way of bringing her own interests on the tapis, re-assumed the topic of our yesterday's conversation.

You can't imagine, Mr Faulkland, said she, how easy I am in my mind, since I have reconciled myself to the loss of Mr Arnold. I own I had a regard for him; but I think it had more of gratitude than love in it; for though he is an agreeable man, to say the truth, he never was quite to my taste: he always had something too formal about him.

I took the liberty to ask her, how she first came acquainted with Mr Arnold; and, as you may not know it, I will give you the story. She answered, with a profound sigh, It was by mere accident I first saw him. After the death of Captain Gerrarde, which happened in a little more than a year after we left Bath, for the gout, poor man, got into his stomach not long after we returned home (and the crocodile pretended to drop a tear), I went to London, in order to sollicit for my pension. As I had formerly been a Roman Catholic, and had not publickly renounced that persuasion, some difficulties arose in the business; and a friend of my deceased husband, who had undertaken the affair for me, happening to be an intimate of Mr Arnold's, and knowing he had an influence with the secretary at war, endeavoured to interest him in my favour, by representing my situation in the most affecting light he could to him. He kindly undertook to interfere for me, and was as good as his word; but could not surmount the difficulty of the objection which was made to my claim. He happened one morning, unluckily for me, to call in at my friend's lodgings, to tell him of his ill success: I, impatient to know how my affair went on, had dropped in to inquire about it a few minutes before him, and was sitting in the dining-room when Mr Arnold entered. I was in my weeds, and my melancholy looks I believe made Mr Arnold conjecture I was the person for whom he had so kindly concerned himself. He told my friend he was sorry to inform him, that though he had used all means in his power, with regard to the affair in which he had employed him, he found it was impossible to effect the business; and I am the more concerned, said he, turning towards me, as I am afraid this lady is to be the sufferer. My relation said I was the person for whom he had been so good as to intercede. I returned Mr Arnold thanks, not without tears, at the uncomfortable prospect I had before me; for I had then nothing to depend on, but my small jointure in Kent. I was about to take my leave; but observing it rained, desired my friend to give his servant leave to call me a chair. Mr Arnold very politely desired I would permit him to set me down, as his chariot waited at the door. I would have excused myself; but my relation said, 'Tis in his way, child; and since you have no hopes of a pension, you ought to be sparing of chair-hire. Mr Arnold very obligingly offered me his hand, and led me to his chariot. He set me down at my lodgings, and at parting desired permission to wait on me. The fatal consequence of our acquaintance it was impossible for me to foresee; for I never had the least hint given me, either from my own relation or Mr Arnold himself, that he was a married man, till he had so far secured my gratitude, by repeated acts of generosity, that it was impossible for me to refuse him the return he demanded.

Too-grateful heart, said I (pretending to believe her cant), what a pity thou wert not destined to reward a purer love! But I thought, madam, you really had enjoyed a pension?

It was not necessary, she answered, that I should let the world suppose otherwise. I was not at all known when I first came to town. Mr Arnold's excessive profuseness (quiet against my inclination) threw me into a more expensive way of living than before. I found myself obliged to account for it, to the few acquaintance I had, by all the probable means I could devise. For this purpose, I pretended that I had not only obtained a pension, but had also a fortune left me by the death of a relation. This was believed, as nobody troubled their heads to enquire whether it was true or not.

Mr Arnold was passionately fond of the country, and always passed his summers there; but as he could not think of parting with me, he was sadly at a loss how to have me near him, without bringing on us both the observation of an inquisitive neighbourhood (such as all country places abound in), if I went down, quite a stranger as I was, into Essex; particularly as he told me there were two families near Arnold-abbey, who made it their business to pry into other people's affairs. These were, a Lady Grimston, a censorious old woman, and the parson of the parish, who was a mighty strict man, of whom Mr Arnold seemed to stand in some awe. He therefore determined against my going to that part of the world: but having casually heard me speak of my little cottage in Kent, where poor Captain Gerrarde and I had lived for two or three years, he asked me whereabouts it was, and was delighted to find it joined his own estate at South Park, and was within a mile of his house. He begged of me to go down to my own house, which he insisted on furnishing elegantly for me, and obliged me also to keep a chariot. I (tho' unwillingly) found myself under a necessity of complying. About a fortnight after I was settled at Ashby, Mr Arnold and his family came down: then it was that, for the first time, I saw his lady. I went to pay my compliments to her, as every genteel family in the neighbourhood did; and I own I never saw her without feeling myself shocked to death at the thoughts of the injury I did her; for I really believe Mrs Arnold is a very well-meaning woman.

Oh! thou scorpion, muttered I to myself, and yet thou hast pursued her to affliction and ruin!

That Mrs Arnold is a well-meaning woman, said I coldly, I have no doubt; yet you see Mr Arnold's opinion of her virtue was not strong enough to be proof against suspicions; for it is most certain, that, if he had not given credit to your representations of his wife's conduct, he would not have gone such lengths as to have parted with her; for Arnold had always some regard to appearances.

My representations, Sir! with a look of astonishment; pray do not lay more to my charge than I deserve: what the particular reasons were, which induced Mr Arnold to part with his wife, I will not say; but whatever his suspicions were, they never took their rise from me.

I found she intended to brazen this denial out; but as it was absolutely necessary to my design to bring her to a confession of this particular act of perfidy, I resolved to lead her into it in such a way as should be least mortifying to her pride.

Come, come, my dear Mrs Gerrarde, said I, I know you are above concealing any past failings that you are resolved to mend. I know very well that it was *your* insinuations, and your's only, that kindled the fire of jealousy in Arnold's breast. Such arts are not uncommon in lovers. You loved him then, and wished to have him intirely to yourself; and a wife, though a forsaken one, is still intitled to so much attention from her husband, as a fond mistress may think robs her of too much. I know this was the case, and it is natural: but were you not an unmerciful little tyrant to involve *me* in the mischief, and put it into the man's noddle, that *I* had designs upon his wife?

The easy manner in which I affected to speak of this affair, seemed to reconcile her a little to the charge; but the last part of it, which regarded myself, struck her all of a heap. She had no notion that I knew it. She was going to speak, to deny the accusation I suppose, and therefore I prevented her; and taking her by the hand, Come now, said I, deal with me ingenuously; and if you persuade me that you are really in earnest, and mean to repair those little lapses which you have inconsiderately been led into, tell me truly, did you really believe that I ever had any thoughts of an amour with Mrs Arnold?

I chose to give my inquiry this turn, that she might, with less shame to herself, by laying hold on the hint, acknowlege her guilt.

She hesitated for an answer, and I guessed she was considering whether to persist in denying the whole charge against her, or avail herself of the handle I had given her, and make a sort of merit of her sincerity, by pretending to believe what she was thoroughly convinced there was not the least foundation even to suspect, but what her own wicked suggestions had encouraged in the unfortunate Arnold. Her silence, thus rightly interpreted by me, made me go on: You see I know all your secrets; and you are not the woman I take you for, if you conceal your real sentiments in this particular: more of my quiet depends on it than you are aware of, and I withdrew my hand from her's with a serious and almost resenting air.

She appeared disturbed, and in a good deal of confusion; but recovering herself, Why really, Mr Faulkland, I can't say but I *had* some suspicion of what you mention. I was no stranger to your fondness for Mrs Arnold before she was married, and there was nothing very surprising in a disappointed lover's renewing his hopes, when he thought the neglect which a lady met with from her husband, might incline her to be less obdurate to a man she was once known to favour so much.

This was enough: I did not think it by any means necessary to press her to a farther explanation; what she said was a sufficient acknowlegement of her fault, though the cunning sorceress had turned the hint (which I had thrown out on purpose) to her own advantage; and had the affrontery to avow an opinion which had never before entered into her imagination.

I found it necessary now to carry on the farce, by assuring her, I had never entertained a thought to Mrs Arnold's dishonour; and that though I made no great scruple of robbing a man of his mistress, yet I thought it a crime of the blackest dye to deprive him of the affection or fidelity of his wife.

The serious manner in which I spoke this a little disconcerted Mrs Gerrarde. Well, said she, I can only say, that I am very sorry I entertained so false a suspicion; and more so, as it has produced such unhappy consequences: but I hope Mr Faulkland will not believe that I meant *him* any injury?

That I am sure you did not, said I; and yet this very affair has given me more uneasiness than you can imagine; for as Mrs Arnold's brother is my most particular friend, he must think me the greatest of villains, if I could entertain a thought of dishonouring his family: the fear of losing his friendship, I own, gives me more pain than I can express, and there is nothing I would not do to exculpate myself to him.

I am very unfortunate, cried Mrs Gerrarde (pretending to wipe her eyes), to have been the occasion of so much uneasiness in any-body's family. I wish I had died before I was so unhappy as to meet with Mr Arnold: if it had not been for him, I might now have been an innocent and a contented woman; and she *really* squeezed out a tear, though not of contrition.

Dear madam (again taking her hand), do not afflict yourself for what is past recalling; contentment, nay happiness, I hope, is yet within your reach; it will be your own fault if you do not lay hold of it: as for the unhappy family that *I*, as well as *you*, have contributed to distress, I wish from my heart there could be a reunion amongst them. Mr Arnold's having lost you might perhaps incline him to turn his thoughts towards his wife, if he were not prejudiced against her by the suspicions he has entertained of her virtue. This I am afraid will be an insuperable bar to their ever living together, unless your influence, which first gave birth to his jealousy, is still forcible enough to remove it.

I wish it were in my power, said Mrs Gerrarde; there is nothing I would not do to effect it: but what influence can I have on Mr Arnold, after what has happened?

Suppose you were to write to him, said I: you and he probably may never meet again; and it would be an effort worthy indeed of a noble mind, to repair the wrongs we have done to others, by a candid acknowlegement of our own faults. Putting Mrs Arnold out of the question, 'tis a reparation you owe *my* character; for however light the world may make of a piece of gallantry with a married woman, it is a matter of serious moment to me to acquit myself of the supposed crime to Sir George Bidulph.

If you think, said she, that my writing to Mr Arnold could produce such good effects, I am ready to do it; though I confess I hardly know how to address him; for he must, to be sure, look upon me as the very reverse of what I *really* am, and thinks me without dispute an ungrateful woman.

We can but try, said I: if it does not produce the desired effect, it will not be your fault; and you will have the satisfaction to reflect, that you have done your duty. I stepped to my escruitore while I was speaking; and resolving not to give her time to cool, took out pen, ink, and paper, and laid them on a little writing-table before her. If this unlucky breach, said I, were once made up, my mind would then be easy.

She took the pen in her hand, but seemed irresolute, and at a loss how to begin. Come, madam, said I, and confute, by your own example, the received erroneous opinion, that if a woman once strays from the paths of virtue, she never returns to them.

A false and ill-grounded opinion indeed, said she, lifting up her prophane eyes as in penitence. What am I to say?

[You are to observe, that my notes, as she went along while I dictated, are put between hooks.]

[Begin] 'Dear Sir' [for I would neither be too familiar nor too cold], 'The terms on which you and I have lived, intitles you to an explanation of my reasons for leaving you so abruptly; and I hope the generosity of my motive will incline you to overlook the seeming unkindness of the action.' [This you may assure yourself it will, when he comes to consider coolly]. 'The unhappiness that I occasioned in your family, by causing the separation of you and your wife, has, for a long time, been a thorn in my heart; and the more so, as besides the robbing her of your affections, I own, and take shame to myself in the confession' [how noble must he think this confession!], 'that those aspersions, which I threw on her, had not the least foundation in truth.' [This is truly great]. 'I always believed her perfectly innocent; but, if I could have had the least possible doubt of it before, I must now be confirmed in that opinion by Mr Faulkland, who can have no reason for excusing or concealing facts of this nature from me at present.' [Here she added of herself, repeating it first aloud to me], 'and I think the preference he has given me to her, now in her state of separation, is a convincing proof of this.' [An admirable argument] (her vanity would not let her slip this observation). [Proceed, madam]. 'The true reasons of my insinuations against her, were no other than that I could not bear to share your affections with any-body' [and a very sufficient reason too, which a man that loves can easily forgive]. 'I knew, that so long as she gave you no cause of complaint, you were too just to withdraw your whole heart from her, and nothing *but* the whole would content me.' [Still you see you shew a great mind]. True, said she, going on; but my reason for leaving him without apprizing him of it, what are we to say for that? [Oh! nothing more *easy* to execute: he will admire you the more for the reason *I* shall give. Come]. 'My departing without first making you acquainted with my design, and going off with another person, may, at first sight, seem very strange; but, to tell you the real state of my heart, I found I could not trust to its firmness on the subject of parting with you. I loved you so, that it was with pain and grief I made the resolution; and I knew too well, that had you used any arguments, which to be sure you would have done, to dissuade me, I, like an easy fool, would have given up all my good designs.' [I am only afraid this will make him love you more than ever]. (She smiled as she continued to write). 'As for the other article' – (This I was more puzzled to excuse than the first; but, putting on a bold face, I said, Madam, I hope you will not condemn me here, while you excuse yourself: the saying you were *run away* with, will knock all the rest on the head, and he may chuse whether he will believe that you really intended to break off with him or not; therefore that particular had better not be touched upon. Well, said she, get me out of this scrape as cleverly as you have brought me into it. Fear not, said I; go on). 'As for the other article, though I shall never love Mr Faulkland as I have done you, yet in him I have found a protector; and through his means, I hope to pass the remainder of my life, in a manner more suitable to a woman of a generous way of thinking, than that wherein she considered herself as encroaching on the rights of another. I hope, by this sacrifice which I have made of my love to a more heroic principle, that I shall expiate my former offence; and that you will follow my example so far as to make what reparation you can to the woman we have both injured.' [How this must raise, how exalt you in his opinion! I think it must, cried she, bridling up her head, as if they were really her own sentiments].

I believe, said I, this is all that is necessary to be said: you may add, in a postscript, that, as he furnished the house for you at Ashby, every thing in it is at his service; together with your chariot and horses, which were also his gifts.

She demurred to this; and in the midst of her heroics, said, I wish I could get somebody to sell them for me privately, and remit the money to me; for, since I *am* here, I should like to see a little more of France before I return.

I told her that would look mean, and below a *great mind*. Well, said she, let them go. I owe all my servants a year's wages, and another person about fifty pounds for a little temple he had just built in my garden, but not quite finished when I came away. I think I had better desire those debts to be discharged: I have always been very punctual in my dealings, and would not for the world *wrong* anybody.

You are in the right, said I: it will look honourable in you to desire those debts to be paid.

She now proceeded to conclude her letter in the same stile she had begun it, and added a postscript to the purport I mentioned. I hastened to make her seal it up, and direct it to Mr Arnold, at his house in London, who, I suppose, has had the pleasure of receiving it before now; for I dispatched it off directly. I flatter myself with the hope that it will have the desired effect on him.

You will think perhaps, that, as I have managed it, I have really given her a sort of merit with him in the acknowlegement of her fault, and the pretended reason she gives for leaving him. No such thing, Sir George. Arnold is a man of too much sense, and knows the world too well, to be so deceived. I have been told by my Lord V—, who knows him perfectly, that nobody judges better when he is not blinded by his passions. All her professions must go for nothing when *facts* are against her. 'Tis plain she went off with another man, and to all appearances premeditately, as her maid and her riches bore her company. 'Tis also plain, by her own confession, that this man stands well with her. As for her recanting her injurious aspersions on poor Mrs Arnold, 'tis the only circumstance in her letter likely to gain belief, as she could have no temptation to that but real compunction, with which people of that kind are sometimes visited; and for the rest of her letter, to any one of common understanding, that lays circumstances together, it will appear, as I intended it should, the contrivance of an artful jilt, who, having almost ruined the wretch she has had in her power, would afterwards make a *merit* of deserting him; for they must be hardened reprobates indeed, that would not, if they could, at least *try* to palliate their evil deeds. This is the light I expect Arnold will consider her in. I know he is hurt deeply in his fortune by this vile harpy. I hope the remnant may be sufficient to support your excellent sister, if not in affluence, at least with comfort, should she regain her influence over him, and submit to live with him again. This, I am sure, will be the consequence, if he is not blind to his own happiness.

I shall be impatient to know how the letter operates on him; but this you are not likely to be let into; and perhaps his pride may make him endeavour to conceal it from every-body. My Lord V—, I am sure, will pick up some intelligence, and send it to me.

I think Mrs Gerrarde's confession, in regard to Mrs Arnold (to which she could have no interested motive), with the corroborating circumstance of *my* going off with her at a time when Mrs Arnold was from under her husband's protection, injured by him in the tenderest point, and aspersed by a barbarous and invidious world; all this, I say, must surely clear from all suspicion that admirable creature: for who, that knows Mrs Arnold, would think that any man (except her husband) would prefer any woman upon earth to her? If this does not remove all doubt of her conduct in Arnold, as well as in the rest of the world, my pains have been to little purpose; and I know no other human means that can be used to disabuse the mad credulity of that man. I pity him from my heart in his present situation; for it will be some time before he will be sensible of the good I have done him; and, I dare swear, the man is at this time so ungrateful, that, if he could, he would cut my throat. I do not want to have him know the extent of his obligation to me: I shall be satisfied to sit down in the contemplation of my meritorious actions, without enjoying the fame of them. This greatness of mind I learnt of Mrs Gerrarde. But to return:

The having gained my material point put me into such spirits, that I could have kissed Mrs Gerrarde; a liberty which, I assure you, however I never presumed to take. She, for her part, seemed as well pleased with what she had done as I was. I praised her for the part she had acted, though I very much feared she would repent of it when we came to explanations, which I resolved should be on that very day. I told her, I hoped she would oblige me with her company at dinner. She consented with a bow. I had ordered one to be got ready earlier than usual, and directed that it should be in her apartment. We were told it was on table. I never saw Mrs Gerrarde so agreeable as she was during dinner; she was in high spirits and good-humour: I almost thought it a pity to let her down that day; but I considered the longer her expectations were kept up, the greater would be her disappointment; and, out of pure charity, I determined to put her out of doubt.

I had been told Mrs Gerrarde was no enemy to a chearful glass; but the designs she had formed upon me put her on her guard, and I observed she drank nothing but wine and water, made very small. This, I was afraid, would not be sufficient to keep up her courage under what I intended to say to her. I pretended to be disposed to drink, and insisted on her helping me out with a flask of burgundy. With affected coyness she suffered me to fill her glass; the second offer I made, her resistance was less; the third she made no objection to at all; and the fourth she filled for herself. The wine was excellent; not that poor sort which is commonly drunk in France. In short, we finished our bottle. I thought her now a match for what I had to say. I had made the glass pass briskly, and had filled up the intervals with singing catches, and rattling on any subject that came into my head.

Mrs Gerrarde, who no doubt expected I should make an advance of some kind or other, seemed to grow a little out of humour at my levity. I found the burgundy had been quite thrown away upon her, and had had very little effect: she was silent for a few minutes, and seemed to be considering of something: at last she opened, and I will give you the conversation that passed between us, by way of dialogue.

Mrs G Mr Faulkland, it is time that you and I should understand one another's meaning a little better than we do at present: you know very well that you have put an end to all my expectations in England: indeed, if I were at liberty, I could not have the face to return there again in any character but that of your wife. (I was glad she began first, and that, though I guessed at her views, she had used so little caution in discovering them, as it at once roused in me an indignation which I could not suppress, and without which I could not have brought myself to mortify her as she deserved).

Mr F My *wife*, madam! (stopping her at that tremendous word) be pleased to tell me if I heard you right?

Mrs G Yes, Sir, it was as your wife I said: if you think you and I are to live together on any other terms, you will find yourself exceedingly mistaken. (I smiled, and suffered her to go on). I thought, Sir (stifling the anger that I saw rising), that the words which you yourself dictated in the letter which I just now wrote, where you say, *I had in you found a protector, and one by whose means I should be able to pass the rest of my life in a manner more suitable to a woman of a generous way of thinking, than that wherein she considered herself as incroaching on the rights of another* – Were not these your own words, Sir?

Mr F They were, Madam. (To say the truth, there was something equivocal in the paragraph, though, when I desired her to write it, this construction never entered into my head).

Mrs G Then, Sir, how am I to understand them?

Mr F I protest, Madam, you have forced a construction that I never once so much as dreamed of.

Mrs G Why, Mr Faulkland (with a very brisk tone), do you fancy that by changing Mr Arnold for *you* on any other conditions, that I am such a mighty gainer by the bargain?

Mr F Why really, Madam, if that *were* to be the case, I don't think you would be a very great loser: you have got as much from poor Arnold as you could expect: I am able to do better for you; and, as I am nobody's property, it would certainly, in *that* respect, be rather a more eligible course.

Mrs G Sir, you use me very ill! I did not expect such treatment.

Mr F How, pray Madam? Did I ever say I would marry you?

Mrs G No, Sir; but your behaviour has given me room to suppose that such a thing was in your thoughts.

Mr F Are you not then the more obliged to me for treating you with such respect as made you fancy so?

Mrs G Respect! respect (muttering between her teeth), Mr Faulkland! (and she stood up) there is not a man in England but yourself, after what I have declared, that would refuse making me his wife.

Mr F What have you declared, Mrs Gerrarde?

Mrs G Why, have I not ingenuously owned my failings, shewed myself sorry for them, quitted them, and made all the reparation in my power?

(I was amazed to see how audaciously she had adopted as her own, the sentiments which I had suggested to her: it was so like her, that I could have laughed in her face).

Mr F Your behaviour, on this occasion, has really been worthy of the imitation of all your own sex, and the praise of ours: for a woman *voluntarily* to quit an irregular life, and that too from mere motives of *conscience* – (I was stopped by a knavish sneer, which I could not subdue. She saw it, and fired immediately; but strutted about the room to cool herself: at last, for I sat very silent, looking at her, and playing with one of the glasses) –

Mrs G Mr Faulkland, if you are disposed to have done trifling, and will vouchsafe me a serious answer, pray tell me, Are you absolutely determed not to marry me?

Mr F Absolutely.

Mrs G You are not serious, sure!

Mr F My dear creature, why sure *thou* canst not be serious in asking me the question!

Mrs G Sir, I *am* serious, and expect a serious answer.

Mr F Why then, – seriously, I have no more thoughts of marrying thee, than I have of marrying the first sultana in the grand seignior's seraglio.

Mrs G Very well, Sir; very well; I am answered; (and she walked quicker about the room than before).

We were both silent. She, I suppose, expected that I should propose other terms, and a settlement; and waited, to try if I would speak. I had a mind to teaze her a little, and hummed a tune.

Mrs G (Advancing to me, and making a low curt'sey, with a most scornful and sarcastical air) May I presume to enquire what your mightiness's pleasure is in regard to me? Do you intend to keep me for your nurse against your next illness, or to send me to the grand seignior's seraglio to wait upon the first sultana?

Mr F Neither (carelessly, and looking another way). I have not yet determined which way I shall dispose of you.

Mrs G Dispose of me! *dispose* of me! why sure the man has lost his senses!

Mr F Look you, Mrs Gerrarde; we will no longer play at cross-purposes: sit down, and be calm for a few minutes, till you hear what I have to say.

(She did so, with a kind of impatience in her looks, that informed me I might have made a very free proposal, without any great danger of her resentment).

Mr F How long have you and I been acquainted?

Mrs G Lord! what is that question to the purpose?

Mr F 'Tis only in order to my desiring you would look back, and, upon recollection, ask yourself, if you ever had any reason to look upon me as your lover.

Mrs G I made that observation to you when we were travelling together: what is the use of it now?

Mr F Did I, in the course of our journey, declare myself to be such, or drop the least hint of devoting myself to you on any condition?

Mrs G We did not talk on the subject at all.

Mr F Did I ever presume, on the advantage of having you in my power, to venture on the smallest liberty with you; or ever deviate from that respect in my behaviour, that I was used, at all other times, to treat you with?

Mrs G I do not say you did; and it was that very behaviour that inclined me to imagine you had other thoughts than those I find you have.

Mr F You drew a wrong conclusion, though it is to be confessed not a very unnatural one. Such a behaviour might have been so construed by a lady otherwise circumstanced than you were; but I think a woman of your sagacity might have concluded, that, with Mrs Gerrarde, a man would first have tried his fortune upon gentler terms than those of matrimony.

Mrs G Well, well (peevishly); I do not understand your riddles: to the point.

Mr F Why, the point, in short, is this; that, without any particular designs on your person, my whole view, in carrying you out of England, was to break off your intercourse with Mr Arnold.

(She seemed thunder-struck; but recovering herself, And is *this* what I am to hear calmly? And she flounced off the chair to the other end of the room.

I followed her; and, taking her hand, begged she would sit down again, and hear me out. I drew her to a chair, and gently set her down in it).

Mr F Now, for your own sake, hear me with patience; violence or perverseness will be of no use to you.

Mrs G Very well, Sir; I am your prisoner; your *slave* at present: say what you please; 'tis *your* turn *now*.

Mr F Well then, Madam, as I said before, I really never had any designs upon you merely on your own account. I allow you to be a very fine woman, and capable of inspiring love in any man that sees you; but I must tell you plainly, that *love* has had no share in my conduct. (I saw stifled rage in her face; but I proceeded). I have already told you the real motive of my carrying you off: it was, as I said, to dissolve the union between you and Mr Arnold, and my reasons for wishing to do so are these: Mr Arnold is married to one of the best women living, for whom I have the highest respect and esteem, and whom I once adored: That lady has, by your influence over her husband, not only been thrown out from his heart, but even thrust out from his house. But the calamity stops not there; she is cruelly aspersed by the world through your suggestions, and I am the person pointed at for the injurer of Mr Arnold's honour, and the destroyer of his wife's innocence. You have brought shame and grief into a worthy family. Lady Bidulph (an excellent woman) has not been able to overcome the shock of the barbarous treatment her daughter has met with. Her brother, the beloved friend of my heart, suffers equal distress; for, though he is conscious of his sister's innocence, he feels the wounds that her reputation has received; nor can he possibly redress the mischief, as his sister's injuries spring from a cause which her delicacy will not permit to be scrutinized. Her two poor children are left without a mother; she herself almost without a friend, and sinking every day under the weight of such complicated misery. As for Mr Arnold himself, I profess no personal regard for him: I scarce know him; but, for his family's sake, I would, on any *other* occasion, risque my life to save him from ruin; for ruin you have almost brought on him. I am no stranger to the sums he has lavished on you; his purchasing an employment for *one* of your brothers, and redeeming another from a prison. You have lost nothing by my proceedings but what I shall make up ten-fold to you, if you behave so as to deserve my kindness. I have now laid before you the true reasons for my conduct. I hope, that by breaking the inchantment that tied Mr Arnold's heart, and blinded his understanding, he may be induced to do justice to his injured lady and her family. If this comes to pass, as I have strong reason to hope, I have no doubt of the lady's character being retrieved. *Groundless* calumnies generally die of themselves, unless industriously kept alive by malice. Mrs Arnold's blameless conduct, the friendship her brother has all along continued to favour me with, joined to this last apparent proof of my attachment to you, will, I am certain, in the eyes of the world, acquit her of all suspicion of guilt. Your letter to Mr Arnold will, as far as relates to your own opinion of her, give unquestionable evidence of her innocence.

Now, Mrs Gerrarde, lay your hand on your heart, and answer me if I have not given you reasons, which, though they may not be satisfactory to you, are in themselves of weight sufficient to justify my conduct.

I had watched her countenance narrowly during my discourse, which she had listened to without once looking at me. I saw I had shocked and even confounded her; but I saw no remorse, no contrition in her looks. All artifice was now at an end, and she unmasked the fiend directly. She started off her chair with the looks and gesture of a fury; and fixing her eyes (which had really something diabolical in them at that instant) steadily on me, You wretch! she cried, with a voice answerable to her looks, you are such a false, dissembling, mean-spirited reptile, that if you had a kingdom to offer me, and would lay yourself at my feet to beg my acceptance of you, I would trample on you like dirt! and she stamped on the floor with the air of an amazon. Do you think you shall carry on this fine-contrived enterprize? No, if I perish for it, I will have vengeance: Mr Arnold shall know how I have been deceived and betrayed, and I will at least have the satisfaction of getting your life, if I lose every thing besides.

A burst of malignant tears now gushed from her eyes; but she robbed them of their efficacy, by mixing with them the bitterest imprecations against me. She curst even the innocent Mrs Arnold, you, and the whole family; and her own folly, in being blinded by the arts of such a worthless milk-sop as myself.

I let her give vent to her passion, calmly walking about the room all the time; only now and then casting an eye on her, for fear she should have rushed on me with a penknife; for I have not the least doubt, if she had had such an instrument about her, she would have made an attempt that might have given a very tragical turn to my adventures.

When she had done sobbing, I addressed her in a very stern voice; for I found I had no baby to deal with, and therefore resolved to frighten her into submission.

I told you before, Madam, that violence would be of no use to you: your menaces I laugh at; you are in my power intirely, and absolutely at my disposal: to think of getting out of my hands would be vain; for it is as impracticable as flying. No mortal knows where you are but the people of this house, who are strangers to your name and circumstances; and if they knew both, they are so totally at my devotion, that it would not avail you. I shall cut off all possibility of a correspondence to England. What then must be your resource? I am prepared against all events; and I would carry you about locked up in an iron cage, like the Turkish tyrant, till I had subdued that termagant spirit, sooner than you should have your liberty to do more mischief. If you have any regard to your own interest, you will endeavour to make me your friend: I have the power and the will to serve you; I have done you no injury; I said I would be your protector; and so I will, if you will suffer me to be so. I said I would be the means of your passing your days in a state more eligible to a woman of either spirit, discretion, or a grain of honour, than you have hitherto done. This I am ready to make good, if you will not be wanting on your part to your own happiness. You have acknowleged that you are conscious of your own errors, are sorry for them, and are willing to quit them (This was turning her own weapons against herself); if you are in earnest in this declaration, I will give you the means of quitting them. The money you have now in your possession, even with the addition of your little jointure, is not sufficient to promise you such a support as would make you easy, if you were to return to England to-morrow; and your story known (as it would be), what could you expect? Do you think Arnold could be so besotted as to receive you again? What must be your resource? Why, to continue, while your beauty lasts, in a wretched, abandoned course. Ten thousand to one you might never light on another whose love would be prodigal enough to enrich you. The only choice left you, is to stay where you are not known, and where, if you behave well, you may gain the respect and esteem which you could never hope for in a place where your history is known. If you will content yourself with an easy fortune, joined to a life of virtue and tranquillity, I will provide you with a husband that many a woman in your circumstances would bless her stars for: I will double the portion you have already, and get it settled on you; and will, on certain conditions, add a handsome yearly income. If you do not like this proposal, I have no other alternative to offer but a nunnery. I know you were bred a Roman Catholic: I am sure therefore I shall do no violence to your religious scruples, if you have any. I can get you admitted with ease: the religious here will think it a meritorious act in me, especially on the terms I shall propose; for I will make it worth their while to receive and treat you as a lady of the first family in France: but remember there is a final period to all intercourse with this world. If you think you can bring yourself to submit to such a life, I would really recommend it to you; for I am sollicitous for your happiness both here and hereafter: if not, you have the other choice to make; and so, Madam, a husband or a convent; take which you like best: I give you three days to consider of it.

I kept up a severe countenance, and a resolute tone. I rang the bell as soon as I had done speaking. Rachael came in before Mrs Gerrarde could answer me. Take care of your mistress, said I, and left the room, without even the ceremony of a bow, or deigning to look at her. I locked the chamber door, which I took care to clap after me; and, putting the key in my pocket, left the lady and her maid to consult at their leisure.

You know, Bidulph, I am not naturally morose; and that I am not very apt to be wanting in that complaisance which all women expect, and which I really think due to *almost* all women: but this one had, in the preceding scene, so intirely thrown off her sex, that I could hardly consider her as a female. I had known many of her ill qualities before; but those she now discovered, if they did not shew her more wicked, certainly rendered her more disgustful to me than the others. In short, I found that all decorum was to be laid aside: I had gone too far not to put the finishing hand to my work; and I had no other measures to observe, but to finish, by dint of force, what I had begun by stratagem. When I mentioned the nunnery to you in a former letter, it was in mere gaiety of heart: I had no serious thoughts of that kind, nor did I now propose it as a practicable scheme. I knew the woman too well to suppose she would acquiesce; though, to confess the truth to you honestly, I think, if she refuses my other plan of accommodation, I must compel her to accept of this: nor ought it to be considered in any other light than that of confining a wild beast, who, having already done a great deal of mischief, would still do more, if left at liberty: but I think I shall not be driven to this. I believe she will accept of a husband with a good settlement, sooner than resign her liberty.

And now who do you think the husband is whom I have under contemplation for her? Why, no less a man than my valet de chambre Monsieur Pivet. He is young and handsome, of good parts, and a man of birth. He tells me he has an uncle that is a marquis, and three or four cousins that are in the high court of parliament. Without a joke, the fellow is of a pretty good family: he was bred a mercer, and in a frolic had run away from his business, when I picked him up at Paris, at the time you and I were there together. He then told me, that he only hired with me for an opportunity of seeing a little of the world, and that he would one time or other sit down and settle to his trade. I have sounded him on the point, and find him very ready to accept of the lady with all her faults.

I told you I introduced him to Mrs Gerrarde, to serve as her interpreter in the house, at the time I was ill. I did not then tell her who he was; and both she and her maid take him for no other than an acquaintance of mine, who happens to lodge in the same house with us. The vain rogue has encouraged this opinion, and I suppose passes for a very pretty fellow with them; for you know Pivet is a Beau, and is really not ungenteel. But do not fancy that I intend to impose him on the lady for any other than what he really is. All disguise is now laid aside, and I shall proceed with the utmost plainness and sincerity, as soon as I know the lady's mind in regard to her choice.

Here, my dear Sir George, I must take breath a little: it has been a busy day. I undertook a difficult voyage without the certainty of a landing-place; a few storms I expected to encounter; I hope I have weathered the worst, and have come at length to some prospect of an harbour. I expect my next greeting to you will be from a fairer shore. – Upon second thoughts, I will not send this off, till I can put both you and myself out of the reach of suspence . . . .

Congratulate me, Sir George, honour me, as the first of politicians, the greatest of negotiators! Let no hero of romance compare himself to me, for first making difficulties, and then extricating myself out of them; let no giant pretend to equal me in the management of captive beauties in inchanted castles; let no necromancer presume to vie with me in skill for metamorphosing tigresses into doves, and changing imperious princesses into plain country nymphs. *All* this I have brought to pass, without the assistance of enchanted sword or dwarf, in the compass of a few days; but take the circumstances in the order they occurred.

I left the lady, as I told you, to utter her complaints to her confidante. Rachael, a simple girl, who had just sense enough to regard her own interest, was not likely to give her mistress much consolation; for she was at least as much *my* friend as her's. How *they* passed the night I know not; for my own part, I slept in perfect tranquillity. I desired Pivet in the morning to go and inquire, as from himself, how the lady rested. Mrs Gerrarde, who was still in bed, no sooner heard his voice in the outer room, as he was speaking to her maid, than she called out to Monsieur Pivet, and desired he would be so good as to step into her chamber. Pivet, not much abashed at being admitted to a lady's *ruèlle*, obeyed her summons, and placed himself in an armed chair by her. He said he hoped it was not owing to illness that he saw her in bed. Yes, Sir, said she, I am exceedingly ill: I have not slept the whole night, and am now in a high fever. Has Mr Faulkland told you any thing in relation to me? I had prepared Pivet, and he had his answers ready. Madam, said he, I am not a stranger to your situation, and am exceedingly sorry for it: I wish the little influence *I* have over Mr Faulkland could be employed for your service; but he is a positive man, very enterprising, and not to be controlled by any-body. Do you know my story, Sir, cried Mrs Gerrarde? He bowed, and looked down. Mrs Gerrarde understanding this as an affirmative, and raising herself up a little, cried out, A base, ungenerous man! Does he intend to expose me wherever he goes? By no means, Madam, answered Pivet: there is nothing in your story that would do you the least injury in any-body's opinion here:

the ladies in France do not think it any disgrace to have lovers.

You are very obliging, Sir, she replied; and perhaps I have as much to say in my vindication as any woman: but sure never was mortal used in the barbarous manner I am. Do you know the proposal he had the insolence to make me last night? Either to take a husband of *his* chusing (*any* low fellow, I suppose, he thinks good enough for me), or immediately to go into a nunnery. Oh! Sir, and she catched hold of his hand, as you are a gentleman, if you have compassion, any humanity towards an unfortunate woman, try to deliver me out of his hands. I have a pretty good sum of money in my posssession; contrive the means of my escape; my gratitude to you shall be unbounded! and she wrung his hand.

Ah! Madam, said Pivet, looking tenderly at her, I would it were in my power; I should think myself but too happy if it were possible for me to accomplish what you request; but I fear it will be impracticable: I declare to you, if I were at my own disposal, I would fly with you to the remotest part of the world; but I am a young man, who have my fortune to make: I am under particular ties here, and have besides such obligations to Mr Faulkland, as makes it impossible for me, consistently with *honour*, to interfere in this business.

Sir, said she eagerly, can't you write a letter for me, or furnish me with the means of informing my friends in England of my situation?

Madam, said he, before Mr Faulkland permitted me the honour of seeing you, he engaged my solemn promise that I would not intermeddle in your affairs.

Lord, what will become of me! What would you, Sir, advise me to do? For as for that wretch (meaning me), I am determined, if I can help it, not to suffer him to come near me.

'Tis a very nice point, Madam: I really do not well know how to advise: but, to be sure, a nunnery is a choice not to be recommended to a lady of your youth and beauty, unless your inclinations lead you that way; then indeed –

She interrupted him. Don't name it to me, Sir; don't name it: I am determined to keep out of *that* snare, if it be for nothing but an opportunity to be revenged on that tyrant: I would marry a beggar sooner than give up that hope.

As for that, Madam, said Pivet, I suppose Mr Faulkland would not be so ungenerous as to compel you to marry one beneath you: there are many young men of good families who would think themselves honoured by your acceptance of them: your personal accomplishments alone are a sufficient recommendation; but Mr Faulkland mentioned to me the additional advantage of fortune. I dare answer for him he will not think of bestowing you unworthily.

I had charged Pivet not to go too far: he thought it time to break off the conversation; and, rising up, he told Mrs Gerrarde he was going into my apartment, and desired to know if she would honour him with any commands.

Sir, said she, I shall only beg you will tell Mr Faulkland, that I never *can* think of his proposal; that I am very ill, and beg to be left in quiet for a few days; but shall be very glad to see *you* whenever you are at leisure.

He bowed, and left her; then came directly to me, and repeated the conversation he had with her word for word. I am glad, said I, to find you are so much in her good graces: it will accelerate my plot; but we must not make you too cheap: if we manage discreetly, she may possibly think herself very well to get off with you.

At present I stand pretty well with her, Sir, said Pivet: she does not suspect that I am your servant: I fear if she did, as the lady seems to have a high spirit, she would forbid me her presence.

I found Pivet had no mind to have this part of his situation explained: his vanity had been highly tickled at passing upon her for a gentleman, and *my* friend. – He had, in obedience to my orders, spent much of his time with her during the few days that I had been too ill to see her. I had, at my first introduction of him to her, cautioned him against letting her know in what capacity he was with me: I did not then give him my reasons for this, and he supposed they were no other, than that, finding it necessary to have him pretty much with her in her confinement, I did not chuse to alarm her pride by the knowlege of his station. I did not hint at my design till the day before I had prevailed on her to write the letter to Mr Arnold. Pivet did not at all disrelish the proposal: he had not been blind to Mrs Gerrarde's charms: he only seemed surprized at my being willing to part with her so soon; for he had not the least conception of my reasons for carrying her off, and very naturally concluded I was deeply engaged in an amour. It was not difficult to guess his thoughts on this occasion.

Pivet, said I, I must premise one thing to you: I assure you there is not, nor ever was, any intrigue between Mrs Gerrarde and me. I do not, however, pretend to vouch for her chastity. It was no secret at V— hall that she had occasioned an unhappy breach in Mr Arnold's family; and that, and that *only* (as I have a most particular value and affection for that family), was my motive to the carrying this lady away. As I hope the disunion (now the cause of it is removed) will no longer subsist, I find it necessary to provide for Mrs Gerrarde some way or other. A good husband I would wish to bestow on her. I do not yet know whether I shall be able to bring her into any measures; but if she should be prevailed on to accept of you, and I should make it worth your while to accept of her, can you overlook the levity she has been guilty of, and resolve to use her kindly?

He promised he would make the best husband in the universe. I bid him not be too sure of success, as I did not yet know Mrs Gerrarde's mind, and feared I should find it hard to bring her into terms; adding, that though I intended to threaten her, I should be very unwilling to make use of compulsion; but if she should happen to like him, without suspecting my design, I might accomplish my purpose with less reluctance on her side, and much more satisfaction to myself.

The conversation he had just had with her elated him highly: she had made him her confidant; she had implored his assistance; she had promised an *unbounded* gratitude; she had prohibited *my* visits, and invited *his*. All this facilitated my work, and I at one time thought of letting her e'en work out her fate, and run blindfold into my trap; for it is plain, if Pivet had given in to it, she would have marched off with him, and even married him, to get out of my clutches; and then, you know, she could have blamed nobody but herself for the consequences. But I resolved not to impose on the gypsey any farther; but let her know what she was to expect before the bargain was concluded, and at least give her her option of having the power of continuing a jilt, or being canonized for a saint.

I found things were now likely to take such a turn as I wished; but it still required management. Pivet, said I, you must let her see you no more to-day; it will make her prize your company the more: keep out of the way, that you may not be seen by Rachael; and give such orders in the house, as that there may be proper attendance for the lady. One of my footmen spoke a little French, and he had been directed to receive and communicate Mrs Rachael's orders in the family.

Tho' Pivet assured me that he thought Mrs Gerrarde was not so ill as she said she was, I yet thought it incumbent on me to have the advice of a physician. The people with whom I lodged said I could not have a better than the doctor who had attended me, as he was reckoned very skilful. I told them, in the present case, I believed honesty was more requisite than skill. They said he was very honest too; so I desired he might be sent for.

Mrs Gerrarde, being determined to carry on the farce of sickness, pretended she was not able to rise; and the doctor was introduced to her bedside. As he could neither understand his patient, nor make himself understood by her, I had ordered the footman, whom I mentioned to you before, as knowing a little French, to wait at the chamber door; for I was resolved so far to keep up my resentment and my importance, as not to vouch-safe assisting at the conference; which, by this means, became the most ridiculous scene you can imagine. The doctor, having felt Mrs Gerrarde's pulse, proposed his questions by the footman, who just peeped his nose in at the door. He explained them (very ill I suppose) to Rachael in English, who re-repeated them to her lady within her curtains; for she would not suffer them to be drawn back. Mrs Gerrarde's answers travelled the same round-about way back to the doctor, who got them mangled in very bad French from his interpreter.

Mrs Gerrarde, provoked, I believe, at the doctor's visit, and very much tired of his questions, asked peevishly where Monsieur Pivet was? This inquiry I expected; and the fellow who told me of it, had been ordered to inform her that Monsieur Pivet was not at home.

The doctor, after leaving his patient, came to me, and confirmed the character I had received of him, both for skill in his profession, and integrity in his practice; for he told me very honestly, that he thought the lady was in perfect health. I thought the doctor deserved a double fee, and accordingly gave it to him; requesting him, however, to continue his visits: for I told him, that, though the lady might really be very well, she was, however, a little vapourish.

I left her to her reflections the whole day. Rachael inquired three or four times of the footman if Mr Pivet was come in, but was always answered in the negative. I was pleased at her sollicitude about him.

I desired him to wait on her the next day, at the time the doctor paid his visit; and instructed Pivet to ask the doctor, in her presence, what he thought of her case, and to report his answer fairly to her; for I was resolved not to let her imagine that she imposed on me.

The doctor, by Pivet's means, discoursed with her more readily than he had done the day before. Pivet asked his opinion of her disorder, and the physican declared it as freely as he had done to me;

adding, he should not have repeated his visit, if I had not insisted on it.

Pivet could not help smiling. Mrs Gerrarde observed it; for, I suppose, she watched his countenance, and asked him what the doctor had said. He says, Madam, what gives me a vast deal of pleasure; which is, that your disorder is intirely imaginary. He is an ignorant fellow, said Mrs Gerrarde; and you may tell him I desire to see him no more. The poor doctor, who knew not what she said, made her half a dozen scrapes, and withdrew.

She then threw back her curtain; and re-assuming the subject she had been upon the day before with Pivet, asked him if he had had any conversation with me about her? and what resolution I had come to?

Pivet (who had begged I would leave this conference intirely to his management) seemed to hesitate a little, and appeared melancholy. We have had some talk about you, Madam, said he; and Mr Faulkland tells me, if you reject the nunnery scheme (which I think *he* seems to be fondest of), that he has a person in his thoughts, who, he believes, will be a suitable match for you, if you are willing to accept of him; if not – here he stop'd. What if I should not, Sir? Pray speak. I hope, Madam, he will not carry matters to an extremity. Extremity, Sir! Do you think he can be brutal enough to force me into a nunnery? Are there no laws in France? I *hope* he will not, Madam; but I can't pretend to answer for him: he is a strange man: he seems out of temper too: the doctor told him nothing ailed you; he believes him, and spoke harshly on the occasion. And what, said she, is the match that he calls *suitable?* One of his footmen perhaps, or his barber?

Pivet affected to look concerned. He tells me, Madam, he has cast his eyes on a young man, well born, and genteelly educated; not contemptible in his personal accomplishments, and one who he is sure will make you a fond and obliging husband.

Pivet sighed deeply, and cast his eyes languishingly on her. You seem concerned, Sir, said she. Do you know the person? It is my doubts on that occasion, Madam, that is the cause of my uneasiness. Pray explain yourself, Mr Pivet. Madam, I dare not, he replied, with great solemnity. I will only assure you, that whoever the person be, whom Mr Faulkland has not yet named to me, I think him the happiest man in the world. What can be his meaning, asked Mrs Gerrarde, for telling you *so* much, and yet concealing the person's name? He says, he has not proposed it yet to the gentleman, Madam;

and as, he tells me, he can't in honour conceal any part of your story, he is fearful – I beg your pardon, Madam; you will excuse me if I do not repeat his scruples on this occasion. I understand you, Sir. He supposes his friend will reject me. Some such insinuation he threw out, Madam, said Pivet. I told him, that he need only permit the gentleman to *see* you; and if he then made any objection, he must be the blindest and most insensible man alive. He spoke this with a warmth that seemed highly pleasing to the lady. She bowed, and answered, *All* men, Sir, are not as generous as you. But what did Mr Faulkland say to this? He only smiled, and said he wished his friend might think as I did; that he would tell me his name another time; and that, in the mean time, it would oblige him if my visits to you were less frequent. Inhuman monster, said she; would he debar me of the only satisfaction I have? Let me but live to get out of his hands! if I can escape him by any means, I will find ways to reckon with him for this. Be so good, Mr Pivet to tell him, that I am content to take the person he offers, let him be who he will: I shall expect nothing from him but insults; therefore shall not be surprized if I see myself sacrificed to some despicable wretch: but any, *any* thing is better than to be in the power of such a tyrant! Madam, answered Pivet, you need not fear the being compelled to accept of an unworthy object: Mr Faulkland declares, that if you should absolutely dislike the gentleman, when you see him, he will be far from constraining you to take him for your husband. The other choice is still open to you, and, by what I can judge, Mr Faulkland seems to wish you would give that the preference. I would die first, cried Mrs Gerrarde – The fool, does he think I can be so entrapped? No, no; the authority of a husband, even of Faulkland's chusing, cannot be such a bar to my revenge as the walls of a nunnery would be. – Sir, I think myself obliged to you, and flatter myself you would have served me if you could. I may yet have it in my power to make you a return for your kind intentions towards me. I presume, when Mr Faulkland has disposed of his property, you will then be absolved of your promise to him in regard to me, and will still have charity enough to befriend an unfortunate woman. She wept, and Pivet owned he was ready to do so too; but constraining himself, protested she should command his life; and withdrew full of seeming uneasiness.

He told me what had passed between him and the lady, and I could not help approving his management of the scene, though the rogue had stretched beyond the truth; but stratagems, you know, are allowable in love, and a lover he was now become in good earnest.

He had taken care to alarm Mrs Gerrarde's apprehensions at every passage of access. He had informed her, that I had a husband for her in my thoughts; and at the same time, that he avoided the most distant hint of its being himself, he engaged her favour by seeming to wish it *were*. Then he took care to insinuate, at least, a possibility of her being refused by the person designed for her, and this he very naturally supposed would raise his own consequence with her, in case any suspicion should fall on him, of his being the intended husband. He pretended I had taken umbrage at his visiting her, still more to inflame her resentment against me, and increase her impatience to deliver herself out of my hands; at the same time he artfully hinted that he was not the man destined to be happy. This, as he saw already he was not unacceptable to her, he thought would make him doubly welcome, when she should find herself no worse off. Then the nunnery was mentioned, in terrorem, with broad hints of my resolution. In short, Pivet played his part so cunningly, that it had all the effect he could have wished; and Mrs Gerrarde, finding her spirit matched, was obliged to surrender at discretion.

I own I did not expect to have succeeded so soon; and without Pivet, who had now a feeling in the affair, I certainly should not. I resolved directly to make the best use of the advantage I had gained. I told Pivet that he should be married the next day. He was so transported at the thought, that he begged I would give him leave to go to Mrs Gerrarde, to declare his love and his good fortune together; for Sir, said he, you know she promises to accept of whomsoever you propose, and I hope she will not dispise your choice so much as she thinks she shall. Softly, softly, good Monsieur Pivet, your violent hurry will spoil all. I do not mean that you shall see her till to-morrow. Not till to-morrow! Ah Sir! do, I beseech you, Sir, allow me; she will think it very cruel. (Poor Pivet, thought I, thou wilt have enough of her). Simpleton (to him), this day's suspence will forward your business more than all you could say to her in seven hours: is it not enough you are sure of her? We have other things now to mind. What plan of life do you purpose to pursue? You know I have promised to do handsomely for you.

Sir, said he, I always intended to follow the business I was bred to; and if this piece of extraordinary good fortune had *not* happened to me, I did purpose, tho' you have been the best of masters to me, to have asked your permission to return to my friends, in order to settle in my trade, as I have some capital of my own. But to be sure, Sir, I shall be directed in this, as in every thing else, by your will and pleasure. I approve of your design intirely, said I; but there are certain conditions that must be previously settled between you and me. In the first place, tell me honestly, what is the capital you say you are worth.

He answered, his father had left him about eight thousand livres, which were in the hands of a banker in Paris, whom he named to me, and referred me to him for confirmation of the truth of what he told me.

Well, said I, this will go a good way towards setting you up in your own business. Where do you think of settling?

He answered, Paris was the best place for his trade.

On that I put an absolute negative; I said Paris was too much frequented by my countrymen, to be a proper place for Mrs Gerrarde to make her appearance in, as she was likely to meet there with more of her acquaintance than might be convenient: I told him I had no objection to any other large provincial town.

He said he was born at Dijon, and should like to go thither, as he had many friends there.

Be it so, said I: What I purpose doing for you is this. Mrs Gerrarde has eight hundred pounds of her own; I will add as much more to it, for which I will give you my bond, till I can have the money remitted from England; and this you shall settle on her, that she may be sure of a support in case of your death, and the interest you shall allow her for her own separate use, but without her knowing that you are tied down to it, that you may have it in your power to oblige her.

He made no reply, but acquiesced with a low bow.

I laughed at the simplicity of his countenance. Pivet, said I, though I have taken care of Mrs Gerrarde's interest, I do not intend to neglect yours, provided you make no demur to the terms. You already know my reasons for proceeding as I have done in this affair. I have great cause to apprehend Mrs Gerrarde's vindictive spirit, if she should find means, which I know she will endeavour at, to lay open the real state of this transaction to some people in England. This might frustrate all that I have been at so much pains to accomplish; be it your care then to prevent it. I cannot wish you to use harsh measures with your wife; but if you have address enough to prevent a correspondence with any one in England, (an elopement, for both your sakes, I am not willing to suppose; though I think, for some time at least, you must keep a strict eye over her) if, as I said, you can prevent a correspondence, I think it will answer my purpose; and that I may make it your interest to do this, I will bind myself, by as strong an obligation as the law can make, to pay you two hundred pounds a year English, so long as you keep your wife within the bounds prescribed; provided, if, after three years, I find those terms no longer necessary, they shall, if I then chuse it, become void. I shall also add something to enable you to fit up a house and a shop, that you need not be under a necessity of breaking in upon your capital.

Pivet's gratitude overflowed at his lips for this (as he called it) noble provision. He said, he made no doubt of gaining so far upon Mrs Gerrarde's affections, as to be able effectually to fulfil his covenant, without using violent methods; but, said he, at all events, I warrant you shall hear no more of her.

Preliminaries thus adjusted, I sent for a notary of reputation, to whom I gave instructions to draw up two separate articles for the purposes mentioned; the latter was to be a secret between Pivet and me, as it was by no means proper for Mrs Gerrarde to be let into it. The other, which regarded her own particular settlement, was intended for her perusal and approbation. I charged the notary to use dispatch, and he promised to have both the papers ready by next morning, as also the bond which I was to give Pivet for the payment of eight hundred pounds.

The lawyer brought the papers according to his promise, and they were signed, sealed, and delivered in due form. That which was to be the private agreement between Pivet and me, was worded in consequence of an article which I drew up myself, and made Pivet sign; wherein I set forth particulars at large.

Pivet was very impatient to see his beloved, but a little uneasy lest she should be disgusted with him, when she should come to know the situation he had been in. I bid him not be discouraged, telling him I should set off that circumstance of his having been my gentleman (for so I chose to call him) in the most favourable light. I presented him with a very elegant suit of cloaths, which I had never worn, and which fitted him very well, as you know he is nearly my size. You cannot imagine how handsome the fellow looked when he was dressed, for he had linnen and every thing else suitable to his cloaths.

I then desired him to wait on his goddess; but he, who had been so eager a little before, was now quite abashed at the thoughts of making his pretensions known to the lady, and intreated me to present him to her. I saw he was quite disconcerted at the serious scene he was going to engage in.

I pitied him, and told him I would go with him to Mrs Gerrarde; but that it was proper first to prepare her a little.

He said he thought so too.

I immediately sent for Rachael, and speaking to her at the door, without letting her see Pivet, I bid her tell her mistress that I purposed making her a visit in half an hour, and should introduce the gentleman, whom I expected she would, according to her promise, receive at my hands for her husband; reserving to herself still the liberty of chusing the other alternative, in case she disliked him.

Pivet shewed the sollicitude of a lover, after this message was sent to his mistress; Poor dear lady, said he, how I pity her? What must she suffer in this interval? But your presence, Monsieur Pivet, said I, will dispel all her fears, and make her the happiest of women.

The poor fellow was out of countenance, and I dare say as anxious as Mrs Gerrarde.

As I received no answer from her to my message, I construed her silence as leave to attend her; and accordingly, at the appointed time, I entered her apartment, leading Pivet by the hand.

She was sitting at a table, leaning her head on one of her hands; she cast a look of scorn at me, and immediately withdrew her eyes, not so much as deigning to glance them at Pivet, little imagining that it was *he* who accompanied me, though she knew it was her intended bridegroom.

Pivet was not able to speak; he trembled, and, like a true inamorato, ran to her, clapt one knee to the ground, and ventured, though with great diffidence, to take one of her hands.

This action obliged the haughty fair one to vouchsafe him a glance at her eye.

Her surprize, spite of her assumed airs of grandeur, was not to be concealed; it was apparent, she coloured, and though she intended to have been solemn and lofty, she even *stared*; and I could discover a litle gleam of pleasure dance over her countenance.

What! Monsieur Pivet? And then she looked at me, as if for an explanation.

Yes, madam, said I, Monsieur Pivet *is* the man. (I was going to say the *happy* man, but I did not mean to compliment her; my business was to make her think I was doing her a favour). It has been your good fortune to make a conquest of him; and in the hope of your making him a good wife, as I am sure he will make you a good husband, I have consented to the match; and I spoke this in the tone of one, who thinking he has conferred a great obligation on an undeserving object, expects to be thanked for it.

The woman, with all her art and assurance to boot, was quite confounded. I did not give her time to recover herself, but taking the settlement out of my pocket, and reading it to her, Look there, madam, and see if I have injured you in the disposal of your person and your fortune.

Mrs Gerrarde, always alert when her interest was in the question, took the paper, and notwithstanding her confusion, read it entirely over. Pivet's handsome appearance, joined to her former prepossessions, had made so good an impression on her, that she began to think the matter worth attending to. When she had read the paper, she put it into Pivet's hands. Sir, said she, it should appear by this that you have acted generously; but as I have already been imposed upon by that gentleman (looking at me) all this may, for ought I know, be a deceit; but as it is not in my power to make terms for myself, it is to no purpose for me to make objections, or to enquire any farther. I am ready to accept your offer, only I should be glad to know who the man is, that I am to make my husband.

She spoke this with such an air of disdain, that the poor lover, shrunk up and diminished in his own eyes, left me to make an answer. Mrs Gerrarde, said I, I declare to you solemnly that there is no deception in any thing which you see, nor any foul play meant to you. This young man, whom I now present to you for your husband, is well born, and has many genteel relations in this country; he has it in his power, to my certain knowlege, to make good the settlement he proposes for you, which I will take care to see properly secured. That part of it which is your own property, you have now in your possession, the other half I know is his. He was brought up to a creditable business, which he intends to follow. I know him to be good natured, and of an obliging temper. He lived with me some time, and accompanied me in my travels. I suppose his having been my gentleman, which station he did not accept through necessity, will not be a material objection (and I smiled and affected to look very proud), and I only mention it to convince you that I have no design of deceiving you, or concealing any part of his character.

Pivet coloured (for I stole a side glance at him) and looked sheepish. He began an aukward compliment with a bow, and 'I hope, madam' – but I relieved him; and speaking to Mrs Gerrarde, You know all now, madam, that can be known; therefore, if you are disposed to keep your word, let us put an end to this business to-day. To-day, Sir! Yes, to-day, madam. What occasion is there for farther delay?

Pivet now plucked up his courage, and begged, since she had consented, that she would not defer his happiness. I told her, between mirth and chiding, that I was in haste to get rid of my charge, and was therefore determined to make her over to Mr Pivet that evening; and telling her I would give orders about the ceremony, left the lovers to make out for themselves a scheme of conjugal felicity. Pivet pleaded his own cause so effectually, that, in the evening, I had the satisfaction of bestowing, with my own hand, that inestimable treasure of virtue and meekness, Mrs Gerrarde, on my faithful Squire, Monsieur Pivet; to the no small joy of the latter, and I believe, if the truth were known, to the no great mortification of the former. Mrs Rachael and myself were the only witnesses of this illustrious union.

When the ceremony was over, I approached, according to custom, to congratulate and salute the bride; but she turned her saucy cheek to me, and affected the whole night vast dignity of behaviour; yet it was so foreign to her nature, that it appeared ridiculous; however it was better than ranting.

I invited them both to sup with me, and treated Pivet with a familiar civility that seemed to please him highly, as it did him credit in the presence of his lady.

After supper, Pivet entreated me to complete the friendly and generous offices I had already done him, by undertaking the settlement of all money matters for him. As he knew I intended to go to Paris, he begged I would receive for him the sum he had in the hands of the banker, which, he said, if I would remit to him, it would enable him to enter upon his business immediately. At the same time he (with no ill grace) presented me my bond again, assuring me he relied entirely upon my honour for the execution of my promise to him, farther requesting that I would put that, together with Mrs Gerrarde's money, if she approved of it, into such hands as I should judge most proper for her advantage.

I was pleased at the openness of his proceedings, and promised to do every thing for their mutual satisfaction; but insisted on his keeping the bond, or lodging it in some proper hand, till I could redeem it, by paying the money, which I should take care should be speedily done. I told him, I thought the sooner he set out for his own province the better. He said, he should be ready the next day, if Mrs Gerrarde (for he did not yet presume to call her by his name) did not object to it. He appealed to her with his looks.

She had scarce condescended to open her lips before; but now answered, You may be sure, Sir, I shall not think it too soon to get out of a prison.

He asked her if she chose to take her maid Rachael along with her?

Certainly, she said; I should not be fond of having a servant about me, by whom I should not be understood.

Rachael was now called in, and the thing proposed to her. She seemed rather inclined to return to England; but I told her, she could not, in gratitude, desert her lady in a strange country; and that if she had a mind to make me her friend, which she should find me upon any future occasion, she would attend her home, and continue with her till her mistress was willing to part with her.

The girl upon this consented to stay, and received Mrs Gerrarde's orders to prepare for their departure the next day.

In the morning I made Pivet a present for his travelling charges, and Rachael another; telling her, according to the account I had of her behaviour, that I would be kind to her. She made me all the promises that I could desire; assuring me, that it was purely to oblige me that she staid with Mrs Gerrarde.

Pivet told me, that he would send the sum which his wife had, in bills to me, to be appropriated in the manner agreed on: for he said, that having that morning mentioned to her my generosity, in relation to the bond, she had owned, that, notwithstanding her resentment to me, she had no distrust of my honour in *those* particulars.

I took this opportunity of telling Pivet, that when he could get his wife in the humour, he might prevail on her to give an instrument, impowering my steward to receive the little income of her jointure at Ashby, which I would take care should be remitted to him; for, trifling as it was, it might be serviceable.

When they were ready to set forward on their journey, I begged leave to speak a few words to madam Pivet by herself. She seemed not inclined to the conference, but her husband very obligingly pressing her not to part with me in enmity, and at the same time quitting the room, she was obliged to hear me.

I then very frankly asked her pardon for the lengths I had gone; telling her, that I hoped time, and her own good sense, would convince her that she was more obliged to me, than her passion would then give her leave to see. Remember, madam, I have kept my word with you. You are now married to a very deserving young man; you have a competent support during your life. Happiness is in your power if you do not wilfully cast it away from you. Shew now that greatness of mind of which you have so often boasted, by forgiving the man, who has, as you think, injured you; and resolving at once on a behaviour that shall, in your turn, intitle you, not only to the forgiveness, but even to the esteem, of those whom you have injured.

I would have preached on, and given her more good advice, but she cut me short, with this decisive answer. Sir, I neither desire your counsel nor your good opinion; Mr Pivet *may* deserve some regard from me, but *you* I will never forgive, and she flung from me.

I called in Pivet, and telling him I was infinitely pleased at the good disposition I found his lady in, I wished him all happiness and a safe journey, and they set out directly for Dijon.

And now, my dear Bidulph, stop, to praise, to admire, to wonder at my virtue! I, who have had one of the finest women in England in my possession, for so many days (and by the way was not her aversion) to yield up her (by me) unpolluted charms to the arms of another! Add to this, that it has cost me more to make one woman honest, than it need have done to have made half a dozen – otherwise. I had like to have writ a strange ugly word, that was just at the nib of my pen.

If you relate my story with the laudable partiality of a friend, judiciously abolishing the context (for which you may have many precedents), and neatly splicing together the useful fragments, shall I not appear to posterity as great as Scipio himself? Ah! Sir George, if we knew the secret springs of many of those actions which dazzle us, in the histories of the renowned heroes of old, it is not impossible but the wonderous page might dwindle into as insignificant a tale as mine is.

Well, I thank my good genius that has led me safely through such a labyrinth as I had got into. In getting rid of that woman (and not disgracefully neither), I feel as if I had shaken off a great load. But what a graceless baggage it is, not to thank me for my kindness. I, who have been more than a father to her, in saving her first from perdition, and then settling her well in the world – but there is no obliging some tempers.

I shall leave this place to-morrow, for I must hasten to Paris, to put every thing on a good footing for the new-married pair; and then I will go and ramble I do not care whither, for another year. I shall lodge at Paris, where I did before, and desire you will write to me directly an account of all that passes within the circle of your family. Let your sister and my lady Bidulph know in what manner I have disposed of Mrs Gerrarde, but besure you do it discreetly, and take care not to mention that paultry circumstance of her settlement, or any other private agreement with Pivet. I know Mrs Arnold's delicacy would be hurt by the knowlege of this; therefore beware of dropping the least hint of it, at your peril. Tell Lady Bidulph I will pray devoutly for her daughter's happiness; if what I have done will promote it, it will not a little contribute to my own; tho' I begin to feel it is not to be expected in this life, at least by such a hopeless wanderer as I am.

I could sit now, and indite melancholy verses, or write an elegy, or make my will, or do any other splenetic thing: in short, I have a good mind to turn monk and go into a monastery. I am sure I should have lady Bidulph's vote for that.

Adieu, my dear Bidulph, you will not hear from me again, perhaps, till I am in another region.

Nov. 30.

December 17

What a strange man this is, my Cecilia! The more I reflect on his conduct, the more I am amazed! What a mixture is there in his nature! Wild to a romantic degree in his conceptions, yet how steady, how resolute, how consistent, in putting those flights of fancy into act! Generous he certainly is; how few men would put themselves to the trouble and expence that he has done, from such a disinterested, such a compassionte motive! Nay, on the contrary, I believe most men would be cruel enough to take a sort of pleasure in the vexation of a man, who had succeeded to the love of a mistress, once so much valued; and would enjoy a mean triumph in being, though without reason, the object of *his* jealousy, who had cut them off from all hope.

Mr Faulkland is above this. I think myself highly indebted to him, whether the scheme he has in so extraordinary a manner undertaken for my service succeeds or not. Yet do I wish from my heart, that the separation between Mr Arnold and Mrs Gerrarde had been brought about by any other means. What if Mr Arnold should ever come at the truth (though I think that hardly possible), might it not leave him more estranged from me than he is even now? or if he should, in consequence of this odd adventure, return to his poor banished wife, repent of his injurious suspicions of her, and restore her to his confidence and love, can he, can he ever restore to her that peace she has so long been a stranger to? Will no latent sparks of former unkindness ever rekindle and light up the fire of discord? How unwillingly do we repair the unprovoked injuries which we find we have done to others! Poor Mr Arnold; if I am so happy as to have my innocence cleared to him, how miserable will his own reflections make him! but if he *is* convinced (which has been my daily and hourly prayers), he *shall* not be unhappy, if I can make him otherwise. Oh! my dear, it is the wish, the ardent longing of my soul, to recover the esteem, though I lose the love, of Mr Arnold! for I call that Being to witness, who knows the secrets of all hearts, that since I have been his wife, I have never, even in thought, swerved from that perfect and inviolable fidelity which I vowed to him. What then must have been my sufferings, deprived of his love, cast out from his house, and branded with the dreadful name of an Adultress? For where is the difference between the intention and the act? To me there is no distinction, and the husband must be gross that makes one.

My mother has suffered me to tell her the substance of Mr Faulkland's letters, though she would not read them. I own I was better satisfied that she should receive her information thus, because his light manner of expressing himself in many places would have given her great offence. Sir George did not consider this when he submitted the letters to my mother's as well as my perusal. Many grave animadversions did she make during my recital, and many times lift up her eyes in wonder at Mrs Gerrarde's behaviour. She often said Mr Faulkland was frantic to undertake such a thing, and wished he had not taken such a *terrible* woman in hand. When I came to that part of the account where Mrs Gerrarde had been prevailed on to write to Mr Arnold, I begged she would give me leave to read the copy of the letter to her, as I assured her there was nothing in it but would give her pleasure.

She consented; and I read it, leaving out Mr Faulkland's apostrophes. My mother did not interrupt me; and finding she continued silent when I came to the conclusion, I looked at her, and saw tears running down her cheeks. Yes, my dear, my innocent child, said she, passionately throwing her arms round me, you *were* wronged; God knows you were wronged; and He now proclaims your innocence even from the mouth of your most inveterate enemy. And lifting up her eyes, Thou hast turned the hearts of sinners to the wisdom of the just; therefore shall the righteous give Thee thanks. And then, God forgive that woman all her sins for this one act, and God forgive Mr Faulkland *his* sins, and reward him for this goodness. Sure your husband will relent now; sure he will long to take my poor, forsaken, virtuous child (and her tears gushed as she spoke), to his bosom again.

I could not answer her for some time; my own tears almost choaked me: at last I said, My dear mother, I have no doubt of Mr Arnold's returning kindness: he will, I hope, be convinced that I am guiltless, and we may yet be happy.

She dried her eyes: God send, God send you may! But what has Mr Faulkland done with his poor penitent? I hope he will behave honourably to her; for this excellent parent had no doubt but that the letter, written by Mrs Gerrarde was, in a great measure, the result of her own contrition; for as I had not been minute in giving her a particular account of all the previous steps taken by Mr Faulkland to obtain it from her, she had not the least idea that Mrs Gerrarde had writ in that manner from any other motive than the good one which appeared obvious to her.

I told her, that I feared Mrs Gerrarde was far from being the penitent she supposed her; and then acquainted her with the true reasons which had induced her to write in the manner she had done. I then proceeded to tell her of her behaviour after writing the letter, and how Mr Faulkland had acted in consequence of that; concluding with informing her of Mrs Gerrarde's being married, and provided for in a very reputable way.

My mother was highly delighted at this last circumstance; for, she said, Mr Faulkland had no right to be the punisher of her crimes; and if he had not made a decent provision for her, she would never have looked upon him but as a dishonest person.

She told me, that though she was very glad, upon the whole, that Mr Arnold and that bad woman were separated, yet she was nevertheless not quite so well satisfied with the manner of it; for I think, said she, that it is impossible but that a man of Mr Arnold's good sense must, one time or other, have been convinced of his error, and, of his own accord, returned to a right way of thinking.

I answered, that might possibly have happened; but that he might have continued long enough under his infatuation intirely to ruin his family: and as for what regarded me in particular, I knew of no means so likely to remove his unjust suspicions effectually, as those which Mr Faulkland had taken.

You are right, my dear, said she; let us hope the best. I am glad Mr Faulkland does not mean to return soon to England: there is but one event which could ever reconcile me to his doing so; and that is, in order to do justice to the unfortunate Miss Burchell. If he would wipe out that blot in his character by marrying her, I should again allow him to be a good man: at present, I own, I can't help being dissatisfied, that one, so blameable as I think him, should have laid my daughter under the obligations which he has done.

I said it would rejoice me if he could be prevailed on to make Miss Burchell the reparation she mentioned; but I feared she had no advocate with Mr Faulkland; though I was of opinion, if he were made acquainted with the life of sorrow she led, as well as her reserved and modest behaviour, he would be inclined to favour her; especially if he were to see the poor little boy.

My mother said, He never could expect quiet of mind, till he had wiped the tears from her eyes.

Miss Burchell came in while we were speaking of her: my mother is always glad to see her. The poor girl had been exceedingly shocked at Mr Faulkland's carrying away her aunt. She thought this action put such an invincible bar between her and her hopes (almost desperate before), that it went near to distract her; for though there was no consanguinity in the case, yet the degree of relationship between her and Mrs Gerrarde, made her look upon this amour (for so she considered it) with the utmost horror. She had so often expressed her sense of it in so lively a manner, both to my mother and me, that had Mr Faulkland even been inclined to offer his hand, she could not, consistently either with virtue or common decency, have accepted of it.

My mother, ever delighted with acts of humanity, was in haste to communicate the true state of the case to Miss Burchell. It was her interest to keep our secret; therefore I made no scruple of trusting her with it; especially as I knew it would so much contribute to her peace of mind.

My mother accosted her with saying, Miss Burchell, I have something to tell you, that I believe will give you pleasure. The unhappy young woman lifted up her melancholy eyes; and, shaking her head, answered, *That*, I believe, Madam, is now impossible. Your aunt is married, said my mother, but not to Mr Faulkland; and, what is more, there has never any thing passed between them that need be a bar to you, if he could be brought to consider you as he ought. Miss Burchell looked amazed; then turned her eyes from my mother to me, as if for an explanation. My mother desired me to acquaint her with the history at large of Mr Faulkland's proceedings; I did so, and took care not to omit the tender manner in which he had mentioned her in one of his letters. She dropped some tears at the recital; and then, turning to my mother, My dear good Madam, you have snatched me from despair by this discovery: I was overwhelmed; I think I could not have got the better of my grief: a faint ray of glimmering hope is once more let in upon me. Mr Faulkland may *yet* be mine without a crime; or, if he is not, I shall at least have the satisfaction to think him not so abandoned as he appeared to me an hour ago. Oh! worthy and lovely Mrs Arnold! said she, addressing herself to me, you see how Mr Faulkland reveres you: oh! that you would but engage in my behalf! *you* can influence his heart; *you* can guide his reason; *you* are his fate!

Her fine eyes, which she fixed on me, filled with persuasive eloquence, let me into the whole of her meaning, and conveyed more to me than it was in the power of words to do. I understand you, dear Madam, said I; and it grieves my heart to think that I cannot, must not interest myself for you in the manner I would most ardently undertake to do, if there were not such obstacles in my way as it is impossible for me to get over. Mr Faulkland, you see, is free from the guilt we all feared he had plunged himself into: he is full of remorse for the injury he did you, and I dare believe retains in his heart a tender sense of your merit: he is still free; nay, he has declared his intention of continuing so. These circumstances give large room for hope: your unobjectionable conduct, joined to paternal affection, may still bring about that wished-for, happy event; but this must be left to time, and the workings of his own heart. You know Mr Faulkland is, in his natural temper, impatient of restraint; he is but a very young man, and has a few of those levities which a little more settled age infallibly will correct, where a good heart and a good understanding are united. Pardon me if I add, that Mr Faulkland is not ungenerous, however blameable he may have been in regard to you. All these circumstances considered, I say, may warrant your indulging a hope, that he will at last be brought to make you the reparation, which is mine and my mother's wish as much as your own. Ah! Madam, said she, but Mr Faulkland is a great way from me: the remembrance of me is already but too much worn out; distance, time, and a variety of objects, must intirely efface it. *Your* hand, the powerful magic of *your* touch, would soon brighten up the colouring of those faint, faded traces, that he but scarcely preserves of me in his memory. What could not your pen, guided by a heart so tender, so sympathizing with the grief of others, effect on the man who considers you as a divinity? If he had any hopes of *you*, Madam, it would be presumption in me to put in my claim; but, as you cannot be my rival, be my advocate: do, dear angelic lady! (and she lifted up her hands to me fervently) write to Mr Faulkland, if you can restore him to me, what prayers will I not pour out for your happiness?

My mother, who was greatly affected by her discourse, said to me, Indeed, my dear, if you could effect that, it would be a very meritorious work. Who knows what the high opinion Mr Faulkland has of you, and the great deference he pays to your judgment, may produce?

I was sorry my good mother's openness of heart had made her enter so suddenly into Miss Burchell's sentiments: it encouraged her to renew her intreatiess; she snatched both my mother's hands, and kissed them; she wanted words to thank her.

I was unwilling to appear cold in Miss Burchell's interest, or to refuse doing what my mother seemed to appove; but the resolution I had long before made, never to see, or on any account whatsoever to hold the least correspondence with Mr Faulkland, determined me. If strict prudence might on so extraordinary an occasion have dispensed with this promise, which, as I had made it to my own heart, I thought amounted almost to a vow, I could not however answer it to that decorum, which I had, as an inviolable law, determined to guide myself by, in so critical a situation. And I resolved to have it in my power to say, in case Mr Arnold and I were ever to unite again, that I had not in the smallest article departed from it.

I told Miss Burchell there was but one reason which could prevent me from complying with her request; but it was one of so much weight with me, that, after my informing her of it, I hoped she would be so good as not to urge me farther. I did, said I, upon my parting with my husband, make a firm resolution, not only never to see Mr Faulkland, but never to receive from, or write a line to him, nor in any manner whatsoever to keep up the least intercourse with him.

I did not know but that Mr Faulkland (if he should learn the truth) considering himself to be (as he really was, though innocently) the cause of that unfortunate separation, might, either with a design of consoling me, or of vindicating himself from any suspicion of blame, have endeavoured to see me or write to me. In this I was mistaken; his prudence, or his respect for me, prevented him from attempting either. The resolution I had made, however, I thought due to my husband's honour, as well as my own. The same cause still subsists; the weight of it perhaps more in my own imagination than in reality; but if it even be so, indulge me, dear Madam (to my mother), and dear Miss Burchell, in this singularity. I have (not improbably) the happy prospect of being restored to Mr Arnold's esteem; let me then be able to assure him, that these eyes, these ears, these hands, have been as guiltless as my heart, and all equally estranged from Mr Faulkland. This is a declaration I think due to that punctilio, or, give me leave to call it, that delicacy, I have endeavoured to preserve in all my conduct. Mother! you always taught me to avoid even the shadow of reproach.

Very true, my dearest, answered my mother; I believe you are in the right. Miss Burchell, I think my daughter cannot, conformably to that discretion by which she has always been governed, undertake your cause at present: it did not appear to me at first in the light wherein Sidney has now put it.

Miss Burchell made no answer, but by her tears; we were both affected, and I wished sincerely to have had it in my power to serve her. I told her, if Mr Arnold and I should ever be re-united, that I would endeavour to draw him so far over to our party, as to obtain his permission to correspond with Mr Faulkland: that I was sure he would join with me in wishing her the reparation she hoped for; and that I would make no scruple of engaging warmly for her in such a case. But then, Madam, said she, with what face can you interest yourself for me, so long as Mr Arnold shall think that my aunt has been criminal with Mr Faulkland? That thought, said I, did not occur to me before, and is indeed a difficulty; for should Mr Arnold know that the elopement of Mrs Gerrarde was against her will, and the letter she wrote him extorted from her by Mr Faulkland, it might perhaps injure me as much in his opinion, as Mrs Gerrarde's false suggestions had done before. Those intricacies, dear Miss Burchell, must be left to time, which I hope may unravel them favourably for us all. The attempt to disclose this affair to Mr Arnold must not be sudden; indeed I must be well assured of his restored confidence and affection before I can venture upon it at all. Whenever that joyful event happens, assure yourself of my best endeavours to serve you, if I have really any influence over Mr Faulkland, and circumstances should so happily concur as to put it in my power to make use of it.

Be contented, good Miss Burchell, said my mother, with this promise which my daughter has made you: if Mr Arnold and she should live together again, Mr Faulkland may probably return to England; as nothing I believe now keeps him abroad, but to avoid giving Mr Arnold umbrage in the present unhappy disunion between him and his wife.

December 18

My brother continues sullen; he seldom visits us, and when he does, the meeting on his part is cold. He has made himself master of many particulars relating to poor Mr Arnold's unhappy connection with Mrs Gerrarde; for since her elopement the affair has been more talked of than it was before, and her whole history traced out. She was the daughter of an innkeeper in a country town, and ran away with Captain Gerrarde, in his march through it, upon an acquaintance of but a few days. The husband, who was passionately fond of her, concealed the meanness of her birth, and put her off to his relations for a young lady of a reputable family, with whom he got a good fortune. This induced his sister, a widow lady, the mother of Miss Burchell, to leave at her death the care of the unhappy girl to captain Gerrarde. The captain, whose infirmities increased fast upon him a few years after his marriage, got leave to retire upon half-pay into the country; and he lived for the most part at Ashby, a little estate which he had purchased and settled upon his wife: it seems he had a pretty good personal fortune, which she had squandered, for his fondness could refuse her nothing, except living apart from him at London, which he could never consent to, though it was always her desire; but being debarred of this, she betook herself to such pleasures as the country afforded, and was always a leading woman at horse-races, assemblies, and such other amusements, as were within her reach; which, together with expensive treats at home, and card-playing (her supreme delight) left her at his death, which happened about five years after their marriage, in the indigent state she in her account of herself to Mr Faulkland acknowleges. It was then Mr Arnold became acquainted with her, and in the manner she represented; for my brother has lately fallen into the acquaintance of that very *relation* (as she calls him) which she mentions, a Mr Pinnick, at whose lodgings they first met. This gentleman, who was in reality nothing more than an humble servant of the lady's, though she called him cousin, the better to skreen a more particular connection, was so provoked at her deserting him in favour of Mr Arnold, whom he said he was sure she had insnared, that he made no scruple of telling all he knew of her. He said, she had two brothers, very great profligates; one of whom had been put into prison for forgery, and would have been hanged, had not Mr Arnold, at the expence of a very considerable sum, saved his life. The other, some very mean retainer to the law, a plausible fellow, and Mrs Gerrarde's great favourite, for whom she had art and influence enough to prevail on Mr Arnold to purchase a considerable employment. It would be endless, said Mr Pinnick, to tell you the variety of stratagems she made use of to get money out of those whom she had in her power, and who were able to supply her. I, for my part, was not rich enough for her, which was the chief reason I suppose of Mr Arnold's supplanting me; and I take it for granted, that those arts, which she practised on me to little effect, succeeded better with him. One time her poor father was in gaol, and his whole family would be undone, and her mother sent a begging, if he was not relieved from his distress, by a trifling sum; fifty pounds would do. Another time her sister's husband, a country shopkeeper, was upon the point of breaking, and would be inevitably ruined if he was not assisted. And then she had a formal letter to produce from her sister upon the melancholy occasion. These circumstances she made no scruple of laying open to me, as she knew I was no stranger to her origin, having resided for some years in the town where she formerly lived, though I did not then know her. Her mother was a Roman Catholick; and in order to have her daughter brought up in the same principles with herself, had her sent to a relation in Dublin, where she received her education in a nunnery. Though her artifices to get money from me were grown quite stale, I make no doubt but she practised them all over again on poor Arnold. She was not contented with the lodgings *I* had placed her in, but obliged him to take a handsome house, elegantly furnished for her: a very fine chariot and horses were the next purchase; for a hired one the lady would not vouchsafe to sit in: and I am sure I have seen her in the boxes at the play, with as many jewels on her as any lady there.

All these ungrateful particulars, which Sir George had received from Mr Pinnick, he took a sort of ill natured pleasure in repeating to my mother and me. Unhappy Mr Arnold, into what a gulph didst thou unwarily plunge thyself! Is it not amazing that this affair was even so long a secret? That it was so to *me* is not strange; for it is natural to suppose that I must have been the last person to receive a hint of this nature; but that my brother should never have been informed of it is surprizing! 'Tis certain Mr Arnold was at first very cautious in his visits, making them generally at night, and even then he never was carried in his own chariot. I am shocked to think of the mischiefs which I fear he has done to his temporal affairs, for his children's sake as well as his own; but since he is delivered from the thraldom in which this woman held him, the rest, I hope, by future good management, may be retrieved. Would to heaven! I had nothing left me to lament, but the waste of his fortune. Sir George says he is sure he is deeply in debt. The law-suit too I hear is likely to go against us; if that is to be the case, it will be a blow indeed!

December 19

How miserable is a state of suspence! I am, if possible, more unhappy now, than when I was without hope of recovering my dear, and now more dear, because undone Mr Arnold. Our cause came to a final hearing many days ago (though I was not told it till this morning), and only prepared for it yesterday, and it is given against us. Mr Arnold by this stroke loses 900 pounds a year, besides considerable costs. Nothing now remains but my jointure. Into what an abyss of misery is my unfortunate husband plunged! Oh! that I could but see him! that I could but regain his confidence, that I might sooth and comfort him in his afflictions!

My brother is very unkind; after telling me the fatal news, he said, he thought I should be much to blame if I returned to Mr Arnold, though he were even desirous of it. What prospect can you have with him but beggary? said he; for I suppose his next step will be to wheedle you out of your jointure, the only support you have now left for yourself and your children.

Oh! brother, brother, said I, you have no heart! I could say no more, for I burst into tears.

Perhaps you may not be put to the trial, answered he cruelly; but if you should, you are to take your own way Mrs Arnold, for my advice had never any weight with you or my mother.

My mother replied, Sir George, you do not use either me or

your sister well. Let her, in the name of God, follow the dictates of her duty. If the unfortunate Mr Arnold sees his error, can you be so unchristian as to endeavour at steeling his wife's heart against him? O son! this is not the way to obtain forgiveness of God for your own faults! Far be it from Sidney to reject the proffered love of a repenting husband. My dear (to me) don't afflict yourself; if your husband has grace, you shall both be as happy together as *I* can make you. Misfortunes, said, Sir George, are mighty great promoters of *grace*; I don't doubt but Mr Arnold will repent most heartily – the having lavished away his fortune; and the hopes of repairing it, may give him the *grace* to take his wife again.

Sir George, said my mother angrily, you will oblige me if you say no more on the subject.

I have done, Madam, said my brother, and took his leave.

I had almost forgot to tell you by what means the widow Arnold carried her suit against us. You may remember I informed you she had at the beginning threatened to produce a witness, who could prove, that her late husband had been with her on a particular night, a very little time before his death. Who this witness was, had been kept an impenetrable secret. She did, however, produce him, when the cause came to be tried; and this witness proved to be Mrs Gerrarde's brother. That very brother whom Mr Arnold had redeemed from a gaol and peril of hanging. This man it seems had been very intimate with her during her husband's life-time, while she was in a state of separation from him: but whether he was at all acquainted with the late Mr Arnold, we have no other testimony than his own. 'Tis however most certain, that she was suspected of an intrigue with him, and in all human probability that child, which is to inherit the Arnold estate, is his.

This concealed villain undoubtedly was the person who first suggested this vile attempt to her, and secretly abetted her in all her proceedings. It was after the commencement of the law suit that he was put into gaol, and Mr Arnold little imagined, when under Mrs Gerrarde's influence he obtained his liberty, that he was bestowing on this wicked wretch power to ruin him.

I do not imagine Mrs Gerrarde was in this secret. I suppose she would not knowingly have contributed to beggar the man by whom she was supported in affluence. But be that as it will, the evidence of this fellow, who was bred an attorney, together with that of Mrs Arnold's maid, established the proof on which the issue of the whole affair turned.

Unfortunately for us, we could find nobody capable of giving any testimony which could overthrow theirs: and the irregularity of the late Mr Arnold's life gave these evidences an appearance at least of truth. God forgive those people the foul play they made use of! I would not possess a king's revenue on the terms they now enjoy the Arnold estate. 'Tis whispered, that the widow is supposed to be privately married to this attorney; she owes him a recompence; for I fear he has risqued a great deal to serve her. The wretch had the affrontery to acknowlege his obligation to Mr Arnold; and at the same time declared, that nothing but the justice which he owed the widow, and the orphan of his late friend, could have extorted a testimony from him to his prejudice.

I need not tell you in what light my poor Mr Arnold looks upon this affair. He said to a gentleman, from whom Sir George had the account, that he was justly punished for having furnished such a villain with the means of undoing him, and execrates the memory of Mrs Gerrarde, who prevailed on him to do it; for he scarce knew the fellow at that time, having only seen him once or twice at her lodgings. But let me drop the mention of such wretches at once. My heart is full of impatience to hear something from Mr Arnold. Mrs Gerrarde's letter I fear has had no effect on him; he must have received it long since. What can this dreadful silence mean? My mother now expects the advances towards a reconciliation should be on *his* side. I would I were rid of my suspence.

December 20

Lord and Lady V— arrived in town last night. They sent a compliment to me as soon as they alighted at their house, which was not till nine o'clock; and this morning at the same hour I was agreeably surprized by a visit from my lord: surprized I say, for he is seldom out of bed so soon. I had him up to my dressing-room; my mother had never seen him, and as she was undressed did not chuse to appear. Well, my good lady, said he, after saluting me, have you heard any-thing from Mr Arnold lately? I told him I had not. I don't know whether you are apprized, said he, that I am in all your secrets: Mr Faulkland and I correspond, and I know how all matters stand. You are not made acquainted, perhaps, that I was aiding and abetting to a certain scheme. I told him that Mr Faulkland had writ my brother the whole account, and that I was sure of his kind participation in every thing that related to me. That you may depend on, said he; the thing cannot be named that I would not do to serve you. I understand from Mr Faulkland, that Mrs Gerrarde has writ to Mr Arnold: have you heard of no effects produced by that letter? I told him, I had never heard a word from Mr Arnold since he had received it. I hope it will not be long before you will, answered he: I called on you this morning on purpose to prepare you; for I suspect Arnold wants to be reconciled: he wrote to me ten days ago, conjuring me in the strongest terms to come to town, and to prevail on lady V— to accompany me: he said he had something of the utmost consequence to consult us upon, in which our friendship might be of most material advice to him: he concluded with telling me, that the whole happiness of his life depended on our complying with his request. Now as this was immediately on his receiving Mrs Gerrarde's letter, for I had regular intelligence of the whole proceeding, I flatter myself that it was in consequence of that letter he made this request, with a design, as I hope, of getting us to mediate between you. As I could not just then attend his summons, having business at V— hall to detain me, I wrote him word, that I should certainly be in town as on this day; and that lady V— would be sure to accompany me. I have not heard from him since till last night, when I sent a message to his house to desire his company to breakfast with me this morning; I expect him at ten o'clock. Now I had a mind to inform you of this opening, which to me seems to promise very favourably for you. I shall not mention my having seen you, so that I can say nothing from you to him. I asked him, was my lady acquainted with the affair as it really stood? He said she was; for that she had been so exasperated against Mr Faulkland on his first going off with Mrs Gerrarde, whom she thought he had run away with upon a very different design, that he was very glad to undeceive her, and that she would presently have done the same by me, after the letter she had wrote me about that affair, but that he prevented her, thinking Mr Faulkland would be better pleased to unravel the mystery himself. He added, that she was too much my friend, not to enter warmly into my interests, and had been extremely impatient to come to town. I thanked my lord for his and his lady's friendship. He then asked me how our law-suit went on? I answered, it had been determined some days ago, and we had lost our cause. He turned pale at the news. Good God! what an unfortunate man your husband is, said he! What will become of him?

He put an end to his visit immediately, telling me, that either he or his lady would call on me in the afternoon, to let me know the result of their conference with Mr Arnold.

I flew to my mother, to tell her the joyful news. She offered up a prayer that it might turn out as my lord V— had suggested; and said, she herself was of the same opinion.

With a heart elated with pleasure, my dear Cecilia, I have scribbled over the occurrences of this morning. God grant I may be able to close my journal of to-day with the happy wished-for event!

I never counted the clock with such impatience as I did this day, waiting the promised visit of lord or lady V—, and I ordered myself to be denied to all company but them. At one o'clock good lady V— came, without my lord. When I heard the rap at the door, and saw from the window it was her equipage, I was seized with such a trembling, that when lady V—, who hurried up stairs, entered the room, I was unable to speak, or salute her. She ran up to me, and taking me by the hand, affectionately embraced me. My mother was present; I made a shift to present her to lady V—. She then led me to a chair, and sat down by me. Come, my dear Mrs Arnold, said she, recover your spirits; all will be well. I began to apologize for giving her ladyship the trouble of coming to me, when it was my duty to have waited on her. Do not mention ceremony, said she, I was in too much haste to bring you good news, to think of forms. We have had Mr Arnold with us till within this half hour, and indeed he more deserves your pity now than your resentment.

Oh! I feared it, said I, and tears started into my eyes. If you are so affected at the barely knowing this, said my lady, I must not tell you the particulars of our conversation; it will be enough for you to know, that your husband is convinced of the injuries he has done you, and desires nothing more than your forgiveness.

Dear lady V—, said I, excuse me; my heart is really so softened by sorrow, that I cannot command my tears. But I beg that may not deter you from indulging me with the particulars of what passed between you and Mr Arnold. If I do weep, as my tears no longer proceed from grief, do not let them interrupt you.

My mother joined in begging lady V— to inform us of all that passed in that morning's interview.

Lady V— obligingly complied, and gave the following account of it.

Mr Arnold came exactly at ten o'clock; my lord was just returned from his visit to you, and had got in but a few minutes before him.

Poor Mr Arnold looked abashed upon seeing me; his countenance and his voice discovered the humiliation of his mind. After the first compliments were over, we sat down to breakfast; your husband drank a dish of coffee, but eat nothing. We were in haste, that the servants should leave the room, and dismissed them as soon as we could. My lord then opened the conversation, by saying, 'Well, Arnold, here are lady V— and I come to attend your summons; now tell us what service you have to employ us in, for I assure you, we are both ready to do you any act of friendship in our power.

My lord, I thank you, said Mr Arnold; the friendship you honour me with, I flattered myself, some time ago, might have been serviceable to me; I must not now think of making use of it. When I requested the favour of lady V—'s presence and your's in town, I meant to intreat your interposition between me and Mrs Arnold. I know I have wronged her so, that were she any other than the woman she is, I could never hope for forgiveness; but from *her* I did hope it, and thought your good offices might bring about a reunion. But that is all over, I neither desire nor wish it now.

I am sorry for that, Mr Arnold, said I; I am sure nothing in this world besides can ever make either your lady or you happy.

Do you know, madam, said he, (and the poor man really looked wildly) that you see an absolute beggar before you? A man without a foot of land, overwhelmed with debts, and who shortly will not have a house to shelter himself in. *I* deserve it all, but Mrs Arnold does not. Do you think, that after all the wrongs I have done her, I will involve her in poverty too? No, lady V—, no. I am not such an abandoned wretch. All I desire now of your ladyship is, to tell my wife that I beg her forgiveness, and request she will take care of our two children; though the scanty pittance that her mother's scrupulous nicety retained for her will hardly enable her to do it; but while lady Bidulph lives, I believe she will not see them want.

He uttered all this with so much eagerness, that we never once attempted to interrupt him.

As I did not know then of the loss of your cause, I was surprized to hear him speak of his circumstances being so desperate, and really feared his head was turned. But my lord soon explained the matter, by saying, he had heard that morning of the Issue of his law-suit, yet still hoped, that matters were not so bad as he represented them to be. He then told Mr Arnold, he was extremely glad to find that his wife had recovered his good opinion; adding, that *he* always had the highest one of your virtue. It amazes me, Mr Arnold, said I, that you ever could entertain a doubt of it. So it does *me* now, madam, said Mr Arnold; but I have been for this year past in a dream, a horrid delirium, from which that vile sorceress, who brought it on me, has but just now rouzed me.

I wanted to draw Mr Arnold to this point. Have you heard any thing of her since she left you, Sir, said I?

He drew a letter out of his pocket, and without answering me, put it into my hands, and desired me to read it; then rose off his chair, and walked about the room.

My lord and I read Mrs Gerrarde's letter together; we were both curious to see it, Mr Faulkland having mentioned it in his correspondence. Mr Arnold, said I, returning it to him, *without* any such proof as this, I believe nobody that knows your lady would think her guilty; nor could I ever entertain so bad an opinion of Mr Faulkland: I have known him from his boyish days, and never had reason to believe him capable of a dishonourable action.

I believe him innocent, as to *this*, answered Mr Arnold, but you cannot conceive the pains that were taken by that vile woman to make me think otherwise; neither would her retracting all she said now work so much on me, as other corroborating circumstances: her running away with the very man, of whom she raised my jealousy, after having plundered me of almost every thing I had to bestow, does not look like a sudden resolution: the scheme must have been concerted for some time, and Faulkland, I suppose, was *her* paramour, at the very time she so basely slandered Mrs Arnold; for I am not so blind, even to the personal charms of my wife, as to imagine the greatest inconstant would grow tired of her in so short a time.

Why, I must own, said my lord, that is a natural inference, which, joined to the perfidy and falshood of Mrs Gerrarde, puts it out of dispute, that she traduced Mr Faulkland and your wife, merely to gain her own wicked ends; one part of which I am inclined to think she confesses in her letter; that is to say, to have you intirely in her own hands, though not for the reason she there gives. Her other motive, I think, now plainly appears by the consequence: she thought, if you were jealous of your wife, you would hardly suspect *her* with the same person, whose visits, to my knowlege, were pretty frequent at her house. Then, said I, (throwing my weight into the scale) the unobjectionable character of Mrs Arnold, her pious education, her modest and affectionate behaviour to you for so long a time, and the recluse life that she had led with her mother since you parted, makes the thought of any ill in her quite incredible.

Lady V—, said your husband, impatiently, I am as conscious of it all as you can possibly wish me. I know I am a blind infatuated monster: What can you say more? Faulkland, I thank you for ridding me of such a pest; Oh! that you had taken her before I was so curst as to see her face! If you had, I should not now be the undone wretch I am! My lord, my lady, will you do me the favour to tell my wife and lady Bidulph, how contrite I am (and he laid his hand on his breast): while I had any thing to offer her besides repentance, I could have thrown myself at her feet for pardon, and conjured her to have returned to my bosom, and to her own deserted house, from whence my madness drove her; but I have now no house to bring her to, and do not desire even to see her face.

His manner was so vehement, that I really feared the agitations of his mind might disorder his brain. My lord told him he was too desponding, and said, he hoped all might be yet retrieved. He then enquired into the particular situation of his affairs, which are, I am grieved to say it, very bad indeed. We were told, when we were in Kent, that a part of South-Park was mortgaged, but did not believe it, as we knew it was settled on you. Upon being asked, Mr Arnold himself acknowleged it, confessing at the same time, that he had been prevailed on to do this, in order to deliver Mrs Gerrarde's brother out of gaol, and that it was the other villainous brother who had transacted the affair for him. I find, besides this mortgage, that, with the costs of his suit, he owes near seven thousand pounds; to answer which, he says, he is not worth six-pence, his plate and the furniture of his houses in town and country excepted.

Though I had shed many tears, whilst Lady V— was describing Mr Arnold's behaviour at the beginning of her discourse, I heard this latter part of her account with a composed attention.

Lady V— took me by the hand: I am sorry, dear Mrs Arnold, said she, that I am obliged to repeat such uncomfortable tidings to you, but you must know all, soon or late, and it as well now as hereafter. I am sure your patient temper and good sense will enable you to bear up against misfortunes.

My lord then proceeded to ask Mr Arnold, if his friends could make his circumstances a little easier, and Mrs Arnold would consent to live with him again, had he any objection to it?

My lord, answered your husband, from the moment I heard of Mrs

Gerrarde's elopement, I flattered myself with the hopes of being restored to my senses, and my peace, by a reunion with my wife; for I own to you, her innocence from that very time became evident to me, and it was mere shame that prevented me from making my application to lady Bidulph, for the purpose of a reconciliation. The receipt of Mrs Gerrarde's letter – (whether the wretch has *really* felt compunction or whether her cruelty to me, in order to make me more unhappy, has drawn it from her I know not) the receipt of that letter, I say, wherein Mrs Arnold's innocence is so entirely cleared, convinced me, I ought not to delay making my wife all the reparation in my power. Though I was shocked to think how much I had foolishly squandered away, I was still in possession of an estate of nine hundred pounds a year; for though it was then in litigation, my lawyers amused me to the last, with a belief that I should carry my suit; and notwithstanding that the payment of my debts would lessen it, I knew, with one of her contented and gentle spirit, it would be sufficient to make us happy, and her jointure (which I hoped soon to clear) added to it, would enable us to sit down in the country in tolerable affluence, and I had come to a resolution to make it the study of my life to render Mrs Arnold happy. I know she is an admirable œconomist; I resolved to imitate her, and hoped in time to retrieve our circumstances. These were my sentiments, my lord, when I wrote to you, to beg that you and my lady would come to town. I own I had not courage enough to make any efforts towards the so much wished-for reunion, without the interposition of friends, whose good hearts I knew would rejoice, could their endeavours bring it about, and whose influence over Mrs Arnold I was certain would make the accomplishment easy. Do me the justice, my lord, to believe, that if I had not thought it in my power, to have made Mrs Arnold amends for the injuries I have done her, this hand should have been sooner employed to send a bullet thro' my head, than to have endeavoured to procure your mediation in this affair.

But as things have turned out, I would not for this earthly globe involve her in my ruin; nor shall her family have it to say, I sought their friendship when I was abandoned of every other hope.

As to that point, answered my lord, I can bear you witness, that your first overture to me, in order to bring about a reconciliation, arrived before there was any likelihood of your standing in need of assistance, either from your wife's friends or your own; for I believe they all, as well as yourself, were pretty sure of your carrying your suit, which, if you had done, your affairs might, with a little care, have soon been, in a great measure, retrieved. Therefore, if they should attempt to make the ungenerous charge you apprehend, I can confute it, and will to all the world; and for the rest, we must manage as well as we can.

My lord then proposed some methods to make his affairs a little more easy; as I am sure his friendship for Mr Arnold and you will make him endeavour to settle them to the best of his power.

My lady V—'s politeness and generosity would not suffer her to mention the particulars of the methods proposed; but I have reason to believe, my good lord V—, will interest himself rather farther than I wish.

When my lord and Mr Arnold, she proceeded, had talked over these matters for some time, in which my lord had much ado to get the better of Mr Arnold's obstinacy, he told him, that I should undertake to explain his situation to you and lady Bidulph. That he made no doubt of your tenderness in forgetting all that was past, and being willing to embrace his fortunes, let them be what they would; for, said he, I am sure Mrs Arnold will think herself happier with you, on three hundred pounds a year, than she would with twice so many thousands without you.

Oh! madam, said I, interrupting her, my lord has read my very heart.

My lady smiled and went on. Lady Bidulph, said my lord, is so good a woman, that as she must look on you in the light of a repenting sinner, you may be assured of her pardon and favour. That he may rest satisfied of, answered my mother. My income is not considerable, and I have never been able to lay any thing by; but if Mr Arnold can be extricated from his present difficulties, so as to be able to retire quietly into the country, I will share that little with him.

My lady V—'s eyes moistened, mine were quite suffused. I assure you, said lady V—, it was not without abundance of arguments used by my lord, and downright quarrelling on my side, that Mr Arnold could be prevailed on to consent that any other application should be made on his part, than that of acquainting you with his penitence, and communicating his resolution, together with his motives for it, of never seeing you more.

He says, Sir George Bidulph never was his friend; and, as he supposes him more now his enemy than ever, he would be sorry to be under any obligations to him.

My mother, who never conceals her thoughts, answered directly, of that I believe he need not be apprehensive; Sir George is not very liberal; he would have persuaded his sister against returning to her husband, and I am sure will not be willing to contribute towards making their reunion happy. Besides, as he is now going to be married, he troubles himself with little else than his intended bride.

Lady V— seemed shocked; I was sorry my mother had spoken so freely of Sir George, to one who was an entire stranger both to him and her; but she is so good, that even her errors proceed from virtue.

Well, said lady V—, we have now seen the worst side of the prospect; let us turn our eyes towards the pleasanter view. What do you mean to do, Mrs Arnold?

Mean, madam, said I! To go directly to my husband.

Well, well, replied she, smiling, *that* I suppose; but how do you purpose to settle your little household matters?

I think, said my mother, the best thing you can do, is, to go directly down to my house in Wiltshire. You know *that*, and the furniture are mine, during my life; they go to your brother afterwards. Send for your two children and honest Martha; dispose of your house in town, and all your effects here, as well as at South-park and in Essex – let the produce be applied to the payments of debts, as far as it will go. You will then have your jointure to receive, to which I will add two hundred pounds a year, which will enable you, by degrees, to pay off the rest of your debts, and I do not see why you may not live comfortably besides.

Extremely well, said my lady, with Mrs Arnold's good management; especially as they will not have the expence of house-rent. I am sure my lord will willingly undertake to manage Mr Arnold's affairs in town for him, and I would have you both get into the country as fast as you can.

I am entirely of your opinion, lady V—, said my mother. What do you think, child? Dear madam, I think that I am the happiest woman breathing. Such a parent as you, such a friend as lady V—, and such a husband, as I promise myself Mr Arnold will prove – How can I be otherwise than happy? I am ready to do, to do joyfully, whatever you direct. Dear lady V—, ought not I to see poor Mr Arnold immediately?

Why, said lady V—, I would not have you surprize him; he is to dine with us to-day, and I will prepare him to receive you in the afternoon at my house, if you chuse it.

By all means, my good lady V—, I will come to your house at five o'clock. Well, said she, bring a few spirits with you, and do not let the interview soften you too much.

Lady V— then took her leave, as she said she should hardly have time to dress before dinner. My mother and I spent the interval between that time and evening, in talking of our future scheme of life. Remember, my dear, said she, that when I die, you lose the best part of your income, as my house, together with my jointure, revert to Sir George; and you have no great reason to expect that he will continue either to you; it therefore behoves you to use œconomy, as well for the sake of *saving* a little, as to accustom yourselves to *live* upon a little. I would myself accompany you down to the country, but as my son's marriage is so near, he would have reason to take it amiss of me; and I know I shall have his imperious temper to battle with, on our making up matters between you and your hubsand; but I shall make myself easy, by reflecting that we have both acted agreeably to our duty.

You never, my Cecilia, experienced such a situation as mine, and therefore can have no idea of what I felt, in expectation of seeing the person, whose presence I most ardently wished for, and yet was afraid of the interview. My fears were not on my account: conscious as I was of my innocence, I had no apprehensions on that head; but I could not bear the thoughts of beholding poor Mr Arnold, in the state of humiliation in which I supposed I should find him. I wished the first encounter of our eyes over; and as the appointed hour approached, my anxiety increased: I was faint, and seized with universal tremors. My mother did all she could to encourage me, and a little before five o'clock, I was put into a chair, and carried to Lord V—'s house.

My lady met me on the stairs; I could scarce breathe. She carried me into her dressing-room, and made me sit down till I recovered a little; she was affected herself, but endeavoured to raise my spirits. I wish, said she, smiling, you had been in my lord's hands, he would have prepared you better than Lady Bidulph has for this meeting; he has been trying to make Mr Arnold drunk, in order to give him courage, he says, to face you. Poor man, he could scarcely credit me when I told him you were to come this evening. She proposed my taking a few drops, which I agreed to; and bidding me pluck up my spirits, said she would send Mr Arnold to me.

I catched lady V— by the hand, and begged she would desire him, from me, not to mention any thing that was past, but let our meeting be, as if the separation had only been occasioned by a long journey.

She left me, and Mr Arnold in a few minutes entered the room.

He approached me speechless; my arms were extended to receive him; he fell into them; we neither of us spoke; there was no language but tears, which we both shed plentifully. Mr Arnold sobbed as I pressed him to my bosom. My dearest Sidney, said he, can it be! Is it possible that you love me still?

If lady V— delivered my message to you, my dear Mr Arnold, sure you would not speak thus to me.

I understand you, said he; Oh! my dear: I never wished for wealth or length of days, till now – but what I can I will.

Forbear, my love, said I; remember my request. I wanted to give his thoughts another turn. My mother longs to see you: When will you visit her?

I will throw myself at her feet, said he; I want a blessing from her, and she has sent me one, throwing his arms again round me.

How much are we obliged to good lord and lady V—, said I.

Oh! they have opened to me the path to Heaven, he answered – if it had not been for them – I think we had better go to them, said I, they will partake in our happiness.

He took me by the hand without answering, and led me into the drawing-room.

I have, my sister, endeavoured to recollect our disjointed conversation, in order to give it to you as well as I could. All that I can remember I have set down, though I am sure a good deal more passed.

Lord V—'s eyes sparkled when he saw us enter together; but my lady and he, I suppose, had agreed before hand to say nothing that could recall any past griefs, for they only smiled at our entrance; and my lord said, Arnold, you really hand your lady in with as gallant an air, as if you were married within these three hours. And so I have been, my lord, answered Mr Arnold. My lady presently called for tea, and we chatted as if nothing had happened. The servants waiting in the room made this necessary; though I could observe the two footmen, who had lived a good while with Lord V—, looked with no small astonishment at Mr Arnold and me.

When the servants were withdrawn, my lady introduced the subject of our going out of town. She had before acquainted him with my mother's proposal, and I repeated what she had said to me on that head, after lady V— had left us. My lord renewed the kind offers of his friendship, and said, as we meant so shortly to part with our house in St James's-street, that he thought it would be better for us not to go into it at all, but make use of his house while we staid in town; as perhaps Mr Arnold might not like to be at lady Bidulph's, on account of Sir George coming there.

I readily assented to this proposal; and Mr Arnold said it would be most agreeable to him. I told him, however, I should be glad of my mother's approbation; and asked Mr Arnold if he did not think it would be right of us both to wait on her together, to let her know of my lord's kind invitation. My lady V— said, by all means, and the sooner the better: if you please, I will order you the chariot; I would have you see lady Bidulph directly. Mr Arnold said, it was what he purposed doing that very night.

The chariot was presently at the door: lady V— said, I have an apartment ready, and shall, with lady Bidulph's permission, expect you back to-night. We promised to return, and drove to my mother's.

I left Mr Arnold in the parlour, whilst I ran up stairs to inform her of his being come to wait on her.

Unluckily, as well as unexpectedly, I found my brother with her. I judged by his voice, as I came up stairs, that he was talking warmly to my mother; he stopped, however, when I came into the room. He was standing, and had his hat under his arm. I concluded he was going, and was not sorry for it; he cast a cold look at me, and, with an ironical smile, I wish you joy *Mrs Arnold*, and he pronounced my name with an emphasis. Tho' I was stung at his manner, I would not let him see it. Thank you brother, said I, God be praised I *have* cause to rejoice. Oh! no doubt on't, said he, so have we all, that your husband has been graciously pleased, after beggaring you and your children, turning you out of doors, and branding you with infamy, to receive you at last into his favour.

Sir George, said I, you shock me exceedingly: where is the need of those cruel repetitions? Indeed you are very unkind; and I could not refrain from tears.

The more blameable Mr Arnold's conduct has been, said my mother, the more cause have we to rejoice in his amendment. We must make allowances for human failings.

Ay, madam, I wish you had thought of that in Mr *Faulkland*'s case, cried my brother.

My mother seemed disconcerted at the rebuke. Sir George looked and smiled, with an air of ill-natured triumph. As my mother was not quick in answering, I replied, the cases are very different, brother; what duty obliges us to pass by in a husband, it is hardly moral not to discountenance in another man.

You say true, child, said my mother; a woman certainly ought not to marry a loose man, if she knows him to be such; but if it be her misfortune to be joined to such a one, she is not to reject him, but more especially if she sees him willing to reform. Where is your husband my dear? Madam, he is below in the parlour: he is come to receive your forgiveness, and your blessing. He shall have both, said my good mother, and my prayers too. Sir George looked a little surprized: I will not interrupt so *pious* a ceremony, said he, but I hope you will give me leave to withdraw before you desire him up stairs; saying this, he bowed slightly to my mother, and left the room: we neither of us said any thing to stop him; my mother rang the bell, but before a servant could attend, he went out, and clapped the door violently after him.

Go bring your husband up to me, said my mother. I begged she would not mention any thing of Sir George's behaviour. I found Mr Arnold impatient at my stay. Poor man, his situation made him jealous of every thing tht looked like a slight. I told him, my brother had been above stairs, and as I did not think a meeting would at that time have been agreeable to either of them, I waited till he was gone. I perceive he knew *I* was in the house, said Mr Arnold, by the blustering manner of his departure. I made no reply; but taking him under the arm, led him to my mother.

That best of women received him with a tenderness that delighted me; he put one knee to the ground while she embraced him with maternal love, then raised him, and taking his hand and mine, joined them, holding them between her own. God bless you my children, said she, and may you never more be separated, till God, who joined you, calls one or other of you to himself. Amen, cried I fervently. Amen, repeated Mr Arnold.

He then besought my mother to forgive him for all the affliction he had occasioned both to her and me; assuring her that his veneration for her, and his tenderness for me, were augmented a hundred-fold, and should for the future influence his whole conduct.

After this, we fell on the subject of our domestick affairs: we informed my mother of my lord V—'s proposal, and said, as we should stay in town but two or three days, we had accepted of the offer of being at his house, rather than by our presence banish my brother from her's.

He is an untractable man, said she; but as I do not wish to quarrel with my children, I think it will be prudent for you to stay at my lord's rather than here. Mr Arnold said his obligations to lord V— were unspeakable; for that he had promised not only to see all our affairs properly settled, but to take the mortage of South-Park into his own hands, as he fears the person who now has it will not be so tender a creditor as himself. He also proposes (as the sale of my effects cannot amount to what my debts come to) to pay what may be deficient, and make himself my sole creditor. If it had not been for such a prospect as this, added my dear Mr Arnold, notwithstanding your goodness and lady Bidulph's, I had resolved never to have appeared before either of you.

We determined to set out for Sidney-castle in three or four days at farthest; and took leave of my mother for this night.

December 21

I told lady V— this morning, that though I was determined never to mention our past misfortune to Mr Arnold, yet I owned I had a great curiosity to know what means Mrs Gerrarde had made use of, to work up his suspicions to the high pitch she had done; but I would rather remain unsatisfied, than mortify him by the recollection of this particular.

I can inform you of her whole proceedings, answered lady V—, as I had it from Mr Arnold himself; for to tell you the truth, I was as curious about that as you, and took the liberty to ask your husband concerning it yesterday, when we had him to ourselves. It was the interval between dinner, and the hour that you were expected here in the evening, that I laid hold of for this purpose, as I found him then composed enough to bear the enquiry.

He told me, that from the time of his going down to South-Park, Mrs Gerrarde had begun to throw out insinuations concerning you, that had a little alarmed him. She asked him, Whether you made a good wife? which he answering in the affirative, she replied, she was glad of it; for that she had been told your affections were formerly deeply engaged to a very fine young gentleman, who, as his fortune was very much above your expectations, your mother, fearing your violent fondness for him might lead you into some act of indiscretion, had carried you out of town on purpose to avoid him; and was glad to marry you as hastily as she could, to put you out of the reach of harm.

Your husband acknowleges, that he believes he had himself casually informed Mrs Gerrarde of the manner of his first becoming acquainted with you, and the suddenness with which his marriage was concluded; yet she pretended to him, she was before apprized of these particulars.

He owns that those hints, though far from giving him any suspicion of your virtue, had nevertheless made some impression on him. You know, Madam, added he, that, madly devoted as my affections were to Mrs Gerrarde, I had always behaved to my wife with great tenderness and respect. This I suppose it was which raised Mrs Gerrarde's jealousy, and made her leave no method unattempted to part us. Mr Faulkland had not been long at V— hall, when she asked me, with uncommon earnestness, whether he visited at my house; I told her he did not, and asked the meaning of her enquiry. She affected to turn it off, and said, she had no particular reason for her question; but her manner was such, as the more excited my curiosity. At length she was prevailed on to tell me, that Mr Faulkland was the man (for she had not yet named the person), whom my wife had so passonately loved. Prepossessed as I was with jealousy, I now took the alarm. I recollected that Mrs Arnold had told me at lord V—'s, upon my first seeing him there, that she *had* been very well acquainted with him; and I even thought that I had observed something particular in his countenance when he addressed her. I was now sure that he had come into the neighbourhood merely on her account. The hell that I suffered is not to be described; for though I really fancied that I had conceived almost an aversion to Mrs Arnold, I yet could not bear the thoughts of being dishonoured. An accident happened which served to strengthen my suspicions: he then related the circumstance of his seeing you at the public house on the night of the fire; and of his finding Mr Faulkland putting you into your chariot. He owned at the same time, that he was there with Mrs Gerrarde, whom he had conducted out of the play-house, having called for her there in his return from making a visit, as he had promised to sup with her that night. Mrs Gerrarde, when she had him at her house, affected to speak with some surprize of your imprudence, in suffering a young man of Mr Faulkland's *known* turn for gallantry, to attend you to *such* a place, and at that hour. Though, added he, Mrs Arnold's own account of this had satisfied me at the time, yet Mrs Gerrarde's insinuations blew up the fire anew in my breast. She pretended to sooth me; but the methods she took rather increased my uneasiness. She told me, she believed my honour as *yet* had received no injury; and to preserve it effectually, she thought I could not do better than to forbid my wife to see Mr Faulkland. The designing vile woman, continued your husband, knowing that this prohibition would cut off her visits at V— hall, no doubt apprehended my wife would not so readily acquiesce under it; and she was sure any resistance on her part would but the more inflame me. But in this she was disappointed; for I no sooner required Mrs Arnold's promise on the occasion, than she, without the least hesitation, made it. My requiring so extraordinary a proof of her obedience, induced Mrs Arnold to enquire into the cause; and upon my explaining it, she acknowleged that Mr Faulkland had once been her lover, and that the match was broken off by her mother, who had conceived some dislike to him. This was so far from gaining credit with me, that it only served to corroborate what Mrs Gerrarde had told me. I was, however, contented for the present with the promise that my wife had made me; of which I informed Mrs Gerrarde.

He then proceeded to tell me of his finding you and Mr Faulkland together one evening at the house of Mrs Gerrarde. I must confess, continued he, this unexpected incident transported me beyond the bounds of patience: I suffered, notwithstanding, Mr Faulkland to go quietly out of the house, more for Mrs Gerrarde's sake than any other consideration, and permitted her to go home with my wife (who I then thought *pretended* illness);, waiting in the mean time at her house for her return, in order to have this extraordinary and unexpected meeting explained.

Mrs Gerrarde, on her return expressed the utmost concern and resentment on the occasion. She told me, that as she had expected me that evening (which was really the case), she had sent to my wife to engage her for the next day, in order to prevent her coming to interrupt us, which was not unlikely, as Mrs Arnold had not been to see her from the time she was laid up by the hurt she received; and she said, she did not care to lay herself so open to her servants, as to have herself denied to the wife, whilst she entertained the husband.

I myself, continued he, having the same apprehensions, had asked Mrs Arnold, on my going abroad in the morning, how she purposed to dispose of herself for the day; and she had told me she intended to stay at home. Mrs Gerrarde said, that notwithstanding her message, she was surprized with a visit from Mrs Arnold just as she was sitting down to dinner; that she however put a good face on the matter, and received her very cordially; but in order to get rid of her soon, told her, she was engaged abroad in the afternoon. Mrs Arnold, she added, however thought proper to stay, and I could not avoid asking her to drink coffee. While we were at it, behold, to my very great surprize, Mr Faulkland sent in his name, and immediately entered the parlour.

As I guessed, continued Mrs Gerrarde, that this was a settled assignation, I own I was extremely provoked at it. Mr Faulkland, with whom I formerly had a very slight acquaintance at Bath, *so* slight indeed as never to be visited by him, now very audaciously made an apology for not having waited on me sooner; but said, that he did not hear of my being in the neighbourhood, 'till a day or two before, and hoped I would allow him the honour of renewing his acquaintance. I had hardly temper enough to make him a civil answer; but said, I was sorry I was engaged that evening, and must be obliged to go out immediately. I thought this hint was enough for Mrs Arnold; and that she would have had the discretion to have taken her leave. She asked pardon for having kept me at home so long, protesting she had really forgot that I told her I was engaged. She begged she might not detain me any longer, saying, she had ordered her chariot to come for her in the evening, and that she would wait for it, as she found herself not very well, and therefore not able to walk home. I now saw into the whole scheme: Mr Faulkland would naturally stay to keep her company, and they would have my house to themselves; but I resolved to disappoint them both; and telling Mrs Arnold I would leave her at home, ordered the chariot to the door. Mrs Arnold opposed this, under pretence of not giving me so much trouble, and pretending to be sick and faint, said she would step to the door, in order to get a little more air; I followed her hastily, and your coming in the instant, I suppose, detained Mr Faulkland in the parlour, for he could not but see you from the window. You know the rest, added Mrs Gerrarde; and I leave you to judge, whether Mrs Arnold be inclined to keep her word with you, in regard to Mr Faulkland.

Can you blame me, Madam, proceeded your husband, if, after what I now saw and heard, I was enraged almost to madness against my wife? The base woman, who had now accomplished her wicked purpose, encouraged me in my desperation. In the midst of my fury, however, I could not help making one observation, which was, that as Mrs Gerrarde's going, or pretending to go out that evening, was a casual thing, they could hardly have expected an opportunity of being *alone* at her house, even though the meeting was concerted. Mrs Gerrarde answered, That was very true; and she supposed there was nothing at first farther intended, than that the *lovers* should have the pleasure of seeing and conversing together, as they had been so long separated; the other, to be sure, said she, was an after-thought, which the opportunity suggested. She then, after making me swear secrecy, told me, that Mrs Arnold had, when she followed her out to the door, conjured her not to tell me that Mr Faulkland and she (Mrs Gerrarde) were acquainted; for, said she, as Mr Arnold is of a jealous temper, and has heard that Mr Faulkland formerly courted me, he would not suffer me to come near your house, if he knew that Mr Faulkland visited you. I promised her I would not, added Mrs Gerrarde; and I make no doubt but that she hoped in time (relying on my good nature, my seeming fondness for her, and the easiness of my temper) to engage me as the confidant and abettor of her loose amour.

Mrs Gerrarde concluded with saying, that she believed nothing criminal had as *yet* passed between Mr Faulkland and my wife, at least since his coming to V— hall; but as there was no with-holding a woman from her will, it was very probable that Mrs Arnold would contrive the means of meeting, though not at *her* house, yet somewhere else. I raved, threatened, talked of fighting Faulkland, and locking up my wife. She artfully dissuaded me from such violent measures by a number of arguments, which I will not trouble you with repeating: Amongst other things, she said, that I had no right to call Faulkland to an account merely from surmise, which was all I had to ground my charge on; and though there was the strongest reason to believe he had dishonourable designs on Mrs Arnold, yet as I could not directly accuse him of them, I should be laughed at for engaging in a quarrel, which to the world would appear to be so ill-grounded. As to what I threatened in regard to my wife, she said, such measures only make a woman desperate, and would be far from preventing the evil; in short, that it would be better to part quietly, without embroiling myself with her friends, or undertaking the hateful office of becoming gaoler to my wife. She found me but too well disposed to follow her fatal counsel. I wrote that cruel letter to my wife, which turned her from her home, at Mrs Gerrarde's house. She kept me with her till midnight, and had worked up my resentment to such a pitch, that I determined not to see Mrs Arnold any more. To avoid expostulations, I went to a friend's house, at the distance of several miles. When I came back, Mrs Gerrarde told me that Mr Faulkland was absent from V— hall, and she concluded the lovers were now together.

I interrupted your husband at this part of the story, pursued Lady V—, and told him, that to *my* knowledge Mr Faulkland had gone to Sidney-Castle, to see Sir George Bidulph, before you left your own house; and did not set out from thence on his return 'till about three weeks after your separation; at the account of which he was exceedingly surprized.

Dear Lady V—, said he, do you think I *now* want any farther arguments to convince me what an injurious wretch I have been to the best of women?

I have one observation to make to you, Mr Arnold, added I; which is, that your lady's misfortune was intirely owing to her great delicacy, and the nice regard she had to your peace and honour.

I do not understand you, Madam, he replied.

Know then, said I, that your wife was well acquainted with your connection with Mrs Gerrarde, from the very night that you found her at the public house, to which the accident that happened to her obliged her to go. She owned to me, at the time you drove her from her home, that she had discovered your amour from a conversation she overheard that night between you and Mrs Gerrarde. This I extorted from her, by letting her know I was no stranger to the intrigue. I then repeated to him the discourse that passed between him and that wicked woman, as far as you had told me, and he very well remembered it. Now, Mr Arnold, said I, to prove the assertion I made in regard to your lady, had she reproached you with your infidelity, as *some* wives would have done, tho' it might have occasioned a temporary uneasiness to you both, yet would it have prevented her from falling a sacrifice to that most artful and wicked of her sex; for you could not then have had such an improbable falshood imposed on you, as that Mrs Arnold would have made choice of the *mistress* of her husband for a confidant, and fix on *her* house as the rendezvous for a love-intrigue. The base woman herself had no reason, from Mrs Arnold's prudent and gentle behaviour, to think she was suspected by her.

Your husband lifted up his eyes to heaven; and striking his breast, Blind, blind wretch, he cried! infatuated, ungrateful monster! are there no amends – no amends in thy power for such goodness?

I could not bear such a description of my poor Mr Arnold's deep contrition. I stopped Lady V—; and, being now informed of all I wanted to know, changed the conversation.

December 22

We are preparing to get into the country with all speed. I have writ to Patty to set out with the two children for Sidney-Castle as soon as possible. Mr Arnold has put his affairs intirely into the hands of our worthy friend Lord V—, and we think, upon a calculation, that what we have in town, at South-Park, and at Arnold-Abbey, will go near to answer the present demands that are upon us.

Lady V— is the best creature living; she knows that neither Mr Arnold nor I chuse to see any visitors, and she has let none in these two days. I am vexed at laying her under such a restraint, though her good-nature will not suffer her to think it one. We shall go out of town on Monday; to-morrow we spend with my mother, as do Lord and Lady V— (who are mightily charmed with her), and then adieu to London, perhaps for ever. If my mother comes down to me, as she intends to do, I shall have no temptation ever to return to it.

Sidney-Castle, December 29.

Here I am, my dear, in the house of my nativity. Your Sidney and her Arnold as happy as a king and a queen! or, to speak more properly, happier than any king or queen in christendom. My two dear little girls are well, thank God! and look charmingly. Poor babes! they could have no idea of their loss when I left them, yet they now seem pleased at seeing me again. My faithful Patty is almost out of her wits with joy. I have no maid but her, and an honest servant, whom my mother left here to look after her house. Mr Arnold has retained but one of his men: the garden is taken care of by an old man in the neighbourhood, to whom my mother allows something for keeping it in order.

With what delight do I recall the days of my childhood, which I passed here so happily! You, my dear Cecilia, mix yourself in all my thoughts; every spot almost brings you fresh into my memory. The little filbert-wood, the summer-house, the mount, and the chestnut-close that you used to love so! but the sight of your old dwelling makes me melancholy. I think I could not bear to go into the house; the deserted avenue to me appears much darker than it used to do; and your poor doves are all flying about wild; and I think seem to mourn the absence of their gentle mistress. Oh! Cecilia, how exquisite are the pleasures and the pains that those of too nice feelings are liable to! You, whose sensibility is as strong as mine, know this. From what trifles do minds of such a turn derive both joy and grief! Our names, our virgin names, I find cut out on several of the old elm trees: this conjures up a thousand pleasing ideas, and brings back those days when we were inseparable. But you are no longer Rivers, nor I Bidulph. Then I think what I have suffered since I lost that name, and at how remote a distance you are from me; and I weep like a child – But away with such reflections: I am now happier, beyond comparison happier, I think, than I was before my afflictions overtook me. Mr Arnold's *recovered* heart I prize infinitely more than I did when he first made me an offer of it; because I am sure he gives it now from a thorough conviction that I deserve it, and therefore I am certain never to have it alienated again.

January 4

It is almost three years since I left this place; and the welcomes I have received from all our old neighbours and acquaintance, have given me more satisfaction than I can express. Mr Arnold is highly pleased with the marks of affection which he sees me daily receive from those who have known me from my infancy. I am the more delighted with it, as I think it gives me an additional value with him. 'Tis a proof at least that I never misbehaved during the long number of years that our former friends knew me, and we must needs be pleased to see the object of our love approved of by others. This I speak from my own experience. Mr Arnold is exceedingly caressed by all our friends, and seems equally delighted with them: you know we have some of the best people in the world amongst our old set of acquaintance. If you, my mother, and good Lady V—, were within my reach, I should think Sidney-Castle a paradise.

January 10

I have had two letters to-day; one from Lady V—, the other from my dear mother. Lady V— tells me her husband is bustling about for us, to put affairs in the best condition he can. She says, he has already got a purchase for the lease of our house in St James's-Street; and all the moveables in it, as they now stand. They have been valued at two thousand seven hundred pounds. As most of our plate is there, as well as our chariot and a pair of horses, this has fallen very short of our expectations; but Lady V— says, she is sure there was not more allowed for the furniture than half their original value, though they have not been a great while in use. She tells me, that my lord has employed a person to go down to Arnold-Abbey, to dispose of the things there; but she fears we shall receive a very indifferent return from thence, as there is but part of the furniture of Mr Arnold's putting in, the old goods going together with the house to the widow. My lord's steward at V— hall has instructions about South-Park: he writes word to his lord that he believes the whole of what is there will not sell for more than four hundred pounds: the house indeed was but small, and the furniture not expensive. Mrs Gerrarde, he says, has had an attachment laid on her house by a person who built some bauble for her in her garden, for which he claims a debt of ninety pounds, though the steward says it is not worth thirty. 'All things, however, my lady adds, shall be adjusted in the best manner we can; and my lord will not let Mr Arnold be distressed on account of any deficiency that may happen in those sales.' What a jewel, my Cecilia, is an honest, warm friend!

The contents of my mother's letter are, That Sir George was married yesterday to Lady Sarah P—. She says, the bride was most extravagantly fine; but looked neither handsome nor genteel. This was much for my good mother to let drop from her pen; but I know she never liked Lady Sarah, nor did her ladyship ever treat her with the regard due to her character, and to the person of one who was to stand in the close and respectable degree of relationship to her, which my mother now does. But I believe I have before told you, that the blessings of good sense and good temper are bestowed but in a moderate degree on Lady Sarah; and for a woman of quality, Lady V— tells me (for I have never seen her), that her breeding is not of the highest form. But you know a great fortune covers a multitude of imperfections in the eyes of most people, and I hope her love for my brother will make her a good wife.

January 23

I am grown a perfect farmer's wife, and have got a notable dairy: I am mistress of three cows, I assure you, which more than supply my family; then I have the best poultry in the country, and my garden flourishes like Eden. Mr Arnold is such a sportsman that we have more game than we know what to do with; but his chief pleasure is hunting.

Your little namesake promises to be the greatest beauty in the county. Dolly, who is a pretty little cherry-cheek, and her father's great favourite, prates like a parrot. How delightful will be the task of expanding and forming the minds of these two cherubs! how joyfully and how thankfully do I look back on the troubled sea which I have passed! My voyage indeed was not long, but my sufferings were great while they lasted. I never, since I was married, enjoyed life till now. You know my match was originally the result of duty to the best of mothers; and though, if I ever knew my own heart, it was absolutely freed from all attachment to any other person, yet was it not so devoted to Mr Arnold, as to have made him my choice preferably to all other men, if I had not resolved in *this*, as in every other action of my life, to be determined by those to whom I owed obedience. When I married Mr Arnold, I esteemed him; a sufficient foundation, in the person of a husband, whereon to build love. That love, his kindness, and my own gratitude, in a little produced in my heart; and I will venture to say few wives loved so well, none better. You know I could never bear to consider love as a childish divinity, who exercises his power by throwing the heart into tumultuous raptures: *my* love, tho' of a more temperate kind, was sufficiently fervent to make Mr Arnold's coldness towards me alone capable of wounding my heart most sensibly; but when this coldness was aggravated by the cruel distrust which he was taught to entertain of me, the blow indeed became scarce supportable; and I did not till then know the progress he had made in my affections.

Sorrows, my Cecilia, soften and subdue the mind prodigiously; and I think my heart was better prepared from its sufferings to receive Mr Arnold's returning tenderness, than an age of courtship in the gay and prosperous days of life could have framed it to. I exult in his restored affections, and love him a thousand times better than ever I did. He deserves it; I am sure he does: he was led away from me by enchantment; nothing else could have done it. But the charm is broke, thank heaven! and I find him now the tenderest, the best of men. Every look, every word, every action of his life, is expressive of a love next to adoration. Oh! I should be too happy, if the blessings I now possess were to be my continued portion in this life! There is, however, but *one* about which I can rationally indulge any fears – My mother – Her years, and her growing infirmities, will not suffer me to hope for her being long absent from her final place of felicity. You always used to say I anticipated misfortunes: this event *may* be farther off than my anxious fears sometimes suggest to me; so no more of it.

March 10

My good Lady V— writes me word, that all our business is finished.

The whole amount of our effects came but to three thousand four hundred pounds; our debts (including some charges which have occurred in the transacting of our affairs) exceeded eight thousand. Our worthy Lord V— has paid the whole, and has made himself our only creditor. We have nothing now, that we can call our own, but my jointure. I do not reckon upon my mother's bounty to us; our income from her, and the house we live in, will be Sir George's, whenever it is our misfortune to lose her. But she tells me she is well, and talks of coming down in about a fortnight.

March 11

I am here in a scene of still life, my dear; and you must now expect to hear of nothing but such trivial matters as used to be the subject of our journals when we were both girls, and you lived within a bow-shot of Sidney-Castle, and saw me every day. The last three months of my life have glided away like a smooth stream, when there is not a breath of wind to ruffle it; and after you read the transactions of one day, you know how I pass all the rest.

I have told you of every-body that came to see me, and all the visits that I returned: I have given you an account of all our old acquaintance, and of some new ones. You know what my amusements are, and what my business. Indeed, what I call business, is my chief pleasure. You, who are surrounded by the gaieties of a splendid court, had need of the partiality which I know you have for your Sidney, to desire a continuation of her insipid narrative. But, I suppose, if I were to tell you, that, on such a day, my white Guiney-hen brought out a fine brood of chickens, you might be as well pleased with it, as I should be to hear from you of the birth of an arch-duchess. Indeed, my Cecilia, there is such a sameness in my now-tranquil days, that I believe I must have recourse to telling you my dreams, to furnish out matter of variety.

March 19

We have had a wedding to-day in our neighbourhood. Young Main (Patty's brother) has got a very pretty young gentlewoman, with a fortune of five thousand pounds. It seems, this pair had been fond of each other from their childhood; but the girl's fortune put her above her lover's hopes; however, as he has, for a good while, been in very great business, and has the reputation of being better skilled in his profession than any one in the country, he was in hopes, that his character, his mistress's affection for him, and his own constancy, would have some little weight with her family. Accordingly he ventured to make his application to the young woman's brother, at whose disposal she was, her father having been dead for some years; but he was rejected with scorn, and forbid the house.

The girl's father, it seems, had been an humourist, and left her the fortune under a severe restriction; for, if ever she married without her brother's consent, she was to lose it; so that, in that particular instance of disposing of her person, she was never to be her own mistress. In the disposal of her fortune, however, he did not so tie her up; for after the age of one-and-twenty, she had the power of bequeathing her fortune by will to whom she pleased.

The brother, who is a very honest man, had no motive, but a regard to his sister's interest, in refusing poor Mr Main: a man of good fortune had proposed for her, whom the brother importuned her to accept of; but she was firm to her first attachment.

The young lover found means to convey a letter to his mistress, in which he told her, that as he was in circumstances to support her genteelly, if she would venture to accept of his hand, he would never more bestow a thought on her fortune. This proposal the prudent young woman declined on her own part, but advised him to make it to her brother, as she was not then without suspicions that he wished to retain her fortune in the family; and that it was only to save appearances he had proposed a match to her, of which he was sure she would not accept. But in this opinion she injured him. She thought, however, the experiment might be of use, in giving the better colour to her marrying afterwards the man whom she loved.

But it was an ill-judged attempt, and succeeded accordingly: for, if the brother should have given his consent, he could have no pretence for withholding her portion; or, if he did so by mutual agreement, his motive for denying his consent before, must appear too obviously to be a bad one.

The young people, not considering this sufficiently, resolved to make the trial; accordingly Mr Main wrote to the brother a very submissive letter, telling him he would, in the most solemn manner, relinquish all claim to his sister's fortune, if he would make him happy by consenting to their marriage; without which, he said, the young lady's regard for her brother would not suffer her to take such a step.

This letter had no other effect than that of making the brother extremely angry. He sent a severe message to the young man, to acquaint him, that he looked upon his proposal as a most injurious affront to his character; but that he was ready to convince him, and every-body else, that he had no designs upon his sister's fortune, as he would not refuse his consent to her marriage with any other man in the country but himself. This was a thunder-clap to the poor lover: he comforted himself, however, with the hopes that his mistress's heart would determine her in his favour, notwithstanding the severity of the brother.

There had been, it seems, besides this gentleman's not thinking Mr Main a suitable match for his sister, some old family pique between him and Mr Main's father.

These transactions happened some time before I came to the country. Just about that juncture, the poor girl had the misfortune to receive a hurt in her breast, by falling against the sharp corner of a desk from a stool, on which she had stood in order to reach down a book that was in a little case over it. This accident threw her into a fit of illness, which put a stop to all correspondence between her and her lover.

In this illness, a fever, which was her apparent complaint, was the only thing to which the physician paid attention, and the hurt in her breast was not enquired after; so that by the time she was tolerably recovered from the former, the latter was discovered to be in a very dangerous way, and required the immediate assistance of a surgeon. You may be sure poor Main was not the person pitched upon to attend her; another was called in, of less skill, but not so obnoxious to the family.

By this bungler, she was tortured for near three months; at the end of which time, through improper treatment, the malady was so far increased, that the operator declared the breast must be taken off, as the only possible means of saving her life.

The young gentlewoman's family were all in the greatest affliction; she herself seemed the only composed person amongst them. She appointed the day when she was to undergo this severe trial of her fortitude; it was at the distance of about a week. The surgeon objected to the having it put off so long, but she was peremptory, and at last prevailed.

On the evening preceding the appointed day, she conjured her brother in the most earnest manner, to permit Mr Main to be present at the operation. The brother was unwilling to comply, as he thought it might very much discompose her, but she was so extremely pressing, that he was constrained to yield.

The attending surgeon was consulted on the occasion; who having declared, that he had no objection to Mr Main's being present, that young man was sent for. He had been quite inconsolable at the accounts he received, of the dangerous state in which his mistress was, and went with an aching heart to her brother's house in the morning.

He was introduced into her chamber, where he found the whole chirurgical apparatus ready. The young woman herself was in her closet, but came out in a few minutes, with a countenance perfectly serene. She seated herself in an elbow chair, and desired she might be indulged for a quarter of an hour, to speak a few words to her brother, before they proceeded to their work. Her brother was immediately called to her, when taking him by the hand, she requested him to sit down by her.

You have, said she, been a father to me, since I lost my own; I acknowlege your tenderness and your care of me with gratitude. I believe your refusal of me to Mr Main, was from no other motive but your desire of seeing me matched to a richer man. I therefore freely forgive you that only act, in which you ever exercised the authority my father gave you over me. My life, I now apprehend, is in imminent danger, the hazard nearly equal, whether I do, or do not undergo the operation; but as they tell me there is a chance in my favour on one side, I am determined to submit to it.

I put it off to this day, on account of its being my birth-day. I am now one and twenty, and as the consequences of what I have to go through, may deprive me of the power of doing what I intended, I have spent this morning in making my will. You, brother, have an ample fortune; I have no poor relations; I hope, therefore, I stand justified to the world, for having made Mr Main my heir. Saying this, she pulled a paper from under her gown, which she put into her brother's hand, that he might read it. It was her will, wrote by herself, regularly signed, and witnessed by two servants of the family.

Sir, said she, turning to the other surgeon, as soon as my brother is withdrawn, I am ready for you. You may imagine this had various effects on the different persons concerned. The brother, however displeased he might have been at this act of his sister's, had too much humanity to make any animadversions on it at that time. He returned the paper to his sister without speaking, and retired.

Poor Main, who had stood at the back of her chair, from his first coming in, had been endeavouring to suppress his tears all the time; but at this proof of his mistress's tenderness and generosity, it was no longer in his power to do so, and they burst from him with the utmost violence of passion.

The other surgeon desired him to compose himself, for that they were losing time, and the lady would be too much ruffled.

The heroic young woman, with a smiling countenance, begged of him to dry his eyes: perhaps, said she, I may recover. Then fixing herself firmly in the chair, she pronounced, with much composure, 'I am ready.' Two maid servants stood one at each side of her, and the surgeon drew near to do his painful work. He had uncovered her bosom, and taken off the dressings, when Mr Main, casting his eyes at her breast, begged he might have leave to examine it before they proceeded. The other surgeon, with some indignation, said, his doing so was only an unnecessary delay; and had already laid hold of his knife, when Mr Main having looked at it, said, he was of opinion it might be saved, without endangering the lady's life. The other, with a contemptuous smile, told him, he was sorry he thought him so ignorant of his profession, and without much ceremony, putting him aside, was about to proceed to the operation; when Mr Main laying hold of him, said, that he should never do it in his presence; adding, with some warmth, that he would engage to make a perfect cure of it in a month, without the pain or hazard of amputation.

The young lady, who had been an eye-witness of what passed, for she would not suffer her face to be covered, now thought it proper to interpose. She told the unfeeling operator, the he might be very sure she would embrace any distant hope of saving herself from the pain, the danger, and the loss she must sustain, if he pursued the method he intended. She was not, however, so irresolute, she said, as to desire either to avoid or postpone the operation, if it should be found necessary; but as there was hope given her of a cure without it, she thought it but reasonable to make the experiment; and should therefore refer the decision of her case to a third person of skill in the profession, by whose opinion she would be determined.

The two women servants, who are always professed enemies to chirurgical operations, readily joined in her sentiments, and saying it was a mortal sin to cut and hack any christian, they made haste to cover up their young lady again.

The disappointed surgeon hardly forbore rude language to the women; and telling Mr Main he would make him know what it was to traduce the skill of a practitioner of his standing, marched off in a violent passion, saying to his patient, if she had a mind to kill herself, it was nothing to him.

The modest young man, delighted to find the case of his beloved not so desperate as he had supposed it to be, begged she would permit him to apply some proper dressings to the afflicted part, and conjuring her to call in the aid of the ablest surgeon that could be procured, took his leave.

The brother of the lady being apprized of what had passed, lost no time in sending an express to Bath; and by a very handsome gratuity, induced a surgeon of great eminence to set out immediately for his house, who arrived early the next morning. But in the mean time poor Main had like to have paid dear for his superior skill in his profession. The other surgeon had no sooner got home, than he sent him a challenge, to meet him that evening, in a field at some distance from the town. They met; Main had the good fortune, after wounding, to disarm his antagonist, but first received himself a dangerous wound.

This accident was kept from the knowledge of his mistress; but on the arrival of the surgeon from Bath, as he would not take off the dressings, but in the presence of the person who put them on, it was thought proper that both Mr Main and the other man should be sent for. The latter was not by any means in a condition to attend; but the former, though very ill and feverish, desired that he might be carried to the house. The Bath surgeon having, in his and the brother's presence, examined the case, declared it as his opinion, that the complaint might be removed without amputation; adding, that it was owing to wrong management that the grievance had gone so far. He consulted with Main, in the presence of the family, as to his intended method of treating it for the future; he agreed with him intirely, with regard to the propriety of it; and having assured the friends of the girl, that he thought him a skilful and ingenious young man, took his leave, being obliged to return directly home.

The testimony of this gentleman, whose skill was undoubted, and whose impartiality must be so too, having never seen any of the parties concerned in his life before, wrought so much upon the brother, that he did not hesitate to put his sister under the care of her lover.

Poor Main, though scarce able to leave his bed for some time, was nevertheless carried to his patient every day, at the hazard of his life. His skill, his tenderness, and his assiduity, were all exerted in a particular manner on the present occasion; and in less than five weeks he had the pleasure to see his mistress restored to perfect health.

The consequence of this incident was very happy for them both; the brother, exceedingly pleased at his whole behaviour, told him, he was an honest generous fellow; and since he was convinced it was his sister's person, and not her fortune he was attached to, he would, with all his heart, bestow both on him; and accordingly Mr Arnold and I had this day the satisfacton of seeing this worthy young pair united in marriage.

Patty is not a little delighted at her brother's good fortune. The honest youth, who has ever since his father's death supported his mother, and as many of the younger children as were not able to gain their own livelihood, has now invited his sister Patty to live with him; but the faithful girl declined the offer; telling her bother, she would never quit me, while I thought her worthy of my regard.

I look upon myself to be much obliged to her for this, as the station she is now in, cannot be so advantageous as I hoped to make it, when I first took her into my service; but I will make up in kindness what may be wanting in profit. Indeed I consider her rather as a friend than a servant, and Mr Arnold always treats her with respect.

March 20

I am very uneasy at not having it in my power to fulfil my promise to poor Miss Burchell; but that is a string I dare not as yet touch upon. Indeed I cannot bear any conversation that leads to the subject. Whenever Mr Arnold begins to accuse himself for his unhappy conduct, in relation to Mrs Gerrarde, which he often does, I always stop him, or turn the discourse to something else. He never speaks of her now, but with a contemptuous indifference; and is so firmly persuaded that she went off willingly with Mr Faulkland, that I dare not as yet undeceive him; which I must necessarily do, should I express even a wish that Mr Faulkland should repair the niece's wrongs by marriage. Mr Arnold knows nothing of miss Burchell's affair. I went once so far as to say I had heard Mr Faulkland formerly liked this young lady. Mr Arnold answered, I am glad it went no farther than liking; if it had, probably I should not have been so soon delivered from my thraldom to her aunt. This reply silenced me; I am exceedingly perplexed about it. Would to Heaven Mr Faulkland would of himself think of doing the amiable unhappy girl justice!

My mother writes me word, that Sir George had informed Mr Faulkland, by letter, of the success of his project; and that his answer was full of congratulations, and expressions of joy. He is now in Italy; but talks of returning to England next summer. He says, he hears sometimes from Pivet, and that he and his wife live very well together.

My mother says she often sees Miss Burchell, and that she encourages her with the hope of what may happen when Mr Faulkland comes back. If this match should ever take place, it would give me most sincere satisfaction. The girl's family is not contemptible; her fortune is pretty large, her person lovely; the unfortunate false step she made, is an entire secret, except to the persons immediately concerned; so that with regard to the world, her character too is good. Mrs Gerrarde, at worst, was only her aunt by marriage; but if that circumstance should be the only rub in her way to happiness, I would sooner declare the whole affair, and run the risk of Mr Arnold's being let into this ticklish secret, than be a hindrance to the poor young creature's welfare. This affair never comes a-cross me, but it makes me sigh. God send a favourable issue to it!

March 26

Alas! my Cecilia, we have received most heavy news! My good lord V—, that stedfast, that worthy, that best of friends, is no more! He was preparing to go to V— hall, three days ago, but was seized with an apoplexy, as he was coming down stairs to go into his coach, and died before any assistance could reach him. Oh! we have a severe loss in the death of this most dear and valuable man! – but why do I mention *our* loss? – his lady – poor lady V— is almost distracted – and well she may – the best of husbands, fathers, every thing! His eldest son, who is abroad, is sent for home on this melancholy occasion – My poor mother is afflicted exceedingly: every body that knew him must be so. Mr Arnold and I have lost more than a father. How *self* recurs every minute; let me think of lady V— again, and not dare to complain on my own account; but my obligations to him were of such a nature, as claim all my gratitude to his memory, and all the tears that I have abundantly shed for him.

Mr Arnold is largely in his debt, we have no room to expect the same friendship from the present lord V—, that we experienced from his father.

This circumstance did not occur to me till poor Mr Arnold put me in the mind of it: my thoughts were too much absorbed in grief, which the death alone of our friend occasioned. My mother hinted at it too, in her letter to Mr Arnold; for it was to him she wrote the mournful tidings.

What a dark cloud of sorrow is spread over Sidney-castle! and how this stroke has imbittered our little domestic joys! But let me not carry my complainings into presumptuous murmurings. I have lost a sincere and truly valued friend; but do I not still possess infinite blessings? My husband, my dear Mr Arnold, my two sweet children, the best of mothers, and thee, my ever-beloved Cecilia, whom I still call mine, though at such a distance from me.

Then I comfort myself with reflecting that lady V— has sons, who, I hope, will be a blessing to her; that her fortune is affluent, and that my lord had passed through a well-spent life, to a pretty advanced age. He was turned of sixty. All these considerations sooth my mind, and I acknowlege, that, upon the whole, I have, by far, more cause to be thankful, than to repine.

March 30

Lady V—'s journey down to V— hall having been so fatally prevented, she is obliged to remain in London. The shock she has received has brought on her a fit of illness. I find my lord has not left any ready money; his fortune was large, but as they always lived in great splendor, he laid none of his income by: the whole sum which he could command, he laid out for our use. My lady's jointure is pretty considerable; if it were ten times more, she deserves it. Oh, may her sons prove worthy of such a parent! The youngest I hear is a very fine youth. He is come to her from Oxford to comfort her, till the arrival of his elder brother.

My mother writes me word, that her old friend lady Grimston is dead! She has left her whole fortune to charitable uses: not a sixpence to either of her daughters. Poor Mrs Vere! She is content with her little income, and has no loss of so unnatural a parent, who carried her vindictive spirit with her to the grave. As for the eldest, she did not stand in need of any assistance from her; but I own, though I had not great esteem for lady Grimston, I could not help being shocked at the brutal behaviour of her son-in-law to her in her last hours. She had never seen either him or her daughter from the time I told you they had quarrelled; but when she found herself dying, she sent a message to this favourite daughter, desiring to see her; her husband, whether out of disregard to the old lady, or his wife, or both, absolutely refused to let her go. My mother remarks on this passage in these words, 'Thus was this unfortunate parent punished in kind, for denying her late husband the satisfaction of seeing his youngest daughter, when he was in the same circumstances with herself.'

My mother is nevertheless very much troubled for the death of her old acquaintance; who, she says, was a valuable woman: she considers her decease as a memento, which warns her of her own approaching end; for they were just of an age.

I fear my mother is not well, though she does not say so; for she has put off her coming to Sidney-castle, without giving me a reason for it.

April 22

I thank you, my beloved Cecilia, for your cordial wish. Your opinion, that all my troubles are at an end, is consonant to your desires, but I doubt far from the real fact. The young lord V— is returned home; but oh! how unlike that honest man, whose title and fortune he inherits! How deceived were his worthy parents in their hopes of him! he is a stranger to every sentiment of virtue. I have had a letter this day from my lady V—, wherein she laments the degeneracy of her son, whom they were made to believe a pattern of excellence: but the tutor to whom they entrusted him was as profligate as himself. In short, she says he is quite a reprobate; she has not the least authority or influence over him; she laments this, particularly on our account; we are indebted to him near five thousand pounds, and my lady says, she fears he will press Mr Arnold. He is profuse, she says, in his expences, without being generous.

What can we do my dear? There is not the least prospect now of our being able to pay this money, but by selling the only remaining stake we have left. Had my lord lived, he made us hope that by his interest he could procure Mr Arnold some employment which would have enabled him to discharge this debt at his ease, without our being obliged to strip ourselves of our all. As we purposed living with the utmost oeconomy, this might have been accomplished in a few years.

This prospect is now lost to us. We must submit. I have begged of Mr Arnold to think immediately of selling my jointure, for we have no reason to expect any lenity from a man of such a character as the present lord V— is. We can subsist upon the income, which my mother is so good as to allow us: it is precarious it is true, but something may happen; I rely on that providence, who has hitherto protected me.

April 28

Lady V—'s apprehensions were but too well founded. We have had a letter from her son's agent. The debt *must* be paid; and we are come to a resolution to sell two hundred and fifty pounds a year. We shall then have but fifty pounds a year in the world which we can call our own! I reckon not upon my mother's life, these afflictions I fear will hasten her departure to another world. From Sir George we have nothing to expect: he is absorbed in vanity; his new alliances engross him intirely.

My dear lady V— writes us word, she will do her utmost to promote Mr Arnold's interest. She has numerous and powerful friends; and says, she makes no doubt of obtaining something for him worth his acceptance. Believe me, my Cecilia, I am not disheartened at this fresh blow. If my dear Mr Arnold could reconcile himself to it, I could be well contented. I will not now (though you used to accuse me of it) anticipate misfortunes; we have still enough for the present to live on decently; and if my lady V—'s kind endeavours should succeed, we may yet be happily provided for. I will not let the thought of my mother's death interfere: let me but calm the anxious fears of my poor Mr Arnold, and all will be well.

May 12

Thank God we have done with the merciless lord V—! his money is to be paid directly to him. I have recovered my tranquility; I enjoy my little in peace; and have the comfort to see Mr Arnold's mind more at ease, and reconciled to his lot. To lady V—'s goodness, as well as my own earnest endeavours, I impute this. She says, she has the promise of an honourable and a profitable post for him; but we are to wait some months for it. The person who is now in possession of this place is to be preferred to a better, and she says, she has the word of an *honest* man on the ocasion; 'he is a very *great* man too, says my lady in her letter, but as it is on the first part of his character chiefly we are to depend, I mention the other only by the by.'

Now, my dear, have I not reason to be contented? A thankless heart should I have if I were not; but I am, indeed, my Cecilia, I am; and I begin again to be happy. Our domestick felicity was but disturbed for a while, it was not over-thrown.

Here will I close; I have an opportunity of sending this immediately by a private hand to my beloved.

[*Here Mrs Arnold's maid Patty continues the journal.*]

May 15

By my lady's orders I take up the pen; and she has charged me to set down every particular. God knows I am ill able to do it! but I will strive to obey her. My poor dear lady is in such trouble, she has not the heart to write, nor scarcely to do any thing.

My master – Oh! madam, how shall I express myself! my poor master, now he is so good, we are going, I fear, to lose him: I must write, according to my lady's custom, every thing in the best order I can.

You cannot think, madam, how happy they have lived together ever since my lady came home to him again. He seemed to grow fonder and fonder of her every day; I believe he perfectly adored her, and he had reason.

You know, madam, my lady was always used to a chariot; but they never attempted keeping one since they came down to Sidney-castle. She asked my master once, if he had a horse quiet enough for her to venture to ride on to church? I observed my master turned away his face, and put his handkerchief to his eyes. I believe he thought of a little favourite pad that he had given to Mrs Gerrarde. I have not one, my love, said he, that I would trust you on. You had once a pretty horse that you were fond of, but my desperate folly has not even left you that; but I will look out for one that will suit you. No matter, my dear, said my lady smiling, and taking him by the hand, I will ride double, I think that will suit me best. Dearest of women! said my master (and he fetched a deep sigh), when shall I be able to make you amends? He lamented hourly the loss of his fortune for her sake. What will become of you, my dearest creature, and my two poor children, said he (when he was obliged to part with her jointure), if I should die before you; and then he cried, and wrung his hands. My lady begged of him to put such melancholy thoughts out of his head, saying, they never disturbed her. I hope, said she, I shall never see your death; but if it pleases God to punish me so far, a little, a very little, will content me for the rest of my days. My master embraced her, and the sweet children; and said, if heaven spared him life, he would yet be the happiest man in the world. Many a time have I been witness to such discourse between them; for they knew my love for them was so great, that they would never scruple talking of their affairs before me. Oh! madam, I believe there was never a truer penitent than my master. My dear lady has said to me, since they were forced to sell her jointure, Patty, though we are now reduced to little more than two hundred pounds a year, I have much more comfort than when we had twelve. I have the satisfaction of seeing Mr Arnold such as I wish him; he is an altered man, Patty; he is truly virtuous, and I am sure he loves me now from right reason. I am content with the little that is left us.

I always prayed for her prosperity; but, madam, God is pleased to order things otherwise than we poor silly mortalls think the best. My lady has always been good and pious, and I hope he will yet bring her out of her troubles, tho' they are great and many.

My lady always charged me to be minute, and to write particulars; but, good madam, excuse the silly way I put my words together. I have not yet come to the dismal part of my story, and I hardly know how to go on, for indeed I am forced to break off every now and then to cry. Reason enough I have, to be sure; but what is *my* sorrow compared to my lady's!

The day before yesterday my master was asked by some gentlemen in our neighbourhood to go a hunting: he had no mind to go, for my lady was not very well, and he was unwilling to leave her; but she persuaded him, because she knew he loved hunting dearly; she has blamed herself for it ever since, but she could not know by enchantment what was to happen. He left my lady in bed, and went out about five o'clock in the morning. At eight, as my lady was sitting at breakfast, and I attending, the other maid called me out. Our man, who had gone abroad with my master, was in the kitchen, and looked as pale as death. I asked him what was the matter? The poor fellow could hardly speak; but at last said, my master has got a desperate fall in leaping a ditch, and I am afraid has hurt his skull: he is lying at farmer Hill's cottage, and one of the gentleman is rid off for a surgeon; but that is no place for him, we must get him home: but I thought it best to prepare my lady before she sees him. My lady rung her bell before I could answer him; I ran in, but I am sure I looked like a ghost, for my lady started when she saw me. Bless me! Patty, said she, what is the matter? Has any thing happened to your master? Not much Madam, said I. He is killed she cried, and sprung out of her chair. Indeed he is not, Madam, I answered, standing between her and the door; but he has got a fall, and is a little hurt. She made me no answer, but flew down stairs, out at the front door, and down the avenue as quick as an arrow. I ran after her, and the other servants after me; we could not overtake her; but she was soon stopped, for she met my poor master borne by four men. I suppose she thought he was dead, for she fainted away directly, and we carried her in after him.

My master was put to-bed; he was alive, but not able to speak. He had got a dreadful cut in his head, and was sadly bruised besides.

As soon as my lady came to herself, we told her my master was not killed. She went into his room, but had not power to speak, but sat like a stone statue at his bed-side. The surgeon came in less than half an hour. I believe he is but a sorry one; for after he had dressed the wound, he said there was no danger in it. At first we were all in hopes that it was so; for about two o'clock my master got his speech again; he complained of sickness at his stomach, and violent pains all over him.

My lady, on hearing him speak, seemed to be rouzed as if out of a deep sleep. Several of the gentlemen, who had been out with my master, had come to enquire how he did; and though some of them came into his chamber, my mistress did not speak, nor seem to regard any of them. The first word she uttered was to call me; Patty, said she, what is the reason I do not see Mr Main here? It was my brother she meant, who is a surgeon; and I believe, madam, she has mentioned him to you, as one that is reckoned pretty skilful in his business. One of the gentlemen immediately said, by all means let him be sent for directly. My brother was soon fetched, and he thought proper to bleed my master in the arm. He would not take the dressings off his head, as the other surgeon had declared the skull was not touched; but said, he would be present when the wound was dressed the next day; and would watch all night by my master.

My lady was not to be removed from the bed-side, nor could we persuade her to take any sustenance the whole day. My poor master was in a high fever all night; and I thought he strove to stifle his groans, that my lady might not hear them. She did for all that; and I am sure every one of them was worse than a dagger to her heart. She stole out of the room several times for a minute, and I could hear her bursting into tears as soon as she was without side the door; then she would come in again, and sit by him, till her heart was again so full, she was forced to go out to give it vent. The whole night passed over in this dismal way.

When my master's head was examined the next day, my brother found that the skull was not touched where he had received the cut, but that it was broke in two other places, and in so dangerous a way, that it was impossible to save his life, as it was not in a part where he could be trepanned. The other surgeon, who found he had been mistaken at first, now joined with my brother in opinion that the world could not save my master's life. Oh! madam, if you had seen my lady when this was declared to her! I shall never forget her looks. I remember a piece of fine painting at your house, which I used to hear your family commend mightily. It was the picture of despair. My lady put me in mind of this piece; she had the very countenance of it; but I think, if she had then sat to a painter, he could have made a stronger and more heart-breaking look even than that picture has.

Such another dismal day and night I believe never was passed in this house. My brother staid with us, though he could do but little service, except to watch my poor master, for he was between whiles quite out of his reason –

No rest did my lady take all last night. She could not be got out of the room; she has tasted nothing these two days, nor slept a wink these two nights – She will destroy herself – What will become of us? – I have wrote to my lady Bidulph, to let her know the deplorable condition we are all in – My God! what will become of the poor children, if my lady goes on at this rate! She cannot hold out to be sure, such a load of sorrow at her heart, without nourishment or sleep – Oh! my good madam, I am not able to go on with my task – We have not the least hopes in the world – My master grows worse and worse every hour: he has his reason now, and is sensible that he is dying. Heaven knows, if I could lay down my life to save his, how gladly would I do it! I should be no loss, but he will be a grievous one –

Lord help me! I am not able to go on – I have writ this by bits and scraps –

[*Mr Main in continuation*].

May 16, Three o'clock in the Morning.

Mr Arnold had been delirious the greatest part of yesterday; but about six o'clock in the evening, having come a little to his senses, he was conscious that he was going fast, and desired that prayers might be read by him. His lady sent for the minister of the parish, but he was gone to London: the gentleman whom he had left to do his duty, was taken ill the night before, and was not able to leave his bed. He sent the messager that went for him, to another clergyman, who lived about four miles farther off, to request he would attend in his stead; but he was engaged on the same duty in his own parish, and could not come, he said, till next morning. The servant had wasted above two hours on this errand; it was nine o'clock when he returned. Mr Arnold during this interval had had several ramblings; but was now again a little composed, though apparently worse. I whispered the apothecary, who just then came in, that he could not live 'till morning. Mrs Arnold observed me, and begged to know what I said. I told her tenderly, that I feared Mr Atkins (that was the clergyman's name) would arrive too late, if he deferred his visit 'till next day.

She made me no answer, but seemed to study a little; then went composedly to Mr Arnold's bed-side. My dear, said she, Mr Downs is unluckily from home; his assistant is sick in bed; and we cannot to-night get any other clergyman to visit you: but as you are desirous of offering up your prayers to Almighty God, I hope it will not be improper if I read the service for the sick by you. He stretched out his hand towards her, and said, in a faint, yet eager voice, Do, do, my good angel! Tears stood in the lady's eyes as she turned from him; but she quickly wiped them off, and requested of me and the apothecary to join with her in the solemn office she was going to perform, which she said, though she was sensible it was an irregular act, yet she hoped, from the necessity of the case, would be accepted in the sight of God.

She ordered my sister to fetch her a prayer-book; and then kneeled down at Mr Arnold's bed-side.

Surely nothing ever appeared so graceful; her fine hands and her fine eyes lifted up to heaven, while the book lay open before her on a little table. Such a reverential, such an ardent, yet such a mournful supplication in those fine eyes! She looked like something more than human! After having in this posture offered up a short petition in silence, she began the service.

Never did I see true devotion before; the fervor of her looks, and the tone of her voice was such, you would have thought she beheld her Creator with her bodily eyes. For my part, I looked on her with such reverence, that she appeared to me like an angel, interceding for us poor mortal sinners.

She went through the office with admirable strength of mind (omitting the exhortation) 'till she came to that part of the prayer, which says, 'yet for as much as in all appearance the time of his dissolution draweth nigh, &c'. Here her voice faultered, and she stopped; but soon recovered herself, and proceeded with an unbroken tone to the end. Every one present wept but herself. She thanked us for our kindness in staying, and begged we would continue by poor Mr Arnold, while there was the least possibility of administering any relief to him.

I told her I would most willingly obey her commands, and sit up all the night with him, though it was not in human power to give him any assistance.

She repeated her thanks, and then sitting down by the bed-side, remained composed and silent.

About twelve o'clock, finding Mr Arnold speechless, I entreated her to retire to her own chamber, and if she could not sleep, to take some little refreshment; for she had taken nothing that whole day, nor for the two preceding ones, but a dish of tea which my sister had forced on her.

Mr Main, said she, suffer me to continue a little longer; my task will soon be over. I was unwilling to urge her; and she remained sitting in her place.

About two o'clock, we heard Mr Arnold give a deep groan: He is gone, said she, and started off her chair. I stepped to his bed-side, and found indeed he had breathed his last. She snatched up one of his hands that lay upon the coverlid of the bed, held it for near a minute to her lips, and then, without any audible token of grief, went out of the room.

I pray God to support and comfort this excellent woman.

[*Patty in continuation*].

Amen! Amen! – Sure my dear unhappy lady is enough to break one's heart to see her. I was not able to go on, good madam, and begged of my brother to set down what happened, and he has put it in better words than I could. My lady shut herself up for the remainder of the night, and would not suffer any one to come near her; it is easy to guess how she spent her time: rest, to be sure, she took none; she could not, if she had been inclined; for there was no bed in the chamber where she locked herself up. In the morning, a lady, who is our neighbour, a worthy good woman, came in her own coach, and took away my lady and the two children. She neither consented nor refused; but seemed to let us do what we would with her; for she said nothing, but suffered the lady and me to lead her down stairs, and put her into the coach. But the sight of the two children, threw her into such an agony, that I thought I should have died on the spot only with seeing her.

I have writ again to lady Bidulph: if she is able, to be sure she will come down; but I had rather she would send for my lady, for this is a sorrowful place for her to stay in.

May 20

My lady has received a message from her mother, desiring her to come to town directly with the children. She says she is not able to come down for her, as her health is but bad; and my lady V— has been so good as to send down her own coach to carry the little family to town.

My brother has taken the care of my master's funeral upon himself. He is to be carried to the family burying place at Arnold-Abbey. As soon as that is over, we must try to get my lady to town; she has no business to go into her own lonely house again; it would be enough to kill her.

May 30

Thank God we have got back safe to London. My lady keeps up wonderfully, under the load of grief that she has at her heart. She does not complain nor lament herself, as I have seen some do, who have not been in half her trouble. She hardly spoke a word during her whole journey, and strove as much as possible not to cry; but I could observe that she never turned her eyes on the two little babes, one of whom sat on my lap, and the other beside me, but the tears ran down her cheeks.

It was a doleful sight, the meeting between her and my lady Bidulph. The poor old lady grieves sadly, and looks mighty ill: I am afraid she will not hold out long; she has had great trials, for a lady so far in years. Sir George came to see my lady; he looked troubled: I hope he will be good to her.

June 1

My lady asked me this morning if I had thought of keeping any journal for this fortnight past. I told her I had, and she desired to see it. She shed so many tears while she read it, that the paper was quite wet when she gave it to me again. She ordered me to make up the packet, and send it off, as she was not in a condition to add any thing to it herself.

[*Mrs Arnold in continuation*].

June 20

Yes, my dear Cecilia, I have need of the tender condolements, with which your last packet was filled. Well may you call me a child of affliction; I am now so exercised in sorrows, that I look forward to nothing else.

Patty, I find, has been a faithful journalist; and has carried down her melancholy narrative to this day: this day, on which, for the first time, I have taken a pen in my hand for more than two months; but my eyes are much better, and I hope I shall not have occasion for the assistance of her pen, unless some new calamity should again disqualify me from using my own.

Yet in the midst of my griefs, ought I not to return thanks to heaven, that I have such an asylum to fly to, as the arms of one of the best of mothers? Oh! my dear, while I have her, I ought not to say, that I have lost every thing. Sir George has been more obliging since my fatal loss than he was before; but still there wants that cordial heart which he formerly had. As for his lady, I know very little of her. She came to see me twice since my arrival in town, in all the formal parade of a state visit. How ill does the vanity of pomp suit with a house of mourning! Her visits were short, formal, and cold. She seems to be intolerably proud, and I thought looked as if she was disgusted at visiting people in lodgings, who were so nearly related to her. My brother and she are to go down this summer into Scotland, to see a nobleman who is her uncle by her mother's side. She is ridiculously vain of her family, and has taught Sir George to be so too; so that now he hardly vouchsafes to own a relation that is untitled.

June 21

Lady V—, whose friendship has been one of the chief resources of comfort to me, went out of town this morning. She is retired, for life I fear, to a distant part of Lancashire, in order to spend the rest of her days with her eldest sister, a widow lady, of whom she is very fond. Her son's ill behaviour has disgusted her so, she has broke with him intirely. Her younger son is gone into the army, not, I find, with her approbation: and she told me, she has nothing now worth living for, at least nothing for which she should subject herself to the cares of life. She insisted on my corresponding with her; and renewed her assurances of that kind attachment, which I have already so strongly experienced.

At another time the loss of this dear woman's society would have affected me more sensibly; but I am so inured to disappointment and grief, that I am almost become a stoic.

Patty has already informed you, that Miss Burchell is often with us; she is more sollicitous, more assiduous than ever in her attendance on my mother. I find she even sat up with her two nights, on an illness which seized her on her first hearing the news of my misfortune. Poor girl! My mother tells me she went so far as to express her apprehensions on my being again single; but my mother quieted her fears on that head (not without a soft reprimand for her doubting), by putting her in mind, that besides the circumstances not being altered in regard to her, she had received my solemn promise, that, whenever it was in my power, I would use my whole influence (whatever that might be) in her favour. I did make her such a promise, and shall fulfil it to the utmost.

Mr Faulkland's absence from the kingdom hitherto put it out of my power; nor would I, without my beloved Mr Arnold's participation, have ever attempted it. Had he lived, fully restored as I was to his confidence and good opinion, I should have ventured to disclose the secret to him, and got him to join with me in such measures, as I should have thought best for Miss Burchell's happiness. It now rests upon myself alone, and I will leave nothing unattempted to serve her.

June 22

You will be surprized perhaps, my Cecilia, when I tell you that Mr Faulkland is now in England. Miss Burchell told me so this day. She mentioned it in a careless manner, rather directing her discourse to my mother. She had too much delicacy to hint at consequences of any kind from this circumstance, and quickly turned from the subject. My mother asked her impatiently, when he came; where he was; and several other questions; to none of which she could give any answer, but that she heard he had been returned above three months and was at his seat in Hertfordshire. I am surprized Sir George never mentioned this to me: to be sure he knew it; he is not extremely nice in his notions; however, this is a decorum for which I am obliged to him. Lady V— doubtless was ignorant of it, or she would have told me.

There is nothing now to prevent me from warmly interfering for Miss Burchell. Charming young woman! how is she to be pitied! The tedious years of suspence, of almost hopeless love, that she has passed, deserve a recompence; and her little boy, my mother tells me, is a lovely creature. Miss Burchell brought him once to see my mother; Mr Faulkland's former house-keeper visits the child often, and has brought his mother frequent and large supplies for his use.

I told Miss Burchell, at parting to-day, that I had not forgot my promise; and that, as soon as decency would permit, nothing should hinder me from being a most strenuous advocate for her. She squeezed my hand, and whispered, dear madam, my fate is in your power!

I would it were, then should she soon be happy. But I will acquit myself as far as I am able.

June 23

I was prevailed on to dine at my brother's to-day, the first time that I have been abroad ever since I came to town. I had no mind to go; but my mother, not being well, had excused herself; and she said, it would be taken amiss if I did so too, lady Sarah herself having made the invitation. Her ladyship said, I need not be fearful of meeting strangers at her house, as it was to be a private day. So much the better, thought I; nothing else should induce me to go.

It was the first time I ever was in Sir George's house, which is a very magnificent one, within a door or two of Mr Faulkland's, in St James's-Square, as lady Sarah did not approve of that which he had before. But, my dear, the ostentation of this woman made me sick; such a parade of grandeur, such an unnecessary display of state and splendor, I thought, looked like an insult upon me. I was carried into a most sumptuous drawing-room; but as this was a private day, as she called it, the furniture was all covered up with body-cloths; and the room, having been newly washed, felt extremely cold.

I was told her ladyship was dressing, though it was then, as I imagined, her dinner-time. After I had shivered here for about half an hour, lady Sarah's woman came to desire me to walk up stairs. As the woman did not know me, and, from the little ceremony she saw me treated with, concluded I was some humble visitor, she took me up the back stairs to her lady's dressing-room, where I found lady Sarah, who was not yet half dressed, in consultation with her millener. The woman was trying some head-dresses on her before the glass. She made me a very slight apology for having kept me waiting so long; and, to mend the matter, told me, as she was not near ready, if I chose looking at the house, I should have time enough to do it before dinner. I thanked her; but said, I had already sat so long in the cold, that I felt myself chilled; and, with her ladyship's permission, would place myself at her fire-side till dinner was ready. She asked her woman, carelessly, why I had not been shewn into the dining-parlour. She then turned to her millener again, to whom she gave a particular charge to have a suit of very rich point, which she had fixed on, done up for her against the next night; by which I found my sister was going to throw off her mourning intirely; that which she had on being so slight, that it was scarcely to be distinguished for such.

My brother entered the room while she was thus employed; and having saluted me, looked at his watch, and asked lady Sarah, had she ordered dinner later than usual? She told him, she had ordered it half an hour later than ordinary, as she had a mind to make a long morning, having dedicated it to trades-people, with whom she had a hundred things to settle. My brother cast a side-glance at me: I thought he looked a little abashed at the impertinence and ill-breeding of his wife.

Lady Sarah had by this time huddled on her cloaths: a laced footman appeared at the door, who summoned us, by a silent bow, to dinner.

The millener gathered up her frippery, and put them into a band-box; telling her, she would wait on her ladyshp again. Lady Sarah answered, You have got a monstrous way to go, Mrs— (I forget the name); and, as I have not half done with you yet, you may stay and dine here, as we are alone, and I will look over the rest of the things in the evening, as I shall not have another leisure day while I am in town.

This was going a little too far: Sir George felt it. I believe, lady Sarah, said he, this gentlewoman has a coach waiting for her at the door (he had seen it, for he was but just come in); perhaps it may be inconvenient to detain her: she may leave the things, and call another time. The woman took the hint, though she before seemed inclined to accept of the honour lady Sarah had done her. She made her curt'sey, and withdrew. As this, however, had brought on a variety of fresh instructions, it detained us so long, that the dinner was quite cold; nor was our repast, had it even been warm, by any means answerable to the elegance of the service, the superb sideboard, and the number of attendants. In short, the dinner was composed of a parcel of tossed-up dishes, that looked like the fragments of a feast. You know there is nobody more indifferent to the pleasures of the table than I am; yet I own that this, joined to the rest of this foolish woman's behaviour, nettled me extremely. There was such a mixture of sordidness and vanity in the whole apparatus, as made it truly contemptible.

I made haste to put an end to my visit, as soon as I possibly could after dinner, with a resolution never to repeat it.

From these few sketches of lady Sarah, you may form some kind of an idea of what sort of creature it is. I should pity Sir George, but that I think her disposition is not extremely opposite to his own.

June 24

I am told that the widow Arnold is actually married to that vile attorney who was the contriver, and more than partner, in her iniquity. I am really glad she has lost the name of a family to which she was a disgrace. Every-body now believes that I and my children have been greatly injured; but how unavailing is compassion; it only mortifies, when it is expressed by the pitying words and looks of people, who have it neither in their power nor inclination to assist you. This Mrs Arnold, bad as she is, is visited and caressed. Favour always follows the fortunate.

June 25

This day Sir George and his lady set out for Scotland. He came to take his leave of us; but made an apology for lady Sarah, whose hurry would not permit her to call on us. My brother says, they shall stay some months at her uncle's, Lord K—. He told me, at parting, he should write to me as soon as he got to his journey's end, having something very particular to say to me.

July 7

I have read over my journal of the last fortnight, and am startled to think what a poor insignificant being I am! Not a single act worth recording, even to *you*. My whole life perhaps may have passed so; yet one is apt to fancy, that they are doing something of importance, while they are engaged in the little bustle of the world, be it in ever so trifling a manner; and when you find you have a variety of incidents to relate, in which you yourself were concerned, that your time has not been spent in vain. But for these last fourteen days, had I kept a journal for my cat, I think I should have had as much to say for her.

July 8

I shall grow busy again: I have received the promised letter from Sir George; an extraordinary one it is: but I will not anticipate the contents; read them yourself.

Dear Sidney, *July 4, 1706.*

I have a serious subject to offer to your consideration, which made me the rather chuse to engage your attention in this manner, than in a conversaton between ourselves; liable as that would be to interruptions, objections, and frivolous punctilios, from which you have already suffered so severely.

I have paid so much regard to that decorum of which you are so fond, as never to have mentioned Mr Faulkland's name to you since you were become a widow, though it is near four months since he returned to England.

As I kept up a correspondence with him when he was abroad, you may be sure I informed him of your reconciliation to your late husband; a reconciliation, which, if you thought it a happiness to you, you were indebted to Faulkland for. This single circumstance it was that inclined him to return to England, which otherwise perhaps he would never again have seen, though the necessity of his affairs here, which he had left at random, required his presence. To avoid giving umbrage to your husband, he repaired privately to his house in the country, where I paid him a visit. Few of his friends, except myself, knew of his being in the kingdom.

Remember, Sidney, the great obligations you have to Mr Faulkland, and let that prepare your mind for what I am going to say.

You are now become a free woman: Faulkland loves you still, with an unparallel'd affection. I had a letter from him soon after your arrival in town, wherein he mentions the revival of his hopes from your present situation, and intreats me to be mindful of his interest. He charged me, however, not to mention his name to you, till a decent time was passed; otherwise probably you would have been acquainted with these particulars sooner: but Faulkland himself has a little too much of that ridiculous nicety which you admire so. I think I have waited till a *very* decent time, as you have now been almost three months a widow.

I have very little reason to imagine that *my* influence, on this occasion, will have any weight either with you or my mother: I have had proofs of this already; but I hope you will not be so blind to your own interest, as to refuse the good that fortune once more throws at your feet. I can hardly suppose you so weak, as to let the absurd objection, which formerly prevented your happiness, still prevail with you to reject the same happiness, so unexpectedly again offered to your acceptance.

My mother and you have by this time learnt how to forgive *human frailties*. Indeed you forgave such enormities, that Faulkland's transgression, in comparison of them, was innocence. But I will not reproach the memory of the dead.

Whatever pretence you might formerly have had to carry your punctilios to an extraordinary height, certain circumstances in your life have now made your situation very different. You are destitute of fortune, incumbered with children. Reflect on this, and let your own imagination supply the rest. To any-body but yourself, I should think all that I have said needless; but I know the minds that I have to deal with.

I must take this opportunity of telling you, that I am surprized at my mother's continued attachment to Miss Burchell; she is an artful creature, and, I think, by no means a proper acquaintance for you. I am far from wishing to injure her; but such an intimacy may be dangerous.

You will certainly hear from Faulkland before it be long. I repeat it again, You owe him more than ever you will be able to repay: the recompence he deserves will ensure your own happiness and prosperity: your gratitude, as well as your prudence, will now be put to the test, and your conduct, on this occasion, will determine me as to the light in which I shall henceforth consider you.

Present my duty to my mother. Lady Sarah desires her service may be accepted.

I am, &c.

What a letter is this, my sister! But Sir George is still himself; gross; void of sentiment: he dreams of nothing but the glaring advantages that fortune and rank in life procure. And how he argues too! Weak arguer! He *will not suppose that the objection* (absurd he calls it), *which formerly prevented my happiness, should still prevail with me to reject the same happiness* – Why not? Is the nature of Mr Faulkland's offence changed? Has he ever repaired it? Has not Miss Burchell the same claim she ever had? Nay, a stronger than ever, if years of unabated love can give it her? *My mother and I have by this time learnt to forgive human frailties; nay, we forgave enormities* – Unkind brother, to rake up the unfortunate ashes of my beloved. We have, indeed, learnt to forgive human frailties; but they were the frailties of a husband, a repenting husband, who was seduced to the commission of those crimes which he abhorred: but surely that is no plea for my overlooking the faults of another, to whom I am under no such tie. I am now *without fortune, and incumbered with children*. Indelicate man! does he think *that* an argument in favour of his proposal? It is a strong one against it. Shall I, who, when I was in the virgin-bloom of youth, flattered with some advantages of person, which time and grief have since impaired, and not destitute of fortune; I, who then rejected Mr Faulkland from motives which still subsist; shall I, now that I have lost those advantages, meanly condescend to accept of this rejected man? This would, indeed, be acknowleging, that the humiliating change had levelled me to those principles which I formerly contemned; would lay me under mortifying obligations to Mr Faulkland, and destroy the merit of that refusal which proceeded from such justifiable motives.

No, my sordid brother! if I *could* recompence Mr Faulkland as he deserves at my hands, I *would* do it; but, with such a mind as I bear, it cannot be done your way. I say nothing of the promise I made Miss Burchell; if I had never made her such, my sentiments would be the same from those other considerations; but such a promise, binding as it is, determined my conduct beyond the possibility of a doubt.

How unreasonable are Sir George's prejudices with regard to this unhappy young creature! He is for ever throwing out some invective against her. It is cruel; but I am tempted to forgive him, as I know it proceeds from his attachment to his friend. He need not put me in mind of the gratitude I owe Mr Faulkland; I am thoroughly sensible of it; but Sir George and I differ widely in our ideas of expressing this gratitude. My *conduct in this affair is to determine him as to the light in which he is hereafter to consider me.* Why, be it so. He has long lost the tenderness of a brother for me; I will not regain it at the expence of my honour. I know the worst that can befall me is poverty. I have already experienced almost every possible ill in life but that, and for that I am prepared. But I will not call myself poor while I have an upright heart to support me; and the means, poor and despicable as they are, of sustaining life. But what do I call despicable? Have I not an estate, my dear, a whole fifty pounds a year, that I can call my own? This much was reserved to me out of my jointure when the rest was sold; and on this, whenever it pleases heaven to take my mother away, will I retire to some cottage in a cheap country, where my two children and I will live, and smile at the rich and the great.

My brother's letter has vexed and disgusted me exceedingly. *Lady Sarah presents her service.* Vain woman! is that a becoming phrase to the mother of her husband? I am so provoked, I think I shall not answer him: he has no relish for such arguments as I could produce in support of my own opinions, and my writing to him would only bring on disagreeable altercations. My mother is in a downright passion with him: Selfish wretch! she called him; and said, he would sacrifice both honour and justice to his own pride.

July 19

Miss Burchell; poor soul, how I pity her! Her anxiety increases every hour. She, you may be sure, keeps a look-out on all Mr Faulkland's motions; for, she tells me, she hears he is arrived in town. I suppose I shall receive a notice of some kind or other from him. The unhappy girl; she grieves me to see her! There was never so extravagant a love as her's: she has nourished it in solitude, and I believe has a heart naturally tender to an uncommon degree; otherwise she could not, for so long a time, and with so little hopes, have preserved so undiminished a fondness; but some accidents have, I know not how, combined to feed this flame. She acknowleges that Mr Faulkland's being disappointed in espousing me, gave the first encouragement to her hopes; for, she said, she had reason to believe that I was the only woman in the world that stood between her and her happiness; and Mr Faulkland's remaining single ever since, confirmed her in that opinion. Then the generous attention that he paid to her welfare, in recommending her to my mother's notice, when he first left England; the noble supplies that he constantly furnished her with ever since for the child's use; his behaviour to Mrs Gerrarde, who, she says, is the most ensnaring of creatures; the tender manner that he mentioned her in his letter to my brother; my mother's constantly indulging her in the belief that she would one day recover Mr Faulkland's affections: all these circumstances, I say, joined together, have kept alive the warmest and most romantic love I ever saw or heard of. Well may the men say, that forsaken women are always the most passionate lovers: it may be so, and Miss Burchell is one instance of the truth of this observation; but I think *I* should never make another. There is something to me unaccountable in this; but Miss Burchell is all made up of languishments and softness. I have heard her speak of Mr Faulkland in so rapturous a strain as has amazed me; and she once owned to me, that she is sure she must have died, if he had not returned her love! Return it! Ah! my Cecilia, how did he return it? How mortifying is her situation! to be compelled to court the man who flies her, and to make use of a rival's mediation too! but let me forget that name; I am no longer so to her, and shall do my best to prove it. She wearied me with importunities to write to Mr Faulkland, now he is come to town; but I beseeched her to have a little patience, till some overture was first made by him toward a renewal of our acquaintance, which, I told her, it was very probable I should soon receive. You may be sure I took care not to let her know of the intimation I had from Sir George. She seems fearful of my seeing Mr Faulkland. Oh! madam, said she, if he beholds your face again, I am undone, unless you can first prevail with him – She stopped. 'I understand you, dear Miss Burchell; I give you my word I will not see Mr Faulkland, unless I am first convinced I can restore him to you.' 'How good you are, madam! your influence, all potent as it is, can work miracles. If Mr Faulkland is *sure* you will never be his, perhaps he may return to his *first* love. My dear, ought she to have said so? But it is no matter; it is nothing to me now, who was his first or second love.

July 20

It has happened to my wish; a billet from Mr Faulkland, sent with compliments and how-do-ye's, to my mother and me. Miss Burchell, who almost lives with us, was present when I received it: her colour came and went several times while our servant delivered his message. I gave the letter into her hand as soon as I had read it. There is nothing alarming in it, madam, said I; see yourself; only a few friendly lines, such as I might expect. Her hands shook while she held the paper. Now, madam, said she, returning it; now you have a charming opportunity of writing to him. I shall not fail, said I, to make use of it, and will let you see what I write.

These are the contents of Mr Faulkland's letter:

Will you, madam, permit a forgotten, though not the least zealous of your friends, to enquire after your welfare? Forgive me, if I renew your grief, when I tell you, that, as I must participate in every thing that relates to you, I have deeply mourned with you on the late calamity that has befallen you. When Lady Bidulph opens her doors to her general acquaintance; if I may presume to mingle in the crowd, and kiss her hands, I shall esteem it as a particular honour; but will not, without her permission, attempt it. She is too good to refuse me this indulgence: you, madam, I hope, will not forbid it to

The humblest, and
most devoted of your servants,

Wednesday morning.

ORLANDO FAULKLAND.

Yes, Orlando, I must forbid you; I know the consequences of thy insidious visits. I'll try you to the quick. You have given me an opportunity of writing to you (I think) without any impropriety. Miss Burchell's interest is uppermost in my wishes, and I will at least try what my influence on this romantic wayward heart can effect.

How happy should I think myself, if *my* mediation, *all potent* as she called it, would have the desired success!

July 21

I wrote to Mr Faulkland last night: my mother approved of the letter, which I shewed her before I sent it. Mr Faulkland was abroad when it was left at his house; but as I received an answer to it early this morning, I will give you copies of the two letters together; and first that of mine to Mr Faulkland.

I thank you, sir, thank you from my heart, for your friendship, and beg you will not think me ungrateful for having thus long deferred to pay you my acknowlegements for the signal favours I have received at your hands. I am sensible, Sir, that it was owing to your compassion, your generosity, and disinterested nobleness of mind, that I was once indebted for the greatest blessing of my life. To you I owe the vindicating of my suspected faith, and the being restored to the affection of my dear husband. For this goodness I have never ceased to bless and pray for you, and shall continue to do so while I live. But oh! Sir, while you have given *me* so much cause for gratitude and esteem, why will you leave one heart to sigh for your unkindness? a heart that admires, that loves, that adores you! a heart worthy of your acceptance, and which has a right to demand all your tenderness. Need I name the amiable possessor of this heart? I need not; there is but one woman in the world who owns this description: for her let me become an advocate; she has won me to her party: indeed, Sir, she, and she only, deserves your love. Her's, I am sure, you have ever possessed unrivalled, though her youth, beauty, and charming accomplishments, must have made her the object of every one's wishes who saw her. 'Tis above four years since you first won her virgin affections. What has been her portion since that fatal time? Tears, solitude, and unremitting anguish. How can a mind like yours, susceptible as it is of pity for the woes of others, condemn *such* a woman to perpetual sorrow? How can that generosity, which has been so active on other occasions, droop and languish where there is *such* a cause to call forth all its exertions?

Do, Mr Faulkland, permit pity to plead in your bosom for the dear Miss Burchell. I should urge paternal affection too; but to the voice of nature you cannot be deaf. Your sweet little son calls upon you to do him and his mother justice; the injured lady herself implores your compassion; my mother, who equally admires and loves her, intreats you; I, whom you once esteemed, conjure you; the secret monitor in your own soul must join in our sollicitations. Why, then, why will you shut your ears against the united voice of reason, of conscience, and of gratitude? You cannot, you will not do it. Miss Burchell's merit and sufferings must be rewarded; and I shall bless Mr Faulkland as the guardian of the injured, the patron of the afflicted, the assertor of his own, as well as of my honour. This is the light, and this only, in which I shall rejoice to see him.

Mr FAULKLAND'S *Answer*

You do well, Madam, you do well to anticipate my suit; and, with so much cruel eloquence, to bid me despair. Yes, I see Miss Burchell has won you to her party; but what have I done to merit such a malevolent fate, that you, you of all created beings, should become *her* advocate? I little thought Mrs Arnold would make such a barbarous use of her power. Tell me, thou dear tyrant, how have I deserved this? Would it not have been kinder to have said at once, Faulkland, do not hope; I never will be yours; I hate, I despise you, and leave you to your fate? Oh! no; you are artful in your cruelty; you would prevent even my wishes, and cut off my hopes in their blossom, before they dare to unfold themselves to you.

But you have furnished me with weapons against yourself, and I will use them with as little mercy as you have shewn to me. If four years are past since I won Miss Burchell's affections, is it not also *as* long that I have loved you with an ardor – Oh thou insensible! Were you not mine by your own consent, with your mother's approbation? Was not the day, the hour fixed, that I was to have led you to the altar? Miss Burchell's hopes were never raised to such a pitch as mine, when an avenging fiend snatched the promised blessing from my grasp. Think what were then my sufferings. I saw you afterwards in the arms of another. Miss Burchell never suffered *such* torture. Had I seen you *happy*, I might have been consoled. If Miss Burchell loved me as I have loved you, she would rejoice in the prospect of my felicity. I should have done so in your's, Heaven is my witness! Had you been happy, I should not have thought myself miserable, though you were lost to my hopes.

Why do you compel me to urge an ungrateful truth in regard to Miss Burchell? Madam, she has no claim to my vows: my gratitude, my compassion, she has an ample right to, and she has them. More might by this time have been her's, if I had never seen Mrs Arnold.

Remember, I do not yet desire permission to throw myself at your feet; I revere you too much to make such a request; but do not banish me your presence. I cannot always be proof against such rigours. Indulge me at least in the hope that time may do something in my favour. I will not desire you to tell me so; but do not forbid it. Lady Bidulph knows I respect her; but she is still obdurate. If *she* relented, would not *you* madam, do so too?

I am, &c.

How this man distresses me, my dear! What a difficult task have I undertaken! yet I will go through with it. I am fearful of letting Miss Burchell see his answer, so discouraging as it is for her; yet how can I withhold it from her sight? 'Tis necessary I should conceal nothing from her on this occasion; she confides in me, and I must not give her cause for suspicion. *She has no right to his vows.* This he always said. It is necessary the lady should be quite explicit with me. I doubt she has not been altogether sincere in what she has said to my mother on this subject. I shall see her presently, and discourse with her more particularly on this head than I have ever yet done . . . .

I have had a conference with Miss Burchell, a long one, and in private; for I told my mother I wished to talk with her alone.

I began with shewing her Mr Faulkland's last letter. It had the effect I expected. She was exceedingly shocked. I laid my finger on that paragraph, *She has no right to my vows.* It is necessary, my dear madam, said I, that you should be perfectly open and candid with me on this head. I have entered the lists for you, and will not give up your cause; but it depends on you to furnish me with every possible argument in your favour. If you mislead me by wrong insinuations, instead of putting it in my power to serve you, you will only create to yourself fresh obstacles.

It is a nice subject, madam, and what I have ever been cautious of touching upon to you; but in the present situation of your affairs, it is of the utmost importance to you, that you should have no reserves to me. When Mr Faulkland first recommended you to my mother's acquaintance, he referred her to your honour, for an explanation of certain points, of so delicate a nature, that I am loath to touch upon them. But pardon me, dear Miss Burchell, you must be open with me. Mr Faulkland was obliged to declare, in his own justification, that he never sought to gain your affections; and was so far from endeavouring to take advantage of the kind sentiments you had for him, that he avoided all opportunities of improving them; that he was even surprized into the fatal step, which has since made you so unhappy, by the artifices of that vile woman, who had the care of you.

Mr Faulkland relied so intirely on your candour, that, as I told you before, he referred my mother to you, for a confirmation of the truth of what he advanced; imagining that your testimony would in some measure extenuate his fault. My mother, I have reason to believe, has heard the story from you in a light less favourable to Mr Faulkland. I was married before she received any information on this subject from you; and as any extenuation on Mr Faulkland's side was then become a matter of indifference to me, I enquired not into particulars; but by what I could judge from my mother's discourse then, and from hints which she has many times dropped since, I am inclined to believe, that either Mr Faulkland concealed some particulars, or that you, from a delicacy very natural to a young lady in such circumstances, chose to draw a veil over some parts of your story. But, dear madam, all disguises must now be thrown aside; depend upon it, your candour will more effectually recommend you to Mr Faulkland's esteem, than any thing else; and, perhaps, your justifying him to *me*, may be no immaterial circumstance in your favour.

Variety of passions discovered themselves on her face while I spoke, but shame was predominant. She was mute, and hung down her head. I took her by the hand, Do not think, my dear, I mean to ensnare you; far be such perfidy from my heart! Have I not promised you my assistance? I declare, by every thing that is sacred, you shall have it to the utmost stretch of my power; but do not let a false bashfulness stand between you and sincerity; you will stop up the way to your own happiness if you do. Speak, dear madam, has Mr Faulkland been just in his representations?

She burst into a flood of tears: Oh! madam, you read my very soul; what disguise can I make use of, before such penetrating eyes as yours? Yes, Mr Faulkland *has* spoke the truth, shameful as the confession is for me, I own it. Mrs Gerrarde, base woman! betrayed me; my own mad passion did the rest. Mr Faulkland told me, a few days after the fatal meeting, that he was the most miserable man on earth for what had happened: he said, there was a lady in the world to whom he was bound to offer his hand; that her brother was his particular friend; that his marriage was then actually negotiating; and he was pressed on that occasion to return to London. He owned he had never seen the lady, but as his honour was engaged to her brother, he could not look upon himself as a free man. He cursed his ill fate, that he had not had an opportunity of informing me of this sooner; which, he said, might have prevented me from casting away my affection on a man, who could not deserve it. What could I say, madam? There was no room for reproaches or complaints. I made none; I had nobody to accuse but myself. I had declared my frantic love to Mr Faulkland unasked; I had implored his in return: in one dreadful moment I fell a sacrifice to my own weakness. The only hope that now remained for me, was built on that circumstance of Mr Faulkland's having never seen his destined bride. Had I known you, madam, to have been the person, there could have sprung but small comfort from that consideration; but ignorant as I was of the lady's merit, I thought it not impossible but that some objection might have arisen either to her person or temper; or the lady, perhaps, (though that I thought almost incredible) might not approve of Mr Faulkland: in either case, some glimmerings of hope remained for me. Mr Faulkland's generous compassion for me, gave me room to think he did not hate me, and I was unwilling to lose the little interest I thought I had gained in his heart, by *fond complainings*, much less upbraidings, for which he had given me no cause. I therefore acquiesced, determined to wait for what my fate was to do with me; resolving privately in my own mind, that in case Mr Faulkland's intended nuptials should not take place, to remind him of my love. I did not confess to my aunt what had been the result of that interview, which she had contrived between Mr Faulkland and me: shame would not suffer me to indulge it. But it was not long in my power to conceal it: I believe indeed, she suspected it before. She reproached me for the error which she herself had caused; but I believe, what most nettled her was Mr Faulkland's having escaped the snare; for I am sure she would have been base enough to have had me retain him as a lover, though I could not secure him for a husband; for he was not the first, that this bad woman would have seduced me to favour, for her own private interest.

In the midst of the horror, into which the condition I found myself threw me, I heard that Mr Faulkland was on the point of being married.

The prospect I had before me drove me to despair. I knew I could not remain long in my uncle's house. I knew not whither to fly. In my distraction I wrote to Mr Faulkland: You, madam, saw the letter, that ill-fated letter, which deprived Mr Faulkland of his happiness.

I soon received an answer, wherein Mr Faulkland related to me at large the unfortunate consequences that letter had produced. He lamented, in the tenderest manner, my unhappy situation; told me, he would provide me a proper place for my retreat; and, as I was an entire stranger in London, having never been there, would recommend me to the notice of one of the best of women, lady Bidulph, from whom, as my unhappy story was known to her, I might expect the utmost humanity. And here, madam, with blushes let me own it, he urged me not to conceal a single circumstance of the truth from that lady.

'You know, said he, my dear Miss Burchell, I am not a seducer; rescue me from that black suspicion; and, as far as the unhappy case will admit, clear my honour to lady Bidulph. See what a reliance I have on *your* honour, when I trust the vindicating of my own to you, in such delicate circumstances. He concluded his letter with telling me frankly, that though he had been rejected by Miss Bidulph, he loved her with such an ardent passion, that it was impossible for him ever to think of any other woman; and till he had a heart to bestow, he should never entertain a thought of marriage.'

You know Mr Faulkland at this juncture went abroad; and thus was I circumstanced when I came to that house, which he had provided for me. And so frank and noble were his proceedings, that I solemnly declare, I was determined, though at the hazard of divulging my own shame, to have acquitted him to the utmost of my power to lady Bidulph; and should have rejoiced, could I have been the means of procuring him the happiness he deserved, in regaining your favour; as I had been, though unknowingly, the unlucky cause of his losing it. But fortune had disposed of you otherwise, before I saw lady Bidulph. This she quickly informed me of, and I will own to you, madam, that as I found there was now an insuperable bar to Mr Faulkland's hopes, I was mean enough not to have the courage to speak truth. I saw it could not avail him, in regard to his prospects with you. Lady Bidulph's eye awed me; yet I think she led me into a justification of myself, so great were her prejudices against Mr Faulkland. Or, perhaps, having already disposed of you in marriage, in vindication of this step, she did not wish to be undeceived. Yes, again, in spite of my confusion, I must repeat it, I was not sincere; I threw out such hints to lady Bidulph, as must have made her think Mr Faulkland had taken pains to undo me: to this act of disingenuousness, my sole motive was, that I might appear in a less culpable light in the eyes of a lady of such strict virtue as your mother. By making her my friend, I was in hopes one day of making you so too. Devoted, as Mr Faulkland was, to the most charming woman in the world, I was not afraid of his making a second choice. I thought, if he *were* to be induced to marry, he might, in time, be prevailed upon to turn his thoughts towards me. In this hope I have dragged on so many tedious years. I was not mistaken in my opinion, that he could find none worthy to succeed Mrs Arnold in his heart. He loves you still, madam; but you have declared you will never be his; he is still free; these are the circumstances that nourish my hope. My heart is in your hand; I have made you mistress of my dearest secret. Can you forgive me, madam? But you have an heroic soul! Remember, Mrs Arnold, to your generosity I now trust what is dearer to me than life. Should Mr Faulkland know, should lady Bidulpoh know, how I have abused their confidence, I think I could not outlive it.

They never shall, madam, said I: I thank you for this frank acknowlegement of your heart; such a proof of your confidence in me, I should be a wretch to abuse; and I hope to make such a use of the candid confession you have now made me, as will greatly promote your interest.

And is it possible, madam, said she, you can yield up the interest you have in Mr Faulkland without a pang? Oh! the exquisite charmer! and she said it with such an emphasis, drawing out her breath in long sighs. But you are heroic, as I said before: Nature did not mold your heart, as she has done those of the rest of your sex. Who that was beloved by Mr Faulkland, would yield him to another? Worlds! ten thousand worlds would I give to be beloved by him as you are! but you are a prodigy of a woman! I stopped Miss Burchell in her transports. There is less merit, madam, than you ascribe to me in my conduct: I readily acquiesced under my mother's rejection of Mr Faulkland, when he *had* some interest in my heart; but there is no self-denial in what I am now about to do for you. My affections have long since changed their object, and now lie buried with him in his grave.

My tears here bore witness to the truth of what I said: Miss Burchell wept too. Her mind was agitated; the confession she had made to me had humbled her; her heart overflowed with fondness; I had filled her with pleasing hopes: all these sensations combined together, melting her into tenderness: she is made up of tears, and sighs, and romantic wishes.

I can now, said I, assure Mr Faulkland, that you have done him justice, and that he is highly obliged to your candour.

She interrupted me; But, madam, if he should know how *late* my acknowlegements came – He need not know it, said I; my mother shall not know it either; leave every thing to my management, and depend upon my word. She snatched my hand eagerly, and kissed it.

But oh! madam, above all things, said she, let not Sir George Bidulph know any thing of your intended goodness, in mediating for me. He hates me, implacably he hates me. I upbraid him not for it: his strong attachment to Mr Faulkland is the cause of it: he accuses me in his heart of being the occasion (which I own I was, though ignorantly) of Mr Faulkland's disappointment. I am sure, were he to know what you design in my favour, he would counterwork you, and use all his influence over his friend to ruin me.

I made her easy on this head, by assuring her Sir George should know nothing of the matter; and put her in mind how lucky it was for her that he was absent.

I cannot help thinking, my Cecilia, that there is a sort of fatality has attended Mr Faulkland's attachment to me. By what a strange accident did we come to the knowledge of Miss Burchell's affair! How strong were my mother's prepossessions against Mr Faulkland; and how many little circumstances concurred her to encourage in this disposition! His letter from Bath to my brother helped to confirm her in her dislike of his conduct; Miss Burchell's letter to Mr Faulkland, though meant very differently, was a strong motive of condemnation. The only means of justification left for him, my mother did not apply to, till it was too late; and then that very circumstances of it's *being* too late to serve him, Miss Burchell acknowleges, was the reason that the very method which he had proposed for his defence, was turned to his condemnation.

Rooted, as my mother's prejudices were, she engages herself, she engages me, in a promise, to use my endeavours to promote Miss Burchell's marriage with Mr Faulkland. Does this not look as if some unseen power, who guides our actions, had set a stamp of disapprobation on the union between this man and me.

I wish I had seen that letter which Mr Faulkland wrote to my brother from Bath: my mother said, she did not read it through. He treated the subject lightly, and there was one circumstance in particular in it that shocked her; and yet surely, if the *whole* might not have borne a favourable construction, Sir George would not have shewn her that account, by way of justifying his friend. This reflection comes too late! Why did it not occur sooner to my mother or to me? We drew no other inference from Sir George's disclosing this letter, than that as Mr Faulkland treated the affair ludicrously, it was therefore expected, both by him and my brother, that we should consider it so too. That could not have been the case. Miss Burchell's confession has opened my eyes. – Poor Mr Faulkland! What wayward fate is thine! But let me beware of relenting; that might be fatal. There is still one indelible blot remains upon his conduct. Miss Burchell, blameable as she acknowleges herself, was still betrayed; and though not by Mr Faulkland, yet sure his having paid the price of her innocence to the wicked aunt, renders him so far guilty, as that he owes her a great reparation. This was a particular I durst not touch upon; the unhappy girl herself being ignorant of it. There is a wide gulph fixed between Mr Faulkland and me. How many things are leagued against him! Alas! he thinks the principal bar to his hopes is removed, and that if Miss Burchell has been just, he ought to be forgiven. But he little knows thy Sidney's heart; critically delicate as my situation is, in regard him, I am removed a thousand times farther than ever from his wishes. Neither knows he the engagements I am under to Miss Burchell; which alone would put an ever-lasting bar between us. Unhappy Miss Burchell! She has bound me to her by stronger ties than ever. She has been ingenuous; she has owned her weakness to me; she declares she would have done this sooner, if it could have promoted my happiness: perhaps she would; shall I not then endeavour to promote her's? I will, I must; my word is given. Yet Faulkland deserves – oh! he deserves a worthier lot.

VOLUME III

June 22

I NOW send you, my Cecilia, my second Letter to Mr Faulkland.

'Why do you compel me, Sir, noble and disinterested as your conduct has been towards me, to accuse you now of unkindness? You call me insensible – oh! it is from my too great sensibility that all my sorrows have sprung. Destitute as I am of happiness myself, or even of a possiblity of ever attaining it here, I look for no other comfort in this life, but what must arise from seeing those whom I most esteem in possession of that tranquillity of mind, which I can never hope to enjoy. If Mr Faulkland were happy, if Miss Burchell were happy, I should be less miserable. Remember, Sir, it was not this lady's fault that you were disappointed in your former hope. She did not try, by female wiles, to engage a heart which you refused her. She used no ungenerous arts to cross your wishes. Loving you as she did, almost to distraction, she yielded you up in silent anguish to a rival; a rival superior to herself in nothing. I acknowlege, Sir, I was to have been yours, and with my own consent; but was it not also with my own consent those bonds were cancelled, by which we were to have been united? I was then convinced Miss Burchell had a prior claim; I think so still, and ever shall. Miss Burchell's fmaily is not mean, her fortune is considerable; her beauty and personal accomplishments inferior to none; and, but for Mr Faulkland, she had been innocent. Yet do not imagine I would aggravate your fault; Miss Burchell's candor could not suffer this. How charmingly ingenuous was her confession! In the midst of tears and blushes, she owned her weakness; you, she said, were not to blame. She praised your generosity, your compassion, the integrity and frankness of your whole behaviour towards her; and could Miss Burchell's suffrage have ensured to you the completion of your wishes, Mr Faulkland would have been indebted to her for what he once thought his happiness. But though her testimony could not avail you in that particular, yet are your obligations to her the same. Does not then Miss Burchell love Mr Faulkland with a generosity equal to his own? Do years of fervent and unalterable affection deserve no return? Does the child, the dear innocent that calls you father, deserve no consideration? He bears your name, Sir; let him not blush to own it: he may one day be an honour and a comfort to you. Put it in his power to make it his boast, instead of his shame, that Mr Faulkland was his father. The amiable lady, whose very life is bound up in you, has, in the midst of her affliction, one great source of comfort; her character has escaped the malignity of cruel tongues, by the privacy with which she conducted her measures, till after the birth of your son. The retirement she has since lived in; her prudent, her modest, her exemplary conduct have created esteem in every body that knows her; this circumstance, as it is a peculiar felicity to herself, so ought it to be a motive of encouragement to you, Sir, to compleat her happiness. The false judging part of the world will have nothing to point at; Miss Burchell's relation, or even connection, with Mrs Gerrarde is hardly known here; she has had no correspondence with that irregular woman since she became a widow; and her character had not suffered before, in such a manner, as to reflect dishonour on the young lady, who was then under her care. How then can you persist in a cruel rejection of this lady? You own she is amiable; I am sure she has a thousand good qualities. Is her love for you, her unparalleled love, to be imputed to her as a crime? If it be one, long and bitter has been her punishment! On you it rests to recompence her sufferings. What may you not expect from a grateful heart that worships you? Such a fervent, such a faithful love (deserving as you are) you perhaps may never again meet with in woman. With her you may be happy, she will make it the study of her life to render you so. Your own heart, conscious of having acted nobly, will confirm your happiness. Would to God I could inspire you with such sentiments as would induce you to make the generous experiment! How would your character rise in the esteem of the two persons whom you profess to revere! How would you be adored by the amiable sufferer! but above all, how delightful must be the exultations of the self-approving mind! There wants but this act to render you the most deserving of men. I would fain esteem, respect, admire you as I ought; but you will not let me; you will be a *common* man, and undistinguished amongst the light ones of your sex.'

I shewed this letter to Miss Burchell; she read it with grateful tears running down her cheeks. In about an hour I received the following answer to it.

'Miss Burchell may triumph, Madam, since she has obtained *you* for her advocate. Well have you acquitted yourself of the task your rigid heart has undertaken. I thank the lady for the justice her charming ingenuousness (as you rightly call it) has done me. But what have I gained by this? Have I not raised the fair complainant still higher in your esteem, given her a stronger claim to your pity, and furnished you with arms against myself? Wretch that I am, I do, I must acknowlege the force of every thing that you have urged. Miss Burchell is amiable, her sincerity, her constancy, and (by me) unmerited love, deserve to be greatly recompensed. I would to heaven I had a heart to give her! but I have not; *you* know I have not; *she* knows it too. Could I have made Miss Burchell the return she deserves, I would not thus long have shunned her presence. I acknowleged the state of my heart to her even at the time I had lost all hopes of possessing you. And in the spite of my own struggles, after years of confirmed despair, I found myself still enslaved. How then could I offer a hand, devoted as my whole soul was to another object, to a lady, whose constant, tender, and delicate affection, demanded all the return that a sensible and grateful heart could make? This, Madam, is all the plea I can urge in answer to those arguments you offer to promote your favourite wish. Consult your own delicacy, let Miss Burchell consult hers, and then perhaps I shall stand acquitted of ingratitude.

'I hoped, Madam, that cleared as I have been of *one* imputation, I might have recovered some favour in yours and Lady Bidulph's thoughts. I was flattered with this consolation, small as it was, when every other hope forsook me. But when an unexpected event again brought happiness within my prospect, this reflection, I own became of more importance, and served to strengthen my then revived hopes. But you dash them with an unrelenting hand; and again build up those barriers between us, that heaven itself had overthrown. What can I say to you, inflexible as you are? has Miss Burchell *all* your pity? You may command my life, Madam; I would lay it down freely for you; but I cannot, must not, will not give up my love; and till you declare in express terms that I *must* be miserable, I will not even give up my hope.

ORLANDO FAULKLAND.'

See, my Cecilia, the heart I have to deal with. Hard to be subdued, and obstinate in all its purposes. I expected difficulties; but was in hopes he would be less determined in regard to his perseverance towards me. I think however I have gained some ground; he acknowleges Miss Burchell's merit, and seems obliged to her for the part she has acted towards him. I have been under some difficulties on this occasion; for as Miss Burchell was not so candid in her acknowlegements to my mother as she has been to me, I cannot let her know the whole of her confession; for this reason, I only told her the general purport of what I wrote last to Mr Faulkland; and in reading his answer to her, I passed over such passages as I thought might induce her to require an explanation. I own I am a little hurt at Miss Burchell's former perverting of facts on this occasion; but, as I have already said more than once, there are great allowances to be made for one in her very critical situation. Neither have I the least right to reproach her for it even in my thoughts; for had she been ever so explicit at my mother's first interview with her, it could not have availed me.

You find, my dear, it is necessary I should speak plainly to Mr Faulkland. I shall write to him again, and here you shall have a copy of what I say; but I must lead this violent spirit with gentleness, and endeavour to convince his reason, without wounding his tenderness.

Mrs Arnold's third letter to Mr Faulkland

'You give me pleasure, Sir; I begin to descry hopes for your and my amiable friend. I know such a heart as Mr Faulkland's cannot be proof against sentiments of gratitude and compassion; it will not be difficult to convert those sentiments into love, when the object is so deserving. Try, Sir, try; the experiment cannot fail. How much to your honour will so noble a triumph be over an ill-fated passion! What delightful returns may you not expect from the obliged, the grateful partner of your happiness! Do not call me inflexible, or rigid; filled as I am with gratitude, and a sense of your merit, I should hate myself, if I did not acknowlege that you deserve more from me than it can ever be in my power to repay. I must be plain with you, since you require it; it is impossible I ever can be yours. Sorry I am, that the necessity of circumstances compels me to make so early a declaration, from which I thought my present situation would have exempted me; but I forgive you, Sir, for urging me on this head, and draw a happy presage from your resting your hopes in relation to me, on my own determination. You appeal to my delicacy, whether you ought, with a heart estranged, to offer your hand to Miss Burchell? Were delicacy alone to be consulted, the answer perhaps might be easy; but there are superior considerations in your case to be taken in. Love, without doubt, demands love in return; but where injured honour is to be repaired, where the disgrace of a darling child is to be prevented, those nicer sentiments of the soul must and ought to give way: and I will venture to pronounce, that Miss Burchell would, with raptures, receive the hand which would confer such valuable blessings on her; leaving it to time, and her own unremiting tenderness and assuduity, to get an interest in the heart, which, by such an act, proved its own rectitude. On this subject, I, from experience, am qualified to speak. You know, sir, the interest you once had in me; you cannot think me so light a creature, as to suppose I so soon after my breaking with you, bestowed my affections on another. I did not; obedience to my mother's commands was the sole motive which engaged my vows to Mr Arnold; and I married him with no other sentiments, those those of esteem and gratitude for the great love he bore me. Yet from these seeds sown in my heart, sprung a tender and ardent affection: never did wife love a husband better than I did Mr Arnold; his kindness merited, and *did* win my whole affections; nor could a temporary alienation of *his* heart, disposses him of the place he held in *mine*. His returning love (for which, with all thankfulness, I own myself bound to you, Sir) made him still dearer to me than ever, and I now profess myself wedded to his memory. You have a right, Sir, to expect that I should explain myself at once to you on this subject; for your own sake, and for Miss Burchell's I must not suffer you to entertain a doubt of my resolution. You compel me to repeat, that I think Miss Burchell deserves your love, and has a just right to your hand. She throws herself upon your honour, without pretending to have any *lawful* claim; if she *had*, I should not condescend to solicit the man who could refuse to do her justice.

'My mother is firm in her first resolves; could you place a crown on my head, her integrity would still oblige her to reject it; nor would a crown tempt me to forfeit the duty which I owe to her.

'See then, Sir, if that *unexpected event*, which you mention (a fatal event to me!) has brought you nearer to your wishes; and here let me add, in justice to my own particular sentiments, that I think Mr Faulkland is the last man who ought to be my choice, even if my heart were disposed to make one. Reproach me not with ingratitude, or caprice, till I have explained myself. It is not long, Sir (blameless and unconscious as you were of the injury, and nobly as you repaired it) since you were the cause of a separation between me and my husband. I know you will say that our mutual innocence on this occasion, and the secret's being known but to a few of our friends, makes that objection of little weight. I grant you, with many it might be so; all minds are not equally susceptible; 'tis my unhappiness to have a too resenting heart. My own honour (scrupulous you might call it) would not suffer me to let the man succeed Mr Arnold in my love, who was the occasion of so much uneasiness to him, and the cause of my being suspected in my fidelity. Would it not be an insult on his memory? Oh, Sir, what is the world's opinion to the approbation of our own hearts! Mine has never yet reproached me, and this has been my support in all my trials. Thus much I say for the reverence I bear my dear Mr Arnold's memory; but I have other reasons to offer in my excuse; refinements you will call them, but my heart feels their force. I am not the same woman you once loved; afflictions have impaired my health, and those little advantages of person which nature bestowed on me, have not been improved by time; my spirits, broken by misfortunes, have left me languid and insensible to joy. Peace is the utmost of my wish, and all that I am now capable of relishing. The bride, whom Mr Faulkland once sought, was in the bloom of youth, admired and caressed, by a flattering world; unblemished in her character, her fortune equal to her wishes, her heart, her virgin heart, was then a present (with pride let me say it) worthy of any man's acceptance. It was then in her power to bestow happiness, and Mr Faulkland would not have been matched unequally. But the scene is changed; what should I now bring to your arms? A person faded by grief; a reputation (though undeservedly) once called in question; a little helpless family without fortune; a widowed heart, dead to love and incapable of pleasure. Oh, Sir! could I bear to be your wife on such conditions? Indebted to you as I am, past a possibility of my ever making you a return, to what a mighty sum would you raise the obligation? How poor would you make me in my own eyes? Humbled as I am by adversity, my soul has still too much pride, or let me call it delicacy, to submit to this. No, if there was no Miss Burchell in the world, no parental sway to guide me, in my present circumstances, I never would be yours.

You have now before you my final determination. I shall trouble you no more on the subject. If your heart relents towards Miss Burchell, great will be your reward. In her you are sure of a tender, faithful, and charming friend; who will more than repay every act of kindness towards her; and he who is the author of justice and mercy will not fail to bless you.

'I am, &c'.

Methinks, my dear friend, I have now eased my heart of a load that oppressed it. What can I say more? Mr Faulkland now knows my determined purpose in regard to myself; and if he is not quite insensible, I think Miss Burchell must at last obtain the wish of her soul. Oh, my Cecilia, I would not have my heart devoured by such a flame as her's, for the whole world. But have I not acted as I should do? I hope I have; I feel satisfied with my own conduct, and I never yet found that to be the case when I acted wrong. There are some nice points, in which our own hearts are the best, as well as the most impartial judges. If Mr Faulkland persists in rejecting poor Miss Burchell, I can urge him no farther; but I am determined not to see him.

June 25

How uneasy has been my suspense these three days! I question if Miss Burchell's is much greater. No answer from this strange man; perhaps he is flown off again. – No, I wrong him, a letter is this minute brought up to me from him – Read it, my beloved, and congratulate me.

> 'You were born to conquer, Madam; what is there that you cannot effect? My heart was made for you, and you can mould it as you please. Enjoy your triumph, if it be one. I will receive Miss Burchell as *your* gift, and since I cannot obtain your love, I will at least compel your esteem. Why should *your* generosity, *your* compassion for an unhappy lady, to whom you have no obligation, exceed that of a man who owns himself bound to her in gratitude? I wish I could repay her the debt of love I owe her, but I will try to repair my fault hereafter; and in her gentle bosom perhaps I may recover that peace, to which I have been so long a stranger. She will forgive the waywardness of a heart, which never disguised its anguish to her; and which she knows has been torn by a cruel passion, that, like a cruel disease, was not either to be resisted or subdued. But thanks to you, Madam, I think I begin to feel my cure approaching. Miss Burchell's tenderness will finish what you have begun. You shall never reproach me more; if I *ever* had an interest in your heart, I will not forfeit it now, but make that proud heart acknowledge, spite of itself, that Faulkland was not unworthy of it.'

Ha! my Cecilia, what do you say to my Orlando now? *My* Orlando let me this once call him. Has he not a noble mind? Happy! happy Miss Burchell! you are at length arrived to the summit of your wishes. Long may you enjoy them, and may you make your love as blest as he deserves to be! My mother clasped her hands together in joy, when I read this letter to her. God bless him, God bless him, said she; he is now indeed a righteous man. How rejoiced I am, my dear, that I have been the means of bringing about his so-much-wished-for event. And yet, methinks, if I were in Miss Burchell's place, though my heart doated on the man to death, I could not receive him on such terms. He accepts her as *my* gift; it is to raise himself in my esteem, he does her justice: Nay, I think the assuming man seems to insinuate a sort of superiority over me, by this concession. Why let it be so, I shall be content in my humiliation, if *my* gift will restore him to his peace. If it does, which I pray heaven it may, ought he not to think himself indebted to me?

I think I should not let Miss Burchell see this last letter; he does not consent with a good grace; and it may damp her joy. Though, upon second thoughts, I question whether she has delicacy enough to be much affected by this circumstance.

I am saved the trouble of observing any decorum towards Miss Burchell. She has been just here wild with transport; and was several minutes in the room before I could get her to speak coherently. She had received a letter from Mr Faulkland, written by his own angelic hand, she said. She made no difficulty of leaving it with me, and here it is.

Mr Faulkland's letter to Miss Burchell.

'Is it possible, Madam, that I can still be dear to you, careless and remiss as I have been towards you, since you first honoured me with your affection? If you can forgive this, I am ready to offer you my hand; and hope, by devoting my future days to you, to make you amends for those years, during which (deserving as you are) I have withheld that heart which was your due.

'I never had any merit towards you but my sincerity; and I will not now give up that virtue to arrogate to myself another to which I have no title. I own to you, Madam, that it is to Mrs Arnold's superior prudence, and nice honour, I am beholden for being brought to a just sense of your worth, and my own obligations to you. If you will give me leave to attend you this afternoon, you will receive a man filled with sentiments of gratitude and esteem for you, and who is determined by his future conduct, to deserve a continuance of your love.

'I am, &c.'

I congratulated Miss Burchell (after reading this letter) on her approaching felicity. She had not words to express her acknowlegements to me. The service I had rendered her was indeed to her a most important one; and there are some occasions where *words* are of no use; Miss Burchell can be eloquent without them. She embraced me a thousand times, and wept in tender transport on my neck.

My mother is as much delighted at this happy event, as if it immediately concerned her own welfare. She recommended it to Miss Burchell, to have her little boy with her when Mr Faulkland came to visit her. It seems he has not seen the child since his last return to England: he did not care to go to the house where it was boarded, for fear of drawing any observation on himself to Miss Burchell's prejudice; and the people never permitted the child to be taken abroad by any one but Miss Burchell (who passes for its aunt) or Mr Faulkland's house-keeper; but this good woman, happening to be sick when he came to town, Mr Faulkland had not an opportunity of sending for it.

Miss Burchell greatly approved of the motion, and flew from us to prepare for this so much desired interview.

And now, Cecilia, do you not think Mr Faulkland has proved himself a disinterested (lover shall I say) of your Sidney? Indeed he has given a noble testimony of his esteem and deference for me, as well as he formerly did of his affection. If Miss Burchell does not render herself worthy of him, how shall I hate myself for having brought about this union! But she loves him too ardently, and is herself too lovely, not to get possession of his heart, when it becomes his duty, as well as his interest, to give it up to her. All acquaintaince between her and me, must now cease: for her sake, as well as Mr Faulkland's, this will be necessary; my presence may disturb, but can never contribute to the tranquillity of either of them.

June 26

Miss Burchell was in too much haste to communicate her joy to us, to defer giving an account of what passed between her and Mr Faulkland yesterday evening. She hurried to us last night, at almost ten o'clock.

He came to her house, she said, at six, the hour she had appointed him; and looked *so* enchantingly. She herself was dressed out very elegantly to receive him, and I thought looked really charming; her countenance was so lighted up with joy, that she did not appear the same woman.

She had endeavoured, she said, to compose herself for this interview, and had tried to assume something of dignity; but it all vanished when her conqueror approached, and the tumult of her heart so intirely banished all recollection, and presence of mind, that she was not able to tell me in what manner she received him. She only knows, she says, that having snatched up her little boy, who stood by her and hung on her gown, she put him into his father's arms, and bidding the babe thank him for his goodness, she burst into tears. Mr Faulkland tenderly embraced the child, not without a visible emotion of countenance; and having gently set him down again, he placed himself by Miss Burchell's side: She was still sobbing. Those generous tears, Madam, said he, taking her by the hand, reproach me too much: I have not deserved this tenderness; I cannot look upon you, nor that dear boy, without blushing, but you have forgiven me: it shall be the study of my life to make you both happy. Oh! Madam, continued Miss Burchell, what an exquisite joy must such a declaration give me from the beloved of my soul. I wrung his hand; Oh, Sir, you are too good: What return can I make you? One thing only say to me, that you do not offer me a *very* reluctant hand, and I shall then be the happiest of women.

Mr Faulkland paused a little while, and then, with a noble frankness, replied: 'You know, my dear Miss Burchell, with what an excess of passion I have ever loved Mrs Arnold: Had no such woman existed, *you* would have been my choice, preferably to any other: but when I first knew you, I looked upon myself as bound to her, though, at that time, I had never seen her: my knowledge of her afterwards confirmed me her's. I made no secret of this to you, and you may remember what my declarations to you were, even at the time my hopes were frustrated. I have loved her fervently ever since; even in the arms of a husband I adored her; and I will be candid enough to own to you, that, as my attachment to her has, during all that time, estranged me from you, so should I still, had I the least hopes of succeeding, have persisted in my suit. But she has cut off all hope; she has declared she can never be mine, and at the same time has represented my obligations to you in so strong a light, that I am convinced I ought to be your's. And let me own, Madam (you who are generous, and know what it is to love, will pardon a declaration which I durst not make to any other woman) to you I will confess that Mrs Arnold is arbitress of my fate; and in approving myself to her, I do so to my own conscience. I do not therefore, though my actions have been guided by her, yield with reluctance to her will; her virtue, her religion, and enlarged mind, have only dictated to me, what my own reason tells me I ought to do. I have been a slave to a hopeless passion too long; I am now resolved to struggle with my chains: you, Madam, must assist me in breaking them entirely; and I make no doubt but that time, joined to my own efforts, and aided by your sweetness of disposition, your tenderness, and admirable sense, will enable me to conquer what I must now call a weakness, and make the triumph equally happy for us both. But remember, Madam, I never see Mrs Arnold more. 'Tis for your peace sake as well as my own, that I make this a preliminary to our marriage. I will, when you shall vouchsafe me the honour of your hand, receive it, if you please, from Lady Bidulph; and as I presume it will be agreeable to you to have the ceremony intirely private, that I may, for our dear little boy's sake, present you rather as my acknowleged wife, than as my new made bride, I will, with the utmost speed and secrecy, have such dispositions made, as shall be suitable to my condition, and your own merit.

'I should like, after we are united, if you have no objection to it, to pay a visit for a while to an estate I have in Ireland; which I have never yet seen, and which I intended to have looked at, if this event, this happy event (and he kissed my hand) had not taken place.'

Penetrated as I was, pursued Miss Burchell, with a sense of the generosity and openness of his heart, I could not forbear raising his hand to my lips; he tenderly withdrew it from me, as if abashed at my condescension. He then turned the discourse to less interesting subjects, and after three delightful hours spent with me, took his leave; not without having first fixed on Wednesday, next Wednesday, to be the blessed day that is to make him mine for ever.

Happy, happy may you be, said I! you *must* be happy; but let me see you once again before you are Mrs Faulkland: there are not many hours to come before that name will be yours. My dear Madam! said she, and patted my bosom with her hand, I hope all is well *here*; she looked earnestly in my face, and then added, but you have a noble heart. 'Tis an honest one I hope, said I, a little disconcerted at her manner. Why did she address me thus, my dear? I hope I did not discover any thing in my behaviour as if I repined her good fortune; if I did, far be such a wretched meanness from the heart of thy friend. Was it not my own act to make Miss Burchell the happy woman she now thinks herself? Yet I own there is something in Mr Faulkland's conduct which has raised my esteem to admiration. Oh may his future days be blessed, else shall I indeed be wretched!

My mother told Miss Burchell, it would give her inexpressive satisfaction to bestow her in marriage on Mr Faulkland; and desired she would let her know to-morrow at what time and place the ceremony as to be performed. She answered, at her own house, as she could be no where else so private; and that Mr Faulkland would engage for the purpose a clergyman, a particular friend of his, and fellow-collegian, on whose discretion he could rely.

Miss Burchell's spirits were too much exhilarated to let her think of rest; she staid with us till it was very late, and having taken occasion to mention how grieved she was at the thoughts of losing my society, and of the necessity Mr Faulkland expressed himself under of never seeing me more, my mother took that opportunity of gravely entering into the subject of matrimonial duties. She highly applauded Mr Faulkland's resolution on that head, and told Miss Burchell, it ought exceedingly to enhance his merit towards her. Let this be a memorandum to you, my dear Madam, said she, how sacred the bond is to be held that is now going to unite you: He will not, you see, run the hazard of being tempted, even in thought, to swerve from that faith which he is going to plight to you; your situation is delicate, and it will require the utmost prudence and circumspection on your part, to secure such an interest in his heart as he now seems inclined to give you. It is not on your personal charms that you are to rely, for subduing, or preserving the affections of such a man as he is. They alone, you see, were not able to effect this: it is to Mr Faulkland's honour rather than his love, that you are now obliged for the justice he has done you: never let this be out of your thoughts; be grateful, but let your gratitude have dignity in it; and by your behaviour convince your husband that honour was with you a first motive to wish this union, love will then come in with a better grace as a secondary inducement.

The freedom of my mother's observations, and instructions, I was not surprized at, because she always speaks her mind; but the emphasis with which she delivered herself was unusual. Miss Burchell expressed herself as obliged to her, and joined intirely in her opinion; I could perceive, however, she was not pleased with the lecture.

When Miss Burchell was gone, my mother told me, she thought it necessary to speak as she had done. Miss Burchell, said she, is not *quite* the girl I took her for; so much modesty and reserve, I thought I had never met with in a young creature before; when she used to speak of Mr Faulkland, it was with affection indeed, but with such a nice decorum as convinced me of the innocence and purity of her heart. But of late I have observed she has been less delicate in her expressions of tenderness; such passionate flights have sometimes broke from her, as I did not think becoming in a young woman, and which indeed almost offended me; and this night her joy has been ungoverned. Great reason she has for joy 'tis true; but there are some considerations which ought to have made her chasten that joy into a sober, and, at least seemingly, moderate satisfaction. She loves Mr Faulkland, but let her beware of disgusting a man of his sense by too strong an expression of her fondness.

My mother's observation, and her uncommonly forcible manner of expressing it, struck me prodigiously. It is true I had made the same remarks myself, but as you know she is not extremely penetrating, and in general, but a superficial observer, I was the more surprized at what she said. Miss Burchell's behaviour must have been formerly very different from what it now is, to have made my mother so sensible of the change. *Some considerations*, she said, ought to have made her chasten her joy. Perhaps, she meant no more than that the young lady, even in the midst of that joy, had, upon reflection, cause for humiliation. I hope, she did not think that her gaiety on this desired event affected me, who had so warmly promoted it. My mother is too open not to give the full meaning of her thoughts. This may be only the suggestion of my own fancy, yet it has mortified me. I had but little rest last night, and rose this morning by day-light, to throw together in writing the above particulars.

June 27

Miss Burchell came not to us till late this evening; pleasure danced in her eyes. I whispered to her, We rejoice with you, dear Madam, sincerely rejoice, at your approaching felicity; but our present state will not suffer us to keep pace with you in that gaiety, however justifiable it may be from the cause: restrain yourself a little; my mother will not think you kind, as we are so soon to part with you. She smiled, and thanking me for the hint, immediately composed her features to such a decorum (I will not call it demureness) that it was impossible to discover she was agitated by any extraordinary emotion. I own, I was amazed at the command she so suddenly assumed over her countenance. I was glad, however, she did so, that my mother might not have fresh cause of dislike towards her.

She told us that Mr Faulkland had settled a thousand pounds a year on her, and that too without ever having informed himself of the state of her fortune: for, in the hurry of her thoughts, she had neglected to mention it to him: (Generous man! whispered I to myself.) She then, with great gravity, applied herself to my mother, and told her, she hoped for the honour of her presence, the next morning, at her own house; where the ceremony was to be performed, before no other witnesses but her ladyship, and the gentlewoman, who had been Mr Faulkland's housekeeper; and that the following day they purposed retiring to Mr Faulkland's seat in Hertfordshire, and, after a short stay there, to set out for Ireland.

My mother commended Mr Faulkland's diligence, for having so suddenly disposed every thing for this important event, and told our friend she would not fail to attend her at the appointed time.

Miss Burchell's behaviour was extremely composed; she either really was, or affected to be, extremely sorry at parting with me; she could not stay long with us, she said, as she had many things to settle in the remaining part of that evening. On taking leave of me, I shall not see you again, worthiest of owmen, said she, at least, for many months; but my love, my respect, and my gratitude towards you will be as lasting as my life. You shall hear often from me, and be so good as sometimes to tell me I am not forgotten. She embraced me with tears in her eyes, but I thought she tripped down stairs to her chair, as if her heart was very light.

My mother liked her deportment; she said, she believed the flightiness of her behaviour before, was owing to her being quite intoxicated with the suddenness of her joy, on so unexpected a turn of fortune; but that since she had time for recollection, she had recovered her wonted bashful and sober air, with which she used to be so delighted. My mother says, she will contrive to carry a rich white brocade gown with her, in order to slip it on at Miss Burchell's house; for she would not, on any consideration, appear in mourning on this joyful occasion. You know the reverence she has for omens.

June 28

The important event is over, my Cecilia. Miss Burchell is now Mrs Faulkland. My mother is just returned, and saw the nuptial knot tied. The lady, she said, looked very lovely; and it was easy to observe she gave her hand with all her heart. Mr Faulkland's behaviour was polite and unconstrained; but his attention to his bride was more gallant than tender; and his whole deportment was that of a man who seemed to endeavour at acquitting himself with a good grace of an act of duty, rather than of inclination. The latter part of the observation is mine, not my mother's; but I collected it from certain little particulars, which she related to me in her own way, without drawing any inference from them.

He thanked her in a most respectful manner for the honour she had done him, and for her former friendship to Miss Burchell; but did not once mention my name. So much the better; I hope he will forget me.

My mother is mighty alert on the occasion, and felicitates both herself and me on our having brought about this very important affair. She joined heartily with me in praying that the new-married pair may be happy in each other. She is quite reconciled to Mr Faulkland. What a pity it was, said she – and stopped; then added, But every thing is for the best. I understood her, but made no reply.

They go out of town to-morrow morning; all happiness attend them!

I expect Sir George will be quite outrageous about this marriage. My second refusal of his friend, with the addition of his now being wedded, through my persuasion, to a woman my brother never could endure, will, I fear, exasperate him beyond a possibility of reconciliation. I cannot help it; I have acted agreeably to the dictates of my duty; that must be my consolation: life is in itself a warfare, *my* life has been particularly so.

July 8

My mother is far from being well; her spirits have been a little heightened for these few days past, but her disorder I see gains ground: the swelling in her legs is returning, and her rest at night quite broken. I am hourly habituating myself to think of her dissolution; or, in other words, am preparing myself for the worst evil that can now befal me. I hope I shall find myself equal to the trial.

July 10

Here is a storm for you my dear; a letter from Sir George. I wanted such a thing to rouse me from the almost lethargic dulness that was creeping on me. Mr Faulkland has acquainted him with his marriage. Pray observe his brotherly address.

Mrs ARNOLD, *June 6, 1706.*

'For I disclaim all relation to you. I have just now had a letter from Faulkland, wherein I am at once informed of your having finally rejected him, and of his being married to Miss Burchell. As for the first, your own folly be on your head. You will have time enough for repentance, and I need wish you no other punishment than what *will*, and for me *shall*, be the consequences of your obstinate adherence to your own romantic wild opinions. But what in the name of blind infatuation could provoke you to urge the man, to whom you owed such obligations, to his destruction? *You* I know have done it; he could not be so mad but under *your* influence. You and my mother I suppose fancy you have done a righteous deed; but you have done what I am afraid poor Faulkland will have reason to – I will suppress the shocking word, that my indignation suggested.

'Why was I not made acquainted with this precious design of marrying my friend to that insinuating little viper? I might perhaps have prevented the mischief; for I cannot think if she had not imposed upon you, that you would have pushed your chimerical notions of honour to such extremities.

'Perhaps you meant well; but it has ever been your peculiar misfortune I think to have your good intentions productive of nothing but evil; this last action I fear will be a severe proof of the truth of this observation. I warned you in time against this woman, but my advice has always been despised.

'I will say no more on the hateful subject; what is done is irrevocable: but I believe you will hardly be able to answer it to yourself, if you find that you have condemned one of the noblest fellows in the world to the arms of a prostitute.'

Lord bless me! my Cecilia, was there ever such a barbarian? with what an implacable aversion does he pursue this poor girl! But what does he mean by the odious epithet with which he closes his horrid letter? Sure Miss Burchell merits not that name. Her weakness in regard to Mr Faulkland cannot bring on her so detestable a charge. If George knows any thing more of her character than I do, why did he not tell me so before? It cannot be; his aversion to her makes him cruel and unjust. He says true; I should not indeed forgive myself if I were the means of making Mr Faulkland unhappy; and his observation would be dreadfully verified, that all my good intentions produce nothing but evil, if this marriage should prove to be unfortunate.

July 20

I have had a letter from Mrs Faulkland. She and her husband are arrived safely at his estate on the borders of the north of Ireland, within less than thirty miles of the capital. It is a pleasant part of the country she says, but as Mr Faulkland has no house there, they have taken up their lodgings for the present at the house of his steward. Her letter is filled with declarations of the felicity she enjoys; she says, she would not change her lot to be the greatest Queen on earth. – May she continue to deserve her happy fortune, and to render her husband as satisfied with *his* lot as she is with *hers!* then shall I triumph over Sir George for his vile insinuations.

I have heard from my good lady V—, in answer to the letter I wrote her, giving an account of Mr Faulkland's marriage. As he had not made her acquainted with his return to England, I knew not whether he had informed her of this particular; and I find he had not. As lady V— was a stranger to his former connection with Miss Burchell (with whom I have already told you she was acquainted, and that she entertained a very favourable opinion of her) she expressed no displeasure at the alliance; but said, she supposed he married, in a tifft, upon my refusal of him; for which I gave her such reasons as I had before given Mr Faulkland, excepting those which related to Miss Burchell; which, for both their sakes, must now be no more mentioned. Lady V— says, she *will not condemn the delicacy of my sentiments, though she owns her wish was, that it could have been got over, as she is sure that Mr Faulkland can never be happy with any one but me.*

[Here follows an interval of near two months, in which nothing material occurred.]

September 13

The time approaches, my Cecilia, when thy friend shall be poor and destitute. I know thy generous heart will more than sympathize with me in my calamity, from the aggravating reflexion that it is not in your power to assist me. The account you have given me of your husband's close disposition has too fully convinced me of this. Nor should I have mentioned my apprehensions to you at this time, but that I am bound not to conceal a thought from the friend of my heart.

Sir George has dropt all correspondence with us, I have nothing to expect from him; nor does that mortal live (yourself excepted) to whom I would, on such an occasion, be indebted. I have already sighed too often under the weight of obligations which I could not repay.

My mother is hastening apace to a better world, She sees her end approaching with such a calmness, such a truly pious joy, as almost makes me ashamed of lamenting her loss; for what is it in me, my dear but selfishness? 'Tis true, the loss of a tender parent, a faithful friend, at a time when all other comforts of life are fled, is an evil one would wish wholly to avoid, or at least to postpone for the longest date possible: but when I consider *her* welfare, ought I to indulge myself in such a wish? Her life is already become a burden to her; her infirmities are painful, and without hope of cure; she longs to be released, and to receive that reward of her righteousness, which cannot be obtained on this side of the grave.

If we had a friend, who, in compassion to our wants or weakness, consented to live with us, though under the pressure of years and bodily pain; and that friend were invited to a remote country, with an assurance of recovering health, of having youth renewed, and of possessing all the riches, power, honours, and accumulated pleasures that this world can bestow; should we not blush to own even a wish to detain him from such a station? What but a love of ourselves, superior to that which we bear to our friend, could suggest such a thought? How much more to be desired then is the change, to which my mother looks forward, with an assured hope!

But there is something dismal in the idea of death! 'tis only our prejudices make it so. I have been endeavouring for many days past to familiarise it to my thoughts, and to consider death only as the name of a region through which my mother is to pass, in order to get at that delightful country to which she is invited, and whither *I* shall assuredly follow her. Such is the present frame of my mind; judge then, my sister, if this philosophy will not bear me up against the unexpected blow when it falls upon me.

September 15

'Tis strange, my Cecilia, that this best of parents, who had always so tenderly loved me, expresses now not the least uneasiness at the forlorn condition in which she must soon leave me. Her thoughts are employed on higher objects, and she seems to have weaned herself from all wordly attachments.

I am going from you, my daughter, said she to me just now, and have no other legacy to leave you but a parent's blessing. Your brother possesses all when I die; I wish you had the means of enjoying life with comfort; but you must be contented. See that you bear your lot as becomes you. I perceive your grief for the melancholy condition to which I am now reduced; but added she smiling, I shall soon be released.

Remember how David behaved on the death of that son, whose life he had so earnestly besought of his maker: let that serve you as an example, not to give yourself up to unprofitable sorrow. Bring up your children in the principles that I taught *you*, and God will take care of them; for *I have never seen the righteous forsaken, nor his seed begging their bread.*

She said, she found herself drowsy, and desired me to leave her for a while. I have left her, going I hope to get a little sleep; she breathes with so much difficulty that she cannot bear to lie down, and never gets any rest but by snatches, as she sits in an arm-chair supported by pillows.

How heavy and cast down do I feel my spirits; but I know the worst – *that* is something. –

It is all over: and my mother, blessed woman! opens not her eyes again but to a joyful resurrection. Oh, my dear, there is no terror in death when he seizes us not unprepared! I went into my mother's chamber, in about half an hour after I had quitted it, at her desire: I found her leaning back in her chair, her eyes shut, and a complacent air diffused over her face, which made me hope that her slumber was sweeter, and more profound than usual. I sat down by her to contemplate her benign countenance; and was some minutes before I discovered that she did not breathe. I took her hand, she had no pulse; and I soon found that the happy spirit had escaped from its house of clay. May *I* die the death of the righteous, and my latter end be like hers! No murmurings, no, no my sister, I will be patience itself!

September 25

I have sent the remains of my venerable parent down to Sidney-Castle, there to be interred with her ancestors. I wrote my brother an account of her death on the day it happened, but have as yet received no answer. Unnatural son! but I will not reproach him; some accident might have prevented his writing immediately on the receipt of my letter. He never intirely forsook the duty he owed his mother, but he has of late been quite estranged from us; his wife, vain, weak and imperious, governs him totally. I must now begin to look about me for a place of abode suited to my present circumstances. My whole income would not pay more than half the rent of these lodgings in which I have lived with my dear mother. My poor Patty! I am grieved for *her*. I begged of her to seek another mistress, who might be able to reward her merit, and provide for her as she deserves; but the worthy affectionate girl told me, it would break her heart, if I talked of parting with her. You must have a servant of some sort, Madam, said she, why may not I do as well as another? If I were able to make you a proper return, Patty, said I, you should not leave me; but I cannot afford to pay a servant of your abilities as you deserve; and I must be my own maid for the future. Never, never, Madam, cried the honest creature, bursting into tears, while I have hands to serve you. Let me but attend on you, and the two dear children; I desire nothing. – I want nothing. Your goodness has all along supplied me so, that I am sure I have clothes enough to serve me during my life; and if I could not put up with the same humble way of living that my mistress does, sure I should be a presumptuous wretch! My tears thanked the grateful girl; and taking her by the hand, I told her, that I would not talk of parting for the present, but when any thing worth her acceptance offered, I should then insist on her embracing it.

I am determined to retire to some village at a distance from London, and either to take a little cottage to myself, or board with my children at some farm-house, as I shall find most convenient. Fifty pounds a year will be but a slender support for three persons brought up in affluence. My little ones indeed will not now be sensible of the change, and by the time they are grown up, they will be so inured to their homely board, that they will not, I hope, aspire after what cannot consistently (perhaps,) with virtue, lie within their reach.

October 27

After paying the expences of my mother's funeral, discharging our lodgings, and some other demands, I find my purse will be so extremely reduced, that I shall have but barely enough to keep out want, till my small income becomes due to me. I must therefore, for the present, defer putting my scheme into execution, as I am not qualified to undertake a journey with my little family; especially as I am as yet uncertain what place to fix on for my residence; neither will I afford my brother (though I have no reason to expect any thing from him), a farther pretence for reproaching me, by giving him room to say, I left London without consulting him, or waiting for his return to it. I shall therefore look out a lodging of a small price, where I will conceal myself from every body that knows me, and wait for Sir George's arrival.

October 28

How happy you make me, my ever dear friend, by your approbation of my conduct; since my receiving your last packet, which came into my hand late last night, I am better reconciled to my present lot than I was before I heard from you. I *could not do otherwise*, you say, after my solemn promise given to Miss Burchell, than use my utmost endeavours to promote her marriage with Mr Faulkland. True; I could not: but I wish you had entered more into my sentiments, in regard to those punctilios, which, you tell me, you think *might* have been got over, if that young woman had been out of the question. I could not help smiling at your wish, unchristian as it was; but my dear, if that *were* to happen, do you think Mr Faulkland so void of reason, nay of feeling, as after all that has past to persevere? Or if he did, that I could be so mean as to owe the very bread that I and my children should eat, to his generosity? Would you, my Cecilia, wish to see your friend so humbled? 'Tis not in the power even of the cold, hard hand of poverty itself, to dash me so low as that would do. But where is the need of forming resolutions, or even making declarations about what never *can* happen? I see notwithstanding, that you think my heart has *again* done itself some violence: You know that heart too well for me to attempt to hide from you its secret workings. I own to you honestly I now feel my own unhappiness in its full extent. I look back, and take a survey of the past, and cannot help thinking that I have had the most wayward fate allotted me that ever woman had.

Disappointment in a first love, has, I think been ever accounted a grief scarce surmountable even by time: but this can only be the case, where the heart, extremely vulnerable by nature (like Miss Burchell's) suffers itself to be so entirely immersed in that passion, that all other duties of life are swallowed up in it; and where an indolent turn of mind, a want of rational avocations, and perhaps of a new object, all contribute to indulge and confirm the disease. This you know was not my case. I loved, 'tis true; but it was with temperance; and though my disappointment afflicted me, it did not subdue me. I got the better of it, I think I got the better of it even before I married; but sure I am, I totally conquered all remembrance of it after I became a wife. I then laid down a new scheme of happiness, and was for a time in possession of it; how I was thrown from this is still bitter to remembrance. You well know what I suffered, when I found myself deprived of my husband's love, and suspected of a crime at which my soul shrunk. But it pleased the just God to deliver me from this heavy misfortune, and I think the happiest days of my marriage were those which I passed with Mr Arnold after our reunion. Then it was, I was thoroughly sensible that the heart *can* love a second time, truly and ardently; but I was soon again plunged into affliction by the death of a husband endeared to me more than ever by his misfortunes. My grief for him was proportionate to my love. Yet, my friend, as time is an universal conqueror, it might have healed this wound as well as the former one; and a few, a very few years would perhaps have disposed me to return Mr Faulkland's still unabated passion, if a variety of circumstances had not interposed, that strongly forbad our union. Convinced as I was of this, I acted agreeably to the dictates both of my reason, and my conscience, in persuading Mr Faulkland to make Miss Burchell his wife. I should have been grieved and mortified had he rejected her, and I had determined never to have seen him more. Yet how deceitful is the human heart! this very act which I laboured with so much assiduity to accomplish, and on the accomplishment of which, I had founded, I know not how, a sort of contentment for myself, has been the very means of destroying what little peace of mind I was beginning to taste before. Sure that man was born to torment me in a variety of ways! If I was disappointed in my early love, I had however duty, and a consciousness of what I then thought superior worth, to support me. If on his account I suffered cruel and injurious aspersions, the innocence of my own self-acquitted heart bore me up under it: but he has at length found the way to punish me without leaving me any resource. My pride is of no use, he has raised himself in my esteem superior to every thing. His whole behaviour so generous, so candid; a love so disinterested, so fervent; what noble, what uncommon proofs has he given me of it! and at length what a triumphant sacrifice has he made of that over-ruling passion, to the sober calls of reason and humanity! He has left me, my dear, to gaze after him with grateful admiration! and sometimes perhaps to sigh that our fates rendered it impossible for us to meet. But if I do sometimes sigh, it is not at the advantages of fortune, which I might have enjoyed with him; no, no, surrounded as I am with distress, I do not envy Miss Burchell's affluence or splendor. If *that* motive could have had weight with me, I might have been mean enough not to have acted as I have done. 'Tis the qualities of the man's mind I esteem; I think our souls have something congenial in them, and that we were originally designed for each other. And if I believed the doctrine which teaches us that there are little officious spirits that preside over the actions of men, I should think that our two evil geniuses laid their heads together in conjunction with Miss Burchell's active demon, to thwart and cross all our measures.

I have nothing now left but to pray for the happiness of one whose lot in this life he has suffered *me* to determine; and to beseech Heaven that he may never stand in that fatal predicament which Sir George, with such outrageous barbarity, marked out in his vile letter.

I now return to myself, and to my present state; which I think I may say brings up the rear of my misfortunes. Let the chastisement stop here, and I shall bow me to it with resignation.

October 29

Ah, my Cecilia, what an aggravation is here to the already too deep regret I began to feel on Mr Faulkland's account! His triumph over me is now complete!

In sorting my mother's papers (as I am to leave these lodgings to-morrow) I found that letter which Mr Faulkland wrote to my brother from Bath. You may remember I told you my mother had, in her resentment, flung it to Sir George, and that, as it happened to fall on the ground, he had quitted the room in a passion without taking it up. My mother, I suppose, when she cooled, laid it by, though I dare say she never looked into it afterwards. Read it, and see by what a fatality we have been governed.

Mr Faulkland's letter to Sir George Bidulph.

Bath, May 9, 1703

'How you mortify me, my dear Bidulph, when you tell me of the happiness I lost by staying so long at Bath! *The ladies are impatient to see me*, say you? Ah, Sir George, thou hast spoke better of me than I deserve, I fear.

'I am sadly out of humour with myself at present. I have got into a very foolish sort of a scrape here. My wrist is quite well, and I should have thrown myself at Miss Bidulph's feet before now, but to tell you a secret, my virtue not being proof against temptation, I have been intercepted.

' 'Tis but a slight lapse, however, a flying affair; neither my honour, nor my heart in the question. A little vagrant Cupid has contented himself with picking my pocket, just lightly fluttering through my breast, and away.

'Are you fallen so low as that, Faulkland, say you? to *buy* the favour of the fair? No, George, no; not quite so contemptible as that neither; and yet, faith, I did *buy* it too, for it cost me three hundred pounds; but the lady to whom I am obliged knows nothing of this part of her own history; at least, I hope so, for my credit sake. The case in short is this: an old gouty officer, and his wife (a very notable dame; a fine woman too) happened to lodge in the same house with me. The man came hither to get rid of his aches; the lady of her money, and her virtue, if she has any, for she is eternally at the card tables.

'Under the conduct of this hopeful guide, came a niece of the husband's; an extremely fine girl, innocent too, I believe, and the best dancer I ever saw. I don't know how it happened, but she took a fancy to me, which, upon my word, and I am sure you have no doubts of me, I was far from wishing to improve. You know I always despise the mean triumph of gaining a heart, for which I could not give another in return. I saw with pain her growing inclination for me; but as we lived in the same house, and met every day in the rooms, it was impossible for me to avoid her as much as I wished to do. The aunt I found, had her eyes upon me, and took some pains to promote a liking on my side. I saw her design, and was so much upon my guard, that she, who I soon found was an adept in love-matters, almost despaired of gaining her ends. The young lady's inclination however seemed to increase; a pair of fine blue eyes told me so every day; and I was upon the point of flying to avoid the soft contagion, when an accident happened that totally overthrew all my good resolutions.

'I had not seen the young lady for two or three days; I enquired for her, and her aunt answered, with a mysterious smile, She is ill, poor thing, why don't you look in upon her, and ask her how she does? I replied, if the lady will permit me, I will do myself that honour, and intended literally to have kept my word, by just asking her at her chamber door how she did.

'You are very cruel, said the aunt; would you persuade me that you don't know the girl is in love with you? Oh, your Servant, Madam; if you think me vain, I thank you for the reprimand. Come, come, said she, this is all affectation, we'll drink tea with her this evening. Upon my word, said I, if I am to believe what you say, I think you ought not to desire me. I am not blind to the young lady's merit, but am so unfortunate as not to have it in my power to make such returns as she deserves. I found the occasion required my being serious.

'If you have not love, said she, you may at least have a little complaisance. Was there ever such a barbarian, not to go and see a woman that is dying for him? I promised to bring you, and she expects you. What is the pretty creature afraid of (patting my cheek). I'll stay by it all the while. There was no withstanding this; I promised to wait on her.

'She knocked at my door about six o'clock, and looking in, asked if the coy Narcissus was ready? I went with her, and she led me directly to her niece's chamber. The young lady looked pale and languishing, but very pretty. I was really grieved to see her, and enquired with an unaffected concern after her health. The tea-things were set, and I tried to force something like conversation, but I believe I was rather formal.

'When we had done tea, the aunt looked at her watch, started off her chair, said she had outstaid her appointment with the party she was to meet at cards, and turning to me, I hope, Sir, you will have the *Charity* to stay with my niece; and then hurried out of the room. I begged leave to hand her to her chair, intending to take that opportunity of slipping away, and resolved to quit the house the next morning. But the determined gipsey was prepared for this motion, and insisting that I should not stir, thrust me back from the door, which she shut, and flew down stairs.

'What was to become of me now, George? My situation was dangerous, and really critical. To be short, I forgot my prudence, and found the young lady's heart too, too tender.

'I never felt remorse before. I never had cause. I accuse myself of indiscretion, but I have not the aggravating addition to my fault of oaths and promises to fly in my face. I made none – love, foolish love did all, and led a willing victim to his altar, who asked nothing in return for the sacrifice she offered; and received nothing but unavailing repentance on my side.

'I know not any thing now that would give me so much pleasure as to find that the girl hated me heartily, though I have given her no cause.

A just reparation I cannot make her. Every thing forbids that thought. I do not consider myself as free; but if I were so, I am not a seducer, and therefore do not think myself bound to carry my penitence to such lengths. The damned aunt has been the serpent. And here let me explain to you what I call buying the lady's favour. You must know the aunt one night (the greatest part of which she had spent at hazard) lost two hundred pounds; at least she told me so the next morning, and with tears in her eyes besought me, in the most earnest manner, to lend her that sum. She said, she should be undone if her husbnd were to know it, and that she would pay me in a very few days, as she had as much due to her from different people who had lost to her at play. Though our very short acquaintance could hardly warrant her making such a request, I nevertheless did not hesitate, but gave her the money directly. She meant indeed to pay me, but it was in a different coin, and this I suppose was the price she set on the unhappy girl's honour.

'My reflections on this unlucky affair make me very grave. I have explained my situation to the young lady, and expressed my concern at not having it in my power to be any other than a friend to her. She blames her own weakness, and her aunt's conduct, but does not reproach me. She cannot with justice, yet I wish she would, for then I should reproach myself less.

' 'Tis a foolish business, and I must get off as handsomely as I can. Prithee, Bidulph, say something to encourage me, and put me into more favour with myself. You have often been my confessor, but I never wanted absolution so much as now; nor ever was so well intitled to it, for I am really full of penitence, and look *so* mortified, you would pity me. I am ashamed of having been surprised into a folly; I who *ought* to have been upon my guard, knowing the natural impetuosity of my temper.

'I must not conclude without telling you, that this very morning, the precious aunt, instead of paying me the two hundred pounds she had of me before, very modestly requested I would oblige her with another hundred, to redeem a pair of diamond ear-rings which she had been obliged to part with for the supply of some other necessary demands; and with abundance of smooth speeches, she assured me, in a fortnight she would pay me all together, having notes to that value which would then become due to her. I was such a booby as to give it to her. – Why, fare it well – I never expect to see a shilling of it. She thinks, perhaps, there is value received for it. Vile woman! The affair fortunately for us all, has not taken wind; and for me, the names of both aunt and niece, may ever stand enrolled amongst those of chaste matrons and virgins. The family quits this place soon, as the old gentleman is better.

'I thank you for your care, in relation to my house. I hope to take possession of it in a week or ten days; you are very good in fixing me so near yourself. Adieu.

'I am, &c.

What do you think of this letter, my Cecilia, written in confidence to my brother? Mr Faulkland could not conceive it probable that any body but Sir George should ever see it; he had no reason therefore to gloss over any of the circumstances. *Had* I seen it but in time – Oh what anguish of heart might we all have been spared! Miss Burchell singly as she *ought*, would have borne the punishment of her folly.

My mother had not patience to read this letter through; nice and punctilious as her virtue was, she passed a censure on the crime in gross, without admitting any palliating circumstance. But I blame her not; the excellence of her own morals, made her scrupulous in weighing those of others; she read the letter in a cursory way, and it is plain but half of it; prepossessed as she was before, by knowing the material point.

The account was given with levity at the *first* mention of the young lady. Then she understood he had bought her of her aunt; there is a paragraph which *looks* like it, and to be sure she attended not to the explanation. Fatal oversight! she read not far enough to have this matter cleared up. She took nothing but the bare facts into her account. A young lady dishonoured, her disgrace likely to be public, then her tenderness for the man who had undone her, and that man rejecting her, and on the point of marrying another. These were the only points of view in which my mother beheld the story. Her justice, her humanity, and her religion prompted her to act as she did; and her conduct stands fully acquitted to my judgment, though my heart must upon this full conviction of Mr Faulkland's honour, sigh at recollecting the past.

I know that the memory of my mother's own first disastrous love wrought strongly on her mind. She was warm in her passions, liable to deep impressions, and always adhered strictly to those opinions she first imbibed. Her education had been severe and recluse; and she had drawn all her ideas of mankind from her own father and mine, who, I have been told, were both men of exemplary lives. From all these considerations, I must again say, that I entirely acquit my dear mother, in regard to her whole conduct, however I have suffered by it.

October 30

I am now fixed in a very humble situation. Shall I own it to you, my Cecilia? I was shocked at the change. A room two pairs of stairs high, with a closet, and a small indifferent parlour, compose the whole of my apartment. Hither did my faithful Patty, my two children, and myself, remove this day. It put us not to much trouble, having nothing to take with us but our wearing apparel, which is all the worldly goods of which I am now possessed.

When I wrote to Lady V—, (which was a day or two before my mother's death) I mentioned not that she was then in so dangerous a way. I know the generosity and good nature of that worthy woman; but I have already been too much obliged to her to lay any fresh tax on her friendship, which I am sure she would too readily pay, if she were acquainted with my situation. I shall therefore, as long as I can, defer acquainting her with my mother's death; and when I do, I shall not give her room to suspect that my brother has cast me off, which I have now too much reason to believe he has; otherwise sure, in more than a fortnight, he might have found time to write to me. I neither expect ceremony, nor tenderness from him; but the occasion of my letter demanded some notice.

November 2

Patty has just now been informed, that Lady Sarah Bidulph is arrived in town. She met one of their servants, who told her that my brother is not come with her; it seems, they parted on the road. He is gone to Sidney Castle, which is now his, and Lady Sarah chose to come to London. She has, I find, been in London four days, though she has not yet vouchsafed to send me any notice of her arrival. She could not be at a loss where to find me, as I left my direction at my former lodging, in case of any letter or message, coming from any of my friends; though I desired the people of the house not to inform any indifferent visitants where I was to be found.

Though George has, in his turbulent way, renounced me as his sister, yet sure his wife, whom I never disobliged, ought not to depart so from humanity and common good breeding, as not to enquire after the sister of her husband, who has an occasion of grief so recent, in which she ought to partake. I shall not however take notice of this slight, but am preparing to send Patty to her, with an enquiry after her health, and to know when my brother is expected in town. –

Patty is just returned from her embassy to Lady Sarah; I will give you the conversation she had with her.

Patty sent in her message, with great respect, by a footman, and waited for her answer in the hall; though her pretty figure and genteel mourning-dress had induced the servant to ask her into the house-keeper's room.

Lady Sarah was alone in the parlour, and desired her to be called to the door. So, young woman, said she, your mistress desires to know when Sir George will be in town. I am really surprised, after the letter she received from him, that she can fancy Sir George means to concern himself about her. Do you know her business with him? you are in your mistress's secrets I suppose. I do not know, Madam, answered Patty, what particular business my lady may have; but I believe it would be a comfort to her to see her brother in her present melancholy circumstances. I don't know that there is any thing uncommonly melancholy in her circumstances, replied the lady; her mother's years and infirmities made her death a thing to be looked for; I suppose your mistress is not in *want*. My poor ingenuous Patty said she blushed at the cruel indifference with which Lady Sarah said this. Not in immediate want, Madam, I hope, but your ladyship must needs think she is in a destitute way, with two children, and but fifty pounds a year in the world. What do you mean, woman, cried Lady Sarah? it is impossible but Lady Bidulph must have left money behind her; Sir George, I am sure, has got nothing but what she could not keep from him. Patty answered, Lady Bidulph, Madam, left no money behind her more than what was barely sufficient to defray some necessary expences that occurred immediately after her death. Well, and so your mistress, I suppose, after having behaved so ill as she has done to her brother, expects he should provide handsomely for her, and her children; *Arnold's* children for the rest of their lives. I know not, Madam, returned Patty, what my Lady's expectations are, but I believe she would be very glad to see Sir George before she goes out of town, or at least inform him of her design. What *is* her design, pray, asked Lady Sarah? To retire into the country, Madam, as she has not wherewithal to subsist on in London. She can't do better, I think, said the Lady. Where does she live now? My poor maid, who thought this question tended to the proud woman's calling on, or at least sending to me, made haste to inform her; she lodges, Madam, at a milliner's, at the corner of the Haymarket, the left hand as you turn – Oh dear! pray stop: you need not be so particular, I have no design of paying her a visit in her corner-shop; my only reason for enquiring was, to know whether she had thought proper to keep those expensive lodgings her mother was in, in expectation of Sir George's continuing *her* in them. My Lady has no such view, I believe, Madam. Well, you may tell your *Lady*, that if she will go out of town with her children, I will prevail on Sir George to allow her something. He will not be in town this month, so that she need not wait for his arrival. She might, if she would have been guided by her brother, have been a credit to her friends, instead of what she now is. Patty owns, she was so full of indignation, that she wished at that moment not to have been a servant, that she might have reproached her with her hard-heartedness. Oh, my dear, these are the stings of poverty! It is not the hard bed, nor the homely board, but the oppressive insolence of proud prosperity; 'tis that only which can inflict a wound on the ingenuous mind.

As for that mean woman, I despise her too much to suffer myself to be obliged to her. *She will endeavour to prevail on my brother*. If his own heart cannot prevail on him, I disclaim her influence; I know she means not to use it in my favour; on the contrary, I make no doubt but she will endeavour to irritate Sir George gainst me by misrepresentations. Her pride makes her wish to have an indigent relation out of the way, yet her avarice would not suffer her to enable me to retire; and she will make my continuing here through necessity a pretence for still with-holding any assistance from me. Let it be so; I would rather submit to the most abject drudgery, than owe a wretched dependant existence to such a woman. I am sure my brother, notwithstanding his resentment, if he knew what my situation truly is, would not behave with cruelty; but my mind is not become so sordid, fallen as I am, as to turn petitioner for relief. But no more, my Cecilia, let not my fate interrupt your happiness.

November 4

I have had a letter from Mrs Faulkland, filled with the overflowings of a joyful heart. She says, Mr Faulkland is so delighted with the country he is in, and finds his estate capable of such vast improvement, that he thinks of making a longer residence there than he at first intended: the rather as he has some suspicions that his agent has not acted faithfully by him; and as he is sure the extensive plan that he has now laid down, will be better executed under his own eye. He purposes building a little convenient lodge on a very charming spot in the centre of his estate, where he may reside whilst his works are carrying on; so that Mrs Faulkland promises herself much pleasure, in spending her time partly there and partly in Dublin. She has already made a large circle of acquaintance, and bestows high encomiums on the great politeness and hospitality with which they are received by all the fashionable people in the county.

She knows not of my mother's death; yet in my answer to her letter, I cannot avoid mentioning it. Though I could wish for obvious reasons to conceal it. Mr Faulkland well knows the ruin of our fortune; and though he cannot suppose while I have a brother living that I am driven to such streights, yet I know what his liberal heart may suggest to him on this occasion, which might lay me under fresh difficulties.

I have but just now apprised Lady V— of the decease of my dear mother, but have not insinuated any other grief than the loss of a tender parent, and an agreeable companion. Indeed I have carried my dissimulation so far as not to desire this lady to change her address to me, lest if I gave her my present direction, she might be led to think, necessity had obliged me to change my former lodgings for worse. I shall use the same precaution towards Mrs Faulkland, as I have obtained permission from the gentlewoman whose house I lately left, to have my letters sent thither: when I go into the country a general direction to the post-house may suffice. I shall now look out for some little spot to retire to, where I can support life on the cheapest terms. In two months I shall have my small pittance due to me, which I reserve to carry me out of town, and to settle me in my new scheme of œconomy in the country. If I could persuade my poor Patty to quit me, and see her settled in some eligible situation, I should then have no material concern to attend to, but the bringing up my children in the paths of virtue and humility. Humility, that happy frame of mind, on which so much of our temporal as well as our eternal welfare depends.

November 9

Who shall say, now is the measure of my griefs complete: Providence thou canst inflict no more! Oh my sister, in the midst of other sorrows, I thought not of one that still remained behind; my children, my two little angels! both dangerously ill. The small-pox is their distemper, and of the worst kind. The disease has been hanging over them for some days, and my close attendance on them, prevented me from using my pen. The cruel distemper now appears with the most malignant symptoms. The eldest always slept with me; I have resigned my bed to her for these three last nights, and have watched by her. Patty has done the same by the youngest. A humane and skilful physician attends them, but my reliance rests not on him.

November 12

Three days and nights of sorrowful anxiety have at length produced a little comfort to me. The distemper has now reached one crisis, whence the physician can form a judgment with some degree of certainty, and he bids me hope. Oh if it were not for that healing word, how could the wretched drag on existence from day to day? I do, I will hope, for there is a merciful providence that superintends his works.

November 21

Thank God! thank God! my Cecilia, the dear babes are out of danger. Fifteen melancholy days and nights has their disconsolate mother watched by the poor little sufferers; but I am fully repaid by having them restored to my prayers. They are now able to sit up, and open their pretty eyes which had been closed for so many days; and to add to my satisfaction I think they will not be marked: but they are still so feeble that it will be at least another fortnight before I can think of venturing their little tender frames out of doors.

The physician's care and diligence deserved a greater recompence than I had it in my power to make him; however what I have done has reduced me to a single guinea. But this affects me not I shall make no difficulty of parting with some of my now unnecessary fineries, which neither I nor my children probably will ever again have any pretensions to wear.

November 22

I have felt the wounds of grief, the pangs of disappointment, and the smart of indignation! yet was my heart never more sensibly affected than it was just now by a circumstance proceeding from a cause very different from all these. I had taken out of my drawers a few superfluous ornaments, which I desired Patty to dispose of as if they were her own, to the woman where we lodge; being things in her own way of business. The poor girl looked at me for some time with a grief in her countenance that pierced me to the soul. There is no need, Madam, said she, with her voice almost stifled, there is no need I hope as yet for this. You don't consider, Patty, said I, that the children's weak constitution requires now a more than ordinary attention to their diet; and I have not sufficient to supply them long with such necessaries as they want. I have no occasion for these trifles, and I cannot see my little ones droop for want of such comfortable nourishment as may restore them to their strength. Nor shall they want it Madam, answered Patty; don't be angry with me Madam, if I beg you will let me use my endeavours to supply them. What do you mean, said I, I know the goodness of your disposition, but how have you it in your power? You know Madam, said she, I am pretty expert at my needle; and as our landlady has always abundance of work on her hands, I undertook to assist her, and have for this fortnight past, while I was closely confined to miss's room, finished a piece of curious work, for which she has this day paid me thirty shillings. You amaze me, said I, I never saw you employed otherwise than in your attendance on the child. I was afraid you would be displeased, Madam, she replied, and always hid my work when you came into the room, which I could easily do, as it was only a fine piece of point which I was grounding; and as I sat up night and day, I had an opportunity of sticking most constantly to it, which enabled me to do in a fortnight, what to another hand would be a month's labour. Now, Madam, with your leave, I can go on in this manner, and though perhaps I cannot always earn so much, yet I am sure I can still procure enough to prevent your being drove to the necessity of parting with your apparel, till we are in a condition to leave such an expensive place as London is. And do you think, my dear Patty, said I, with tears of affection and gratitude in my eyes, that I will consent to take the fruits of your ingenious and honest industry from you? No, no, if you can find time by these means to procure a little supply for your own pocket, do so; but I will not suffer you to expend a farthing of what you can earn, on my account. I saw she looked distressed and confounded; excuse me, Madam, said she, but I have made bold to lay out part of the money already; I thought the poor children would want a little wine to nourish them, and indeed, Madam, your spirits want some support after your long fatigue. I have bought a few bottles of wine, Madam, and some other little necessaries; I hope you will not take it ill.

I pressed the affectionate creature's hand; I cannot be angry with you, Patty, for your goodness, but such proofs of it as these distress me more than my wants could. I accept of your kindness for this time, but insist on your not doing such a thing again. If there be occasion for it, I can apply to my needle as well as you, and would sooner do so, than part with any of my things, since it gives you so much uneasiness.

The poor girl was rejoiced at my acceptance of her friendly and tender offer, and produced her little purchase, which was indeed both seasonable and useful.

November 23

I had this day a letter from Lady V—. I send you a copy of it.

> 'I condole with you, my dear Mrs Arnold, on the afflicting loss you sustained in your good mother's death. You mention not any particular consequences from this accident; but I know, that by Lady Bidulph's death, you are deprived of a considerable part of your income, and on this account I have taken the liberty of friendship, to send you a supply, which your family-calls may require, till your affairs are settled upon a better footing.
>
> 'Let me know how you and your brother stand; if he should not be so kind to you as he ought, I insist upon your looking on me as your banker, who know not how to make so good a use of my income, as sharing it with those I love as I do you.
>
> 'I am, &c.'

The supply which Lady V— mentioned, accompanied this letter, and was a bank bill of three hundred pounds.

I own to you, my Cecilia, that my first emotions were only those of joy, surprize, and gratitude, for so unexpected and important a donation; but when those were a little subsided, I began to reflect on the nature, and manner of this noble act of friendship. I know Lady

V— is one of the best women living; she is generous, and compassionate, and has always honoured me with a particular regard; yet I must confess to you, her present now comes to me suspected. I believe I told you, that Lady V— had retired into Lancashire, to live with an only sister she has there: this Lady is a widow, and I have since been informed, was left with a very numerous young family, and an income scarce sufficient to support them genteely; they are now most of them grown up, and all the girls, of which there are five, unprovided for. Since Lady V—'s departaure, I have been told, that it was principally on account of these young girls, of whom she is extremely fond, that she went to reside with her sister, in order to support them more agreeably to their rank; their father having been a general officer, and a man of high birth. Lady V—'s jointure is a thousand pound a year; but as I hear the family make a respectable figure in the country, and I am sure Lady V—'s fondness for her nieces, would induce her to save what she could, in order to leave them something at her death, I cannot reconcile it to her prudence, notwithstanding the liberality of her spirit, and the friendship she has for me, that she should make so considerable a present, at the same time give me as it were an unbounded letter of credit on her. Had she sent me the sixth part of the sum, I should not have doubted its being only the effects of her kindness towards me; and in her present situation, as considerable a proof of it, as she ought in regard to have given to one whom she has already bound under strong obligations. But the largeness of the sum renders it suspicious; and to tell you the secret inspirations of my heart, I fear it comes from a different quarter.

I made Mrs Faulkland acquainted with my mother's death, about the same time that I informed Lady V— of it. To neither did I give the most distant hint of my circumstances, yet Mr Faulkland knows they cannot be happy. He too knows better than any body, how far Sir George's resentment may carry him. Is it not natural then, my dear, to imagine that this man, who is generosity itself, should have taken this method of making Lady V— the channel through which he conveys his liberality? I am sure it must be so. It is three weeks since Lady V— had the notice of my mother's death; Why thought she not sooner of reaching out her supporting hand, if she imagined I stood in need of it? I gave her no cause to believe I did; otherwise I make no question of her ready friendship, as far as her abilities would go: but *she* could not know as well as Mr Faulkland how much my brother was exasperated against me, and therefore could not suppose me to be as destitute as I really am. She desires to know how my brother and I stand. This question is not Her's; Sir George, for his own credit, perhaps has not told Mr Faulkland what his conduct has been towards me, but he wants to be informed. Contriving man! I will disappoint him; nor shall he heap such obligations on me as must sink me under their weight. I will not receive this suspected gift of Lady V—'s; but it is a delicate point, and, whilst I refuse, I must take care not to offend. I will send Lady V— her bill back again, but in such a manner as to shew her, I refuse her gift for no other reason but its being too valuable.

November 24

See, my Cecilia, whether I have succeeded in my endeavours to refuse, with a good grace, my Lady V—'s offered kindness.

This is my answer to her.

To Lady V—.

'You oppress me, my dear and ever honoured Lady V—, by a generosity and friendship that knows no bounds. Why will you force me to appear proud, or ungrateful, by refusing the favours of so true a friend? But, my dear Madam, do not believe me either the one or the other. Had you sent me a trifling token of your love, you would have been convinced of my respect for you, by the thankfulness with which I would have accepted it; but do not seek to humble me so far, my good Lady V—, by heaping favours on me, which I can never have a prospect of returning. With equal respect and gratitude, permit me, Madam, to return your too considerable present. I cannot in honour, receive a liberality, which I am so little intitled to; and the less, as Justice now demands, that your bounteous heart, so diffusive in its generosity, should a little restrain itself.

'I cannot say that my circumstances are as happy as they have been; yet have I, I thank Heaven, accommodated my mind to them. My brother has not been in town since my mother's death; but I am not without hope that he will make my situation easy. On this account, I know my dear Lady V— will the more readily pardon my refusal of her obliging offer, and believe that her goodness is not bestowed on an unthankful heart.

'I am, &c.'

In this letter I re-inclosed her bill, and have sent it off. Did I not well, my Cecilia? If, as I strongly suspect, this present came from Mr Faulkland, I should never endure myself, had I retained it. If it should have really come from Lady V— herself, I must still approve my own conduct. The sum (circumstanced as she now is) was certainly too much for *her* to bestow, or *me* to receive; and in the manner of my refusal, I think I have insinuated this, with as much deference for Lady V—'s judgment as I could shew. She will see my motive, and I think that will be a sort of touch-stone, whereby I shall discover, from her behavour, whether my doubts are well grounded or not. –

Patty has, by her inquiries, heard of a little pleasant retirement in the country, about fifty miles off, where my children and I can be tolerably lodged and boarded for thirty pounds a year, at the house of an honest farmer, a relation of hers; thither I shall repair as soon as my little girls are in a condition to be removed.

[*Continued by Patty.*]

November 26

The dismal task is fallen upon me again, to keep an account of our melancholy days. My dear suffering lady is seized with a fever, and confined to her bed. She orders me, Madam, to write down every thing as it happens. Lord keep us! there is nothing but sorrows in this world: I am sure, at least, my poor lady has had her full share of them. Her close attendance on the children, and the loss of rest for so many nights, has brought this new affliction on her. Oh, Madam, the loss of health is a grievous thing, even when there are riches: what must it be in my lady's circumstances? But she has the patience of Job himself. To be sure, Madam, her trials are enough to put another beside themselves; but I think my lady's courage increases with her troubles. I was obliged, to-day, with an aching heart, to dispose of a fine lace head of my lady's. I heard her say, it cost sixty pounds; but, though it never was wet but once, I got but fifteen for it, and this, perhaps, may all go to the doctor, if my lady's illness continues long. What does it signify? We cannot buy health too dear.

November 30

My lady is better between whiles; the doctor says, her disorder is chiefly on her spirits; and, though it is not dangerous, he is afraid it will be very tedious. Lord! what will become of us if it is?

December 3

My lady has had a letter this day, from Lady V—, which she has ordered me to send you, Madam, a copy of.

To Mrs Arnold.

'You cannot imagine, my dear Mrs Arnold, how uneasy you have made me, by your not accepting of the bill I sent you, because I too well know the occasion you have for it. But, since you *have* refused (and I know the sincerity and strength of your resolutions) I must not take to myself the merit of this friendly and generous offer; too liberal indeed, as you, with great delicacy, hinted, for *me* to make. To let you into the secret at once, and that your gratitude may be directed to the proper place, it was from our noble friend Mr Faulkland that I received that sum, with instructions to send it to you, as from myself, for he well knows you would not have accepted it from him; but, since I see you are determined to reject it, as coming even from me, I think I ought, in justice to him, to place this act of friendship to the right account.

'I had a letter lately from Mr Faulkland, wherein he tells me, that having heard, from your correspondence with Mrs Faulkland, of Lady Bidulph's death, he fears you are by her loss, rendered extremely unhappy in your circumstances. He is not a stranger to the losses you formerly sustained in your fortune, and he says besides, he knows your brother's warm temper so well, that he is apprehensive he will carry an unreasonable resentment he has taken up so far, as to deny you that brotherly kindness and assistance, which you have a right to expect from him. "If this be the case" (he adds) "what must be Mrs Arnold's situation?" He then conjures me to convey to you that trifle (as he called it) under the sanction of my own name, that being the only one from which he had a hope it would not be refused; and he farther said, that if you should be prevailed upon, on account of the friendship which he knew there was between you and me, to accept of my service, he would contrive, from time to time, to furnish you with such little supplies, as might make you easy, 'till

Sir George and you should be on better terms. Now, my dear Mrs Arnold, you have the truth of this whole affair. I own it was with great reluctance I lent my name to impose on you, but, as it was so much for your benefit, I overcame my scruple.

'I could wish your extreme nicety had not forbid you to accept this offer: I have reason to be angry with you on this account; yet my amiable, sagacious friend, perhaps you had your doubts. Be that as it will, remember you said you would not have refused a small token of my love; I wish I could send you one worthy of your acceptance, and the love I bear you; we should then see whose punctilio should get the better. As it is, I send you a very small token, which I insist on your taking, if you have the least occasion; if this should be the case, I know the candour of your heart, and that you will be too ingenuous to grieve me by a refusal.

'I hope Mr Faulkland will not be angry with me for betraying his secret; But what would it now avail to keep it? I would have *you*, as well as myself, know his worth. Oh how I lament – but it is to no purpose – Adieu, my dear good creature! you are tried like fine gold, and your excellence is become the more conspicuous by adversity –.

'I am, &c.'

My Lady's spirits were greatly affected by reading this letter; she wept bitterly, and was so cast down all day, I was afraid it would make her disorder much worse. The good Lady V— inclosed a bill of fifty pounds in it. My Lady said she must not refuse it, but would thank her ladyship whenever she was able to take a pen in her hand. God knows when that will be; for though she struggles with her illness, it still gets the mastery. The two young misses mend but slowly; they do not gather the least strength, and one of them has such a weakness in her eyes that she cannot bear the least light. Indeed, Madam, this is a most melancholy family. I pray to God night and day to keep me in health, more for their sakes than my own; for I think it would quite break my heart if they should want my attendance, and I should not be able to give it to them. –

December 6

I write on, Madam, as I am ordered, though I have but little to say, in the confinement of a dismal sick room, where I never see any body but a doctor and an apothecary: but my lady is unwilling to let this packet go, till she is able herself to tell you (with her own hand) that she is better, for fear my dull account should make you uneasy.

December 7

There is such changes and turns in my lady's disorder, that we do not know what to make of it. One while we think she is a little better, and then again the next hour she seems much worse than before. The doctor would have a consultation, though my lady is quite against it; but these doctors love to bring in one another. My Lady V—'s present came in good time, but if they go on at this rate it will not last long. My lady said to me to-day, Patty one would think that I was of great consequence, and mighty happy, by this bustle to preserve my life; but there is the tie (pointing to the two children); for their sakes I must try to get well.

[After an interview of six weeks written by Mrs Arnold in a hand scarce legible.]

January 20

Restored at length by the mercy of God from the jaws of death! restored to my children, to my dear Cecilia, and just able to tell her with a feeble hand that her Sidney lives –.

January 25

I am now able, my dear, to reassume that task, once the most pleasing of my life, when health, joy, and prosperity gilded all my days. The scene is now changed; and I think I have nothing the same about me, but the feelings and affections of my mind. You cannot imagine, my Cecilia, how I am altered; you would not now say, that you envied my white and red; you would hardly know me, and it is not to be wondered at, preyed on as I have been for near two months by a slow but tormenting fever. It is with difficulty that I hold my pen, but my willing hand obeys my heart when it would pour itself out to thee. I have made a shift to scrawl a few lines to my good Lady V—, to thank her for her kindness. I could not refuse it! it would indeed have been disingenuous, considering the footing on which she put my acceptance of it. I should have been driven to extreme streights, if it had not been for her present, confined as long as I have been to the languishing bed of sickness.

January 26

Patty heard to-day that my brother has been in town some time, but he takes no notice of me. I have not a relation in the world but himself. He could not sure be so cruel, if he knew all. But Lady Sarah keeps it from him; she thinks perhaps I am slunk into some obscure corner, where she leaves me to distress. Sir George is not of a savage nature, yet his humanity is not strong enough to seek out the afflicted. His pride too I know is gratified by having me out of the way of observation, and so long as I do not call upon him, I find he will not enquire after me.

The winter is now so far advanced, and I am in a condition so extremely weak, that I cannot, till the spring advances a little, think of taking my flight to my peaceful retreat in the country. I look eagerly forward to the time of my enlargement; such I may call it, for indeed, my dear, my spirits are quite exhausted with my long confinement in a little close lodging in this irksome town.

January 27

The gentlewoman with whom I lodged in St Alban's-street, told Patty, who went to her house to-day to enquire if there were any letters for me, that there have been, at different times, several people of my former acquaintance to look for me; but I do not find that one enquiry has come from my brother. I had given the gentlewoman instructions not to tell any stranger where I lodged. I believe this caution was needless, there are few who give themselves the trouble to trace out the steps of the unhappy; and I dare say, that those whom common form obliged to pay me a visit of condolence on my mother's death, were none of them much hurt at the disappointment of not finding me. –

January 30

I have been laying down a little sort of plan for my future life. I told you the terms I could live upon with the farmer whom Patty found out for me; but as I cannot expect to be boarded at so cheap a rate when my children are grown bigger, I have been devising the means how to enlarge my scanty income against the time that our wants must necessarily increase; for I am firmly resolved my kind Lady V— shall never augment the debt I already owe her. You know, my dear, I am pretty dexterous at my needle; the woman where I lodge deals in embroidery, which is much in fashion, and I think I have not seen any, though she pays largely to her artificers in this way, equal to some pieces of my own work. Now, my Cecilia, I have resolved to apply myself to this when I get into the country. I shewed the woman a small fire-skreen wrought by me when I was a girl, the same which I remember my poor Mr Arnold accused me of neglecting for my Horace, and which had never been made up; she said the work was so curious, that she would give any price for such a hand. Patty is well skilled in this sort of work too, and as I find she is determined not to quit me, I must, in return, endeavour not to let the poor girl be too great a sufferer for her kindness.

I think we shall between us be able to do a good deal, and my landlady has promised to receive and dispose of our work for a small consideration; as fast as we can send it to her; which we shall have constant opportunities of doing.

You cannot imagine how pleased I am with my scheme. Patty is in raptures at the thoughts of her being permitted to continue with me. I would even now set about my project if my health would allow me; but alas! my Cecilia, I am still so feeble, I am not able to sit up more than an hour or two at a time; and cannot walk a-cross my narrow room without help. Fresh air and a little gentle exercise would I am sure, more than any thing, contribute to restore my strength; but the means to procure these, are not conveniently within my power; so that I must wait that slow, but generally sure remedy, patience.

February 10

I have a wonderful incident to relate to you! you, my Cecilia, I know will join with me in admiring and praising God for his gracious providence!

This morning I was but just risen and got down into my little parlour, when Patty came to tell me, a man desired to speak with me. I immediately ordered him to be admitted. Patty accordingly introduced the person, who had stood in the entry whilst she was speaking to me. He seemed to be a man between forty and fifty years old, mean in his apparel, though clean. I nodded to my maid to leave the room, which when she had done, I civilly demanded of the stranger his business.

I was standing when he entered the room, and continued doing so while I spoke to him, not thinking from his appearance that he was intitled to sit down with me. You know I am not proud, but there is a sort of usage established, which we naturally fall into. The man who had advanced some steps into the room, looked over his shoulder as if for a chair; so I understood the motion, and accordingly sat down myself, and bad him do so too. He did, and with an air as if he considered the civility to be only what was due to him.

I believe, Madam, said he, though you do not remember me, that you cannot be ignorant of your having had a relation of the name of Warner, who went to the West-Indies about five and twenty years ago. I answered, I do remember to have heard of such a person.

You see that unfortunate man before you, he replied; I am your near relation, Madam, your father was my mother's only brother: I have been very unhappy; I lost, in my return to England, what almost five and twenty years industry had scraped together: the sum was but a moderate one, yet sufficient to have supported me decently for the remainder of my life. I asked him, how it happened? I began, said he, to grow sickly abroad, and was told that my native air might restore me. This advice so well agreed with my own inclinations, which were, for a long time past, bent upon returning home, that I took the first opportunity of a ship bound for England; but we were unluckily met by a French privateer, who stripped me of every thing but the clothes on my back, and set me on shore on the coast of Spain, whence I begged my passage to England, having nothing to support me but a few shillings, part of a collection, made for me and my fellow-sufferers, amongst some English gentlemen.

Whilst he spoke I thought I could discover a likeness in his face to my father. He was reckoned extremely to resemble his sister, the mother of this unhappy Mr Warner; she was a fine woman, and I had seen her picture. His story was credible; and I had no reason to doubt the truth of what he said.

And here I will give you a brief account of what occasioned this unfortunate relation to be thus long an alien from his family.

His mother, as you have just now heard, was my father's sister, who threw her person and her fortune away upon a broken officer. This act disobliged my father so much, that from the time of her marriage, to the hour of her death, he never would see her. Her husband died, when this their only child was about nine years old; the poor mother survived him but a short time, and the orphan boy was left to my father's mercy. I have often heard him say he was very unlucky, and never could be persuaded into a love of his book; he was, however, put to school, and my father bestowed the same expence on his education, as if he had been his own son. When he was about sixteen years old, as he wrote a good hand, and had a great capacity for figures, he bound him apprentice to a merchant, in which situation he had been above a year, (and during that time he had made several elopements, and was with difficulty reconciled to his master, through my father's mediation) when he committed such a misdemeanour in his master's family as obliged him to abscond. Accordingly he stole, unknown to any body, on board a ship bound to the West-Indies, of which his master was partly owner, where he hid himself, and nobody could tell what was become of him, 'till my father, about nine months after his departure, received a letter from him, dated from Jamaica, wherein he begged pardon of him, and his master, for his elopement, told him, that he had been taken into a merchant's compting house, and declared, that he meant, by his diligence and good behaviour, to make amends for his past ill conduct. This was the only letter my father or any of his friends ever had from him. He answered it; but had no return; nor could he, from repeated enquiries, made two or three years after, learn any thing of him; so that all his relations concluded him dead.

These particulars I had heard before from my father, and his relations perfectly agreeing with them in every circumstance, I could have no doubt but that he was the man. Sir, said I, I very well remember to have heard your story; your likeness to my father, who was the image of your mother, leaves me no room to question your being the Mr Warner, of whom I have so often heard: you are indeed my near relation, and it grieves my heart to see you in such distress; and the more so, as I have not the ability I could wish to assist you; but we will talk over more particulars after breakfast. I rang the bell, and ordered Patty to get some coffee. While we were at breakfast, I asked my new-found kinsman by what means he had discovered me so soon? (for, by the way, I should have told you that he said he had been arrived but two days in London.) He answered, that one of the English gentlemen, who had been so kind to him at Cadiz, had given him a letter to a gentleman in London, for whom he was to leave it at a coffee-house in Pall-mall; that as he was delivering it, he perceived another letter lying on the bar, directed to Sir George Bidulph. The two names struck him, remembring them to be those of his cousin. His uncle, he supposed, was dead; but he determined to enquire who that gentleman was, and if he found it to be my brother, to apply to him for assistance. He had soon an opportunity of being satisfied; my brother happened to come in his chariot to the door, just as Mr Warner was going out; he knew the arms, and had some recollection even of his features. It was past three o'clock, and I heard Sir George direct his servant home. I concluded he was going to dinner, and that the morning was the properest time to call on him, and having informed myself where he lived, I accordingly went yesterday morning.

He stopped, and sipped his coffee for some time without speaking.

And did you see him, Sir? Yes, Madam, I saw him, and heard him too. He has got a fine house, and seems to have every thing very elegant about him. When I was let into the hall, I desired the footman to acquaint his master that a gentleman, newly arrived from the West-Indies, wanted to speak with him, being commissioned by Mr Warner, a relation of his, to enquire after him. The footman went up stairs, and returning presently, asked me if I brought a letter from the gentleman I mentioned. I said, No, but I had something to say to him.

The servant, after delivering this message, came half way down the first flight of the stairs, and leaning over the banisters, he bid me walk up. I found your brother, and his lady (I suppose) in her dressing-room, at breakfast. There was tea and chocolate on the table. I bowed very respectfully; the lady scarce moved her head; your brother said, Your servant, Sir, and viewed me from head to foot, but fixed his eyes earnestly on my face. The footman who had introduced me had withdrawn. Sir, said I, have you quite forgot me? I remember you well. He answered hesitatingly, and with a change of countenance that boded me no good, I protest, Sir, – I – I know nothing of you. 'Have you forgot your cousin Ned Warner?' He looked at his wife, and she at him; he forced a smile at her, which she returned, without knowing for what. 'I do remember there was such a one related to the family, whom we all supposed to be dead; as for recollecting his person – 'tis really so long ago – that I – can't say I do.' All this while he let me stand, he was lolling in an easy chair, and had a dish of chocolate in his hand, of which he sipped and spoke to me by turns. His wife was feeding a monkey that was perched on her shoulder.

I am indeed more altered than you, Sir George; the hardships which I have undergone, and my long residence in a warmer climate, may readily account for that; but have you no traces of my features? No recollection of my voice? I have carried you many times in my arms. 'Sir, I do not dispute the *identity* of your person, but I should be glad to know your commands with me.' *Commands* I have none, Sir: the poor must entreat, not command.

I then proceeded to tell him my unhappy story in the same words I just now gave it to you. His lady seemed not to mind me, but kept talking to her marmouset. He listened to me, but with so much impatience in his looks, as quite abashed me. I was still standing, but a little to take off the aukwardnes of my posture, I had ventured to rest one arm on the back of a chair.

When I had done speaking, your brother got up in a violent passion, to which he seemed to have been working himself up during the time I took to explain myself. He whisked away the chair on which I was leaning, and walked to the other end of the room; then turning to his lady, Is not this a pretty fellow to force his way in upon us, by a sham story of a message from a relation? and now truly by way of an agreeable surprize he turns out to be that very relation come a begging in his own proper person. Sir, said I, I ask your pardon for the liberty I took to gain admittance to you; but you will be the more inclined to excuse me, if you please to consider that it was out of respect to you that I would not in the mean appearance I now make, acknowledge myself to any of your servants; for the same reason I imagined, that had I not sent a message which I was in hopes would have a little interested you in my favour, I might have been ordered to send up my business by your footman, which would I thought have been quite improper. You might have writ, said he, interrupting me. Ah Sir, (shaking my head) if I *had* – and I stopped short. 'You might not have been much the better for it: is that what you would say? (with a contemptuous half sneer.) In short, Sir, I can do nothing for you; what is it that you expect I *should* do?' I do not mean to be a burden on you, Sir, I replied, I was bred to business, I write a good hand, and understand accompts. I hope to get into some merchant's house; but in the mean time I am starving. I am an utter stranger here, though in my own country. I observed he had slipped his hands into his breeches pocket, and seemed to be feeling for a bit of money. Sir George, said the lady, (who had observed him as well as I) 'tis to no purpose to give any thing to these sort of people; assist one, and They will send another to you, and so there is no end to such claims. Your brother withdrew his hand from his pocket, as if checked by his lady's looks. 'Sir, it is not in my power to assist you.' I then asked him if you were living, and where I could find you? for though you were not born when I left England, I heard afterwards that Sir Robert Bidulph had a daughter. Your brother replied peevishly he knew nothing of you, as you preferred the friendship of strangers to that of your relations. He then rang the bell, and calling his man to dress him, went out of the room without casting a look at me. I ventured to ask his lady your name (if you had changed it) and where you lived. She told me your name, but said she knew not where you lodged, adding I might spare myself the trouble of enquiring you out, for to her knowlege you could do nothing for me.

I took my leave, but enquiring of a footman whom I found in the hall, he directed me to St Alban's Street, where you formerly lodged. I went there, and it was with difficulty that I could prevail on the woman of the house to tell me where you now lived; but my necessities made me urgent, and I waited on you this morning, Madam, to make my distress known to you; but I am afraid the information I had from your sister-in-law concerning you has but too much truth in it. As he spoke this he cast his eyes round my meanly furnished parlour, looked at the poor equipage of my tea table, and again sipped his unfinished and now cold dish of coffee.

Sir, said I, when my sister informed you that I was poor, it is certain she spoke truth; I am not, however, I thank God, *so* poor but that I can spare you a little; if you will take a cheap lodging near me, I will supply you with enough to pay for it; and if you can eat as I and my little family do, you shall be welcome to us every day till something can be done for you. I see but very few people, but I will speak to such as come in my way to try to have you recommended to some one for employment. I then put my hand in my pocket, and taking out five shillings (all the silver I had) I put it into his hand: Sir, you may owe some little trifle where you have slept these two nights, I fear your lodging has been but poor, but if this will not discharge it tell me freely.

He suffered me to drop the shillings into his unclosed hand. He fixed his eyes eagerly on my face, but instead of replying to what I said, he only cried out, Good God! good God! and undoing two or three buttons at his breast, he sobbed as if his bosom was bursting. I was affected with his gratitude, and tried to disperse the tears that mounted to my eyes. I wish I could weep, said he, but I can't; and may these be the last tears that ever you shall have occasion to shed! my worthy, my generous, my pious relation! God forgive me for trying such a heart, but I will reward it, amply will I reward your goodness.

He then drew a red letter-case out of his bosom, and, opening it, he put a bill into my hand for two thousand pounds on the bank of England. Think, my dear, how I started at such a vision! Sir, you amaze me! was all I could say. I beg your pardon for deceiving you, said he, but it was with a good intent. I suppose it is needless to tell you that I am not that poor forlorn wretch that I represented myself to you. Hear the real truth of my circumstances. You see before you (of a private man) one of the richest subjects in these dominions. You have heard that my setting-out was no other than that of a common writing-clerk in a merchant's counting-house at Jamaica; from whence I wrote twice to your father, but never had any answer. I interrupted him to tell him, I had heard my father say he had got one letter from him, and had writ to him in return, and afterwards made many enquiries after him without success. Perhaps he might, said he, but I never received it, nor heard of any enquiries made, which piqued me so, that I resolved never to write again. In a little time I made myself so useful to my master that he grew exceedingly fond of me; and having no heir but an only daughter, who it seems had conceived an inclination for me, though without my suspecting it, but which her father had by some means discovered, he frankly made an offer of her to me in marriage; with an assurance of leaving me all that he was worth at his decease, and an immediate proffer of entering into partnership with him. The only return he required on my part, was to change my name, and assume his, which was Collett. I made no scruple of complying; for though my regard to the young lady had never risen to what is commonly called love, I yet thought her in all respects an unexceptionable match. I married her; my patron punctually fulfilled his promise; and at the end of three years I found myself by his death in possession of a considerable estate. The following year I lost my wife in childbed of her first child, who died with its mother. The changing my name was probably the occasion of my not being found out by those employed to enquire after me; and I perhaps ought now to acknowlege myself careless in not acquainting my friends with my good fortune.

I had such uncommon success in trade that my wealth increased amazingly. In about five years after the decease of my first wife, I married the widow of a merchant, with whom I got an immense fortune. This lady I truly loved. She was an amiable creature. I had one son by her, a fine youth, and we lived happily together for twelve years; at the end of which it pleased God to take from me both wife and child. Poor man! his tears began to flow here. He proceeded. After this loss my own life began to grow.tiresome to me; I had more riches than I knew what to do with, and had nobody to leave them to; my health began to decline; I grew weary of the place, and resolved, partly to divert my melancholy, and partly through affection to my native country, to see England once more. I settled my affairs in the best manner, sent considerable sums of money over before me, and brought a large one with me. During my voyage the whim took me, that I would enquire privately after your family, and present myself to you as I have done, in order to make trial of your dispositions, resolving, according as I found you worthy of it, to share my fortune amongst you, as I knew I had no other relations in the world.

I have been in England above a month. The first thing I did was to go down into Wiltshire, where I was soon informed that your father and mother were dead, and that your brother was married and resided for the most part in London; you, I was told, had been married and was a widow, but I could learn no more about you. On my return to town I soon found where your brother lived, and had the pleasure to hear a good character of him; but I had determined to make my own experiment on him, and I did intend, had he received me ever so kindly, to have made the same experiment on you, before I disclosed my plot to either of you.

I dressed myself in these old clothes on purpose, and what the success of my scheme has been you know. Your brother, narrow hearted, inhuman wretch, I blot forever from my thoughts: it will be the better for you, though I have more than enough for you both.

Your kindness, I tell you again, my valuable relation, I will repay an hundred-fold. Accept of that bill in your hand for your present use. I am sure you want it; and accept of it only as an earnest of my future friendship towards you. That brother, in affluence himself, who could see his sister, *such* a sister want, must have lost all regard to ties of blood, and 'tis no wonder that I, so much further removed in kindred, met with such treatment at his hands.

See, my Cecilia, what an amazing turn of fortune! What could I do but lift up my eyes, as I did my heart, in silent adoration of that God, who is a father to the fatherless, and defendeth the cause of the widow!

It was some time before I could frame my mind to discourse on ordinary subjects. I gratefully accepted my cousin's noble present. He enquired minutely into my situation; there was no need of concealing any thing from him, nor did I attempt it. He was very inquisitive as to my brother's behaviour towards me. I told him the whole of it; he was even bitter in his invectives against him, and Lady Sarah. But, said he, I will have my revenge on them; I will make you triumph over him, and that proud upstart his wife. What lodgings you are in my poor dear creature! Is this your best room? I told him I had nothing but that and a bed-chamber where the children and I lay, and a closet for my maid. He desired to see the children, and I had them both brought it. He kissed them tenderly; poor babes! you have a cursed uncle, but you have a very good mamma, and I will take care of you all.

I will dine with you to-morrow, said he; let us eat a comfortable morsel together, and for your life not a word of what has past to any body. He then took an affectionate leave of me and departed. – Let me here lay down my pen and wonder at my fate!

I have got into a flow of spirits, my dear. What scenes of happiness might now open upon me, if happiness consisted in riches alone? but no, no, it does not. My heart, broken by vexation, cannot recover its tranquillity so soon. Yet is there room for joy, joy springing from a rational, from a humane, from a commendable motive; and I will a little indulge it. I can now in part return the vast obligation I owe Mr Faulkland, as far as at least relates to pecuniary debts. I can now repay many-fold the kindness of my good lady V—. I can provide for my affectionate worthy Patty. I have the delightful prospect of giving my children an education suitable to their birth; and, if my life is prolonged, of seeing them honourably and happily settled in the world. I shall have the glorious power of diffusing benefits! Oh, my dear, 'tis good for me that I have been in trouble, it has so enlarged my charity, that I feel transports which prosperity is a stranger to, at the bare idea of having it in my power to succour the afflicted. Who would not suffer adversity to have the heart so improved?

February 11

My new-found relation dined with me to-day according to promise. Patty had provided two dishes of the best things in season, and dressed them admirably; I need not tell you in what satisfaction Mr Warner and I enjoyed our little chearful meal. He had sent me in the morning a hamper of excellent wine, and seemed to relish his bottle with an extraordinary good goust.

When Patty had carried the children up stairs, and we were left alone, he told me that he had been that morning looking out a house for me; you must quit these lodgings directly, and submit a little to my management; for I *will* mortify your paltry brother and his wife. You shall have as handsome a house as his, and better furnished too, or I'll know why. You must know I mean to set you out like a dutchess, and you shall roll by that worthless puppy's door in a better equipage than his minx is carried in. But I do not intend to live with you as well as I love you; for though I am an old weather-beaten fellow, you are young and handsome, and the world I know is full of scandal. I shall therefore content myself with a lodging some where in your neighbourhood, and come and see you now and then. I thanked him for the prudence of his consideration, but begged he would restrain his generosity, and suffer me to live in that moderate state, which, if I had ever so much riches, would be my choice. Don't oppose me coz, said he; pray don't. I *must* have my way in this, I have set my heart upon it. You shall *blaze* for a while at least; when I have had my revenge, you may live as you please afterwards. I was unwilling to contradict him in his odd humour; yet was very much afraid of the consequences of *blazing*, as he called it, all at once. But dear Sir, said I what will the world think of my emerging thus from obscurity into the splendour you talk of? though you do not live with me, as I am still young, may it not give room for censure? busy people will pry into the source from whence I draw my affluence, and envy will not be backward in putting wrong constructions on an appearance by which it will be so much excited.

He listened, looking at me earnestly in the face; then nodding his head, with a very grave countenance said, You are a sensible woman, coz, and I commend your prudence, but I must have my will for all that. I could not forbear smiling at his manner; and going on, if, said I, I were to enter again into public life with a moderately genteel appearance only, nobody's curiosity would be excited, as it might easily be supposed that my brother had enabled me to support a decent figure in the world. – I soon found that I had made use of a wrong argument, which put my friend into a violent passion. A fiddle-stick for you and your brother too, said he; do you think I will let that whelp have the credit of what *I* mean to do for you? no, no, set your heart at rest about that; what I do, all the world shall know, and my reasons for it too. I'll have my own way; there is no hurt I hope in providing for a near kinswoman, that is left to starve by a still nearer relation. I make you my heir, look you, and I will spread it all over the town. Is there any harm in that? God knows I have no more ill in my heart than one of your children; but I am a little resenting may be, so say no more of it. I found Mr Warner was pretty positive, therefore thought it the wisest way to insist no farther upon the argument; but told him I would submit intirely to his discretion. It will be best for you, said he; consider me as your father, and I will *be* a father to you. He then told me that he had been trying to get a house for me near my brother's, that I might *nose* him as he called it; but that as there were none empty in the square, he had fixed on a very handsome one in an adjoining street. I did not like the furniture, said he, so I ordered it out, and have bespoke new of an upholder, who promises me, in a week or ten days at farthest, to have every thing completely fitted up. In the mean time I can't bear to see you in this sorry room; poor soul! how long have you been here? I told him near four months, and that, with his permission, I would continue in these lodgings till the house was ready, as it was not worth while to change them for so short a time. Well, said he, you may do as you will for that; I'll see that every thing is to your satisfaction. He took his leave with an affectionate shake by the hand.

How miraculous is all this, my dear! this messenger of good tidings, is he not sent to me by providence? as I found he intended not to make a secret of his designs in my favour, I was in haste to divulge the joyful news to my friends. I have accordingly writ to my Lady V—, giving her an account of the wonderful revolution in my affairs; and I intend, as soon as I can fix upon some curious present worth her acceptance, to make her a large return for her favours. I have also acquainted Mrs Faulkland of the happy turn in my fortune, and I design a magnificent present for her as soon as I have time to prepare it. To neither of these ladies have I hinted at my brother's behaviour, either to myself, or Mr Warner. I have made the good woman, with whom I lodge, stare wonderfully at the relation. I could get nothing from her but exclamations of astonishment, her hands and eyes lifted up, 'Good God! Lord bless us! what strange things come about! what luck *some* people are born to! and this was your *own*, *own* cousin that you never set eyes on before? My goodness, what a swarthy gentleman he is! but tumbling in gold, I warrant him. It would be long before such good fortune would happen to me, though I have a cousin beyond seas too.' I could plainly see that this poor woman envied my prosperity, though she tried to congratulate me; but it is the less to be wondered at, as she knew not that I was born to any better prospect, than that of working for my bread in a two pair of stairs room.

February 15

I have not seen my honest kinsman these four days; but he sent me a note to inform me that he was busy in seeing every thing put in order in my new house; and that he abstained from visiting me out of *discretion*, this word he marked, the more to impress his full meaning. He says I shall not see any thing till all is ready, neither has he yet so much as told me the street where I am to live. I find he *will*, as he himself says, have his own way.

February 22

Now, my Cecilia, I may reasonably hope that my afflictions are at an end: as far as wealth can promote felicity, that felicity is mine.

I have just settled with my landlady, and having paid her for her lodgings, made her a present, a little to reconcile her to my prosperity, when a new chariot most superbly gilt stopped at my door; a black and a white footman in rich laced liveries behind it. One of these brought me a note from Mr Warner, who informed, me that he had sent my *own* equipage to carry me home, where I should find him waiting to welcome me to my *own* house.

Patty seemed to have got wings to her feet; she flew up to me with the welcome notice, and begged of me to observe from the window, that the servants were in our own family livery; with this difference, that the lace was silver instead of what we used to give.

On expressing my surprise at this, Patty told me that Mr Warner had, at his second visit, enquired of her, as she let him out, what liveries we used to give, but bid her not mention it to me; which she said she would not do, as she guessed he meant to surprise me. But this was not all, he had been so minutely correct, as to have the Arnold arms in a lozenge elegantly painted on the doors; what these were, he was at the pains of informing himself elsewhere. My Patty almost frantick with joy hurried the two children down stairs, and stuck them up in the chariot, telling them both it was their own as she put them into it; but the poor babes fell a crying, and were not to be pacified by the novelty or finery of the thing till I came to them. She staid behind to send our little baggage after us, and I drove to my new house in Pall-mall; where I found my generous benefactor waiting, as he had promised, to receive me.

Oh my dear he is a princely man! such grandeur, such elegance! he led me thro' every room, where wealth and magnificence were displayed even to profusion. From top to bottom there is not the smallest article wanting that luxury itself can imagine. The carpets, skreens, cabinets, and an abundance of fine china, are beyond comparison more beautiful than any thing of the kind I have ever seen. 'Tis but eleven days since my kinsman mentioned his design to me, and you must believe he has been indefatigable in his diligence, since he has left nothing for me to do, but at once to take possession of this splendid mansion. All the necessary domesticks are hired, and ready in their respective stations; and I am already as much settled in a few hours, as if I had lived here so many years.

Mr Warner told me that as a trifle would not be sufficient to keep up every thing in proportionable state about me, he intended to allow me three thousand pounds a year. This appointment, said he, you are to consider as your own property, and just call upon me as you would on your steward. I am sure you will employ it well, you gave me a proof of that in *your five shillings*. You need not be afraid of being too profuse in your charities; when I die you will find yourself possessed of the means of continuing them.

Dear Sir, said I, long may you live to feel and rejoice in the blessings which *your* bounty will, through me, I hope, draw down on us both. I leave you to enjoy yourself, said he; but I am impatient till your brother knows what he has lost by his hard-heartedness. He cannot long be ignorant of it, Sir, replied I; but indeed I flatter myself that he is not quite so much to blame in regard to me, as we have both imagined. You see he seemed to know nothing of my situation when you enquired after me, and even threw out something like a reproach for my having withdrawn myself without acquainting him where I was; I am very sure lady Sarah never informed him of my having applied to her. – It was his duty to have enquired you out, said he; did he not know you were poor? He knew, said I, that my circumstances were very much streighten'd, but he did not know *how* much. Well, well, answered Mr Warner, it is good in you to excuse him, but *I* know him to be a narrow-hearted poltroon. He took his leave, and said he would see me soon again, having taken lodgings for himself in my neighbourhood.

February 23

I begin to doubt, my Cecilia, whether I am really awake or not! 'Tis all enchantment! I am afraid my old kinsman is a wizard . . . . I have been talking to, and examining my servants, to see if they are real living people, or only phantoms; I look at, and handle the rich furniture of my apartments to try if it be substantial! – 'Tis all so – every thing real – I beg my cousin's pardon for suspecting him of sorcery; I believe he deals in no charms, but that all-powerful one – money.

Now, my sister, what a spacious field is there opened before me! Three thousand pounds a year! how many hearts will it be in my power to make glad! and I will make many glad.

'O Lord God, who hast showered down thy blessings in abundance on my head, vouchsafe me such a portion of thy grace, that I may become an humble instrument of thy mercy, to those whom the rod of adversity has laid in the dust. Teach me so to use this thy bounteous favour, that *Thy* honour, not *my* worldly desires may be promoted; that *Thy* priase, not *my* pride may be exalted. And if, O Lord, thou hast chosen me to be the dispenser of thy fatherly kindness to the afflicted that cry unto thee, quicken in my heart such diligence, humility, and integrity, as may render me not unworthy of the important trust. But if, O my God! thou has sent riches only to be a trial of my strength, unsupported by thee; be merciful, take them from me, and restore to me that poverty, which first taught me to know myself.'

Upon my knees I have poured out this prayer to the Almighty, and it is the fervent wish of my soul that he would grant it.

February 26

You will smile, my dear, as I did, in pity of the meanness of poor Lady Sarah; but proud people are always mean. I have been here but four days, yet I find she has already heard of my metamorphosis. Indeed she could hardly do otherwise, so near her as I am. Mr Warner has been very urgent with me to drive out in my new chariot; this I readily complied with, as both the children and I wanted air and exercise, and yesterday we drove to Hyde-Park. I did not however go at the hour when there is most company, but I conclude I was seen either by Lady Sarah herself, or by some one who told her; for this morning, prodigious! she sent her woman to me with a message. I had her called up stairs, and enquired very civilly after my brother and his lady.

She told me that Lady Sarah sent her humble service to me, and was very much surprised that she had not heard from me in so long a time; that she supposed I was gone out of town, but as Sir George seemed uneasy that I never wrote to him, her ladyship had sent her to enquire for me at my old lodgings in the Hay-Market, from whence she had been directed to me here; and that she was ordered to tell me that her lady had talked to my brother about the affair that I knew of, and that Sir George would act agreeably to her request, if I would call or write a line to him.

I found the woman had been instructed to feign an entire ignorance on her lady's part of the change in my circumstances, but I was resolved to let her see I had detected this paltry artifice. I could observe that the servant, though she endeavoured to avoid it, eyed every thing in my apartment with surprise and curiosity; and I concluded that Lady Sarah had sent her for no other purpose, but to satisfy herself from her maid's account, whether the report she had heard concerning me was true. Tell your lady, said I, she needed not to have been at the pains of framing such a message to have gratified her curiosity; my house is open to any one who has a mind to look at it, even to Lady Sarah herself. You shall see it all over, and may report to her ladyship what my cousin Warner's bounty has done for me; and she may then judge whether I stand in need of the assistance she now pretends to offer me. The woman looked abashed, and though she seemed inclined to ask questions, was ashamed to do so. This was that very servant who had so unceremoniously led me up the back stairs when I went to visit her lady; but I appeared in a quite different light to her now; I rang the bell, and ordered a footman to *shew her the house*. She curtsied in silence, and withdrew.

What a poor creature is Lady Sarah! Mr Warner called upon me before her woman went away. I told him the whole passage. Oh! how he chuckled, and rejoiced, shrugging his shoulders, and rubbing his hands! He wanted to see the servant, but I was afraid he would be too strong in his insults, and turned him from the point.

He told me, he invited himself to dine with me; and accordingly he favoured me with his company, and staid during the greatest part of the evening. He is a man of a strong natural sense, though he is careless of improving it. He has passed his life in business, and in acquiring riches. He does not let me into the particulars of these, though he is in other respects very communicative and entertaining.

There is a whimsical vein runs through his conversation. He now, for the first time, desired me to give him the particulars of my life from my childhood, which he had but a partial account of, at different times, from myself. I took up the story at the earliest period of my life, wherein any thing interesting had occurred, and traced every circumstance minutely to the hour he first saw me.

I could easily see that he had a tender sympathizing heart, for he was moved to tears more than once during my relation; nor was he ashamed of them, for he suffered them to run down his cheek, whilst he listened with mute attention to my story. He praised Mr Faulkland highly, said he was a man after his own heart, and deserved the best woman in the world. I wish you had married him, said he, such a princely fellow deserves a princely fortune. He owned my brother had some reason to be nettled at my refusal of such a man. Our sex, said he, have not such *chimæra* notions as you women have; but still that does not excuse his sordidness.

I took this opportunity of telling Mr Warner that my brother did not really know the very great distress I was in, and that I had reason to believe, from the general tenor of Lady Sarah's character, that she had either concealed it from him, or made misrepresentations of my case; doubtless she had not informed him to what streights I was reduced immediately upon my mother's death; and who knows but Sir George, having left me for a while to feel the effects of that resentment, with which he had threatened me in his last letter, still meant to shew himself a brother; for if he were ignorant, as I am willing to believe, of that particular which I have mentioned, he could not suppose that I was driven to absolute want; and from Lady Sarah's insinuations, perhaps he thought that my mother left a sum of money behind her. He knew not of the illness that my children and I were visited with; and indeed it appears to me, from what he hinted to yourself, that he was quite unacquainted with my situation.

To say the truth, Cecilia, as you know I am of a placable disposition, I should be glad to be on good terms with my brother, the only relation (my kinsman excepted) that I have in the world. I was willing therefore, if possible, a little to reconcile Mr Warner to him; as I durst not, without his permission, seek a reconciliation with Sir George.

There *may* be something in what you say, coz, answered my friend; perhaps he had a mind to let you bite on the bridle for a while, and I am willing to suppose with you, that hereafter, may be, he would have given you some dirty trifle; for a generous thing I am sure he is not capable of, from his sordidness to me. I found this stuck most with the good man. Oh, Sir, said I, but consider Lady Sarah's influence stepped in *there* too. My brother, you acknowlege, *was* going to give you something, 'till she interposed. – Half a crown, I suppose, said he: To say the truth, I believe she is the worst of the two. She has a great deal of pride. Sir, answered I; she has communicated some of it to my brother; probably he was mortified and disconcerted at the sight of so near a relation, in his wife's presence, whose exteriour appearance could do him no credit; perhaps, had you applied privately to him, he would have behaved better. You have not much worldly wisdom, replied my cousin, to excuse him thus; however, I think the better of you for it, whatever I may do of him. But speak honestly now, don't you want to be friends with Sir George, that he and his wife may have an opportunity of seeing you in all your finery? As I knew Mr Warner's temper, I was resolved to humour him in it, and thought I could not give my desire of seeing my brother a better turn than this, to one of my kinsman's disposition. To deal with you openly, Sir, said I, I think our triumph over Lady Sarah will not be complete, unless she herself is a witness of that high fortune, of which she might have been a partaker, had it not been for her own meanness of spirit. And to be sincere with you, my Cecilia, I did think Lady Sarah deserved this mortification, though it did not so far influence me as to make me desirous of being on terms with her: as for my brother, I was governed by no other motive than affection towards him.

Well, said Mr Warner, suppose you were to invite them both to dine with you, and to have me at table, handsomely dressed out (for I can dress fine when I please) and let them see that the man, who was not thought worthy to sit down in their presence, they had better have used with more ceremony. Oh, Sir, said I, that would be too severe an insult; besides, I doubt whether my brother would come; you know he is angry with me, and thinks he has reason. If you will permit me first to call on my brother, when we are reconciled, I can afterwards ask both him and his lady to my house; and though I am sure you have too much good nature and politeness to shock them all at once, by violating the laws of hospitality in this house, which your bounty has made mine, yet will you have sufficient room for retaliation, by treating them, in your turn, with neglect.

Thou art a milkly thing, answered Mr Warner; but as I am willing to please you, you may do as you like; but by – , and he swore a tremendous oath, they shall never have a cross from me.

February 27

Having obtained Mr Warner's consent, I went this day to my brother. He was not at home; but I was introduced to Lady Sarah, for whom I enquired. Poor woman! how she looked! My resentment was disarmed; and I felt nothing but pity. Her confusion was so great, she knew not how to receive me; she curtsied, without knowing what to say, or how to behave. I would not embarrass her too far, but taking a chair by her, As you favoured me with a message yesterday, Lady Sarah, said I, in as obliging a tone as I could speak, I thought it a sisterly duty to wait on you and Sir George: I hope my brother is well, I long to see him, and flatter myself he will forget all former coldness, and again be my brother.

I spoke this long sentence on purpose to give her time to recover herself. She rubbed her hand over her forehead, I believe to hide the glow that was in her face from my first entrance: 'Lord, Mrs Arnold – I am so surprized – this visit was so unexpected – I thought you were in the country' – (her woman you know had been with me the day before, I passed this by however) I have not been out of town at all, Madam, I was detained by illness – 'I am mighty sorry for it – I hope you are quite recovered – pray, why did not you let me know you were ill?' As I had heard nothing from you, Madam, after my first message, I was afraid that the mediation, you were so kind as to promise me, had failed, and that my brother's resentment was so great, he would not hear of me.

'Oh dear, that is true indeed – it was a sad affair – I mentioned you to your brother when he came to town; but he was in *such* a passion, I durst not name you to him again.' (She durst not name me, observe that, my dear; poor George, whom she governs with despotic sway). Then probably, Madam, my brother knew not *all* my distress? I protest I don't know – said she – you know your brother is very warm, and whenever I attempted to speak of you, he always stopped me short – so – I don't know how it was; but I never could get to tell him your situation – I should think I had great reason to resent my brother's cruelty, Madam, said I, if he had known those particulars of which my maid informed *you*, but since he did not, I will not reproach him; neither will I accuse your ladyship of unkindness in concealing them from him. My sufferings are, thank God! at an end, and I am now come to offer you, and Sir George, my sisterly love; I hope he will not refuse me his love in return, I have nothing else now to ask for. She blushed again, and seemed in great confusion; 'You are very good, Mrs Arnold, we must forget and forgive.' – Shall I not be permitted to see my brother, Madam? By the message I received from you, I was in hopes you had prevailed on him – The *poor* woman was now struck dumb. She felt for her snuff-box, and *would* not find it in her pocket; but got up to look for it to gain a little time; rumaged her toilet, and at last, took it out of her pocket; offered me a pinch of snuff, then sat down again. Why, that message, to tell you the truth, said she (forcing a conscious silly smile) your brother knew nothing of; but not having heard from you in so long a time, I was resolved to enquire after you; and was determined myself, out of my own pin-money, to allow you what I could spare, till I could get Sir George in better temper; but I made use of his name because I thought you would more readily accept of any thing from him than from me. Your brother thought you were actually in the country, till we were surprized with the account of the *wonderful* fortune that has come to you lately. 'Then you *had* heard of it, Madam, interrupted I, before you sent to me?' an untoward question, my dear; it plunged her again in the mud, and she flounced and floundered to get out, which only sunk her the deeper. We had heard a strange flying report, said she, of which I did not believe a word, and therefore sent Holmes (that is her woman's name) to you to offer you my service.

I was not ill-natured enough, my Cecilia, to persist in embarrassing this mean woman any farther, though the insincerity of her whole behaviour, and the low falsities she had recourse to, very well deserved reproof. I was glad to find my brother was not so culpable as he had at first appeared; for I could easily discover from the whole tenor of her discourse, she was so far from giving him any intimation of my distress, that she had prevented him from enquiring after me, by telling him that I was gone out of town; probably too with some aggravating circumstances, either of a pretended neglect on my side towards them both, or, perhaps, some other falshood still more injurious. It was very apparent that she had sent her maid only as a spy, and, by way of passport, with a sham offer of kindness, of which she knew I stood not in need: and she depended on my pride and resentment so justly provoked, for my never coming to any explanation either with her or my brother. No wonder then she was so confounded at the sight of me, and the more so as she apprehended I might reproach my brother, who could so well excuse himself by pleading ignorance of my situation: and her conduct must then appear so despicable to her husband, that hardy as she is, she would be at a loss to justify it.

All this being very obvious to me, I determined to make her easy at once. I shall think no more of what is past, Lady Sarah, said I, I only wish to be on terms of friendship with my brother and you; and since he knows not of the message you sent to me, I will not mention it to him, nor any thing else that can recal past unkindness. I hope this visit will be taken as it is meant, out of pure affection, and that you, Madam, will be so kind as to make my peace with my brother; whom I am very sorry I was under a necessity of disobliging; but as I never did offend him, and I am sure never should but in that one instance, wherein *I* was so much more nearly interested than himself, I hope he will think no more of it; but restore me to a share of his love, which is all that is now wanting to my happiness.

This declaration (as I intended it should) entirely restored Lady Sarah's tranquillity. Her countenance brightened up; I'll take upon me to answer for Sir George, said she, that he *shall* restore you to his affection; I shall insist upon a general act of oblivion being passed on his side, and I beg, sister, on your part, that you may not, by reproaching your brother, revive the memory of your past coldness.

The weakest people are often very cunning; this caution of Lady Sarah's, artfully enough introduced, conveyed an obvious meaning to me, very different from her pretended reason; she was afraid of an eclaircissement. I promised her I should meet my brother, whenever he would permit me, as if nothing had ever happened to disturb our friendship.

See, my dear, how this woman, do *durst* not name me when I was poor, took upon her now to *make* her husband, whose anger had so much intimidated her, subscribe intirely to her opinion: but I was now become an object of attention; a finer house, and a finer equipage than her ladyship's, gave me an indisputable title to that regard, to which, as a *sister*, and in distress, I had not the least claim.

She now ventured to ask me some particulars relating to the very extraordinary change in my fortune. I satisfied her minutely, not without mentioning the cause of Mr Warner's having made me the *sole* object of his bounty. Poor Lady Sarah could not conceal her vexation at the thoughts of what she had lost by her ill-timed pride and parcimony. A strange whimsical old mortal, she called him, to come upon them so abruptly, and in such a scandalous garb, that Sir George was quite ashamed of him. I am glad, however, Mrs Arnold, that he has made *you* the better for him; I hope he will continue his fondness; but such odd humourists are not to be depended on. Don't tell him, however, what I say; I should be glad to shew him any civility in my power, for his kindness to you.

I took my leave of her ladyship, with a cordial invitation to come and see me; which she said she would not fail to do.

Mr Warner called on me for a few minutes in the evening to know the result of my visit, as I had told him I intended to make it. I related every thing that had passed between Lady Sarah and me; he enjoyed her confusion as I described it; with a triumphant satisfaction, which nothing but a very strong resentment could have excited in so good-natured a man, as he really seems to be.

He has added to my store of china to-day (of which I have already an abundance) a pair of most magnificent jars, above four feet high, which he values at a hundred and fifty pounds; these, with an entire service of the finest Nankeen china, and a most beautiful Persian carpet, I have set apart as a present for Lady V—, and shall send them to her the first opportunity.

I have also got him to bespeak a set of jewels to the amount of fifteen hundred pounds, with which I intend to present Mrs Faulkland. This sum will not exceed my debt to Mr Faulkland, if his agreement with Pivet stands in force for the term prescribed.

Mr Warner, who mightily loves to be employed, has undertaken to get these jewels made up for me in the most elegant taste.

This man's generosity is as inexhaustible as his riches; I fancy he is still some way concerned in trade, though he does not tell me so. These jars he said he had just received by the arrival of an East-India ship, and I understand that his former dealings were extremely extensive: all over the world, he said, where there was commerce, he put in for his share.

February 29

Lady Sarah has returned my visit; she was not slow you see in her ceremony. *So* obliging, *so* polite; every thing praised, and admired; and *sister* at every second word, and the children caressed, *Arnold's* children. What a fine thing it is, my dear, to be independent! I shewed her all my house; but not with ostentation. I thought it would have looked affected not to have recommended so much wealth and elegance to her notice. My sideboard she says is absolutely the handsomest she ever saw; indeed both for workmanship and richness it does surpass any I have seen.

She told me she had talked to my brother and that though he still resented my obstinacy, as *he* called it, yet as I had made such advances towards a reconciliation, he was very ready to meet me, and desired every thing might be forgotten on my side, as it should be on his. He would have come to see you, added Lady Sarah, but as he does not chuse to meet Mr Warner, he would rather that the first interview between you were at his own house. I told her ladyship I would breakfast with her the next morning, and we parted upon wonderful courteous terms. –

February 30

Just returned from my brother's. Sir George received me with open arms, and I returned the embrace with the utmost cordiality of affection. Surely, my dear, there is something wonderfully powerful in the natural affections; Sir George, spite of his resentment, his turbulence, and the threats denounced against me, could not at sight of me, after an absence of so many months, resist the first impulse of his heart, in giving me strong tokens of brotherly love; though probably had he not seen me, the latent tenderness might have lain for ever dormant in his heart.

I entered immediately on the topic of my extraordinary acquisition, as I was determined not to lead to a subject which might bring on explanations so much dreaded by Lady Sarah; and I could observe that my brother avoided any thing tending that way as much as I did.

He congratulated me heartily on my good fortune, but said, between jest and earnest, that if he could have divined his cousin Warner had come to him to make experiments, he should have taken care to have treated him better. But I don't know how it was, said he, he came in an evil hour; and I was in an ill humour.

Lady Sarah kept up the conversation with a great deal of vivacity; always taking care to keep us clear of the rock she was afraid of, till a lady, with whom she was engaged to go to an auction, called to take her up. Sir George would fain have detained me, but she insisted on my going with her, to have *my* judgment she said on the things she intended to buy. It appeared to me that she did not chuse to leave my brother and me together, for fear mutual confidence (in the fullness of our hearts) might have brought her disingenuous proceedings to light; but cunning people often over-act their parts; she was so extremely pressing, tht my brother could not but take notice of it. I acquiesced to avoid giving her uneasiness; having first engaged my brother to dine with me on Friday. Lady Sarah and he both consented, but premised that Mr Warner was not to be of the party; this I ventured to promise, as I was resolved if Mr Warner invited himself, which is his usual way, to put him off by fairly telling him the truth, and trusting to his good-nature for the consequence.

March 2

After the trivial incidents of these last two days, my Cecilia, now hasten to more interesting particulars. But first a word or two of my cousin Warner. I had not seen him since the day that my brother and I met, till this morning; when he called to ask me how I did, and to know how the puppy George, as he calls him, had behaved to me. After having satisfied himself in this enquiry, in a way the most favourable I could for my brother, I told him that as I had really found both him, and his lady extremely penitent and mortified, I had asked them to dine with me that day. I am glad of it, said he (very quick) I'll be here to snoutch them. Dear Sir, said I, for heaven's sake have a little compassion; you cannot conceive how humbled they are; they dare not look you in the face, and it was one of their conditions with me, before they would consent to come, that they should not see you. Ho, ho, said he, exultingly, have they changed their Note? Well, I will not distress you so far in your own house, as to mortify them with my company at dinner, but if I should take it in my head to drop in, in the afternoon, you must not take it amiss. I only want to see them look a little like fools.

I could not venture to oppose him in this, but resolved to make it as easy as possible by preparing my brother and sister for his visit.

I told him that would do extremely well, and he went away rejoicing at the thoughts of his intended triumph.

Mr Warner had but just left me when I was surprized with a message that Sir George was below. I went down to him directly, and seeing him in his morning-dress, imagined that something had happened which prevented their dining with me, and that he called to excuse himself; but he undeceived me presently. As I had not an opportunity, said he, of asking you any questions the other day, and shall be prevented probably in the same manner this day, I am come to have an hour's chat with you before dinner. And first pray inform me, Sidney, where you have lived ever since my mother's death, and how it comes to pass that in all this time you never took any notice of either Lady Sarah or me? As to your first question, brother, it is easily answered, I have never been out of London: for the rest, lest us avoid all retrospection, which can now answer no end to either of us.

You surprize me, said he, I understood you had been in the country; Lady Sarah told me that you were gone to Lady V—.

She was misinformed, I replied –

What was the meaning, then, said he, that you never called, or sent to her? *She* had no resentment to you, though *I* had.

Dear Sir George, ask me no more questions. I thought it had been premised that we were not to talk of the past.

I see, Sidney, answered he, there is something you have no mind to explain; you know I love and respect my wife, and that I cannot easily be brought to take any thing ill of her; but she was so extremely earnest with me not to ask you any questions, that it made me suspect there was something she had a mind to conceal from me. What confirms me in this opinion is, that as I know you are ingenuous and open to conviction you would have made me some apology for a neglect both of me and Lady Sarah, which, you could not but suppose, offended me, if you had not looked upon yourself as by much the most injured Person.

You urge me very home, brother; I thought I was injured when you disclaimed all relationship to me, if I did not comply in a certain particular, which I was not at liberty to do.

I *was* very angry with you, said he, but should not have carried my resentment any lengths after my mother's death, if you had made any concession, or desired to throw yourself under my protection, instead of a stranger's, for Lady V— comparatively is one. I could not suppose you were in immediate want of my assistance, as I understand my mother's private purse was not inconsiderable, and to tell you the truth, I was resolved till you did condescend to inform me of your situation, not to give myself any pain about you.

I can only tell you in two words, Sir George, that you have been extremely misled in regard to me; I wish not to revive so disagreeable a subject, pray say no more of it.

But one word more, said he, just for my own satisfaction, and then I have done: was Lady Sarah made acquainted with your circumstances? You must have lived in miserable obscurity to be so long in London without my knowlege.

You love and respect your wife, brother; you must not take any thing ill of her.

I am answered he replied: He walked about the room, and I could see he was ashamed and affected.

You will make me very unhappy, Sir George, said I, if you resent any thing on my account to your lady; she did not think perhaps that things were quite so bad with me as they really were; but if she heard (which by the way I knew was an invention of her own) that my mother left any thing behind her, she was deceived, there really was nothing. But let us call another subject. – When did you hear from Mr Faulkland? It is some time since I have had a letter from his lady.

His lady he repeated, and stamping with his foot, cursed be hour which gave her that title!

Dear Sir George, you shock me! how can you be so uncharitable, so unchristian?

If you know her as well as *I* do, said he – and shook his head.

You are so strong in your indignation against her, I replied, that you almost make me suspect that you *do* know more of her than I do; her weakness in regard to Mr Faulkland excepted; I could never entertain an ill thought of her; but you have raised a curiosity, which, though I tremble to have it gratified, yet I must beg you to speak out.

Do not think me malicious, Sidney, said he, a woman's reputation is too sacred a thing to be trifled with; if her weakness, as you call it, had been confined to Mr Faulkland, *hers* should be so with me: but I cannot think with temper on the sacrifice that noble fellow has been forced to make to caprice.

Dear brother, explain yourself, you terrify me.

My heat on this occasion, he answered, would be unjustifiable, if I had not *proof* for what I say; Miss Burchell, for I will not call her by my friend's name, is that monster, a female libertine, a rake in the worst sense of the word.

Monstrous! cried I, your prejudice makes you believe every cruel tale you may have heard. –

Heard, he interrupted with an indignant smile, the d—l's in it if I have not more than hear-say for my knowledge.

Lord! brother, you make me shudder, what do you mean?

He replied, you will not believe me perhaps when I tell you that *I* am as much obliged to Miss Burchell's favour, as Mr Faulkland was.

If Sir George had plunged a dagger in my heart, I could not have felt a sharper pang. He saw me struck with amazement and grief.

I knew it would shock you, said he, but you extorted the secret from me; for a secret it has, and ever should have remained, but in my own justification you compelled me to disclose it.

You know, said he, that from the first I never considered Faulkland's engagement to her, as a serious one, nor in any shape binding: this judgment I formed without knowing any thing of the woman, but from Faulkland's own representation of the fact; tho' to say the truth, he always spoke of her with more tenderness than she deserved, and imputing her frailty to her love of him, was, as most men are apt to do on such occasions, disposed to judge favourably of her. The first time I saw her was at Sidney-castle; that time when my mother invited her, and when, you may remember, I went down there in compliment to my mother. I own I thought her extremely agreeable, which was alone sufficient, to make me a little more than barely polite; but my mother's extraordinary attachment to her, engaged me to go still farther, and to oblige her, I was more than ordinarily attentive to please Miss Burchell. When I assure you upon my honour that I had no farther views, I believe you will not doubt my veracity; but whether Miss Burchell mistook my civilities for fondness, or whether, as I rather believe, her natural disposition was so loose that every man she saw lighted up a flame in her heart, I know not; but certain it was, she made me such advances that I must have been extremely stupid not to have understood her, and absolutely frozen to have repelled her.

My good mother's unsuspecting temper permitted us too many opportunities, and the light ones of your sex do not easily forgive the neglect of those.

In short Miss Burchell yielded to the impetuosity of her wishes, and I followed her lead, more through vacancy, and a want of better employment, than out of inclination. I was very glad when she was recalled home, for I was heartily wearied of her. The day before she left Sidney castle, when we were alone, she said to me, I have too great a reliance on your honour, to suppose you capable of injuring my reputation by ever divulging what has passed between us; I am easy therefore on that head. But there is one circumstance on which you must give me the most solemn promise that is in your power to make, without which I shall be the most unhappy creature in the world. I know there is a friendship between you and Mr Faulkland, and I am not ignorant that you men in your unreserved moments of confidence, do not scruple to disclose such secrets as I have trusted you with; I do not fear your imprudence with regard to any one else; but it is of the utmost importance to me that *He* in particular should never know what my tenderness for you has led me into. You know I have a son by him; he has hitherto provided liberally for the child's maintenance; and to let you into a secret, which nobody besides must know, I myself am indebted to him for the principal part of my support; though he, as well as the rest of the world, believe that I have a fortune. Now though I do not entertain the least hope, nor indeed wish, ever to be Mr Faulkland's wife, yet would it be of terrible consequence to me to forfeit his regard, which you may naturally suppose would be the case if he were to come to the knowlege of what has happened. He has given me to understand by his house-keeper that when he comes to England he will provide for me; the woman hinted something like a design of his making a handsome establishment for any worthy man of whom I should make choice; insinuating at the same time that this depended on my conduct. I have no thoughts of marrying, but as mine and my child's future welfare must be chiefly owing to Mr Faulkland, you see the necessity there is for my preserving his good opinion. For this reason then, my dear Sir George, you must swear to me that you will never betray me to him.

The reasons were so plausible, and the request so natural, that I made no scruple of giving her a solemn oath to preserve the secret inviolable from Mr Faulkland's knowledge; for so she herself worded the promise she urged me to make: in regard to any one else, she said she was satisfied all assurances were needless.

You see, continued my brother that by this declaration she laid me under a double tye of secrecy. As I had no conception that Faulkland could ever be brought to think of marrying her, I thought myself bound not to injure her in his opinion: and therefore religiously kept my promise. Faulkland was not then in England, but when returned, and came to visit me at Sidney-castle, just at the time you parted from your husband, he spoke of Miss Burchell in a manner, which though it convinced me he had a regard for her, and wished to see her happy, yet was it far from alarming me on his account; I therefore should have thought it the highest baseness and cruelty to have hurt her in his esteem.

I never have had the least intercourse, either by letter, or otherwise, with Miss Burchell, since we parted. I make no doubt but she has dispensed her favours wherever her inclination has led her, and you see she has had the good fortune to keep all her amours secret. But what hope can there be that such a profligate will keep her faith to *one* man, though that man is the most amiable in the world.

Oh brother, what a scene of iniquity have you disclosed! I would to Heaven you had kept the horrid secret to yourself, or divulged it time enough to have prevented the misery into which I, unhappy that I am! have precipitated your friend. But I ought not to blame you, you acted agreeably to the dictates of honour. Detestable woman! I cried in the bitterness of my heart. I do not wonder at her cautioning me against letting you into my design of urging Mr Faulkland to marry her; I then little knew the reason you had for the opposition she said you would give to this fatal match: every thing fell out to her wish, and coincided to promote her successful guilt. – Your absence from London, mine, and my mother's urgency, and the too generous yielding of our dear unhappy Faulkland. I burst into tears – my heart was torn with anguish, and in that instant my tenderness for him revived. Sir George strove not to comfort me. He was too much affected himself.

I have but one hope, said I, and that is in the extraordinary love she has for Mr Faulkland, and his uncommon merit, which may probably ensure to him the continuance of it.

You know not what you say, answered my brother; the merit of an angel could not secure the fidelity of such a heart as her's. Her love is gross; a new object will always have charms for her. Had I been as credulous as Faulkland, I should have thought myself the idol of her soul, so lavish was she in her expressions of tenderness.

Is it not strange though, I asked, that with so loose a mind, she should have so long preserved an attachment to Mr Faulkland? for most certainly her affection to *him* has at least been sincere.

Her affection to his estate, answered my brother, has, I believe, all along been sincere: Do you not know she is a beggar?

I told him, in this she had imposed on him, to answer her own ends, in engaging him the more firmly to keep her secret; for to my knowledge, she has seven thousand pounds, as I was informed by Lady V—, who knew her circumstances.

Sir George vented two or three curses on her head. I am not surprized at any instance of her falshood, said he; she is made up of deceit. Such characters as her's are not uncommon; but none of them ever fell in your way before, and I hope never will again. If you will look back on her whole conduct, however it may surprize you, you will find there is nothing inconsistent in it. She is only a sly rake in petticoats, of which there are numbers, that you good women would stare at, if you knew their behaviour. She considers men just as the libertines of our sex do women. She likes for the present; she seduces; her inclinations cool towards an old lover, and are warmed again by a new face. She retained not Faulkland long enough to grow tired of him, and therefore possibly still preserved some tenderness for him; indeed his uncommon attractions must have made an impression even on *her* heart; but this did not hinder her from indulging her inclinations elsewhere. You must throw into the account too that she had by accident got a sort of hold on him, of which, by my mother's indulgence, and some other concurring circumstances, she hoped one day or other to avail herself. With so pretty a person as she has, and the fortune you tell me she is mistress of, do you think she could have failed of marrying creditably, if that had been her view? No, no she meant not to confine herself. Her passion for Faulkland, whether real or pretended, gave a colour to her preserving that liberty, in the licentious use of which she placed her happiness: nor would she in the end have confined herself within the bounds of marriage, if an immense fortune had not sweetened the restraint.

I pray heaven it may, answered I; 'tis all we have now to trust to. You have given me an idea of a character, which I thought was not in the female world.

I own, replied Sir George, I live in perpetual fears of her relapsing into vice. A woman without principle, Sidney, is not to be relied on. Love (if in such a breast it can merit that name) even towards the most deserving object, is never permanent. Fear, and even shame, are subdued by repeated crimes; what hold then remains? Interest alone (where that happens to interfere;) but if detection can be avoided, even that can have do farther influence.

Sir George took his leave of me, in order to go home to dress; but I was not to say a word of his morning visit, so that I found I needed not to be under any apprehensions of reproaching Lady Sarah with her behaviour towards me; for he meant not to let her know he was informed of it. So much the better; I should be extremely sorry to be the occasion of any difference between them.

They came at the appointed hour; I entertained them magnificently; and we were all harmony and good humour. When dinner was over, I told them, they must not be surprized, if we should have a visit from our West Indian relation, in the evening, for that it was very probable he would call, and if I should be denied, he would never forgive me, as he possibly might find it out. Lady Sarah looked frightened, and said she would not stay; but Sir George declared he would arm himself with a few bumpers, and stand his ground.

I affected to treat the interview with pleasantry and reconciled them both to it; for I was really apprehensive that Mr Warner would take it very ill, and think I betrayed him, if I let them escape. I supposed too, that after he had indulged himself in a short triumph, all would be over, and they might afterwards meet on better terms.

In less than half an hour, we heard a loud rap; Lady Sarah turned pale; Sir George laughed at her, but was himself a little disconcerted. The parlour door flew open – a footman entered – Mr Warner – and in stalked my kinsman, with a very stately tread. He was dressed out, I assure you. A large well powdered wig, tied with a rose; a suit of the finest cinamon-coloured cloth, and over it a surtout of the richest mohair and silk, with gold frogs; and a fine clouded cane, with a gold head; silk stockings of the same colour with his coat; a fine lace-cravat, his hat under his arm. He really looked very gentleman-like, and venerable; for he appears older than he is.

He glanced his eyes with a supercilious scorn, over my brother and sister, who stood up at his entrance, and making up directly to me, saluted me, and took his place by me. A short silence ensued, which was broken by my asking Mr Warner to drink a glass of wine. I could almost have smiled at the embarrassment of my brother and Lady Sarah; the old gentleman enjoyed it, and looked at them both, but as if he knew neither. My brother had recourse to the bottle, he drank my health, and civilly enough bowed to Mr Warner, just pronouncing the word Sir! – the other scarce returned it by a slight inclination of his head.

At last, addressing himself to me, cousin, if you have no aversion to tobacco, I should be glad if you would indulge me with a pipe; 'tis my custom after dinner, but I have not smoaked yet.

As I had never observed him to do this, when he had dined with me before, I took it for granted the compliment was meant for Lady Sarah.

I said *I* had no objection, and referred myself by a bow to Lady Sarah.

She made no reply, and my kinsman, without seeming to mind

any one else, rang the bell, saying, if *you* don't dislike it, there is no more to be said. The black, whom he had given me, presenting himself at the door, Mr Warner desired him to step to his lodgings for his pipe and some tobacco. The man quickly returned with a long japaned reed, with a boll fixed at the end of it. Mr Warner called for a lighted taper, and throwing himself back in his chair with one leg crossed over the other, lighted his pipe with much composure, puffing large clouds of smoak-a-cross Lady Sarah's nose, who sat at his right-hand. My sister, who had really an unaffected aversion to tobacco, could not bear this; she coughed excessively, and, with tears in her eyes, rose off her chair, and retired to the other end of the room. My old gentleman laughed till he weezed, nodding his head after her, and looking at me, as much as to say, I am glad I have sent her off.

Sir George, though determined not to be put out of humour, thought this was going too far; I was really uneasy myself, and hardly knew how to act; for if I shewed any mark of distinction to Lady Sarah, I knew it would be construed by Mr Warner as an affront to him. I ventured, however, to tell her that if she would step into the drawing-room, I should order coffee, and wait on her immediately.

Ay, said my brother, approaching his lady, and taking her by the hand, let us get out of this horrid atmosphere that this honest gentleman has raised about us. The honest gentleman vouchsafed not to look at him, and my brother and sister withdrew into the adjoining room.

As soon as they were gone, Mr Warner threw down his pipe, and striking the table with his clenched fist, burst into a loud laugh. Lord, Lord! said he, pride *will* have a fall. I think I have brought them down a little; how like asses they both looked! Well, now I am satisfied – I have had my revenge, you may go and drink your coffee with them, I'll bid you good-by.

He immediately withdrew, and I joined my brother and sister, who were heartily rejoiced that they had got rid of him.

Sir George said, he saw his design, but was resolved not to give an opportunity for insults, and so held his tongue. As he is your friend, Sidney, said he, I would not distress you by engaging you as a party on either side, which must have been the case; for that old fellow would not have suffered you to remain neutral.

I told him our kinsman was whimsical, but that as he was now thoroughly satisfied at having paid them in kind, I was sure he would never again seek to give them any offence, and they ought to forgive him by the law of retaliation.

They laughed at the singularity of his manner, and the whole passed off in mirth: though Lady Sarah declared he had made her quite sick with his nauseous tobacco.

March 3

The ridiculous scene, my Cecilia, for a while called off my thoughts from the melancholy subject which is now nearest my heart, I mean the shocking account which Sir George gave me of Mrs—, can I bear to call her – Faulkland! but it now recurs to me with all its horrors. Oh, my dear, what a fatal wretch have I been to Mr Faulkland! my best purposes, by some unseen power, are perverted from their ends. I wonder the food which I take to nourish me is not converted into poison when I touch it. But I will calm my troubled mind with this reflexion, that I *meant* not to do evil. Mr Faulkland, ignorant of his own misfortune, may (as hundreds of others in the same situation are) still be happy, if that light creature has but a single grain of honour or gratitude. I will not think of it – anticipating as you used to call me, I will banish the hateful idea from my mind.

March 12

What do you think, my Cecilia? Mrs Gerrarde has eloped from her husband, and is now at Paris in quality of mistress to a young nobleman who maintains her in vast splendour. I had this news in a letter from Mrs Faulkland to-day.

Poor Pivet wrote his master an account of it. You know the agreement to pay this young man an annual sum was conditional. Upon Mr Arnold's death, Pivet tired of the termagant spirit, and intolerable coquetry of his wife, was very glad to relax his discipline; and declared, were he to have had a thousand a year, he would not undertake to keep her within bounds; and that nothing but his great respect for Mr Faulkland could have engaged him in the task so long. He acknowleges that he is very glad to be rid of her, and as Mr Faulkland enabled him to set up very handsomely in his business, I really think he is happy in his loss.

March 14

I have been deeply affected, my Cecilia, within these two days. If it had not been in my power to relieve the distress I have been a witness to, how unhappy would it have made me!

I was stepping out of my chariot yesterday morning, when a young woman who stood at my door, in an old linnen gown, presented to me a little band-box, open and filled with artificial flowers; she spoke not, but the silent anguish in her looks drew my attention. She seemed about eighteen, and very pretty. As an appearance of industry I think doubles the claim which the poor have to our compassion, I took out of her box a small sprig of jessamin, very naturally imitated, and asked the young woman if she made those flowers herself.

She modestly replied, she did. And cannot you, child, said I, find any one who would give you constant employment in this way to prevent your wandering about in the streets to dispose of your work?

She answered, Yes, Madam, but I have a poor decrepid father in jail, who cannot be without my assistance. I live with him, and only come out once a week to sell my flowers. I might go to service, but he would die if I were to leave him. Her gentle speech, her youth, and the unaffected tender sorrow that appeared in her face, when she spoke of her father, touched me to the heart.

I bade her come in, and taking her into the parlour, was desirous to ask her some questions.

You look, said I, as if you had not been bred in poverty; pray what is your father?

She blushed, and with down-cast eyes replied, A clergyman, Madam.

A clergyman, I repeated, what misfortunes (for such I must suppose they were) drove him to the distressed situation you mention?

It *was* a misfortune, Madam, and not any crime, answered the girl, with tears in her eyes; my father is as good a man as ever was born.

I asked his name, and she told me it was Price.

My curiosity was excited by her manner. I desired her to sit down, and relate to me the particulars of her story.

She obeyed with a sensible politeness that pleased me.

About twelve years ago, said she, my father had a little cure in Berkshire; he was reckoned a fine preacher and a very great scholar, and what was more than either, one of the best of men. In the parish to which my father belonged, lived a gentleman of a very great estate, his name was Ware; he was himself a very worthy man, and had so high an opinion of my father, that he pitched upon him to go abroad in quality of governor to his only son, then a youth of about nineteen. As my father had travelled in the same capacity once before, he was very well qualified for the employment; and had no objection to the acceptance of it but his leaving my mother, of whom he was very fond, and me his only child, then scarcely more than an infant. The elder Mr Ware assured him he would be a friend and guardian to us both (and so he was) and that he would, in his absence, allow us double the income which my father received from his cure.

This, together with the appointment, which he was to receive as his son's governor was too handsome an offer to be refused, especially as the gentleman promised he should never want a patron in him while he lived; and every body knew he had interest enough to make this promise of consequence. My father was then past fifty, but as he was of a very healthy strong constitution, he did not think it too late to undertake, for the good of his family, what he said was a very troublesome task.

I could not help interrupting the young gentlewoman to ask her how it came to pass that her father, such a man as she represented him to be, was no better provided for at this time of life, especially as she said he had before been intrusted with the care of a pupil, whom I presumed to be a person of fortune, as scarce any others are sent to travel.

She said, he had a small patrimony of his own, and that his original design was to study physic; but being persuaded by the love he bore a young gentleman, to whom he was private tutor at the university, to go abroad with him, he had for some years, while they continued on their travels, been obliged to decline this study. When he had brought his pupil safe back to England, he intended to pursue it, and for this purpose was preparing to go to Leyden; but the gentleman, who really had an affection for him, declared he could not part with him; and that if he would consent to stay and take holy orders, he would get him a living which was in his father's gift (a nobleman then alive,) as soon as it should become vacant, of which there was a good prospect, on account of the age of the incumbent; and that in the mean time he should live with him. As the young gentleman had been married immediately after his return from his travels to a lady of vast fortune, and was settled with a family of his own about him, my father who fondly loved him, did not disrelish the proposal; and without much difficulty consented to it. He now laid aside the thoughts of physic, and turned his attention to the study of divinity; nor was he in haste for the promised living's being vacated, as he was resolved not to take orders till he was properly qualified for the holy profession he was now destined to. He continued thus four years with his young patron; the gentleman who possessed the living, though very sickly still holding it.

My father then being inclined to go into orders, his friend got him nominated to a cure in town, the duties of which he constantly performed for two years, still living with his benefactor: but it was his misfortune then to lose him. He was drowned in crossing a deep water on horse-back which he thought was fordable. My poor father had now lost, as it proved, his only friend; though he then lamented him as a son he loved; and I have heard him say he was more afflicted for his death, than his real father was.

As that nobleman was well acquainted with his son's intentions in regard to his tutor, my father had no doubts of his fulfilling them, especially as he had given his promise to do so. About this time the curate of the parish in Berkshire which I mentioned to you before, having a mind to make an exchange for one in London where all his friends lived, proposed it to my father who had been at college with him. As he had now no attachment in town, and preferred a country life, he readily agreed to the change; and having first waited on the father of his late friend to remind him of his promise, which he again confirmed, he went down to Berkshire. Here it was he fell in love with my mother, who was the daughter of the rector whose cure he served; she liked him, and as her father looked upon him as a man certain of preferment, and every way esteemable in his character, he did not scruple to give her to him.

In a few months after their marriage, the incumbent of the long-promised living died.

My father immediately waited on the nobleman, so sure of success that he thought he should have nothing to do but to thank him for it; but that Lord told him with a pretended concern, tnat he had disposed of it, having heard that my father was well provided for in Berkshire, and had married a lady of great fortune.

He returned home shocked and disappointed, more on account of the family he had married into, than on his own. He now found himself at near forty years of age, with a family coming on him, and no other provision than a curacy of forty pounds a year. My grandfather pretended he had been deceived by him, and made that excuse for withdrawing all his favour from him. My mother had children pretty fast, but they all died young excepting myself; and as he loved her too well to let her feel the inconvenience of streightened circumstnaces, he was content to let his own little patrimony, which he had preserved till now, gradually waste; for my grandfather never gave her any fortune. At his death, which happened a few years after, it appeared he could not, for he left but little behind him. In this situation, my father having lost all hopes of being better provided for, with the melancholy reflexion of having thrown away the best part of his days in a fruitless attendance and expectation, dragged on a life of obscurity and toil for eleven years; and then it was that Mr Ware applied to him in the manner I have mentioned.

I told this amiable girl, I was glad I had interrupted the thread of her story, as by that means she had obliged me with so many interesting particulars of her family, and then requested she would proceed. She bowed with a pretty modest grace, and went on.

I informed you, Madam, that my father, having accepted of the tuition of Mr Ware's son, prepared to attend him on his travels. He took his leave very reluctantly of my poor mother and me, whom he tenderly recommended to Mr Ware's patronage, and set out with the young gentleman, having given up his cure, as his absence was to be of a long continuance.

Mr Ware, who was a truly good man, was punctual in the performance of his promise towards my mother and me, and behaved while my father was away like a second parent. His son continued abroad upwards of four years, and returned a very accomplished gentleman.

Mr Ware was exceedingly pleased with my father's conduct, for which he told him both his son and himself owed him the utmost gratitude. He was now far advanced in years, and grown indolent from infirmities, he thought it better to be himself the rewarder of my father's merit, than take upon him the trouble of soliciting other people to provide for him; and accordingly resolved to give him an annual income of two hundred pounds during his life. He told him, at the same that as his estate was entailed, it was not in his power to confirm this grant by a will; but he was sure his son was too sensible of what he owed him, not to promise in the most solemn manner to continue to him this income, when he should come into his inheritance. The young gentleman, who was present, handsomely acknowleged the obligations he had to my father, and assured him he thought he could never sufficiently repay them.

My father, who now wished for nothing more than to sit down peacably on a competency, thought himself very happy; he retired to his little house in Berkshire, where my mother and I still lived, and gave himself up to domestic contentment.

The old gentleman was punctual to his agreement, constantly paying my father fifty pounds every quarter. He died in something less than three years; his son immediately on his accession to his fortune, being at that time in London, wrote my father a very affectionate letter, assuring him of the continuance of his friendship. Nor did he fail in his promise; for two years he was punctual in his remittances to my father. He did not during that time come down to Berkshire, having another country-seat, of which he was fonder. At this time I lost my dear mother, who had been for some years in a declining way; and though during her health, as she was an exceedingly good œconomist, my father might have laid by some of his income, yet the frequent journies she was prescribed to Bath, and other places, for change of air, together with the expence of physicians at home, put it out of his power to save any thing: which on my account gave him great uneasiness; but as he was still strong and hale, he was in hopes he might yet live to lay by something for me. I was now about fifteen, and the darling of my father's heart. He was inconsolable for my mother's death, but I endeavoured to comfort him, and at last in some measure succeeded. Mr Ware, whom my father had not seen since the death of the good old gentleman, came down now to revisit his paternal seat. He would not omit paying a visit of condolement to his old friend and tutor, and accordingly came to our house the day after his arrival in the country. Though I had seen him before, as it was in my childhood, I had taken but little notice of him; he is indeed a handsome genteel young man.

The innocent girl blushed as she spoke these words, but I seemed not to observe it.

She proceeded with a sigh. My father who loved him, was rejoiced to see him; Mr Ware behaved with a tenderness and respect almost filial towards him, and very obliging to me. He continued about a week in the country, calling to ask my father how he did every day. When he was about to return to London, he pressed my father to pass a few weeks with him in town: you are melancholy here, said he, changing the scene a little, will divert both your daughter and you.

My father thanked him for the honour he did him, but modestly declined it.

Mr Ware guessed at his motive, and told him, smiling, I know your objection, but to obviate it at once, I must tell you that I have prevailed on my sister to come and keep house for me, and I expect to find her at home on my return. I knew his sister, a maiden lady some years older than himself, who had on the death of his father gone to live with a near relation of theirs. My father smiling in his turn, told him he had guessed his mind rightly, and since that was the case, he would not deprive his poor girl (looking at me) of the happiness of the good lady's company for a while.

Mr Ware said, we might go to town with him in his coach, and as we had but little preparation to make, we set out with him next day.

When we arrived at his house in London, he welcomed us with all the marks of politeness and respect. I was surprized we did not see his sister the whole night, but as she was not apprized of our coming, I thought that either she was abroad, or had not yet quitted her friend with whom she lived.

The next morning at breakfast Mr Ware made an apology for his sister's absence. He said, that the lady, at whose house she lived, was ill, and that she could not possibly leave her till she was better, which he supposed would be in a few days, as her sickness was no other than the consequence of her lying-in; mean while he hoped Mr Price would not be uneasy, as he was himself his daughter's guardian.

Though my father was not pleased at this excuse, he however concealed his thoughts from Mr Ware; but told me if Miss Ware did not come home in a few days, he purposed that we should take our leave and return into the country.

We had very handsome apartments assigned us; and my father was put in possession of Mr Ware's library; a very noble one, where that gentleman knew he would pass his most agreeable hours.

For my part as I did not care to go abroad, 'till I had a proper person for me to appear with, I declined the offer Mr Ware very obligingly made of getting some ladies of his acquaintance to take me to public places. I expected his sister every day, and if she came, as I knew my father purposed staying for a month, I thought I should have time enough to see every thing; so I chose to entertain myself with working, and reading in my own room.

But, Madam, I soon found that Mr Ware was a very base man. The third day after we came to his house, his behaviour towards me began to change intirely from what it was before; he took every opportunity of being particular to me in his compliments. I received them at first with that distant civility which I thought would neither encourage nor offend; I looked upon him as a worthy young man, and my father's friend and benefactor; and thought in my humble station I should not be too quick at taking exceptions, as there had nothing as yet appeared in his behaviour which exceeded the bounds of respect: but he did not preserve this long; on the fifth day he came into a closet where I was reading, and there in the warmest manner declared himself my lover. I would fain have turned his discourse into pleasantry, but he had recourse to oaths and protestations, and swore he could not live without my favour. I represented the cruelty of the insult he offered me in his own house, and begged he would leave me, as I was determined to depart immediately. I will not, Sir, said I, let my father know the unkind return you have made for all his care of you, but I can easily prevail with him to leave your house. He fell at my feet, begged my pardon, and talked all that sort of stuff which I have read in romances. At length I got him out of the closet, and locked the door; resolving never to sit alone, without using the same precaution while we staid in his house, which I hoped would not be above a day or two longer; for I concluded there was no sister to come, and that this was only made use of as a snare to draw us to town.

As I had a mind to try the young girl, I asked her, How came you to receive Mr Ware's addresses in the manner you mentioned? how did you know but he intended to marry you?

Ah no, Madam, said she, I could not entertain such a thought; I have not troubled you with the particulars of what he said to me, but young as I was, I knew too well what it tended to; besides the fear he shewed lest my father should know of his pretended courtship, was enough to convince me what his designs were, without any thing else to guide me.

Did you like him, I asked? The ingenuous young woman blushed.

I *could* have liked him, Madam, she replied, better than any body I had ever seen, if there had not been such a distance between us. I desired her to proceed.

I told my father that same evening, that as I saw there was no likelihood of the lady's coming to her brother; and as I led but a melancholy life, having no woman to converse with, I had much rather be at home amongst my neighbours and acquaintance, and begged he would return to Berkshire.

My father said, it was what he had determined on after completing our week in town, unless Miss Ware came in the interim; I have just told our friend so, said he; he seems to take it unkindly, and says he is afraid he has disobliged me; but I assured him my only reason was, that I did not think the house of a handsome young batchelor, a proper place for a pretty little country girl, even though her old father was with her. He assures me his sister will come, and wants to protract our stay a few days longer; I hardly know how to refuse his entreaties, but I shall be uneasy till we are at home.

I told my father, Mr Ware had too much sense to take his refusal amiss, and begged of him to stick to his day.

I gave Mr Ware no opportunity of speaking to me the remainder of that day, nor all the next; though he came to my closet door where I always sat, and entreated for admission; but I was peremptory in my denial, and he went away reproaching me with cruelty.

Mr Ware made an apology to my father, on account of his being obliged to spend the evening abroad, the first time that he had been absent from us since we came to his house. He had twice entertained us with a very agreeable concert, at which there was a great deal of company, both gentlemen and ladies. He had got it performed at his own house, on purpose to amuse my father, who was a great lover of music; but excepting those two mornings, I had never seen any company with him, as he said he would not invite strangers, 'till I had got a companion of my own sex to keep me in countenance. My father and I supped alone; we were to go out of town the next day, and we retired to our respective chambers about eleven o'clock, in order to go to bed.

The poor girl paused at this part of her story, as if she were ashamed to proceed.

I hope, said I, Mr Ware did not violate the laws of hospitality, by intruding on you that night. Oh, Madam, he did, he did, said she; the vile wretch hid himself somewhere, I know not where, for it was not in my closet. The house-keeper slept in my room, in a little tent-bed, which had been put up for that purpose; but she was not as yet come up stairs. The chamber-maid, who had attended me to my room, told me there was to be a great deal of company to dine with her master the next day, and as the house-keeper was very busy in making jellies and pastry, she was afraid she should sit up late, and hoped I should not be disturbed at her coming into the room. I always dismissed the maid immediately, as I was not used to have a person undress me. I went to bed, but not being a very sound sleeper, and knowing a particularity I had, which was, that if once rouzed, I could not compose myself to rest again, I resolved not to attempt it at all 'till the house-keeper came to bed. I placed the candle on a stand near me, and took up a book that I found on a chair, by my bed-side, which I had been reading in the evening. I had been about an hour thus employed, when I heard somebody treading softly in the room: as I had not heard the door open, I called out, in a fright, to know who was there. I received no answer; but immediately Mr Ware presented himself, on his knees, at my bed-side, and half leaning on my bed. I shrieked out; I knew not what he said, but I remember the most wicked of men held me fast, and talked a great deal; I continued shrieking incessantly, and struggling to get loose from him, which at last I did, by giving a violent spring, which threw me out of bed on the floor.

I had hurt myself sadly by the fall; but dragging the quilt off the bed after me, I wrapped it about me and shrieked louder than before. The vile man tried to pacify me, and said I should disturb my father.

Providentially for me, my dear father had not gone to bed, for his room was a great way from mine, but was reading in the study, which was over my bed-chamber. He had heard my shrieks from the first, but, little dreaming it was his poor daughter's voice, he imagined the noise was in the street, and had lifted up the sash, and looked out to try whence it proceeded. Finding every thing quiet without doors, he ran down stairs, and was led, by my cries, into my room, for my vile persecutor had not locked the door, very well knowing none of his own people could dare to molest him, and he did not think my cries would have reached my father's ears, as indeed they would not, if he had gone to bed. Think, Madam, what my poor father must feel, when he saw me on the floor (for I was not able to rise) such a spectacle of horror; my cap was off, and my nose bleeding with the fall.

The wretch was endeavouring to lift me up, and I trying to resist him. Good God defend me! said my father, what is this I see? Oh, Sir, said I, clinging round him, carry me out of the house! carry me out directly from this monster! my father looked aghast. You do not mean Mr Ware, my child, said he, it cannot be *He* who has put you in this condition? Mr Ware quitted the room the minute he saw my father, which was not till I catched hold of him: for he had his back to the door, and, I suppose, was in too much agitation to hear him coming in.

My poor father, speechless with astonishment, took me into his arms, and put me sitting on the bed; then stepping into my closet, brought out a bottle of water, some of which he made me drink, and afterwards washed the blood from my face, which he soon found only proceeded from my having hurt my nose a little.

When I had recovered breath enough, I told him all that had passed. His despair, Madam, is not to be described; he tore his hair, and was like a madman. Where is the ungrateful villain, said he? I will go this minute and upbraid him with his treachery; he ran to the chamber-door, but it was locked on the outside. My father thus prevented from going out, had time to cool a little: he considered it would to be no purpose to reproach a powerful tyrant with the injuries he did us; he resolved to quit the inhospitable house as soon as any one in the family was up to open the door to him, and without ever seeing his face again, commit himself to providence for his future subsistence.

It would have been happy for us if he could have executed this design; but the profligate man prevented us. We spent the remainder of the night in lamenting our misery. At day-light Mr Ware entered the room in his night-gown, for I suppose he had gone to rest after he left us.

He told my father he was sorry for what had passed, and imputed it to his having drunk too much. I own, said he, I love your daughter to distraction, and could not bear the thoughts of losing her, as I found you resolved to go out of town so suddenly. My father answered, I will not reproach you as I ought, but my tender care of your youth did not deserve this return: suffer us to depart out of your house, and you shall never more be troubled with us.

Mr Ware entreated to speak with my father by himself, and with much difficulty prevailed on him to go into his study with him. They staid together near half an hour, and I heard them talking high; my father then entered my room with tears streaming from his eyes. He threw himself into a chair in an agony of grief. The villain, said he, has finished his work – he has stabbed your father's heart – I ran to him almost frantic; I thought he had made an attempt upon his life. When I found he was not hurt, I asked him the meaning of his words.

He would have me *sell* you to him, said he; he would have bribed the father to prostitute his child. Oh, Sir, said I, why, do we stay under this detested roof? There is no safety for us here, said he, come, my dear, let us get out of the house, and then we will consider which way we are to turn ourselves.

My father laid hold of my hand, and I followed him, just as I was in my morning gown. We thought if we could once find ourselves in the street, we should be happy, though neither of us knew where to go, having no acquaintance in London. I had never been there before, and my father had been so long absent, that he was forgotten by every body.

We got out of my room into a little sort of anti-chamber, but found the door of that fast locked.

We now gave ourselves up for lost; our despair is not to be expressed: we sat down, and consulted what was best to be done. I saw now that there was nothing that our base persecutor would not attempt, and I told my father I was resolved at all events to make my escape.

He said that the shocking wretch had given him till the next day to consider of his proposal; and he hoped, by that time, both father and daughter would come enough to their senses, to think he had made them a very advantageous offer.

I told him in that lucky interval I hoped to be able to affect my deliverance; which I thought I might accomplish, with his assistance, by tying the sheets of my bed together, and so from the window, sliding into the street.

We were both pleased with this expedient; but the next thing to be considered was, what place I should go to, as I could not make this attempt till late at night, and must go alone; for my father being in years, and pretty corpulent, I could not think of letting him run the same hazard, which might have put his life into imminent danger, especially as I could not give him the same help which he could afford me. This was a difficulty, till I recollected a mantua-maker, who was then making some clothes for me; and I happened to know where she lived. To her house I resolved to go (having first settled all my previous steps) and to remain concealed there till my father should get an opportunity of coming to me. I told him as *I* was the unhappy object on whom Mr Ware had designs, I supposed he would not detain my father after I was gone. He shook his head, but said, he hoped he would not.

Having now settled our little plan, we were more composed. A servant brought breakfast into my apartment at the usual hour, and dinner, and supper, in the like manner. We did not appear, troubled, but as carefully avoided seeming chearful, for fear of giving suspicion.

The house-keeper was generally the last person up in the family; so that I was either to seize the opportunity before she came up to my room, or wait till she was asleep. The last I thought was the securest method, as she was an extremely sound sleeper. I lifted up the sash in the bed-chamber, to be in readiness, and closed the shutters again.

Very fortunately my father having received his quarterly payment from Mr Ware just before we came to town, had fifty guineas in his purse, half of which he insisted on my taking in case of any emergency.

About twelve o'clock the house-keeper came into the room where we were sitting, as she was obliged to pass through that to go to the room where we lay.

We heard her at the door, and my father suddenly changing the subject of our discourse, made me a sign which I understood; and as the woman entered, affected to be representing to me the charms of wealth and grandeur, whilst I seemed to listen, with a sort of pleasure to him. He stopped when the woman came in, but not till he was sure she had heard what he said, for we observed that she staid at the outside of the door a little while, as if to listen to our conversation. On seeing us engaged in discourse, she made a motion to withdraw, saying she would come up again when Mr Price was retired to rest; but I told her she might if she pleased, then go to bed, as we should not sit up long. But as I suppose she had orders to lock me in after my father had left me, she did not chuse to do this. She said she was not sleepy, but would come up in half an hour, and left the room smiling.

This was an opportunity which I thought was not to be lost. I repaired to the window, and hearing a watchman cry the hour, I waited till he came under it, and having prepared a piece of paper, in which I had put a weight to carry it down, I lighted it and dropped it at his feet; it was fastened to a string, and at some distance from it above, was fastened another large piece of white paper folded up, in which I put a guinea, and in two lines written in a large plain hand, beseeched him to assist me in getting down, for which I would reward him with another guinea.

The lighted paper (as I concluded it would) attracted the man's notice, he stopped and took it up, and finding another paper hanging to the string, looked up at the window. I leaned my body out as far as I could, and, in a low voice, but loud enough for him to hear me, bid him read it. He opened the paper, and, by the light of his own lantern, read the lines, at the same time taking out the guineas, which I could perceive he also examined by the same light.

He then said, I'll help you, stay a little.

He made what haste he could away, and I was now afraid he intended to leave me, and return no more. My terror was inexpressible during the man's absence, especially as several people in that interval passed by; however, he soon returned with a companion; and the street being now clear, I saw he had brought a sort of plank, or board, under his arm, which he fixed from the iron pallisados a-cross to the stone-work which jutted out from the bottom of the lower windows, on this he without difficulty mounted, and being now much nearer to me, he told me he would receive me, if I could contrive to get down to him.

My poor father hastily kissed, and blessed me, and having my apparatus ready for descending, he had the farther precaution to fix some strong ribbons, which I had tied together for the purpose under my arms; these he held in his hands, whilst I slid down by the sheets which I had fastened together corner-ways with a knot.

The trusty watchman caught me in his arms, and lifted me over the pallisados, to his comrade, who set me safely down in the street.

It was very dark, but I could distinguish when my father drew in the linen, and heard him shut the window. I then told my deliverer that I must beg a farther act of kindness from him, which was to see me safe to the street where I wanted to go.

He readily complied, and leaving it to his comrade to carry away the plank, took me under the arm, and we got without being molested to the mantua-maker's house. The family were all in bed; when after repeated knocking, a maid looked out of an upper window, and asked us what we wanted. I told her an acquaintance of her mistress had urgent business with her, and begged she would step down and speak to me from the parlour window. After keeping me a long while waiting, she at length came down, I then gave the watchman the other guinea I had promised him, and dismissed him, very well pleased with his night's adventure.

After he was gone, I told the woman my name, and begged she would let me come in, which she immediately did. I without scruple acquainted her with the manner of my escape, and the occasion of it; she was shocked and affected with my story, and promised to keep me concealed till my father should come to carry me to some place of greater safety; for she said, as Mr Ware's house-keeper was her acquaintance I might be discovered at her house.

This terrified me exceedingly, but the good-natured woman gave me the most solemn assurances that I should be safe for the short time she supposed I should stay with her. She invited me to part of her bed, as she told me she had never a spare one, and I readily accepted of her offer.

I remained all the next day in the utmost grief and anxiety, at hearing nothing from my poor father. In the evening of the second day, a porter brought a letter to the mantua-maker, which served only as a cover for a note directed to me. Seeing it writ in my father's hand, I eagerly opened it; but oh, Madam, how shall I tell you my grief, and horror, when I saw it dated from a prison! My poor father told me, that our cruel persecutor, enraged at my escape, had charged my father with it, who immediately acknowleged he had assisted in delivering me from ruin; that Mr Ware, after treating him with the most injurious language, demanded payment of him for the sums he said he had lent him from time to time since his father's death.

To this my father making no other reply, than that Mr Ware knew he had it not in his power to refund any of that money, which, though it was a free gift, he would restore sooner than lie under any obligation to such a base man, the villain was barbarous enough to have him arrested, and sent to jail, where he said he should remain till his stubborn spirit should be glad to yield up his daughter to him.

My father desired me to come to him directly, and to bring some body with me to protect me by the way. I instantly obeyed, and sending for a hackney coach, the mantua-maker got her husband, a decent tradesman, and his apprentice to accompany me. We drove directly to my poor father's melancholy habitation, where they delivered me safe into his hands. His joy at seeing me again, made him for a while forget the sorrows which surrounded us.

He told me that after he had seen me get safe into the street, and had recommended me to the care of providence, he had put every thing out of the way which had assisted me in my escape; and putting out one of the candles left it in my room, that the house-keeper, when she come up, might suppose me in bed; he then went to his own. He concluded that the woman, when she went into my room, supposed me asleep. Mr Ware was at home the whole evening, and had before that retired to rest, so that there was no discovery made that night.

My father now informed me that Mr Ware had said, when he first made the odious proposal to him, that if I complied, he would allow my father four hundred pounds a year, and settle the like sum upon me for life; at the same time, in case of refusal, insinuating the threat which he afterwards put into execution. Thinking, no doubt, he should by this intimidate my poor father so much, that upon reflexion he would use his endeavours to prevail on me to comply; and it was for this wicked purpose he was permitted, or rather compelled to pass the whole day with me. I would not, added my father relate this particular to you, for fear your tenderness to me might shake your virtue; but the trial God be praised! is now past; you are here my poor child at least in safety. We have some money to support us for a while, perhaps the wicked wretch may relent. If he gives me my liberty I may still obtain a livelihood; and if I can get you received into some worthy family, that will protect you from his violence, I shall be contented.

My father, unwilling to expose his ungrateful pupil, and thinking when he cooled a little he would be ashamed of his conduct and release him, resolved not to apprise any of his friends in Berkshire of his situation; but wrote a long expostulatory letter to Mr Ware, which he concluded with requesting no other favour but his liberty.

To this, Mr Ware wrote in answer, that he was still ready to make good his first proposals, and since he now found that he had got his daughter with him, he should obtain his liberty on no other terms.

My father still loath to believe him so lost to humanity as to persist in this barbarous resolution, patiently waited another month; at the end of which he again wrote him a very affecting letter; but to this he received no answer, being told Mr Ware was gone into Berkshire. He wrote to two or three gentlemen of his acquaintance there, informing them of his deplorable situation, and begging them to use their influence with Mr Ware on his behalf. He did not disclose the enormity of his behaviour, but only said, that on a quarrel he had with him, he had confined him under colour of a debt, which it was not in his power to discharge; this he did as much in tenderness to Mr Ware's character, as to avoid exasperating him more against him.

He ordered me at the same time to write to an old maid-servant, who took care of our little house in the country, to send me my clothes, my father's books, and such other things as belonged to him. As I had come to town but for a month, and was in deep mourning for my mother, I had left the best part of my apparel behind me, and I had taken nothing with me from Mr Ware's but a little bundle of linnen; my father had been permitted to carry his with him to the prison.

As the furniture in this little house was of no great value, my father having purchased it as it stood in the house of the former curate, he made a present of it to the old servant, who had lived with him from the time he married.

He received no answer to any of the letters he wrote to the gentlemen; but I got a letter from this old servant, at the same time that she sent the things which I wrote for. And you will scarce believe, Madam, to what a height this abandoned wretch carried his crimes.

Not contented with having plunged my poor father and me into the deepest distress, he endeavoured to blast and destroy our characters in the country. He gave out that my father, taking advantage of his (Mr Ware's) being a little overcome with wine one night, had put his daughter to bed to him, and would have insisted the next day that he had married them. To punish the ungrateful designing old rogue, he said he had put him into jail where he intended to keep him a month or two till he repented.

Though the respectable character my father bore in his neighbourhood made this story incredible, yet Mr Ware's power and influence was such, that people seemed to believe it, and applauded Mr Ware's clemency in my father's punishment. No wonder then his letters were unanswered; they were shewn to Mr Ware, and laughed at. The old servant, who was sure we were both cruelly belied, lamented our unhappy fate, but poor creature she could do nothing *but* lament. This last blow quite subdued my father's courage; he fell sick upon it, and languished many weeks in a most melancholy condition.

When he recovered a little from his sickness, he was suddenly struck with the dead palsey on one side, by which he lost the use of his right hand; so that I am obliged to dress and undress him like a child.

When the money which we had brought with us to the prison was spent, we were obliged to sell most of my father's books, and the best of my clothes.

We had repeated messages from the merciless mann, by his vile house-keeper, who used all her rhetoric to persuade us to compliance; but my father constantly repulsed her, with contempt and indignation; 'till at length Mr Ware, tired, I believe, with persecuting us, left us to perish in peace. He supposed my father could not hold out long; and he then concluded I should be at his mercy; for as I never stirred out of the jail, he had no hopes of getting me into his power whilst my poor father lived.

If I had even a place of refuge to go to, I could not think of leaving him in the wretched hopeless condition to which he was now reduced. I thought therefore of applying myself to something, by which I could obtain bread for our support. I set about making those little artificial flowers, which had formerly been one of my amusements; and a woman, who was confined in the same prison with us, and worked for some shops, undertook to dispose of them for me. She had a daughter, who came often to see her, and used to carry her work and mine to the people who bespoke it.

In this manner we have languished, Madam, near eighteen months; when hearing lately that Mr Ware was gone to Bath, and the girl who used to visit her mother being sick, I ventured out myself with the work. The person who employs us did live in the city; but has lately taken a shop in this street; and though it is a journey from what I now call my dismal home, I have come to her once a week, for this month past, with the product of my own, and, I may say, my fellow prisoner's labours. She told me this day she was overstocked with such flowers as I brought her, and, having picked out a few of the best of them, she left those, which you see in my band-box, upon my hands. I was returning home very disconsolate, when, to avoid your chariot, which drew up close to the house, I stood up on one of your steps, not knowing it was going to stop; and something in your countenance, Madam, I know not how, encouraged me to offer my little ware to you.

I have given you this affecting story, my Cecilia, pretty nearly in the girl's own words. I was much moved by it. If this be all fact, said I, what monsters are there among mankind!

She replied, It was all very true.

Though the girl was very young, and, as I told you, had a modest and ingenuous look, yet as I had seen such cheating faces before, I would not yield up my belief implicitly. This story might be invented to move compassion, at least, the most material circumstances of it; and though I could not suppose she had contrived it on the spot, yet I did not know but it might have been contrived for her.

I have a mind to see your father, child, said I.

She answered, quite composed, Then, Madam, you will see an object, that would greatly move your pity.

She rose up as she spoke this, saying, her poor father would be very uneasy at her staying so long, and was preparing to go.

I was seized with a strong inclination to visit this unhappy father directly. If, said I, the case be as she represents it, I cannot be too speedy in my relief; and, if she has falsified in any thing, I shall probably detect her, by not giving her an opportunity of seeing and preparing him first.

It was not more than eleven o'clock; and I resolved not to defer the charity I intended. I desired the young woman to stay a while, and ordering Patty to bring down a plain black silk hood and scarf of her own, I made the poor girl, to her great astonishment, put them on. I then ordered a hackney coach to be called, and said, I would go with her to her father. She looked surprized, but not startled, which made a favourable impression on me. She appeared decent, and I desired her to get into the coach, which I ordered, according to her direction, to drive to the jail, where her father was confined.

When we arrived at this mansion of horror, for so it appeared to me, I let her go up stairs before me. She stopped at a door, and said that was the room where her father lay. I bid her go in first; she entered, and I stood without-side the door, where (as the lobby was dark) I could not readily be perceived.

I saw there a man of about sixty; and as she had told me her father was corpulent, I did not at first take him to be the person, for he looked worn out, pale, and emaciated. He wore his own grisled hair, and had on a cassock, girded about him with silk sash. One of his hands was slung in a black crape; he sat pensively, leaning on a table, with a book open before him, which seemed to be the Bible.

Upon his daughter's going into the room, he lifted up his eyes to see who it was: he had a fine countenance; candour and sincerity were painted on it.

My dear, you made a long stay, said he, in a melancholy voice, I was afraid something had happened to you. What has detained you?

Oh, Sir, said she, looking towards the door, I believe I met with a good angel, who is come to visit you in prison.

I entered at these words: the venerable man rose. – A good angel indeed, if her mind be like her face! He bowed respectfully.

Pray, Sir, keep your seat.

I took a chair, and placed myself by him. He did not seem in the least embarrassed, but gravely and modestly demanded to what it was that he owed the honour of a visit from a lady of my appearance; for, said he, affluence and prosperity seldom seek the dwellings of the wretched.

I informed him, that, having met with his daughter by accident, she had given me a melancholy account of his situation, and that I wished to hear the particulars from his own mouth. He made an apology for the length of his story; but said, if I had patience, he would relate it. I told him, I had come for that purpose.

He then repeated to me every particular, as I had before heard them from his daughter, enlarging on certain passages, which she had but slightly touched upon. He shewed me copies of his two letters to Mr Ware, and that gentleman's answer to the first, as also the old servant's letter to his daughter, which convinced me of the truth of every thing he had said.

I asked Mr Price, what Mr Ware's demand on him might amount to?

He said, four hundred pounds, which was what he had received from him, since his father's death.

Take courage, Sir, said I, you shall not long remain here.

Ah! Madam, cried he, may God be the rewarder of your goodness! but my enemy is a hardened man; he is not to be influenced by honour or virtue.

I perceived by this that the poor gentleman had no thought of my paying his debt, but supposed I would endeavour to soften Mr Ware on his account. Have a little patience, said I, and we will try what is to be done.

I requested he would give me Mr Ware's letter, wherein he promised to make good his first proposal, if he would consent to yield up his daughter to him.

I took my leave, and slipped my purse, which had ten guineas in it, into his daughter's hand as I went down stairs.

As soon as I returned home, I sent for Mr Warner, and related to him circumstantially the distresses of this worthy father and child. His honest indignation burst forth against the base betrayer of them both; honest I must call it, though he vented his wrath in oaths and execrations on his head.

These are proper objects, said I, to exercise our humanity on; I mean to pay his debt, and make the remnant of his days comfortable. You are a good girl, said, he, you know my purse is open to you.

Oh, Sir, said I, there is no need to tax your generosity upon this occasion, the two thousand pounds you so lately gave me is but little diminished. Psha, psha, said he, I gave you that to make ducks and drakes of; it is not to go into the account; you know your quarter's income is commenced, you may have what you will.

I begged he would immediately write to Mr Ware, who is now at Bath, and make him a tender of his money, that we might get the poor man discharged from confinement as soon as possible.

I gave him that vile fellow's letter, and advised him to let him know that he was acquainted with the whole truth of the story; which, perhaps, might frighten him into better terms than insisting on his whole demand.

Mr Warner said, there was a merchant of his acquaintance at Bristol, to whom he would write immediately, and order him to pay the money directly, if it was insisted on. He said, he knew his friend would readily undertake the thing, and execute it as soon as possible.

He called for pen, ink, and paper, and wrote before me the following letter to his correspondent, which, as he left it with me to seal, and send it to the post-office, I first copied.

'Dear Sir,

'I beg immediately on the receipt of this, you will take the trouble of riding to Bath, and there enquire for a man of fortune, one Ware, who is the greatest villain in England, and you may tell him I say so. He has kept a poor honest clergyman starving in jail this year and a half, because he would not sell his daughter to him. He pretends the parson owes him four hundred pounds, which is a lie; for though he received that sum from him, it was paid him for value received by agreement. However, as the man can have no redress, I request you would immediately tender him that sum, and get a discharge, for I will have the poor fellow out.

I herewith send you inclosed a letter which that scoundrel Ware wrote; pray shew it to him, as a token that the parson's case is known, and that he has got friends to stand by him.

Your speedy execution of this affair, and answer, will oblige,

'Your friend and servant,

'EDWARD WARNER.'

To Mr William Blow,
merchant, at Bristol.

London, March 14, 1707-8.

My honest kinsman desired I would immediately send this letter off. I suppose his correspondent will have more discretion than to let Mr Ware see the contents, but I hope we shall have a good account of this negotiation.

March 22

I have been very impatient, my Cecilia, for an answer to Mr Warner's odd letter, and this day he received one. His friend at Bristol I take it for granted acted very prudently, for he says, that having *waited* on Mr Ware (which word Mr Warner took great exceptions to) he acquainted him with his commission, and at the same time produced his letter to Mr Price by way of identifying the person, as Mr Ware at first seemed not to recollect any thing of the matter. He said, Mr Ware blushed upon seeing his own letter, in the hands of a stranger; Aye, I remember the silly affair now, said he; the man is an old hypocrite, and his daughter is a young one; but as I never meant to ruin him, I will forgive him the debt; and accordingly wrote a full acquittal, which the merchant transmitted with his answer.

Nothing now remained but to pay the usual fees, and get the poor old gentleman out as fast as we could. Mr Warner undertook to do what was proper on the occasion, and instantly set out it with an alacrity that shewed the goodness of his heart.

How wonderfully shame operates on some minds! this wretched man, Ware, whom neither the laws of God nor man could restrain, has, by this single passion alone, been subdued. He found his base conduct was known by people whom he could not impose on; and his forgiving the pretended debt, no doubt, was meant as a bribe to prevent his disgrace from being propagated: for though he could sit down and enjoy himself under the accumulated guilt of fraud, perfidy, cruelty, oppression, and ingratitude; he was not proof against the reproach and ridicule of the world. This shews at least that he was not long practised in crimes of this sort.

March 24

I did not see Mr Warner again till this morning, when he entered my room making flourishes with his hands. Mr Price and his daughter were with him – Here they are for you, said he, and it has done my heart good to deliver such honest people from their misery.

The good old man poured forth such fervent prayers, and thanks for my goodness towards them, that my heart exulted with rapture, at being the means of conferring such happiness, as this worthy parent and child seemed to enjoy. The young girl's gratitude was silent, but not less ardent than her father's. She had kneeled down before me, and kissed my hands. I was greatly touched with the humility and tenderness of her acknowlegement.

I put an end to the grateful effusions of these honest hearts. I have done but little for you, said I, as yet; as Mr Ware had the grace to refuse the offered sum, I shall apply that money which I intended for him to your future use, or your liberty will avail you but little.

We shall think of some method of settling you comfortably for life; in the mean while your daughter and you shall be welcome to live with me.

I stopped him from renewing his thanks, and insisted on his saying no more on that subject. The poor old gentleman is extremely feeble and languishing from his long confinement, but I hope with proper care, as he is naturally strong, he will recover his health.

April 1

What true delight springs from benevolent actions, my dear! I never expected such heart-felt satisfaction as I have received from restoring comfort to these truly deserving people. I have bought the young lady some new clothes, plain, but genteel; and you cannot imagine what a pretty creature she is, now she is dressed. I find the old gentleman a man of admirable understanding, and great reading. He has a simplicity in his manner that is truly engaging, but at the same time a politeness that shews he is no stranger to the great world. Of his integrity he has given convincing proofs. Praised be the Lord! who has made me, and honest Mr Warner, the instruments of delivering such a man from the depths of affliction. He mends apace in his health, but I am afraid he will never recover the use of his hand; though, as it is not painful, it seems not to give him any uneasiness. –

April 10

I am infinitely charmed with the conversation of this couple; for the girl is very sensible, and prettily accomplished. I wish she were married to some honest man that knew her value; for I find she has still terrors on Mr Ware's account, nor is her father without his apprehensions.

He said to me to-day, if I were to die, Madam, I would conjure you as my last request to take my daughter into your service. With such a pattern before her she must be virtuous, and with such a protector I am sure she would be safe.

I told him he might rely on me, but that I hoped he would live long enough to see her happily disposed of in marriage.

If I could see that day, said he, I should then have no other worldly care to disturb me.

Here, my dearest Cecilia, I will close my very long narrative. The pacquet is already swelled to an enormous size, but you never think them too large.

May 14

After so many trifles, my dear, as my journal for nearly a month past contained, you will be glad of somehting a little more serious. I mentioned in my last week's journal, that I had cast my eyes on a young man, who I thought would make a suitable match for Miss Price, if he were approved of by her, and her father. This person is a linen-draper in the Strand, a second brother of my Patty's. You can't have forgot Harry Main, my dear, whom we both knew as a boy, remarkable for his sober behaviour, modesty, and sweetness of temper. He is just now out of his time, and his eldest brother has set him up in a handsome shop. You may be sure I am his customer. 'Tis on this lad then that I have turned my thoughts, as a fit husband for the amiable girl. I went yesterday morning to buy some linen for Miss Price, and carried her with me, as I had done once or twice before. After we made our markets, I told young Main, with a freedom which a long acquaintance gave me, that I thought he was so well settled, he wanted nothing but a good wife to complete his happiness. He replied, he should think himself very happy if he could light on some good young woman as a partner for life. Why do you not look out for one, said I? They are not so hard to be come at. I believe, Madam, he answered, I must get some one else to do it for me, my friends laugh at me and say I am too bashful to speak for myself, but I fancy were I to meet with a person that really touched my heart, I should make a shift to find courage enough to tell her so.

And have you never yet seen such a person, said I? He blushed, and by an involuntary motion his eyes were turned on Miss Price, of whom I concluded his sister Patty, as she often visits him, had given him the history. He said if I commanded him to tell his secret, I should know it another time.

This was enough; I asked in a jocose way, would he take a wife of my chusing? Sooner than of any body's in the world, Madam, he replied.

We took our leave, and I asked Patty when I went home, whether she had ever mentioned any thing about Miss Price to her brother? Poor Patty coloured for fear she had committed a fault, but owned directly she had told him every circumstance of her story; her brother having been very inquisitive about her, from the first time he had seen her with me; and added, that she believed he was down-right in love with her.

I told her if Miss Price liked her brother, and her father did not disapprove the match, I saw no reason why they might not make each other happy, as I should give Miss Price a fortune worth a young man's acceptance.

Patty said, she was sure her brother would rejoice at the offer, and that she herself could not wish him to make a better choice.

It only remained now to know how the young lady herself stood affected towards him. I put Patty (for whom Miss Price had conceived a great affection) upon this task. I thought she would speak her mind with less reserve to her, as I feared the obligation she thought herself under to me, might have such an influence on her gratitude, as to prevent that freedom which I wished her to use; for I was resolved not to put the least shadow of constraint on her inclinations.

Patty succeeded so well, that without seeming to have any design in it, she drew a confession from Miss Price very much in her brother's favour.

Being now sure that the young people liked each other, I thought I might open my design to the old gentleman, which I did in few words. How the good man was delighted with the happy prospect which his deservedly-beloved daughter had before her! he has left the affair intirely to me, so that I hope to have the girl disposed of very much to all our satisfaction.

May 18

I am charmed with Mr Warner's noble behaviour. I claim an interest, said he, in these honest creatures that you have taken under your protection. I like the old fellow mightily, and admire the little girl so much, that, if you had not provided a better husband for her, I should have been half tempted to have taken her myself; but since it is as it is, we must do handsomely by her.

I told him I had enquired into the young man's circumstances, and found that about a thousand pounds would set him forward extremely well, and that this was the portion I intended to give him with the young gentlewoman.

Well said he, I believe that will do; but I must make the poor thing a present myself for wedding-trinkets. And the old man too, must we not take care of him?

Dear Sir, said I, how good you are? You would remind me of my duty, if I myself were forgetful of it. But I have already settled a hundred pounds a year on him.

Is that enough, said he? will it make the good fellow easy?

Oh, Sir, it exceeds his wishes; he intends to live with his daughter, as his growing infirmities require her tender care.

Every thing is to be this day settled. Mr Price is exceedingly pleased with his son-in-law elect; and the wedding will be no longer delayed, than till Mr Main receives the answer to those letters which he has wrote to his friends in the country, to apprize them of his approaching marriage.

May 26

I am sure my dear Cecilia will rejoice with her friend in the acquisition she has received to her own happiness by conferring so much on a worthy family. The bride is this day gone home to her own house; her delighted father with her. Their prayers and blessings, poured out from truly grateful and virtuous hearts, remain with me. A reward, my dear, and a rich one too, for the self-satisfying part I have acted.

My worthy Patty, whose merit alone raises her much above her station, I shall no longer consider as my servant. She has been my friend in the tenderest and most enlarged sense of the word, and she shall continue so. I have hired another maid to wait on me, and with a sort of merry ceremony enfranchised Patty on the day of her brother's marriage; for I had her dressed elegantly as bride's maid to her new sister, and she sat on her right-hand at the wedding dinner. I look on her as my companion, but I cannot persuade her to forget that I was her mistress. She shews this by actions, not by words.

[Here follows an interval of thirteen months, in which nothing material to the thread of the story occurs. The journal contains only a continued series of such actions, as shewed the noble and pious use which Mrs Arnold made of the great fortune which providence had blessed her with. The rest is filled up with a variety of little incidents, many of them relative to her brother and his lady, to Mr Warner, and several letters from Lady V—, with whom she constantly corresponded. At the end of that period the journal proceeds thus.]

June 28, 1708

And shall I really be so blessed, my ever beloved Cecilia, as to see you at the time you mention? Oh, my dear, after an absence of five long years, how my heart bounds with joy at your approach! The two months that are to intervene before we meet will appear very tedious to me. But it is always so with happiness, that is within our view. Before I expected you, though I regretted your absence, yet did I patiently acquiesce under it, and could entertain my thoughts with other objects; but I am now, I cannot tell you how anxious and impatient to see you. And yet, my Cecilia, we shall have nothing new to say to each other, knowing as we both do every circumstance of each other's life since we parted. Mine has been a strange one; but my lot is now fallen on a fair ground, where, I hope it will please heaven to continue me whilst I am to remain in this world. The noble, I may almost call it, princely fortune that my kinsman has settled on me, will enable me to live my children greatly provided for, whenever it shall be God's pleasure to call me away. Let me but live to embrace my Cecilia, and then, providence, thy will be done!

June 29

Gracious God! for what I am yet reserved? My trembling hand can scarce hold my pen, but I will try to tell you the event which yesterday produced.

I was but just set down to dinner; nobody with me but Patty and my children. A note was brought into me, which, they said came by a porter, who waited for an answer. I opened and read it. My eyes were struck with the unlooked for name of Orlando Faulkland at the bottom; the contents filled me with terror and surprize. I know not what I have done with the note, but he informed me in it that he was just arrived in town, and begged I would appoint an hour that evening to see him alone, adding, that his arrival was, and must be, a secret to every body but me.

Troubled and shocked as I was, I returned for answer, by the same messenger, that I should expect him at six o'clock. I need not tell you how I passed the interval 'till that hour. It was impossible for me, amidst a thousand conjectures, to form one which could probably occasion this amazing visit. So strangely introduced! so unthought of! and from one I imagined to be in another kingdom.

Precisely at six o'clock, I heard a coach stop at the door; Patty was in the way to receive him, and presently Mr Faulkland himself entered the drawing-room. Distraction was in his looks! I rose to receive him, but shook from head to foot; and I felt the blood forsaking my face. He ran to me, as if with a design to salute me, but started back without making the offer. I made a motion to a chair for him, and sat down myself, for I was not able to stand. You are welcome to England, Sir, I am glad to see you – scarce knowing what I said. I hope your lady is well? He looked wildly, as if in horror at the question. Then suddenly catching both my hands, he fell on his knees before me, his eyes fixed mournfully on my face, and it was some time before he could answer.

I could not speak; I burst into tears: – there was something dreadful in his silence. He kissed both my hands, but I withdrew them from him. Sir, Sir, speak I conjure you. You shock me to death! I see I have, said he; and I am afraid to proceed: you will die at the relation. For God's sake, Sir, explain yourself. –

You see a man, said he, whose life is forfeited to the law – My wife is dead – and by my hand –.

I don't know whether he said more, for I fainted away. It seems he did not call for any help, but by his own endeavours at last brought me to myself, and I found him weeping bitterly over me.

The sound of the last horrid words I had heard him speak still rung in my ears. I begged him to explain them.

That wife, said he, that woman whom *you* persuaded me to marry, I caught in adultery, and I punished the villain who had wronged me with death. She shared in his fate, though without my intending it. For this act of justice, which the law will deem murder, I myself must die, and I am come but to take a last look. – What recompence then can you make the man, whom you have brought to misery, shame and death?

His looks, and the tone of voice with which he spoke this, made my blood run cold, and my heart die within me.

I wrung my hands, and redoubling my tears, I do not need your reproaches, said I, to make me the most miserable woman on earth –

What recompence indeed *can* I make you – None, none, but to tell you that if you will fly this instant, my fortune will be at your disposal, and I will take care to supply you in what part soever of the world you shall chuse for your residence.

And can you after all that is past, said he, persist in such barbarity as to drive me from you? or are you determined to see me perish here? If that be so, I will soon rid you of this miserable hated wretch.

He drew his sword like a madman, and with a dreadful imprecation, which made me shudder, swore that if I did not that minute, promise to bear him company in his flight, he would plunge it into his breast, and die before my eyes. – Good God, what a scene of horror was this! I will, I will, I cried. I will go with you to the farthest verge of the earth. I catched his arm, fell down on my knees, and was more mad, if possible than himself.

I begged of him to put up his sword, which he did, seeing me almost dead with fear. You know, said he, the means of dying are always in my own power; take care you do not trifle with me, nor plead in excuse for falsifying your promise, that you made it to save me from immediate destruction.

I beseeched him to calm himself a little, and to permit me to send for my brother. Sir George you know has an intire affection for you, said I, you may trust him with your life in safety.

I had forgot him, said he; poor Bidulph! he will be afflicted when he hears my story.

I instantly wrote a line to my brother requesting to see him immediately. By good fortune he was home, and came to me directly.

In the mean time, as I saw Mr Faulkland's mind was exceedingly disturbed, I endeavoured, by giving him an account of my own situation, to divert his thoughts from the trouble that preyed on them; for I was apprehensive of his relapsing into the same phrenzy that had so much terrified me, if I touched on the cause, and therefore chose to defer enquiring into the particulars of his misfortune, till my brother should be present.

Sir George was equally astonished with me at the sight of Mr Faulkland; they embraced tenderly; poor Mr Faulkland wept upon my brother's neck. It was easy to discover he laboured under some extraordinary affliction.

My brother looked at me as if for an explanation; he seemed to guess at least part of the fatal truth. Are you come to England alone, Faulkland, said he? I prevented the reply; he is alone, said I, he has a dreadful story to relate to you. Mrs Faulkland is dead. I durst not ask the manner of her death, till you were by, to calm the transports of your friend.

My heart forebodes, answered my brother, addressing himself to Mr Faulkland, that the ungrateful woman you married has betrayed you. She did, replied Mr Faulkland, but I did not mean to stain my hands with her blood, perfidious as she was; her death be on her own head.

Sir George looked astonished; that she is dead I rejoice said he, but how my dear Faulkland, were you accessary to it?

We were that instant interrupted. Mr Warner passing by, called to ask me how I did, and as my brother's chariot stood at the door, I could not be denied to him, though I had ordered that nobody should be let in.

I was called down to him, and indeed was not sorry to have an excuse for absenting myself a while, for my spirits were quite overpowered.

Mr Warner quickly observed that something extraordinary had happened, and as he was already acquainted with the greatest part of Mr Faulkland's history, some particulars relative to his wife excpted, I made no scruple, relying on his prudence and secrecy, of telling him the cause of my present distress; in which he seemed to take a friendly and even paternal share.

When he was gone, I returned to the room where I had left my brother and his friend. They both seemed in extreme agitation, they were walking about.

This is an unfortunate affair, said my brother, and may be attended with dreadful consequences, if Faulkland does not shew more regard to his own safety, than he seems inclined to do. I have been persuading him to retire to a place which I can provide for him, where he may lye concealed for a day or two, till he is recovered from the fatigue of his journey; for he has travelled night and day for these three days without sleeping.

Sir George looked at me, and by a sorrowful sign which he made, I apprehended he feared his unhappy friend's head was disturbed.

For heaven's sake, Sir, said I, be advised by my brother, who loves you; suffer him to conduct you to some place of security; when you have had a little repose we will both come to you, and concert such measures as shall be best for your safety.

He snatched my hand, Sir George is my true friend, said he, take care that *you* do not deceive me. I find myself giddy for want of rest. I am satisfied to be disposed of for to-night how you please. But give me your word of honour that I shall see you in the morning.

You shall indeed, Sir, I replied.

Depend upon it, answered Sir George, I'll bring her to you myself.

He looked irresolute, and as if he knew not what to say; then turning to my brother, and leaning on his shoulder, Do, dear Bidulph, carry me to some place where I may lie down, for my spirits can hold out no longer.

Come, said Sir George, taking him under the arm, my chariot is at the door, I will bring you to a house where you may be quiet at home.

Mr Faulkland rivetted his eyes on me, as my brother led him out of the room, but he did not speak.

Sir George whispered me that he would return again. They went into the chariot together and drove away.

It was ten o'clock before my brother returned. He told me he had lodged Mr Faulkland safely at a friend's house in whom he could confide, as he did not think his own, in case of a search, a place of security.

He said he had seen him in bed, and hoped a little sleep would compose his mind, which seemed very much disturbed. I requested my brother to give me the particulars of that terrible affair, which Mr Faulkland had mentioned. Sir George related to me what follows, though Mr Faulkland, he said, told the story but incoherently.

Mr Faulkland said he had no reason to be displeased with his wife's conduct for more than a year after their marriage; her affection for him seemed lively and sincere; and he had made her the most grateful returns, it being the study of his life to render her happy. Her love abated not of its ardor, and he had all the reason in the world to imagine himself intirely possessed of her heart.

Whilst Mr Faulkland's house in the country was building, he had been invited by a neighbouring gentleman, who lived at the distance of about three miles from his own place, to stay at his house; which obliging offer Mr Faulkland had readily accepted, as by that means he had daily opportunities of seeing, and expediting his own improvements.

Mr Bond (that was the gentleman's name) had a wife and two or three daughters, all very agreeable women; with whom Mrs Faulkland had, by living so much in their family, contracted a great intimacy; but particularly with the eldest, a sprightly fine young woman, of about twenty years old. They had been three or four Months at Mr Bonds; their house, which was nothing more than a little lodge, was finished; and they only waited till it was thoroughly dry to remove into it, as Mr Faulkland had laid out extensive gardens, in the finishing of which he proposed to amuse himself some time; for he acknowleged to my brother, he was in no haste to return to England.

During their residence with this gentleman, they had made two or three excursions to town. On their return from one of these, after an absence of about a fortnight, they found a visitor at Mr Bond's; his name was Smyth; he was an officer, a genteel handsome man, and they were given to understand he made his addresses to the eldest daughter; of whom he had been an admirer a long time, but durst not make his pretensions known to her father, till having lately been promoted in the army to the rank of a major, the young lady's parents admitted his visits to their daughter. She had long before that acknowleged to Mrs Faulkland in confidence, her attachment to him. Mr Faulkland, who had learned this secret from his wife, was very glad to find that Miss Bond, for whom he had great esteem, was likely to have her wishes accomplished, as he saw that Major Smyth was treated with distinction by her parents, who complimented him with a bed at their house; for he generally staid two or three nights with them, every time he paid them a visit, as his regiment was then quartered at a town about fifteen miles distant from their house.

The Major, without being a man of very shining parts, had such talents as made him acceptable to the women. He sung prettily, was lively to extravagance, full of agreeable trifling, and always in good humour. Miss Bond loved him; and as he was considered in the light of a person who would shortly be one of the family. Mr Faulkland soon contracted a friendship with him, which the Major on his part, seemed very solicitous to improve.

The marriage was now agreed on, and was only deferred till the young lady's brother should be at age, as he was to join with his father in making a settlement on his sister. This desirable event was at the distance of four months; but as the lover was in the mean time permitted to enjoy so much of his mistress's conversation, he seemed to submit to the delay with patience.

Things were in this situation, when Mr Faulkland, thinking it time to remove to his own house, proposed it to his lady; but she objected to it, declaring she did not think it safe, as the house had been so lately built. Though indeed it was now perfectly well seasoned; for the shell had been intirely finished some time before Mr Faulkland had gone to Mr Bond's house, and it was only the inside work, and a kitchen that was built apart from the lodge, that wanted to be completed. Mr Faulkland was unwilling to oppose his lady in any thing; but he was the more solicitous that she should comply with his request in this particular, as he thought he had observed that the eldest Miss Bond, had, of late, behaved with more coldness towards her than usual. Though he was far from guessing the cause of this, he thought it, however, a sufficient reason for their removal. He was afraid they had already staid too long; and that, perhaps, notwithstanding the good nature and hospitality of the family they all now secretly wished their absence. This, though he intended to make a suitable return for their friendly reception of him during so long a time, made him resolve not to continue there; and the more so, as Miss Bond, who was present when he proposed it to Mrs Faulkland, seemed to wish for their departure; as she dissented from that lady with regard to her opinion of the state of the new house, and seemed to think there could no danger attend their immediate entrance into it. Mrs Faulkland seemed nettled at this, and immediately assented to her husband's proposal; the next day they took their leave of Mr Bond's family, and repaired to their own house.

Mr Faulkland, from this period, remarked a change in his wife's behaviour; she grew melancholy and peevish; but as she complained of not being well, he imputed the alteration in her temper to that alone; and the more so, as she did not abate in the tokens of her seeming affection for him.

Mr Bond's family frequently visited them; Major Smyth always made one of the party, and often came without them. Though they lived but at the distance of three miles from each other, yet as the road for carriages between the two houses, being a-cross one, was very bad, the ladies were often prevailed on, if they staid late, to lye a night at Mr Faulkland's, and in consequence of this, Mr Bond and the Major had frequently done the same when they were of the party.

Though Mr Faulkland was far from having any injurious suspicion of his wife, he could not help observing that all her complaints vanished, whenever this family were at her house. This, however, he ascribed to nothing more than her being fond of the company, though he thought a coolness between her, and the eldest Miss Bond, was still apparent. The principals of the family, however, behaved with their usual frankness and good-humour, and Mr Faulkland thought there might be some little female pique between the two ladies, which was not worth enquiring into.

As they punctually returned the friendly visits of these agreeable neighbours, Mrs Faulkland always proposed passing the night there, to induce them, as she said, to use the same obliging freedom at her house. Mr Faulkland, on those occasions observed, that his lady always rose much earlier than usual, but unsuspecting as he was, he was satisfied with the reason she assigned for it, that of enjoying the pleasant hours of the morning in a very delicious garden; a pleasure which they could not have at home, as Mr Faulkland's improvements were only in their infancy.

The mutual intercourse between the two families was thus carried on for more than three months, when the time drew near, that Miss Bond and her lover were to be united, and every thing was preparing for the purpose. The young Mr Bond was come home from the college, and the house on this occasion was more chearful than ever. Mr Faulkland and his lady were there at a ball one night, when the latter, after dancing a long time, complained suddenly of being violently ill and either really did, or pretended to, faint. She was immediately conveyed to bed, and, at her request, another room prepared for Mr Faulkland. He, extremely alarmed at her indisposition, came to her bed-side, purposing to sit up by her the whole night; the youngest of the Miss Bond's offering to do the same, but Mrs Faulkland absolutely refused them both, and about midnight, saying she found herself inclined to sleep, insisted on their retiring; nor would she admit a servant to stay in the room, but contented herself with having a candle burning on the hearth.

Mr Faulkland, who really had an affection for his lady, was impatient the next morning to enquire after her health; he found her in bed, the complaints of the preceding night all renewed.

The family were extremely disconcerted at this unlucky accident, and expresed the utmost uneasiness, all but the eldest Miss Bond, who was silent; and heard her mother and sisters condoling with Mr Faulkland, not only with unconcern, but a suppressed smile of contempt, which did not escape Mr Faulkland's observation. He now began to resent such a behaviour, which he thought very unkind; and told his lady he wished she was in a condition to be removed, as he was fearful in her present situation it might be very inconvenient to the family to have her remain sick in their house; especially as it quite broke in on the mirth and festivity which were now going forward.

To this she replied, that she found herself so weak and dispirited, which she said was always the consequence of those faintings, to which she had been subject from her childhood, that she could not think of leaving her room. She made a shift, however, to rise, and said she hoped in a day or two to be able to remove.

Mrs Bond, who was of an extremely humane and tender disposition, begged of her not to think of stirring till she found her health perfectly re-established: Mrs Faulkland thankfully accepted her offer, and Mr Faulkland, though reluctantly, was obliged to acquiesce.

They remained thus two days longer, Mrs Faulkland's complaints still furnishing her with a pretence for sleeping alone; and, under colour of not giving trouble in the family, she would not suffer a maid to sit up with her.

Major Smyth, who had been in the house all this time, had now some call to his regiment, which obliged him to go to the town where it lay, and Mr Faulkland heard him give his man directions for their journey.

Mrs Faulkland still kept her room, and had not left it since the time she was first taken ill. It happened that the chamber which was assigned for Mr Faulkland, immediately joined his lady's, and was only separated from it by a wainscot partition, by which means he could hear the least stir in her chamber.

The unsuspecting injured husband, whose anxiety for his faithless wife had always made him watchful and attentive to her motions, happened this night to be more than ordinarily so. The family had now been for some hours buried in sleep; every thing was profoundly silent for some time. Mr Faulkland, who hoped his lady was settled to rest, was endeavouring to compose himself to sleep, when he heard her stir. This immediately roused him, and raising his head off the pillow, he found she got out of bed. Though she seemed to use the utmost precaution, he nevertheless heard her very distinctly open her door, and go out. Surprized as he was at this motion, no other thought occurred to him, than that perhaps Mrs Faulkland, finding herself ill, had got up to call some of the female servants. Prepossessed with this belief, he started out of bed, and hastily slipping on his clothes, ran into his lady's room, where he found her candle still burning.

As he concluded she would presently return, he waited some

minutes in her chamber; at length, perceiving her clothes lying on a chair at her bed-side, he was afraid she had gone out without putting any thing on her, and though the night was not cold, he was apprehensive, that in her apparently weak condition, her health might be farther injured.

On this account, he determined to go in quest of her; and concluding she had gone to the apartment of the female servants, which was on the floor over that on which they lay, he ascended the stairs as silently as possibly.

As he was passing by a room on the top of the first flight, he heard some one speak in a low voice, and listning, fancied it was his wife's.

As he knew not who lay in that room, he made no doubt but that it was she, who was calling the person that slept there; and, without farther reflection, hastily opened the door, and went in, with the candle, which he had taken in his hand. On his sudden entrance, the person, who was in bed, eagerly called out, Who is there? He soon perceived by his voice, that it was Major Smyth. He was about to make an apology for his intrusion, when he perceiving his lady's wrapping gown, which he had seen her wear that morning, lying on the floor, and in the same instant recollecting that he had heard a woman's voice when he was without-side the door, the horror of her guilt rushed upon him at once, and without making any answer to the major, he suddenly drew back the feet curtains of the bed, where he plainly perceived that the major had a companion, though she had hid her head under the clothes.

The major instantly leaped out of bed, and though he saw Mr Faulkland was unarmed, he snatched up one of his own pistols, which lay on the table, and which his man had charged that night, as they were to go a short journey the next morning. Mr Faulkland, in the first transports of his rage, seized the other; the miserable woman, observing their fatal motions, threw herself out of bed. Mr Faulkland was too much distracted to be able to give a distinct account of this dreadful incident; all he can say is, that Major Smyth snapped his pistol at him, which, he thinks, missed fire, and he instantly discharged his with more fatal success; for Mrs Faulkland, who had in the instant rushed between them shrieked out, and dropped on the ground; and the major reeling a few steps, fell against one of the pillars of the bed, and cried out, He has killed us both.

Mr Faulkland says, that, after this dreadful action, without knowing what he did, he ran down stairs, and opening the front door, made the best of his way home on foot. The phrenzy of his mind was such that he thought not of providing for his safety; but having got into his house, he had no intention of going farther, when, in less than a quarter of an hour, one of his servants, whom he had left behind him at Mr Bond's, a faithful fellow, who had lived with him many years, came to him, scared and breathless, having ran himself almost dead to overtake his master.

Oh, Sir, said he, for heaven's sake, get away as fast as you can: Mr Bond's family are all in an uproar; you will be taken, if you do not make your escape this instant.

Have I killed any body? demanded Mr Faulkland.

Oh, Sir, answered the man, you have killed my lady, and Major Smyth is mortally wounded.

I know not what I did, cried Mr Faulkland, but I did not mean to hurt your mistress.

I believe it, Sir, replied the servant, but I fear nobody else will, for that wicked wretch, though they think he cannot live many hours, would take away your life if he could. The report of the pistol alarmed the family, and we all ran into his room, gentry and servants and all; the major was able to speak, but my lady was quite dead.

The account he gives is, that my lady's candle having gone out she got up to get it lighted, and was endeavouring to find one of the maid's rooms, when passing by his, and seeing a light, for he was but just got into bed, she stepped in; and before she had time to retire again, you rushed in like a madman; and seeing his pistols lie on the table, you snatched them both up, and discharged one at your lady, which killed her on the spot, you fired the other at him, while he was leaping out of bed. I am sure, Sir, this is a false story, yet, as the family may all believe it, I beg you on my knees, to provide for your safety. Miss Bond was tearing her hair for her lover; but I heard her say, she was glad that wicked woman (meaning my lady) had lost her life.

They had sent off some of the people for a surgeon, and I ran as fast as I could to warn you of your dangers.

This honest fellow, not contented with urging his master, soon saddled a very swift hunter, which he had in the stable; and Mr Faulkland, now convinced of the necessity of flying, mounted it directly, and, attended only by one groom, galloped off to Dublin, which he reached by seven o'clock in the morning, and was lucky enough to arrive just as a packet, which was going off with an express was ready to sail. He went on board, and landed at Holly-head in twelve hours, from thence, without stopping night or day, except to change horses, he rode post to London, and presented himself, in the manner I have already told you, before me.

Such, my Cecilia, are the dismal particulars of this sad story. My brother staid with me 'till it was very late; our time was past in consulting on measures for Mr Faulkland's preservation. He said, he would advise him, by all means, to get over to Holland as fast as he could; for if that story, which the execrable Smyth had invented, should be believed, and it was very likely to gain credit in case he died of his wound, and persevered in it to the last, Mr Faulkland, having no witness to disprove any part of the charge, would be in imminent danger of losing his life.

I need not describe to you the horror in which I passed last night. I rose this morning at day-light, and was but just dressed, when I was informed Mr Warner wanted to speak to me. I went down stairs to him directly.

I could not sleep all night for thinking of your affairs, said he, without any previous salute; and I am so impatient to hear Faulkland's story, that I could not rest 'till I came to you to be informed of it, for I suppose you heard every thing last night.

I related all the particulars minutely as I have done to you, Mr Warner never once interrupting me. When I had ended the story, what do you intend for Faulkland, said my kinsman? I know not what to do, Sir, I replied; but this I am sure of, that if it were in the power of wealth to relieve his afflicted mind, he has an undoubted right to a large portion of the fortune I possess; this I think myself bound to bestow on the man, who, when I was destitute, offered me his. If we can prevail on him to take care of his own safety, which, when he is a little more collected, I hope we shall be able to do, I must entreat your assistance, Sir, in helping me to make him as easy as his unhappy circumstances will admit of. – And is this *all*, demanded Mr Warner sternly? Does not your gratitude suggest a warmer recompence than giving him a paultry income?

I was startled at the question, and not replying immediately, You must marry him, said he in a peremptory tone; there is nothing now to hinder you; the heavy misfortune which has fallen upon him, puts it in your power to make him such a return as his prosperous days would not have allowed you. You can confer an obligation on him now; so *that* scruple is rubbed out. As for any former idle aspersions, you have already done more than enough to convince the world they were without foundation. I could wish indeed that Jezebel of a wife had been cut off in the common way; but since he was guiltless in his intentions, it would be barbarous to make *that* an objection, and I dare answer for it, all mankind will acquit him, though the law perhaps may not, of that scoundrel's death, who so well deserved it at his hands.

I told Mr Warner, that though Mr Faulkland had proposed something like this, I was sure it was owing to his distracted mind, for that he had at first declared he only came to take a last look at me, and that I hoped, when he came to the cool use of his reason, he would be far from urging such a request – The more are you bound then, said he, interrupting me, to deal generously by him. – What does your brother say upon the subject? He has not touched upon it, I replied, I was so taken up with hearing Mr Faulkland's melancholy story from my brother, that I mentioned not to him his wild proposal; and as Sir George told me Mr Faulkland was much more composed when he left him to his rest, I presume he hinted nothing of that kind to my brother.

Ay, ay, cried Mr Warner, Sir George to be sure will change his note. Mr Faulkland is now a fallen man, therefore depend on it he will not be for your marrying him; but for this very reason, I insist on your doing a noble thing. If you have a grain of honour, or of gratitude in you, you will not hesitate a moment. I will not desire you, continued he, finding me silent, to carry your gratitude so far as to marry a madman, if he should prove to be so; but if on your visit to him this morning, you find him composed, and in his right mind, make him a frank offer of your hand, and see you do it handsomely; consult not George, upon the subject, I will have it all *my* doing. Go, added he, if I did not know that at the bottom of your heart you *love* Faulkland, I would not make this a point with you; but notwithstanding all your pretended demurs I am sure that is the case.

I should be disingenuous to deny it, answered I; far from doing so, I will own that I should prefer him before all the world, if the strangeness of his present situation did not frighten me. Trouble not your head about that, cried Mr Warner, if the man is in his senses, do as I bid you, and take care that you acquit yourself with honour.

He left me without waiting for a reply. What can I say or do, my Cecilia? My heart and my reason are at variance. What a strange dilemma am I driven to? nobody to advise me. Mr Warner, precipitate and fanciful in his determinations, urges me on to I know not what. Marry Mr Faulkland! receive a hand stained with – Oh the very thought is terrible!

What would the world say to such an union? It cannot be. He will not sure when he comes to the use of his cooler reason insist upon a promise, which my own terror, and his desperation, extorted from me.

I must try to convince Mr Warner's judgment? I hope he will not obstinately persist in pressing me to what I dare not comply with . . . . My brother is just come to carry me to Mr Faulkland. Heaven grant I may find him restored to his right mind! . . . Just returned from my visit to Mr Faulkland. What a scene! He wrung my very heart. I would I had never seen him.

We found him up, and walking about his room; his looks much more composed than they were last night.

On our entering his chamber, his eyes sparkled with pleasure. He ran to my brother, and embraced him. Thank you my dear, dear Bidulph, said he, you at length give her to me, and with her own consent too. My bride! turning passionately to me, and snatching my hand.

My brother seemed shocked, and cast his eyes mournfully at me: mine moistened, and I was obliged to apply my handkerchief to them, turning my head away.

Tears! cried Mr Faulkland, in a tone of surprize, and on our wedding-day! I could not bear this, I sobbed aloud. My brother was willing, if possible, to give his thoughts another turn, for not knowing what had passed the day before, he thought this was some sudden start of phrenzy.

My dear Faulkland, said he, you affect my Sister too much; we have been consulting for your safety, and came to talk with you upon it.

I think there is no time to be lost, and that you ought immediately to retire into Holland.

I am ready, said Mr Faulkland, but Mrs Arnold goes with me, I have her promise for it.

Sidney shall follow you, answered my brother, making a motion to me to shew he would have me humour him in his ravings. I will not go without her, cried Mr Faulkland; the universe shall not now part us.

I was almost distracted with apprehension, and knew not what reply to make; my brother looked confounded, and was silent.

Mr Faulkland approached me, and with a look of gloomy despair, You are both mute, said he; Bidulph, I always thought *you* loved me. Mrs Arnold I hoped did not wish my death; but I am deceived in you both – I have no farther business with life – The friend I most confided in betrays me; the woman whom my soul worships, and to whom I sacrificed all my hopes of happiness, repays me with ingratitude. Why should such a wretch any longer submit to life? I have borne it too long already; but there's my remedy, pointing furiously to his sword, which lay in the scabbard on a table.

I could no longer contain myself, but bursting into tears, Oh, Sir, said I, accuse me not of ingratitude; I would to heaven *my* death could repair the heavy afflictions I have brought upon you; if it could, I would welcome it this hour. Your reproaches, cruel as they are, I forgive. I own myself the unhappy cause of all your misfortunes; we have been mutually fatal to each other. You know I always valued and esteemed you, and have in your calamity already been sufficiently punished for the share I have had in bringing it on you. What shall I say to you, Sir? My whole fortune I think too small, too poor a recompence, to the man who has obliged me beyond a possibility of return. Yet what have I to offer more? Can you, Sir, can you urge me to a marriage at so strange a juncture? Think how it will expose us both to censure. Your long attachment to me has not been a secret. Think what dreadful constructions may be put on *your* conduct, nay, on *mine*, should a union now take place, brought about, as it must appear, by so terrible an event.

Mr Faulkland was silent, his eyes fixed on the ground. My brother took up the argument. Indeed, my dear Faulkland, my sister has reason for her fears. You know I ever was your sincere friend; you know too I always was of opinion that Sidney ought to have been your wife; her former objections I thought were romantic scruples, and hardly forgave her refusing you. The present obstacle has more weight in it – Do not mistake me, added he hastily (seeing Mr Faulkland raise his eyes full of resentment at him) I wish my sister still to be yours, and will consent to your marriage with my whole heart; but let me conjure you to take a more favourable juncture; withdraw yourself but for the present; your affairs may not be so desperate as you imagine. If that villain Smyth should chance to recover, perhaps his conscience may awaken remorse, and he may be prevailed on to do you justice. In that case you must be cleared from the most distant imputation of what my sister hinted at, and what has but too justly alarmed her. Cleared as your character will then be, and conscious as we both are of the innocence of your intentions there will remain no bar to Mrs Arnold's giving you her hand.

Smyth *cannot* recover, interrupted Mr Faulkland, suddenly – there is no hope can spring from that. Then answered my brother, at worst you can but live abroad; all parts of the world are alike to such a philosopher as my sister is; and probably, circumstanced as your marriage will appear, she may like best to reside out of England. –

Mr Faulkland shook his head, and with a smile of indignation, Leave me, Bidulph, cried he, I cannot bear *your* attempting to deceive me. You think me mad, and are cruel enough to endeavour at imposing on me – I know my mind is disturbed – but who has driven me to despair! to madness! to death! and he cast a look at me that chilled my blood.

Be satisfied, Madam, you shall soon be rid of this fatal – hated – betrayed – abandoned wretch! he spoke this with his hands grasped eagerly together, and his eyes lifted up to heaven. Then striking his breast, he burst into tears, and rushing suddenly into his closet, he shut the door violently, locking it on the inside.

He wept aloud, and his agonies reduced me almost to the same condition with himself.

I begged my brother would endeavour to prevail on him to open the door, for I was fearful of his making some dreadful attempt upon his own life; but Sir George a little quieted my fears, by shewing me his sword, which still lay on the table, and which, at my desire, he put out of the way.

My brother approached the closet door, and in the most soothing language beseeched him to open it; but he could get no other answer from Mr Faulkland than to beg he would leave him to himself.

I found this was not a time for arguing. I told my brother, we had better suffer him to vent his passion alone, and that, perhaps, when he had time to reflect a little on what had been said, he would permit his cooler reason to govern him.

Sir George was very unwilling to leave him in such a distracted state of mind; he renewed his efforts to persuade him to come out of the closet, but to no purpose.

I beseech you to leave me, Sir George, said he, I am not in a condition to talk – I cannot bear the sight of Mrs Arnold – let me recover myself – another time perhaps I may be better able to discourse with you.

Will you promise me then, replied my brother, that you will in the interim do nothing that may be injurious to your life or health? Indeed, my dear Faulkland, you distress my sister and me more than you can imagine. Name the hour when you will permit me to come to you again; and for heaven's sake think of your own immediate preservation: *that* once secured, there is nothing which my sister and I will not afterwards do to make you happy – Can I rely on you, Faulkland? do you promise me not to be rash? You have my sword in your possession, answered Mr Faulkland, (still speaking within the closet) I have no other weapon about me – leave me, Sir George – I cannot talk.

Say but that you wish to see me again, replied my brother, and I will go, and give you no further trouble. Mr Faulkland sighed deeply. Say, I wish to see you! he repeated, ah, Bidulph! and his voice seemed choaked. My brother could not refrain from tears. I will come to you in the evening, Faulkland – You will find me your true friend. – I should be loath to lay you under any restraint here, in the house of my friend; do but say there is no need of it. Promise me – the slightest word will suffice. I know my dear Faulkland will not break his word.

Well – I will not attempt my life, cried he impatiently, let that satisfy you – leave me, and let me not be exposed to any insults here.

I leave you, answered my brother, and hope to find you more composed a few hours hence. Mrs Arnold too begs you will be calm, and think of preserving a life which is so dear to us both.

Mr Faulkland was silent, and my brother and I withdrew; he thought it best I should not speak to him.

Sir George left me at home, and said he would call again on Mr Faulkland in the afternoon, and bring me word how he should find him. My brother is exceedingly affected with his situation, and says he knows not what to advise. He is fearful that Mr Faulkland's phrenzy is not to be calmed, but by consenting to marry him, and circumstanced as he now is, that thought is terrible. Yet, if I persist in my refusal, I drive the noblest of minds to desperation. Oh, my Cecilia, is this the return I ought to make to the most generous of men? whose fervent love for me has been a constant source of torment to him for so many years! Yet how can I yield him my hand? All my former scruples, weighty as they appeared to me, were light to the dreadful bar that now interposes.

Had that ill-fated woman died the common way, with what joy, what exultation could I have rewarded his honest persevering love! all my duties fulfilled, obedience to my mother, justice to the woman I thought injured, reverence to the memory of my husband, the respect due to my own character. Should I not, my Cecilia, after thus being acquitted of all other obligations, have been to blame, if, after a series of misfortunes, all brought on by my strict adherence to those duties; should I not have been to blame for refusing at length to do justice to the most deserving of men? When I reflect on the past, when I survey the present, and my foreboding heart whispers to me the future sufferings of our dear unhappy Mr Faulkland, all my philosophy forsakes me. I have borne up under my own sorrows – his quite subdue me – I must lay by my pen – my eyes are brimful of tears . . . . Ah, my dear, what will become of us? I am almost dead with apprehension. Rash, rash, unhappy Mr Faulkland! He has fled from the house where my brother had concealed him: I know not what I am writing, my fears distract me. 'Tis but two hours since we left him, Sir George relying on his promise, and unwilling to provoke him by any appearance of constraint, gave no caution to the gentleman with whom he was lodged to observe his motions; he is ready to kill himself for this neglect; but relying on Mr Faulkland's promise not to make any attempt on his life, he suspected not that he would endeavour to escape. Escape do I call it? rather let me say, to throw himself into certain destruction. – He is set out on his way for Ireland. Heaven knows what will be the consequence of this, if my brother does not overtake and persuade him back. He is gone after him, my cousin Warner with him; both rode post.

My thoughts are so confused, I can put nothing in order. It seems we had not long quitted him, when he called up his servant (that groom who, as I informed you, had come over with him) and telling him he was going out of town ordered him to go directly to an inn somewhere in the city, and hire two post-horses, and that he would follow him presently.

The man obeyed, and in about half an hour, his master came in a hackney-coach to the place where he had directed him to wait for him.

Upon the inn-keeper's enquiring whither the horses were to go, Mr Faulkland replied, to St Alban's. The man objected to the length of the stage, and named Barnet. Mr Faulkland seemed impatient and angry; his unusual earnestness, his wild looks, and the road he purposed taking, alarmed his servant (a discreet elderly man) and he had the prudence immediately to dispatch the master of the house, whom he prevailed on by a piece of money, to go directly to my brother with this intelligence.

He had the precaution not to mention his master's name, only bade him find out Sir George Bidulph, and tell him that his friend was set out for St Alban's, and that his man had dispatched him with the news, and would, if possible, endeavour to detain him on the road, that Sir George might overtake him.

The man was punctual in delivering his message. My brother, wild with amazement and horror, just called as he past my door, to tell me this new and unexpected misfortune. Mr Warner had that instant come to enquire what had past between Mr Faulkland and me in our interview this morning. I had no time to tell him any thing. He looked very much displeased at my brother and me, upon hearing Mr Faulkland was gone; but said he would accompany Sir George, and they both hurried away together.

The man said, Mr Faulkland had set off before he could leave his house, the servant having scarce time to give him the message.

I fear it will be impossible for my brother to overtake him – He will be lost forever – what then will be my portion? Happy had it been for me indeed, as my dear mother once said in the bitterness of her heart, that I had died in my cradle!

Tuesday-night twelve o'clock

Heaven be praised, they are returned! *All* returned; Mr Faulkland has been prevailed on to come back, Mr Warner has prevailed on him. He has saved his life; but, my Cecilia, thy friend's temporal happiness, and peace of mind, is the only price that could ransom this desperate self-devoted victim!

Mr Warner has bound himself by a solemn oath that I should become his wife, or Mr Faulkland, determined on his own destruction, would, spite of all they could do, have pursued his fatal journey to Ireland, in order to deliver himself up to justice.

It was near ten o'clock before they returned to town. My brother carried Mr Faulkland back to the gentleman's house, where he was before lodged; and my kinsman left them together, in order to come and give me an account of what passed.

He said the gentleman, at whose house he was lodged by my brother was extreamly surprized at seeing him again, Mr Faulkland having with great composure taken his leave of him in the morning; and after thanking him for the shelter he had afforded him, told him he was going out of town.

My brother and my kinsman overtook him above a mile on this side St Alban's, for which success they were intirely indebted to the prudence of the servant who attended him: For the poor man, finding himself pushing on with the utmost eagerness, and Mr Faulkland no longer making a secret of this intention of returning to Ireland; resolved at all events to prevent his ruin; and hoping that by a little delay, Sir George might overtake them, contrived at their first stage so dexterously to slip a nail in between the horse's shoe and his hoof, that he knew he could not go far without being lame.

This succeeded so well, that the poor animal was soon disabled, and Mr Faulkland not having it in his power to mount himself better, was obliged to go on at a very easy rate 'till they arrived at the next stage.

Mr Warner and my brother overtook him in this situation: Sir George knew him as soon as they came in sight of him, and followed him at a proper distance, still keeping him in view, 'till he lighted at the post-house. They then at once entered the room, into which he had retired, whilst fresh horses were getting ready.

Mr Faulkland started at the sight of my brother; he looked earnestly at Mr Warner, whom he had never seen before; but spoke not to either of them.

Sir George, pursued my kinsman, accosted him affectionately: Dear Faulkland, was this kind of you, thus to fly from your friends that love you? He presented me to him at the same, naming me as his relation.

Mr Faulkland grasped the hand, which I reached out in salutation to him; he fixed his fine sparkling eyes on my face: Is it Mr Warner whom I have the honour to salute? Sir, I am no stranger to your worth: I honour, I revere you. You are too good to interest yourself thus for an unhappy wretch, cast off, and forsaken by all the world.

Do I forsake you, Faulkland, cried your brother, kindly enough? No, Faulkland, I am your constant sincere friend, and will prove myself so, if you will but let me. Mr Faulkland made no reply.

Dear Faulkland, am I not your friend? You are Mrs Arnold's brother. – You are not the man you were. Indeed Faulkland, I am; I am your true friend; suffer me to be so, come back with me; Mr Warner and I have followed you, in the hope of prevailing on you to return with us; do, Faulkland, let us persuade you to preserve a life so dear to us all.

What am I to live for, answered Mr Faulkland sternly? *You* have tried to deceive me; the man I loved most, now I am fallen, rejects me. Your sister persists in her obstinate cruelty towards me; she breaks her promise, and you encourage her in it. I have neither friends, fortune, or country! and do you talk to me of life on *such* conditions? No, Bidulph, it is a burden of which I will rid myself – Mr Warner, *you* are a generous man, *you* have an enlarged mind; may a stranger ask a favour of you?

I could have wept, continued my kinsman, to see such a frank noble fellow driven to such desperation. Command me, Sir, I replied, there is nothing I would not do to serve you.

I thank you, Sir; I have a little son; let me recommend the unhappy orphan to your protection. He will soon want a father: will you be one to him, Sir? I will send him over to you; he laid hold of my hand, and repeated his question, Will you Mr Warner? *You* have an enlarged mind, and do not despise the unfortunate.

I cried downright; he touched me to the very quick. I never was so affected in my life; and I own I was heartily displeased both with you and your brother, for driving him to such extremities: *You* especially, on whom I laid injunctions to act in a contrary way. As for Sir George, I am not surprized at *his* behaviour.

From Mr Faulkland's discourse, proceeded my kinsman, it was apparent to me, that his distraction proceeded from no other cause, than his belief that you and your brother slighted him in his misfortunes. It was plain when he fled to England, that he was sufficiently in his senses to be anxious for his own safety; and though the sight of you, joined to the hurry of his spirits, his fatigue, and want of sleep, might, in a man of such violent passions, have created a temporary phrenzy, yet I am very certain it would all have subsided, if you had behaved to him as you ought to have done, and as I desired you would: nor do I see how you can answer it to yourself, after the miseries you have already brought on such a glorious man (for I never saw his equal either in mind or person) to persist in a behaviour which has already turned his brain, and must in the end occasion his death: for death he is determined on, if you refuse to become his wife.

Oh, Sir, cried I, leave him not to himself, I conjure you; you see the influence you have over his mind; you have done wonders in bringing him back. –

Hold, replied Mr Warner, till I inform you of the means I was obliged to use.

I have told you how I was affected with his situation, and the request he made me to take care of his child. This was not the suggestion of madness; it was plain to me, that if the cause were removed, he would soon be restored to the perfect use of his reason, and I could not bear to see the desolation of such a noble frame, and all charged to your account.

Sir, I hope you do not mean, said I, to return to Ireland, do you not know the risque that you run by putting yourself into the power of an exasperated family from whom you can expect nothing but the most malevolent persecution?

I deliver myself up to the laws, replied Mr Faulkland; my life is devoted, 'tis indifferent to me how I die.

Suppose, said I, Mrs Arnold should consent to marry you, would not that reconcile you to life?

Oh, Sir, and he shook his head, I am not to be deceived *twice*. (Your brother walked about the room without taking part in the conversation.)

I do not mean it, Sir, Mrs Arnold must be yours; *I* can influence her; do but return back with me, I give you my honour I will do my utmost to prevail on her to give you her hand immediately. Her heart is hardened, Sir, she will not consent, replied he. I have no friend to urge her, I am an outcast, and not fit to live – *I* will urge her, Sir, she respects me, she will be guided by me; she shall fulfil the promise she made you – Oh, Sir, you but deceive yourself – she will find out new excuses, I am not to be again allured by false hopes.

He stepped towards the door as he spoke these words, and was about to open it. Your brother followed, and laid hold of his arm; I did the same. Sir George, said he, expose me not to insults, why do you persecute me? Leave me, Sir, I am *not* a madman – but I am *determined* – and he spoke as if he were *indeed* so.

For heaven's sake, Faulkland, said your brother, be composed: You have Mr Warner's word of honour; you shall have mine too, that we will do our utmost to persuade Mrs Arnold to consent to your wishes. You have *my* full consent, you have won Mr Warner to your interest, my sister will yield to our joint entreaties. *Yield*, he repeated, no, no, Sir George, she has a stubborn heart. I once thought it otherwise; but it is turned to stone, nothing but my death will satisfy, her, and she *shall* be satisfied.

He made an effort to break from us. Stay Mr Faulkland, said I, again laying hold of his hand, and I here swear to you by every thing that is sacred, that if you will suffer me to conduct you back into Mrs Arnold's presence, I will insist on her immediately accepting of you for her husband, or I will for ever renounce all friendship with her: I know she esteems and values you above all men, I am therefore sure, I do no violence to her inclinations; and if she perseveres in her obstinate punctilios, I swear to you by the same oath, that I will no longer oppose you in your resolutions, let them be what they will.

Sir George, added I, Do you join with me in giving your friend the same assurances? I do, answered he, solemnly addressing himself to Mr Faulkland, and swear by all my hopes of happiness hereafter, to act in conjunction with Mr Warner in every particular that he has promised.

Mr Faulkland seemed to be moved, he looked whistfully at us by turns, as if willing, though afraid, to yield to our entreaties.

At length, I *think* I may rely on you, said he, you will not break an oath (to Sir George) but that woman has such an *inflexible* heart! you cannot change *that*.

We will do our utmost, we both answered together. Remember, then, said he, stretching out a hand to each of us, you have sworn, if she persists in her resolution, that you will leave me to myself, and oppose me no longer. We have. I will go back with you then cried Mr Faulkland, and stepped again nimbly to the door.

It will be best, said I, if we can hire a coach to carry us; there is no necessity for our riding post, and we shall be less liable to observation than if we were on horse-back. Mr Faulkland looked as if he suspected some design; do you not mean, said he, to go directly back to London? Certainly, I replied. And shall I see Mrs Arnold to-night? Without doubt, if you desire it. Let us go then, said he; I think a coach is a tedious way of travelling, but I submit to *your* guidance.

I left Sir George with him, and went out to enquire whether we could be provided with a coach and four; which after some delay was procured for us. We prevailed on Mr Faulkland, whilst it was getting ready, to take a little refreshment. He asked us, by what means we were informed of his departure.

Sir George, unwilling to let him know that his servant had discovered it, evaded the question; and only replied, Do you think, Faulkland, that in the humour I left you, I could be inattentive to your motions? I am not a madman, Bidulph, I must not be treated like one. I do not think you one, answered your brother, but I know you are warm, and too fearless of danger.

When the coach was ready, Mr Faulkland very willingly got into it with us. He spoke but little, and appeared very thoughtful during our journey.

The coachman stopped at an inn, after we had driven about fifteen miles, to bate his horses for a while. He seemed startled at it, and said he would not alight. We told him there was no occasion, but your brother and I chose to go into the house, that he might not think we watched him. He seemed pleased at this, and smiled when we set forward again, but did not speak.

When he arrived in London, Now, Sir, said I, we will, if you please, go directly to Mrs Arnold's house. As I am sure your absenting yourself in the manner you did, exceedingly afflicted her, so am I certain your return will give her sincere joy. I am ready therefore to attend you immediately to her; but if I may advise you, I think it were better that I should first see and talk to her. It will be proper to prepare her, by giving her at least one night to reflect on the important event, which I expect will take place to-morrow. Sir George, what are your sentiments? I am of your mind, replied your brother? I think my sister ought by all means to have so much time given her for recollection. If Faulkland has no objection to it, we will go to my friend's house, where he was before. When you have seen my sister you may come to us there with her determination.

I have submitted myself for the present, answered Mr Faulkland, to your guidance. To-morrow remember I am to be at liberty. Bidulph, beware how you watch my motions again.

Your brother then directed the coachman to his friend's house, Mr Faulkland not opposing the motion. I went in for a few minutes merely to satisfy myself in what manner Mr Faulkland had escaped from thence in order to inform you.

Mr Faulkland was very urgent with me to go to you. Keep me not long in suspence, Sir, said he, I may as well know my fate to-night, as to-morrow.

I left him with a promise to return with your final answer. You know *my* sentiments, you know your brother's, and it rests on you to pronounce sentence of life or death (for your answer imports no less) on a man who is worthy of the greatest queen in the universe. What do you say, Mrs Arnold, must Faulkland die?

Heaven forbid, cried I, no, Sir; I should be inflexible *indeed*, if, after what you have told me, I were any longer to resist. I yield, Sir, to your request, to Mr Faulkland's, and to my brother's; and I will own at the same time that my heart strongly impels me to consent. Yet, my dear Sir, believe me I should have resisted *that* impulse, if I could hope that my refusal would not be followed by consequences too dreadful to be thought on. There is therefore *no* alternative, I *must* be the wife of Mr Faulkland.

The sooner the affair is finished then the better, said he; Faulkland stands here on slippery ground; perhaps some of the Bond family may by this time be arrived in England, and in pursuit of him; therefore let your marriage be dispatched immediately, and send him away directly to Holland. I suppose when he has made sure of you, he may be prevailed on to go without you. Oh, Sir, said I, urge this request to him I beseech you, it is of the last importance to me that he should comply with it, and the only preliminary that I have now to make to our marriage. Yes, yes, answered my kinsman, I think we shall convince him of the necessity of this. I shall escort you to Holland myself, for I have business at Rotterdam; and I had thoughts of taking the voyage, if this occasion had not offered. We will but just stay to settle some affairs here, and observe what measures can be taken for his service, and then follow him. Take courage, my dear, continued he, seeing me look sad, all may come right again. I love out-of-the-way adventures, and this I think *is* one. We will live like princes, let us go where we will. I only wish that your brother were *against* the match, that I might have the more pleasure in forwarding it; but I need not grudge him that *once* in his life he has shewn some tokens of generosity.

I will return to Faulkland, I long to set his noble heart at ease. Strange perverse creatures your sex are! It amazes me that any thing could tempt you to reject such a man! Were I a woman, I should run mad for him. Well, I will go to him, and let him know without any farther demurs you will give him your hand to-morrow morning. Our honest friend Price I think may join you. I will call on him, after I have seen Faulkland, to bid him prepare for the business. I will myself have the pleasure of giving you away. Good by – and away he went with a pleased busy countenance.

I took up my pen as soon as he departed, and have scribbled thus far without suffering any reflections to stop me. Let me now lay down my pen, to pause before I leap into the frightful precipice that opens before me .... To-morrow! Ah, my Cecilia, what is that morrow to produce? it joins me for ever to Mr Faulkland! the chosen of my heart, my first love! the man who adores me; who deserves all my affection, who has obliged me beyond all recompence. Who has a claim to my warmest gratitude, to my esteem, to my whole heart. I save his life, I have the power to make him happy; my brother, my kinsman urge me; my own heart too prompts me. Why cannot I then reconcile myself to my lot? Oh that question is answered by a fearful image that starts up to my fancy – I am not superstitious, yet believe me, my dear, I am at this instant chilled with horror.

I am ashamed to confess my weakness, but I must call Patty to sit with me the remainder of the night. I cannot think of rest!

Wednesday Morning

I have passed the whole night in endeavouring to fortify my mind against the important event that a few hours will accomplish. If Mr Faulkland's mind should again become tranquil, which my kinsman gave me room to hope would be the consequence of gratifying the ardent wish of his soul, I must take care not to disturb it by shewing any reluctance in yielding him my hand. Had an Angel *once* told me that I should give my hand *reluctantly* to Mr Faulkland, I would not have believed it; yet fatally circumstanced as our marriage *now* is, it cannot be otherwise.

And yet I *ought* to be his. I owe him a great sacrifice, and I am about to pay it. I am dressed and ready. I wait for my kinsman or my brother, one of whom, or both perhaps, will be here presently . . . . Mr Warner is come; I have but just time to tell you that my brother and Mr Price are with Mr Faulkland. My kinsman says he is quite a new man. They wait for me, I go. Heaven guide my steps . . . .

Thursday

My fate is accomplished! What a change! Join with me, my dear Cecilia, in beseeching heaven to look graciously down on me in my new state, and to guide and protect my beloved Mr Faulkland, my ever destined husband. Alas! my dear, he is now many miles separated from me.

The worthy Mr Price performed the sacred ceremony. Mr Warner did the office of a father. He and my brother were all who were present.

There is something so amazing in all this, I can scarce credit my senses; but my life has been a series of strange, strange events!

I am so bewildered, I cannot connect my thoughts; but I will try to give you my yesterday's *vision*, for I can hardly persuade myself that what I recollect really happened.

I broke off just as Mr Warner called on me, to carry me to the house of my brother's friend.

While we were in the coach, he told me, that having the night before informed Mr Faulkland of the joyful news of my consenting to marry him the next day, he seemed at first to doubt, and repeatedly conjured him not to deceive him; 'till having received the most solemn assurances of its being true, Mr Faulkland gave himself up to such ecstacies as made them apprehensive his joy might have effects almost as fatal in their consequences, as his despair was likely to produce before.

Mr Warner had a mind to lower him a little, and thought, by putting him in mind of his danger, somewhat to allay his transports.

Mrs Arnold's consent to make you happy, said he, fills me with extreme joy; but it is not now a time to indulge it: you are here in peril of your life; you must preserve it now for Mrs Arnold's sake. For Mrs Arnold's sake! he replied, with ecstasy, yes, yes, 'tis now worth preserving. Mr Warner, Kinsman, Friend of my life, (grasping his hand) dispose of me as you please; you shall guide all my steps. Will not Mrs Arnold go with me after we are made one?

If, after having considered what may be urged to you on that head, you should still continue to desire it, replied my cousin, she will without doubt accompany you. But, my dear Sir, consider, circumstanced as you now are, what will the world say, should she accompany your flight? It will fix an indelible stain on her character, which is dearer to her than life, and which I am sure, upon cooler thoughts, you will prize at an equal value. This marriage will be a profound secret to the world; it may remain so as long as we please. I have business in Holland, which will demand my presence there in a very short time. Her accompanying me thither can give rise to no suspicion. I will dispatch my affairs with all possible speed, and conduct her to you.

The joy that before lighted up his countenance, pursued my cousin, seemed a little clouded. He took a turn or two about the room, as if to consider of what I had said; then, addressing himself jointly to your brother and me, You are both cooler than I am; perhaps you may judge better; let me but call her *mine*, I will then do as you would have me. I cannot determine on anything now.

As soon as my sister and you are married, said Sir George, I think, Faulkland, you ought to get out of England with all the speed you can. It will be but a short absence; Sidney will soon follow you. What do you purpose doing in regard to your son? I had forgot him, cried

Mr Faulkland. Poor child! My heart has been in such tumults since Mr Warner came in, that I could think of nothing but the blessed news he has brought me. But I must not neglect my boy. I will write to the honest servant that I left behind; he shall bring him over: you, my dear Bidulph, will take care of him, 'till an opportunity offers of sending him to me.

I hope there will be no need, replied your brother, of sending him out of England; your affairs may yet turn out so as to permit your return into your own country. – Impossible! interrupted Mr Faulkland; if Smyth should ever recover, *his* representation of the other accident cuts off every hope. He will not, for his own sake, confess the truth, but impute the error of my fatal hand to premeditated guilt. Heaven knows, base as she was, I would not have attempted her life; but I was born to be the avenger of those crimes into the commission of which I, perhaps, first led her. As for the contemptible villain who wronged me, I do not repent of the punishment I inflicted on him; though probably, had I been allowed a moment's time for recollection, I might have taken vengeance in a manner more worthy of myself.

I was delighted, proceeded Mr Warner, to find him so cool and rational in his reflections. He continued talking calmly and reasonably on the subject of his misfortunes; but on the mention of your name, started again into transports; but they now seemed to be only those of joy, upon the prospect of what was to happen the next day.

After I left him, I went to Mr Price, who promised to be in readiness at the appointed hour.

We were now got to the house of my brother's friend. Mr Warner led me up stairs into the room, where Sir George, Mr Faulkland, and Mr Price, were sitting together.

Mr Faulkland was so agitated at the sight of me, that having risen to salute me, he was not able to speak; but seizing both my hands, he kissed them fervently one after the other, tears dropping on them as he held them to his lips. Every one was silent; we were all too much affected to speak. My brother was the first that broke silence. Well, Faulkland, said he, have we not kept our promise?

Mr Faulkland turned towards him: Oh, Bidulph, forgive me for doubting; I am afraid I have used you ill: Can you pardon the madness that I was driven to by despar? – Mr Warner, Mrs Arnold, I believe you think me distracted. Indeed I am not. I was only – (and he seemed to hesitate for a word) weary of life. – I thought I had lost every thing. – The world was grown a desart. – No one in it for me.

You formed a wrong judgment, my dear Sir, answered Mr Warner; you find yourself now with your sincere friends; Sir George and myself are both so; and your bride, your dear Mrs Arnold, is ready to give you her hand. I *am*, Sir, said I, and if your happiness still depends on me, it gives me joy that I have at length the power of *bestowing* it.

I have no *words*, he replied, I can *find* none, it is all *here*; and he laid his hand on his heart, his eyes fixed with delight on my face.

I beheld him now, my Cecilia, in a light in which I had never before viewed him; overwhelmed by misfortunes, of which I accused myself as being the author. I saw him an exile, likely to be deprived of a noble fortune, his heart pierced with remorse for an involuntary crime. I saw too that he loved me; loved me with a fervent and unconquerable passion. Of this, in the anguish of his soul, at a time when he was wrought up to phrenzy, he had given but too strong demonstration. Shall I own it to you, my Cecilia, I think I never loved him as I did in that moment.

My heart was at once assailed by a variety of passions; amongst which, gratitude, and the softest compassion, were predominant.

I continued silent, whilst Mr Faulkland remained ardently gazing at me.

My brother, I believe, thought us too solemn; the occasion indeed required it: but his fears for Mr Faulkland made him wish to give the scene a livelier turn.

Come, sister, said he, let us not defer the happy event for which we are now met, we have no time to waste in ceremony. You remember what our mother used to say, 'Many things fall out between the cup and the lip.' My brother rose off his chair as he said this. Mr Warner taking the hint, approached, and took me by the hand, Let *me*, said he, to Mr Faulkland, have the happiness of bestowing this best of Creatures on the man that I think *best* deserves her.

Mr Faulkland made no reply; but in taking the hand that my kinsman put into his, his looks spoke the rapture that swelled his heart; though I saw he put a constraint upon himself, and endeavoured to assume a deportment suitable to the important and solemn occasion.

After the indissoluble knot was tied, my brother desired Mr Faulkland to retire with him into the next room for a few minutes.

I concluded it was in order to press his departure, and to prevail on him to submit to going without me.

This I found afterwards was the subject of their conversation.

They returned to us in about a quarter of an hour, Mr Faulkland's countenance less embarrassed than it was at going out of the room. On their entering, Mr Price took his leave. My brother addressed Mr Warner and me. Faulkland, said he, is convinced of the necessity there is for his immediately withdrawing from England, and he is determined to depart from hence at three o'clock to-morrow morning; for I would by no means have him leave London by day-light, as we know not who may be on the watch to trace his steps. He has consented that you, sister, should remain behind till Mr Warner's affairs will permit him to conduct you over. In the mean time, Master Faulkland is to be brought from Ireland; and if you should not be ready to depart before his arrival, you may take him over with you to Holland.

Mr Faulkland seemed rather to *suffer* my brother to make this explanation for him, than to assent chearfully to it. Mr Warner and I however laid hold of it, and immediately entered into discourse on the subject of our domestic concerns, and the measures proper to be observed on so critical an occasion.

Mr Faulkland joined in the conversation with the utmost composure; and to my unspeakable joy, seemed perfectly settled and collected in his mind. I thought indeed he appeared a little constrained, and that he seemed to keep a constant guard over himself, lest he should betray any symptom of a too much heated imagination: but my kinsman afterwards observed with pleasure to me, that this denoted nothing more than a consciousness in Mr Faulkland of the unhappy wandering that had before so much alarmed us all; and into which he was sure there was not the least danger of his relapsing, as his heart was now perfectly at ease.

Mr Faulkland told us he had letters to write to Ireland, which he would dispatch, that he might have nothing to interrupt the few short hours we had to pass together in the evening.

Mr Warner said he had business to do that called him away, but that he would return after dinner: and my brother (that Mr Faulkland might be quite undisturbed) proposed my going home with him, and that we should come back together in the afternoon.

Mr Faulkland did not object to this, and I went with Sir George.

We returned early in the afternoon to Mr Faulkland. As my brother had let his friend into our secret, we passed up stairs without any notice being taken of us.

Mr Faulkland had writ two letters; one of them very long, to Mr

Bond, which he gave my brother to read, but I know not the contents of it. The other was to that careful honest servant whom he had mentioned to us, with orders to bring over Master Faulkland with all convenient speed, and put him into Sir George's hand.

Mr Warner but just called in upon us in the evening, he said he had been making the necessary preparations for Mr Faulkland's journey; and that having resolved himself to attend him as far as Harwich, he would, at the hour appointed call on him in a coach, which should carry them a few miles out of town, where the horses were to wait for them.

Worthy, compassionate, and generous kinsman, how I love you for the honest warmth of your heart!

My brother and Mr Faulkland had a great deal of discourse about the necessary measures that were to be taken by us all; and we passed the evening in a kind of chastened satisfaction, which could not arise to happiness from the near prospect we had of parting.

About ten o'clock my brother took an affectionate leave of his friend, he excused himself from accompanying him on his journey, on account of Lady Sarah's not being well.

To see *such* a parting, would at another time have deeply affected me, but my own hour of separation drew near. It came, and Mr Warner punctual to his time, hurried Mr Faulkland almost by force into the coach, and drove off with him.

I threw myself into a chair which he had ordered for me, and was carried home. I went not to bed; but had recourse to my pen. God preserve my dear fugitive; I can do nothing but weep.

July 2

My mind was too much unsettled yesterday to dictate any thing coherent. I am now, thank heaven, more composed. Sir George and Lady Sarah have been with me during the greatest part of the day; both kind and consoling. My brother seems to have all his former affection for me revived in his heart; he is indeed charmed with my justice, as he calls it. Lady Sarah, who at the bottom of her heart is no way concerned about this event, affects however to think as her husband does, and commends me for my generosity.

I feel myself easier in proportion as I think Mr Faulkland gets farther out of the reach of danger. Sir George says by this time he may be on his voyage.

I shall certainly wait till the child arrives, in order to take him with me. My two little girls will be fond of such a brother, for he is a charming boy.

My brother flatters me with a possibility at least of Major Smyth's recovering; and if so, he says that Mr Faulkland may stand his trial for the other accident, as he is in hopes Smyth will not persist in his villainy so far as to add perjury to his other crimes.

I have but little expectations of justice from so bad a man, but I would not discourage my friends in their endeavours to comfort me.

July 3

Mr Warner is returned from Harwich, after having seen Mr Faulkland safe on board the packet, and even under sail for Holland.

What a benevolent heart has this good relation of mine! Indeed I dearly love and respect him. His return has revived my spirits, and I begin to lose my fears. He brought me a short letter from Mr Faulkland; short it is, but his heart speaks in every syllable of it. I will not give you the contents, my Cecilia, you will think it too extravagant, too romantic, for a husband to write so to his wife.

July 6

I long, yet dread to hear accounts from Ireland. I fear that wretched Smyth is dead. No mail has arrived from thence these eight days. Contrary winds they tell me detain the packets on the other side very often for a fortnight together. If that be so, how fortunate was Mr Faulkland in seizing on a lucky hour for his departure from the Irish shore.

I suppose Mr Bond's family, whom he must have rendered very unhappy, particularly the daughter, are all now his implacable enemies; and are tormenting themselves in being detained from the pursuit of their vengeance. But let them come now when they will, he is far out of the reach of his foes.

I would it were possible for my Cecilia, to arrive in England before my departure for Holland. Indeed, my dear, I shall not be sorry if I am detained from Mr Faulkland, till I have the happiness of first embracing you, as our separation may be afterwards of a long continuance. I shall wait for the arrival of Master Faulkland, and who knows what adverse winds may detain him till your return. O! that I may pass though it be but one day, with the dear companion of my youth before we are again divided!

I will not send this packet off, till I am ready to depart from

England, as that will be closing an important period of my life. What would I give that my dearest friend would come, and instead of this tedious narrative which I have written, receive the account from my own lips! If my wishes should not be granted in this, cannot you make Holland your way home? Mr Faulkland purposes staying at the Hague till I go to him.

July 9

Cecilia! have I been a murmurer at the decrees of providence? have I been an impious repiner when heaven has poured down its wrath upon my head? if not, why am I marked out for divine vengeance? before I lose my senses, or my life, for both I cannot retain, hear the last act of your friend's tragic story.

My brother called on me this day; he gave me a letter directed to Mr Faulkland, which came under a cover to him. Read it, said he, it is from Ireland, and may contain something material for us to know.

It was from the honest servant Mr Faulkland left behind him. See what he says, and then tell me if I ought to live any longer.

'Honoured Sir,

'I have the happiness to send you a piece of good news, which made me wish for wings to have flown over to you with it.

'My lady, Heaven be praised, is not dead, nor so much as hurt. I am thankful for this, Sir, on your account, not her's.

'I don't know what possessed the people at Mr Bond's, to tell me she was dead; the mistake, to be sure, was occasioned by the great confusion the family were thrown into, and indeed, from what I myself saw, I was sure she was actually dead.

'Major Smyth lived 'till the surgeon came; but had been speechless for two or three hours, and died whilst his wound was probing.

'My lady had only fallen into a fit, and the major having bled prodigiously, she received a great deal of his blood upon her linen, and as he afterwards contrived to throw himself on the bed, which was at some distance from the place where she had fallen, it gave occasion to Mrs Bond (who was herself the first person that entered the room, after the sad accident) on finding my lady lying senseless, pale, and bloody, on the floor, to suppose she had been killed.

'This alarm ran through the family, and was confirmed to me

by every one in it, as we servants soon quitted the chamber; and the major himself said, that you had discharged one of the pistols at your lady, and the other at him.

'I returned to Mr Bond's in the morning, after you were gone off, to enquire whether Major Smyth was alive or not; he was just then dead.

'The waiting-maid informed me, that my lady, to their great surprize, was recovered, having only been in a fainting fit, which held her above an hour, without her shewing any signs of life; and that she had fallen from one to another 'till morning: and she farther said (begging your honour's pardon) it would be no great matter if she had died in one; for she believed it was for no good she went into the major's room at that time of the night.

'I staid about the house all the day to pick up what intelligence I could from the servants. Young Mr Bond, with two or three men, went to your house, and not finding you there, I suppose, rode in pursuit of you; but, Heaven be praised, you have escaped their hands.

'The waiting-maid, who is a very civil young woman, told me, in the evening, that my lady, being come a little to herself (though I believe not in her right mind) was informed of the major's death; at which she was so exceedingly terrified, that finding herself ill besides, she confessed the whole truth of the matter, and proved, that the major died with a lie in his mouth: so that I hope Mr Bond's family will not be so spiteful as to prosecute the affair any farther.

'My lady was sent home directly in the chariot, as they could not bear the sight of her any longer in the house. She takes on mightily; but we all bless ourselves, that she is alive.

'I shall make bold to inclose this, according to your order, to Sir George Bidulph; and as soon as I receive your commands about Master, shall make no delay in this unlucky place. I am.

'Honoured Sir,

'Your dutiful and obedient servant,

'FREDERICK HILDY.'

June 26

Adieu, my Cecilia, adieu; nothing but my death should close such a scene as this.

Here, to the editor's great disappointment, Mrs Arnold's interesting story broke off; that unhappy lady not having continued her journal any farther.

But as this seemed to be one of the most affecting periods of her life, his curiosity induced him to enquire of the gentleman from whom he received those papers whether he could give him any farther light into her story; as he thought it not improbable that he might have learned, from his mother, some other particulars relating to her.

His friend told him, that he knew his mother had drawn up a narrative of the subsequent remarkable events in the life of Mrs Arnold, at the request of a particular friend; that he had once heard it read; but, as he was then a boy, it made but little impression upon him; that afterwards, when he wanted to have his curiosity gratified, his mother told him, she could not find the manuscript, and feared it was lost. However, he said, he would search her papers and, if he recovered it, it should be at his service.

After some time, the gentleman informed the editor, that he had made the strictest scrutiny into his mother's papers, and could find nothing relative to the subject of Mrs Arnold, excepting a few loose sheets, which seemed to have been the foul copy of the beginning of her narrative; and, at the same time, put them into his hands.

These the editor offers to the publick, as he received them, without any alteration or addition.

CECILIA'S NARRATIVE, &c.

BEING
A SUPPLEMENT TO MRS ARNOLD'S
JOURNAL

I SET out on my return to England, immediately after the receipt of her last journal, the melancholy close of which had exceedingly terrified and afflicted me.

Immediately on my arrival in London, I flew to the dear friend of my heart; she was still at her house, in Pall-mall.

I found the dear Sidney alone, in her bed-chamber. She had been prepared to receive me; but though I had endeavoured to arm myself with resolution for this affecting interview, I was not mistress of myself at the sight of her.

The tears I shed did not spring from that sweet emotion, which long severed friends feel at seeing each other again; I wept in sorrow for the heavy misfortunes of the best of women.

But Mrs Arnold, still herself, and superior to adversity, received me with the tenderest marks of friendship, and with a composure that amazed me.

Piety, meekness, and patience, were ever Mrs Arnold's characteristics; and they now all appeared blended, and so strongly impressed on her beautiful face, that I could not look at her without admiration.

As I was astonished to find her so calm under so trying an affliction, I could not help expressing myself to that purpose; but Mrs Arnold checked me, with this reply: 'I have been set up as a mark, my Cecilia; let me fulfil the intention of my Maker, by shewing a perfect resignation to His will. I hope, my task is almost finished, and that he will soon permit me to return to the dust from which I came.'

Frederick Hildy had arrived from Ireland above a fortnight before, with Master Faulkland, a beautiful child of about five years old. They were both lodged in Mrs Arnold's house.

She told me, that Sir George Bidulph and Mr Warner had set out together for Holland, immediately after the receipt of the letter, which informed them of Mrs Faulkland's being alive.

My brother, said Mrs Arnold, thought it necessary himself to be the bearer of news so fatal in its import to his friend. He hoped besides he should be able to return and stand his trial for having killed Major Smyth, as there is no doubt of his being acquitted; all Mr Bond's family being now convinced, from Mrs Faulkland's own confession, that there was nothing premeditated in this fatal event, and that what Mr Faulkland did, was in defence of his own life.

I have writ, continued she, to Mr Faulkland, to endeavour to console him under our mutual misfortune.

At my request, she shewed me a copy, of this letter; wherein she assured him, she would take the tenderest care of his son, 'till the child could be delivered safe into his hands; and conjured him, for that child's sake, to be careful of his own interest and preservation; adding, that as their ill fated marriage was an absolute secret to every one but the persons immediately concerned, she hoped he would not suffer the thoughts of it to break in upon his future quiet; and concluded with beseeching him to forget her, as they were never more to meet.

This was the substance of what she wrote. There were no murmurings at her fate, no womanish complainings, mixed with the tender, yet noble sentiments of her heart. She endeavoured to conceal her own anguish under the mask of contentment, that Mr Faulkland might the better support this final destruction of all his hopes.

I asked her, whether she had heard since from Mr Faulkland? She told me she had as yet received no answer from him to this letter, but that she had heard severally from Sir George and Mr Warner, who both informed her, that Mr Faulkland, after his first transports of surprize and grief were over, at receiving this new and unexpected blow, had grown more calm, and seemed inclined to return with them to England. Sir George added, in the last letter she had from him, that they only waited 'till Mr Warner had accomplished the business that he had to do in Holland, and hoped, before a fortnight was at an end, to return home, and to have the pleasure of conducting Mr Faulkland back.

It is ten days, continued Mrs Arnold, since I received this account, and I flatter myself, that they may now be on their journey homeward.

Mrs Arnold said, that she waited but for Sir George's return, in order to deliver Master Faulkland into his hands, and that she then meant to retire into the country, with her two children, and Patty, the faithful companion and partner of her grief.

Lady Sarah Bidulph, who would gladly have gone with Sir George to Holland, had been persuaded by him to stay behind, in order to bear his sister company in her affliction; and Mrs Arnold said, she had dedicated much of her time to that friendly purpose.

Her Ladyship came to pay her a visit whilst I was there. I had never seen Lady Sarah before; and we were introduced to each other.

I took my leave of Mrs Arnold, and promised to see her again the next day.

In the morning, as I was preparing to go to her, I received a note from Lady Sarah Bidulph, earnestly requesting the favour of seeing me, at her house, in St James's Square, before I went to Mrs Arnold.

I obeyed this unexpected summons, and immediately waited on her.

I took the liberty, Madam, said she, of desiring to see you here this morning, at Sir George's request: he arrived late last night, and brings most melancholy news from Holland.

Sir George entered the room while she spoke. After the first greeting of friends long parted were over, I am afraid to ask, Sir George, said I, yet am impatient to learn something of Mr Faulkland, your lady has terribly alarmed me; Mr Faulkland is not returned; I dare not, enquire the reason. Tears instantly sprung into Sir George's eyes. He returns no more, said he, his remains are soon to be conveyed to England to be laid with his ancestors.

Ah, Sir, cried I, what will poor Mrs Arnold say to this fresh misfortune?

It was on that account Madam, he replied, that we are now requested to speak with you, before you saw my sister. You, who are her bosom friend, can more tenderly disclose this melancholy event than any one. I have not the courage to see her. We must beg of you, dear Madam, to prepare the unhappy Sidney for the news.

I asked him the manner of Mr Faulkland's death. I cannot positively say, answered Sir George, but much I fear he precipitated his own fate.

Mr Warner, or I, constantly staid with him from the time we disclosed the fatal account we brought concerning Mrs Faulkland. Knowing as we did the violence of his temper, we were apprehensive of sudden and dreadful consequences; but he deceived us both; for after the first starts of passion were over, which though they shocked, did not alarm us, as we expected them, he assumed a calm resignation to his fate; and talked with such a rational composure of the strange circumstances of this incident, that we began to entertain hopes, that the efforts of his reason, joined to our constant endeavours to sooth and console him, would in time so far succeed, and though we never expected to see him restored to a tranquil state of mind, we yet flattered ourselves he would submit to life upon such terms as Providence thought fit to impose on him.

I was with him, proceeded Sir George, when he received a letter from my sister. His hands shook so on perceiving by the superscription that it came from her, that he let the letter drop. Read it for me, Bidulph, said he, and tell me how it fares with Mrs Arnold.

I instantly complied with his request. I found by the date of the letter that it had been delayed much longer than it ought to have been, which I immediately observed to him, as he had often expressed his uneasiness at not hearing from my sister.

Mrs Arnold is well, said I, giving him the letter; read what it says, and let her teach you fortitude.

He withdrew to a window to peruse it. After he had read it, I admire your sister's stoiscism, said he, stepping back to his chair. This is true philosophy, laying his finger on the letter which he still held in his hand. *Her* heroic soul is still unmoved, and above the reach of adversity. Happy Mrs Arnold – What a vain fool was I to think that such a mind as *hers* could be subdued. He paused and seemed for a while buried in thought. Then putting the letter up in his pocket, he began to discourse on some other topic.

We passed the evening together, continued Sir George, and though Faulkland was far from being chearful, I thought he appeared more tranquil than he had done since my arrival.

I talked to him of his returning to England with me. He said with a smile, I think I ought to go if it were for no other reason but that I may have my dust mingled with that of my forefathers; and this office, Bidulph, I expect from you, if you should outlive me.

I laughed at him, and said I thought he had a much more material reason that pressed his return.

Your estate, said I, is unsettled; and if you were to die abroad in the predicament in which you now stand, what is to become of your son?

I have already done for my son, said he, all that I thought in justice was in my power to do: I have long ago settled my personal fortune on him, that in case my next heirs should on account of the illegitimacy of his birth, claim the family estate, he may have a handsome support without it.

And indeed I never wished to debar my lawful heirs in favour of this child; though I love him tenderly, and they are worthless people, whom I despise, and with whom I never had any intercourse.

I replied, if that were so, as the manner of the child's birth was a secret, I wished he might, undisturbed, inherit his father's fortune, when he should come to pay the last debt to nature.

He answered, where such a vast property was at stake, there would not be people wanting whose interest would engage them to discover the secret; and he doubted not but the irregularity of his wife's conduct, had already occasioned enquiries to be made.

Supposing, said I, you had had another son by Mrs Faulkland since your marriage – as you could have no objection to the bequeathing your fortune to him, would it not have appeared strange in the eyes of the world that you should disinherit your eldest son.

It might have appeared so, said he, but I certainly should have done it: and for that reason, as I have no child but him, I have made such a disposition of my fortune as I now tell you. If I live, I may increase my son's patrimony; if not, he must be contented with that which I have bequeathed to him, and let my kindred scramble for the rest.

We staid together till it was late; he discoursed on a variety of subjects, but mentioned not my sister's name during the whole time.

I thought I left him well, and his mind tolerably composed. We were to set out on our return in six days; but an account was brought to me in the morning, that Mr Faulkland was found dead in his bed.

There were no symptoms discovered on the body that could let us into the occasion of his death; but as my own fears suggested too much, I chose not to be particular in my enquiries. Wishing rather that his fatal story should be buried in silence.

Mr Warner found that his affairs were likely to delay him longer than the time proposed; and as I had nothing farther to detain me in Holland, I set out the day after my unfortunate friend's death, leaving to Mr Warner, the care of conveying his remains to England, agreeably to the desire he had expressed, which I now considered as his last injunction laid on me.

Thus, proceeded Sir George, by a series of fatal events, each of which was occasioned by motives in themselves laudable, has one of the bravest and most noble-minded men on earth been cut off in the prime of his youth – O! Faulkland, why did you suffer that gallant spirit to be vanquished? –

Sir George's emotion stopped his farther speech, I was too much affected to say any thing to him, but took a hasty leave of Lady Sarah, in order to go to Mrs Arnold.

As soon as I entered my friend's room Cecilia, said she, if your countenance be as faithful an interpreter of your mind as it used to be, you have some thing disastrous to relate; you may say anything, misfortune and I have been so familiar, I shall not shrink as its approach.

Sir George is returned, I replied, you will see him to-day.

Is he come alone, she asked? Alone, I replied. You but repeat my words, Cecilia, without adding any thing from yourself. Shall I interpret the meaning of that mournful echo? Mr Faulkland no longer lives!

I was silent – Oh I knew him too well, said she, raising her voice with energy, to think he would survive this last blow.

His death was natural, said I, for any thing that appears to the contrary. God be praised for that, cried Mrs Arnold! *If* so, I am satisfied that he is at peace.

She then enquired after Mr Warner, and her brother, without making any farther mention of Mr Faulkland.

Whilst we were in discourse, Master Faulkland ran into the room. He had been at play with the two little Miss Arnolds, who were in pursuit of him, And he flew to Mrs Arnold to hide him. She folded him tenderly in her arms; then turning to me, Look at this boy, said she, he is the perfect image of his father.

When am I to go to my papa, cried the child, as he hung round her neck? This innocent unexpected demand quite vanquished Mrs Arnold's fortitude. She set him down without being able to answer his question, then said, Excuse me, my Cecilia, I would wish to be alone for to-day. It was not yet a season to administer consolation, and I withdrew.

She staid in London but two days after this; when, as she had before resolved, she retired to an estate in Buckinghamshire, which her kinsman had purchased and settled on her for ever.

With her brother's consent, she took Master Faulkland with her, and prevailed on Mr Price to accompany her into the country, to whom she committd the care of the child's education.

Mr Warner, whom she had acquainted by letter with her intention, approved of the step she had taken. He returned to England in about three weeks after her departure from her house in town, which she had left for his reception just as he had fitted it up for her.

Before I accompany Mrs Arnold into her solitude, I shall just briefly mention some other persons who were connected with her story.

The relations of Mr Faulkland, as he had foreseen, claimed his estate, and at length obtained it, the illegitimacy of the child being proved.

The wretched Mrs Faulkland, abandoned and despised, returned to England; but as she was there hated and shunned by every one, she remained in obscurity for a few years, and then died unpitied and unlamented.

I now return to Mrs Arnold, who, settled in her quiet retreat in the country, it might be hoped would have passed the remainder of her days undisturbed by any new calamity.

That only source of true heroism of soul, religion, had all along supported, and prevented her from sinking under the most trying afflictions. Many and bitter were the sufferings she had already endured; but she was, to use her own words, *Set up as a mark*; and the deep afflictions that still pursued her, and clouded even her latter days with misfortunes, may serve to shew that it is not *here* that true virtue is to look for its reward. I saw her at a time when this reflection, as it had been her chief, so was it her last and only consolation.

Possessed as she was of an admirable understanding, and an enlarged mind, in the deepest solitude she had always resources of entertainment within herself. Her natural disposition ever sweet and complying, was improved by her sufferings into a patience very rare in woman; and a resignation imbibed at first from a rigid education, was heightened by religion into an almost saint-like meekness and humility.

I shall pass over the first ten years of her retirement, in which nothing material happened but the marriage of the amiable Patty Main to a gentleman of a large estate, and the death of her worthy kinsman Mr Warner, who bequeathed her his whole fortune.

Miss Arnold, her eldest daughter, was now something more than fifteen, and fulfilled the promise her childhood gave, of her being a perfect beauty, Miss Cecilia was about a year younger, and though not so handsome as her sister, was accounted one of the finest young ladies of her time.

With what delight have I seen this excellent mother, while these two charming young creatures were all attention, relate to them the extraordinary and affecting incidents of her life.

This, said she, I do, not as a murmurer at my fate, nor to move your pity at my misfortunes, but to teach you by my example, that there is no situation in life exempt from trouble. It found *me* under the tender care of the best of parents, it pursued me into my husband's house. In my virgin state, when I was a wife, and in my widowhood, I was equally persecuted.

Poverty, I once thought, would have exempted me from every ill, but what its own hand inflicted; and had it remained my companion, the bitterest misfortune of my love would have been prevented; for, if wealth had not accompanied my hand, the world could not have persuaded me to yield it to Mr Faulkland.

Do not therefore pride yourselves on the great fortunes you are likely to possess: I have received no other satisfaction in mine, than what arose from the benefits I have conferred on others.

By such lessons as these, did this tender parent endeavour to fortify their young minds against the vicissitudes of fortune, and to teach them not to place their confidence in riches.

She dwelt so often upon this theme, that she seemed to have a presentiment of those evils, which were now ready to pour in like a torrent upon her.

Gracious Heaven! how inscrutable are thy ways! Her affluent fortune, the very circumstance which seemed to promise her, in the eve of life, some compensation for the miseries she had endured in her early days, now proved the source of new and dreadful calamities to her, which, by involving the unhappy daughters of an unhappy mother in scenes of the most exquisite distress, cut off from her even the last resource of hope in this life, and rendered the close of her history still more . . . .

Here the lady's narrative breaks off, and the editor, not having it in his power, after the most diligent enquiry, to recover any more of the manuscript, is, to his great mortification, compelled to offer this fragment.

The END of the THIRD VOLUME.